Katheryn Dubois
Mlyn Hurn

Elemental
Desires

ELLORA'S CAVE
ROMANTICA PUBLISHING

An Ellora's Cave Romantica Publication

www.ellorascave.com

Elemental Desires

ISBN #1419951963
ALL RIGHTS RESERVED.
Wynd Temptress Copyright© 2003 Kathryn Anne Dubois
Rayne Dance Copyright© 2003 Mlyn Hurn
Fyrebrand Copyright© 2003 Lora Leigh
Edited by: Kari Berton
Cover art by: Syneca

Electronic book Publication: December, 2003
Trade paperback Publication: May, 2005

With the exception of quotes used in reviews, this book may not be reproduced or used in whole or in part by any means existing without written permission from the publisher, Ellora's Cave Publishing, Inc.® 1056 Home Avenue, Akron OH 44310-3502.

This book is a work of fiction and any resemblance to persons, living or dead, or places, events or locales is purely coincidental. The characters are productions of the authors' imagination and used fictitiously.

Warning:

The following material contains graphic sexual content meant for mature readers. *Elemental Desires* has been rated *S-ensuous* by a minimum of three independent reviewers.

Ellora's Cave Publishing offers three levels of Romantica™ reading entertainment: S (S-ensuous), E (E-rotic), and X (X-treme).

S-ensuous love scenes are explicit and leave nothing to the imagination.

E-rotic love scenes are explicit, leave nothing to the imagination, and are high in volume per the overall word count. In addition, some E-rated titles might contain fantasy material that some readers find objectionable, such as bondage, submission, same sex encounters, forced seductions, etc. E-rated titles are the most graphic titles we carry; it is common, for instance, for an author to use words such as "fucking", "cock", "pussy", etc., within their work of literature.

X-treme titles differ from E-rated titles only in plot premise and storyline execution. Unlike E-rated titles, stories designated with the letter X tend to contain controversial subject matter not for the faint of heart.

Contents

Dedication:

To the readers:

Because you make writing fun.

Thank you for all your emails, your support and encouragement.

Prologue

The files had finally arrived. Shannon Riedel, head of the Psychic Sensory Investigations Agency stared at the computer screen with a sense of resignation. The email cover letter said it all. File contained. Information, re: The Elementals. Executive clearance required.

"Computer, open file," she commanded softly.

"Executive level clearance passcode, please," the computer asked with its hollow monotone.

She typed in the first part of the code. "Pass code: Dream walker, seventh order, warrior rights. Zebra, seven of the sixth key." The oral passcode gave her level of clearance, the typed code gave a set of number and letters unique to her. The third key was her own unique voice, combined with the infrared eye scan that suddenly activated and her thumb scan from the small pad at the side of the flat keyboard.

She waited only seconds for the file to open. She felt her chest tighten in remorse when it did. Another death warrant, she wondered? There was nothing she hated worse than preparing evidence against a psychic. If they were psychic.

There were three young women rumored to be Elementals, the grandchildren of Tyre, a demon whose psychic abilities had nearly destroyed the world fifty years past. If these three women truly possessed Tyre's powers, then there wasn't a chance in hell she could save them. The Agency would demand their execution. Unless their powers could be neutralized by the PSI agents. Which was rare. Very rare.

She read through the information, frowning at the brevity of it, the lack of conclusive evidence. If the women held the most feared of psychic powers, then there was little evidence of it. The most damning fact was the evidence that Maile, daughter of the Tyrea, had claimed the girls as her granddaughters, though each child had carried different surnames. Different fathers? She rubbed at the tension settling in her brow.

Shannon sighed wearily. Psychics had once been a benefit to the world, now any good they could do was immediately reviled for the very power that could accomplish it. The horror of the psychic wars was too well remembered. Many cities within the U.S. were still rebuilding from the rubble that had been left in the wake of the final battle.

It was now Shannon's job, as director of the PSI agents, to evaluate the power the women held and make a determination of life or death to be passed to the Council. No mistakes could be made. She had risen among the ranks to take her seat as Director of the PSI Agency because she didn't make mistakes. And with these three women, her very life would be on the line. If she determined innocents should die, then her conscience would destroy her. But if she allowed such three powerful threats freedom, then the world could pay for her mistake.

She had to move carefully. If their powers could be controlled by the PSI agents, then there was a chance of saving their lives. But only a chance, and only if. She pushed her fingers through the short fall of her black hair and narrowed her eyes. It wasn't feasible to destroy them all. It wasn't humane.

As yet, there was no conclusive proof of psychic power, no reports of the women conspiring or socializing with known or suspected psychics. But, neither had they turned themselves in to the Psy-Guardians as the law required. A mark for them, a mark against them. She bit off a curse as she stared at their pictures once again. They didn't look like rebels or conspirators, but how many of that sort resembled the evil of their plans? Tyre had been one of the most handsome men known to be born. But his soul had been a cesspool of evil.

She drew in a deep breath. She needed more information. She couldn't condemn three women who had done nothing to warrant such extreme measure to death, without first being certain. She would have to send out three agents capable of learning this information for her. And of course, all restrictions on the ways they gained their knowledge must be lifted. There could be no doubts.

Wynd Temptress

Kathryn Anne Dubois

Chapter One

Adam Wydner would have recognized Jezermiah Cameron, a.k.a. Jesse Calhoun, self-elected mayor of Chinook, even without the detailed information he had been given to locate her. Purple eyes were as rare in 2150 as fuel-injected engines. Even from this distance of twenty-five feet, her eyes were clear and bright against a mass of the blackest hair he had ever seen on such a fair-skinned woman. She was an unusual mix in every way, down to the fragile build that graced her tall frame.

He focused in on her, blocking out all other stimuli.

She was ordering around a group of muscle-bound males who looked intent on doing damage to anyone who crossed her. And yet, the merest of breezes looked sufficient to whisk her away. Although that was impossible, since she *was* the wind. The wind to her two sisters' fire and water. All believed to be level five psychics.

Until now he hadn't understood why he was called out of retirement for this mission.

Now, in his mind, there was no question.

She was his.

The conviction wrapped around him and settled within his soul like a long awaited homecoming. He couldn't take his eyes off her. The slender column of her throat disappeared under a flannel chambray shirt that looked two sizes too big for her, and the heavy work pants she wore did nothing to hide the delicate curve of her hips. He could feel her intensity.

As he sat in his parked skimmer watching her, he concentrated his gaze on the graceful hollow where throat met collarbone, wishing he could press his lips to the translucent skin. He watched her fidget. While she issued instructions, her slim fingers stroked her neck, and she gave a furtive glance around before returning her attention to her men.

It pleased him that she could sense him. That is, she sensed something. She wouldn't yet know that she belonged to him.

And he suspected that convincing her would be considerably harder than the mission itself. His groin stirred at the suggestion of how he would accomplish that.

At first he had hoped to be assigned to kidnap the one who was fire, which sent his imagination into overdrive with images of what her name might imply. But looking now at the oldest of the sisters made him change his mind. The heat simmering within him as he studied her would prove enough for them both.

As he continued to watch her, he invaded her mind, planting a thought. *You will come to me.*

He paused a moment longer before he started his skimmer and drove past the row of vehicles lined along the wooden planked sidewalk until he came to the end. He pulled into the last space and cut the power. The sleek vehicle hummed to stillness.

As usual, when he stepped out he felt embraced in a time warp. After the successful global rebellion fifty years ago, few towns had escaped unscathed and this small town in Alaska was no exception. But while the major cities had been completely destroyed, other more isolated regions like this had enough intact to start up again.

Satellite dishes stood tall in the distance, but the hard-packed mud street he walked on held only traces of the smooth white stone for which Alaskan streets had been famous. With a plentitude of oil at its disposal, the fiberglass-kinetic material was developed by Alaska in 2100 and had been imported worldwide.

The planked sidewalks and log storefronts that now graced Main Street made the town look like a two-hundred-year-old western starring John Wayne and was a necessary result of a sector that cherished its autonomy. The newly self-proclaimed nation of Alaska had no intention of being dependent on anything it couldn't produce or mine itself, like brick or stone, but it had plenty of trees.

And water and space—even oil, if things got really desperate. Which was the problem. The newly formed League of World Government Sectors needed Alaska to join them. They needed its resources to help rebuild the rest of the North American continent. And if Alaska stubbornly refused to do so, it might encourage other rebellious sectors to follow suit.

To be fair, Alaska wasn't the only government looking to take a break from a unified anything.

He half-agreed with them. He understood their caution. Which is why he had wondered why Shannon Riedel, the Psychic Sensory Investigations Agency Director, wanted only him and no others on this mission to determine Jezermiah's intentions and her level of psychic abilities. When his long-term friend and mentor had insisted that he held the key to Jezermiah's cooperation, he had trusted her too much to question. Whatever the reason, she would reveal it in time.

The tall, lithe goddess was now standing with her hands on her small hips and ordering a group of her lackeys to haul every bench they could find into the meeting hall as the streets and sidewalks continued to teem with people.

She grabbed a tangle of her long thick hair with one hand and was threading it through a cloth tie as Adam approached the door to the hall. He would hardly draw attention today since strangers from all over gathered for the first meeting to discuss California's water needs and how Alaska could benefit by trading its water for food.

His boots clicked along the wooden sidewalk. He lowered the wide brim of his black hat, planning to slip right past her, when she turned suddenly and faced him dead on. For the briefest of seconds her eyes flared and then turned impassive again. She gave a generic nod of acknowledgement, about to face her men, when she fixed her gaze on him again.

There was no way she could have recognized him from anywhere. Unless, of course, it was true that she *was* a psychic of the highest level. His blood warmed at the thought of colliding with a beauty so powerful. As powerful as him.

"Who are you?" She blinked her thick lashes and seemed startled by her own question.

Had she felt him transferring his desire to her? He withdrew the transfer lest she grow wary of him.

"That is," she shifted her weight, "are you here representing some special interest group? You look familiar."

She had a husky voice so at odds with her feminine stature. But one that fit with her tough stance.

If he lied, she would know it. He carefully blocked any thoughts of his purpose or the lustful ideas running rampant in his system.

"We have never met, ma'am." He tipped his hat. "My name's Adam Wydner." He stepped forward and extended his hand.

She nodded. "Jesse Calhoun."

As soon as he got within a foot of her, the aura surrounding her nearly knocked him flat. His body was like a magnet drawn to its polar opposite. Her scent filled him with a rich mixture of female musk and lilac. The urge to touch her was powerful. He stuffed down his reaction lest she sense it, reeling himself with the strong sensation.

Damned if he didn't feel an erection stirring in his coarse denim pants as he gazed down into her face. If he didn't rein in his lust for her it was bound to be noticed.

She seemed hesitant to take his hand. She licked her lips and took a little breath. Then, business-like again, she extended her hand. "Mr. Wydner," she said with a curt nod.

When their fingers touched, his body lit like a torch.

He forced himself not to squeeze her small hand in a fierce grip, willing himself instead to break the contact. But he couldn't seem to do it. He was sure his expression showed no sign of his inner turmoil, but his pulse was beating at a frantic pace and he could feel the head of his cock sliding down his thigh. It was as though she had cast a spell on him even though he knew better. He should have been prepared after all these years. It was bound to happen that fate would one day deliver his soul mate.

He forced a smile and slid his fingers along her palm in an effort to let go of her, but it didn't come easy. A small gust of wind kicked up through the wooden slats beneath their feet, stirring up dust. Was she warning him off? He mentally berated himself—she was a psychic, not a witch. If she chose to use her power over wind, she could do better than that.

He finally broke contact. She looked a little stunned and stepped back as soon as he released her. Her bodyguards formed a protective circle around her.

Barely two seconds in her presence and he had almost blown his cover. Pretending that he hadn't noticed the cavalry forming, he gave a nod. "Well, ma'am, I'll just grab a space in there before it gets too crowded."

His quick exit saved him from answering her other question about whether he represented a special interest group. If she guessed he was here for the PSI Agency she'd bolt. It had taken them years to find her. It had taken him a lifetime.

Chapter Two

Jesse sat off to the side of the stage, listening to the engineer she had just introduced explain the plans for the proposed pipeline. She gave a small sigh of relief that the meeting was proceeding smoothly.

After she had recapped California's proposal to purchase water from Alaska, she had fielded questions about user fees, royalties, and who would pay for the pipeline bringing the water.

Chinook sat in the heart of the largest lake system in Alaska, so if the proposal went through, it would be a major supplier to California. The impact on the small isolated town would be impossible to predict, but still every contingency needed to be addressed and considered.

The food that California couldn't grow without water was sought by Alaskans. Although fish and game were plentiful, Alaskan's needed a year round supply of grains and vegetables. Jesse couldn't help but think of her sister Rayne struggling in California.

She wished she could see her and her youngest sister, Carmella, too. The last she knew Carmella was in Ohio. Carmella had been only ten and Rayne twelve when, for their own safety, their grandmother Maile had separated them, keeping each of their destinations secret from each other.

As the engineer explained where the proposed pipeline would go, she thought about the last time she had seen her small family. Jesse barely remembered her mother since she had died giving birth to Carmella, but her grandmother had taught Jesse everything she knew. The one who warned her about her psychic gifts and her unusual power over the wind. Jesse had seen evidence of it here in Chinook. Like a gentle breeze that stirred the long grass, Jesse, with the mildest of comments could cause an entire group of citizens to change direction, no matter what the controversy. When she was younger, she credited it to her confident demeanor or an uncanny conviction in her voice, but now she knew it for what it was. A legacy left to her by her evil great-grandfather.

Whether a gentle breeze that naturally turned people in her direction or a fierce wind that could destroy everything in its wake, Jesse wanted no part of her paranormal power over the wind. She finally understood what her grandmother tried to counsel her about. She just wished she understood better her grandmother's other counsel for her to be careful with whom she fell in love. Jesse missed her and had regretted her last words to her.

Her grandmother had been heart-broken over separating the girls and sending them away. Even at that time, Jesse had understood that her grandmother feared for them due to another wave of paranoia seizing the region. The climate for psychics was once again becoming dangerous.

Still, Jesse had always been the one to look out for her younger sisters, repeating the warning of her grandmother to hide their powers, even from their grandfather. She argued with her grandmother that day, telling her that she was old and her powers were weakening, but that she and her sisters were strong. They knew how to be careful and it was wrong of their grandmother to separate them. When her grandmother refused to listen, Jesse railed at her, saying that she hated her.

It was the last thing she remembered, besides the image of Carmella crying and Rayne comforting both Carmella and their grandmother.

Jesse had been fifteen at the time and had run away rather than be sent to some compound where she would be protected for the rest of her life. No one was going to cage her in. She had been careful, reinventing herself continually until years later when she finally found a place where she could blend in. It was another piece of advice her grandmother had often recommended they do when they grew up. She settled into the isolated town of Chinook. It had been perfect.

For many years after their separation, she and her sisters had contacted each other on that anniversary, chaining a communication. But it had been a very long time since they had risked it again. When bands of renegade psychics had been discovered trying to take over new governments, the climate for psychics had become more hostile. The quest by the PSI agents to root out any others had stepped up and rumors circulated that any high level psychics were being hunted and killed. She and her sisters had to suspend use of their powers until it was safer.

Although it saddened Jesse to have no contact at all with her sisters, she had no trouble putting aside her powers. She had no interest in being a level five psychic. The knowledge of her gifts had brought her sorrow all her life. And the legacy of her great-grandfather, Tyre Leyton, was one that she abhorred. Every female in her line had suffered as a result of his evil machinations.

All the female descendants of Tyre Leyton had been born with gifts. None of their mates were psychic or held powers of any kind. Nonetheless, Jesse believed that the worst possible thing she could do was to breed with a psychic, especially one as powerful as herself.

What if she created the next Tyre Leyton? The thought sent a shiver down her spine.

In Chinook, Jezermiah had always been just Jesse. She never did anything that would cause her neighbors to think she had special powers of any kind. She intended to keep it that way.

She felt a sudden sense of unease.

The strange sensation that had traveled along her neck earlier returned, but now it was sliding over her breasts like a warm caress. Her nipples tightened. She drew in a sharp breath and sat straighter as though she was caught doing something naughty. Then a sexual heat flared in her belly and moved down between her legs. A rush of moisture flooded her.

She squirmed in her seat on the stage, trying to shake off the peculiar sensual tremors as her eyes skimmed the audience below her.

Her gaze halted when it settled on the man she had seen earlier. He was leaning against a back corner wall, his long legs crossed in front of him in a casual stance that did nothing to erase the dangerous look of him.

She mentally corrected herself. It wasn't his look that had signaled danger to her, although the hard angular lines of his face and rough shadowed jaw didn't help. And his eyes were mesmerizing. Black, intense, as though he could hypnotize a person who was lulled into staring into his eyes longer than it was safe.

Rather, it was an impression she received, a hunch. All level fives had the gift without having to call it up. It was just there, surfacing at unexpected times. With this man it was triggered by his scent when he had moved close to her. A rich masculine scent to his skin that had alerted her, called up her senses, and sent knowledge she didn't know she possessed. The knowledge that this man was a danger to her. It wasn't clear, yet, in what way.

She could call up her powers to discover what he was up to. Touch his thoughts, even plant an opposing idea in his mind, but she refused to do that.

She would not use any of the powers gifted to her by her evil great-grandfather. She would find out this man's intentions the same way everyone else did — through logic and intelligence.

She gave a mental shrug and tried to turn her attention back to the engineer, but like a magnet drawn to its opposite, her eyes couldn't pull away from him. Yet, this time he was too far away for its cause to be the aura that had surrounded him and that had captured her on the front porch.

She frowned. And then without warning, the sexual heat that teased her turned to a molten fire that swelled her sex. The feeling was so powerful she bit her lip to keep from crying out.

She couldn't see his eyes, hidden beneath the wide brim of his hat, but even from this distance she could see his jaw move and see the strong chords of muscle that ran along his throat flex with tension.

She narrowed her gaze, trying to detect if he was staring at her and purposely trying to make her uncomfortable. A woman didn't have to be psychic or telepathic to feel when a man was undressing her with his eyes. And if that was the only danger he posed it was a relief. She could certainly handle him.

While she simmered, he crossed his arms over his broad chest. Then, to her annoyance, he tipped up the brim of his hat and stared openly, his gaze unflinching. She raised a brow, but he didn't so much as blink.

Arrogant bastard. What was his game anyway? A small trickle of sweat pooled between her breasts.

Whatever it was, she wasn't playing.

And he wasn't worth brooding over.

Except that when he stared at her, she wasn't uncomfortable exactly…she was aroused.

Chapter Three

Adam slipped out of the meeting before it was over. He had seen enough.

If she was living as a psychic or even exercising undue influence over the population of Chinook, he couldn't see it. In fact, other than her classic beauty, she blended in as well as anyone.

He wouldn't find out anything more hanging around here. Not until he isolated her in the Agency's protective environment would he know.

He would spend the rest of the day reviewing his plans to kidnap her.

* * * * *

Adam slipped into her bedroom later that night, glad that he decided to kidnap her while she slept, because it gave him the advantage of having her half-naked when he did.

He gazed down at her sprawled figure lying across the bed, tummy down and long limbs tangled in the sheets. Her luscious bottom was barely covered by a delicate scrap of ivory lace and the T-shirt she wore was hiked up past her waist.

All he could see of her face under the tumble of dark waves were full lips relaxed by sleep, glistening with moisture in the moonlight, and a light flush coloring high cheekbones. Every cell in his body reacted. In the space of a breath, he was hard...throbbing hard.

He ran a hand through his hair and grimaced. How was he going to make it through the next several days of interrogation while sporting a constant erection?

Maybe he needed to resolve that conflict first.

But even as he thought it, he doubted she'd cooperate.

He eased down beside her, wanting to wake her before he administered the Bellaveter. It was a powerful yet harmless drug. When she came to, he wanted her to remember the preceding moments so it would lessen the shock of her kidnapping.

He lifted a thick curl off her cheek and stroked lightly along her jaw line. She frowned, her small straight nose crinkling until she gave a soft sigh and then relaxed again.

He suspected she slept deeply and wondered what collective thoughts she was picking up during these unguarded moments, what thoughts from those Akashic records that stored every thought that has ever occurred on the astral plane.

He could plant a thought in her mind now. Whisper in his perfected hypnotic tone that he was her completion. That only together could they be whole.

But he wouldn't. He wanted her to recognize him through her female senses first. He wanted her to feel the powerful pull of her sex that drew her to him in the same way he felt it.

He ached now, groaning at the fullness that stretched the fabric of his pants and the seam that cut into his balls.

He pulled out the small plastic package and ripped gently. "Wake up," he murmured, close to her ear, holding the opened packet. He allowed her to breathe in the herbs from the scented cloth, but held it far enough from her nose that it would take effect slowly.

Her huge purple eyes opened wide. "What…" She lifted her head and gave a puzzled frown, then rolled over in slow motion. But while her actions grew more slumberous her eyes sharpened. "Why…are…"

"Shhh…" He lifted an errant curl that stuck to the moist skin of her cheek. "You're coming with me, honey."

Panic filled her eyes, but while he knew her sight and hearing would be the last of her senses to weaken, the Bellaveter was already paralyzing her physical responses. She gave a slow shake of her head. Her hand came up off the bed and then dropped.

"I won't hurt you, Jezermiah." Terror filled her eyes when he called her by her given name. "Trust me," he urged as he continued to run a lazy finger along her cheek. She looked as though she wanted to murder him. Although her facial expression hadn't changed, her violet eyes torched into flames. He touched the tip of her chin, tilting her face up, tempted to kiss those full, relaxed lips. Her eyes flared, but she was powerless to react.

The thought occurred to him that he might not find her this vulnerable for some time.

Unable to resist, he gave in to the impulse.

He drew close to her and ran his nose along her cheek, inhaling her delicious scent. Then he ran his tongue along her lower lip for a small taste of her. The rush of blood that pounded through him with the contact jolted him.

He drew back and frowned, just as her thick lashes closed, feathering pale cheeks. Though he was unwilling to break the pleasurable contact, he was annoyed by how little control he had around her. If he wanted to keep the upper hand, and he definitely needed to, he had better curb his appetite for her.

Was it the pheromones she emitted? He knew they had to be strong. It explained why the males at the meeting today had hovered around her like studs circling a mare in heat.

For the first time he wondered what he would do if he discovered that she *was* a threat. Would he have the strength to turn her in?

But the idea was impossible. How could his eternal mate be evil? And there was no question in his soul that she was his mate.

He knew it with every fiber of his being. That she was a psychic was also without question. It was only the level of her powers that he needed to determine.

A dark thought edged into his mind. What if his attraction to her was purely physical and so strong due to her pheromones that he was confusing his sexual need for her with his spiritual need to become as one with her soul?

But in his thirty-six years he had always trusted his psychic ability and never before had he recognized anyone as his soul mate. Why should he doubt it now?

Except that he had also never felt such a strong sexual pull before either.

He slipped an arm under her shoulders and the other under her knees and lifted her easily off the bed. The contact of his forearms sliding beneath her satiny thighs was torture, but he ignored it and carried her out of the bedroom and toward the backyard where his skimmer waited.

After settling her comfortably on the lamb's wool blanket spread out in the skimmer's back, he started to drape a silk sheet over all that bare skin that shimmered like pearls in the moonlight, but then stopped. He shouldn't look at her while she lay unconscious and unable to protest. But he did. Her tits were small and high, beautifully shaped with large nipples that darkened the lavender T-shirt.

He guessed her nipples were not pale like the rest of her skin but ruby-red dark. His cock swelled at the thought of taking a taut nipple into his mouth and rolling his tongue along the sensitive tip.

He cursed at the bite of pain his zipper caused. His arousal was becoming unmanageable, even annoying.

He could end it by simply reaching into his pants. Looking at her spread out before him, it would take only a few smooth strokes to get him off.

His eyes dropped to the small triangle of lace between her legs.

A small mound of curly hair darkened the lace and then he groaned when he realized it disappeared. It was clear her sex lips were smooth. She was damp and the full fleshy folds were clearly outlined against the silky fabric between her thighs. The thought of his tongue tracing along the hairless swell of her sex had his cock throbbing.

This was stupid. This paralysis of lust. He closed the door of the skimmer and, turning his back on her, unzipped his fly. He would not visually rape her when he jerked off, assaulting her with his eyes and his thoughts while she lay unresponsive, but he definitely needed to relieve himself.

He frowned when he took out his cock and the cool moist air drifted over his heated flesh. It looked like some aberration of his body, sticking straight out like a flagpole from his fly, the skin red and smooth compared to the dark rough skin of the rest of his body. Like most men, he wondered how women could even take the ugly beast seriously. He would have laughed if he weren't so strangled with lust.

Maybe it was true that men were led by their cocks.

But even as he thought it, he knew it wasn't true. It was the lovely creature he had just drugged and kidnapped that had captured him and now ruled his hungry responses.

He didn't have to look at her. Every detail of her was already etched on his brain. He leaned against the skimmer's door and wet the tips of two fingers. Then he slid the moisture along the thick purpled vein that ran his length and imagined her tongue slipping along his hot skin, fluttering lightly and then with more pressure before she took the angry head into her mouth and poked her tongue into his slit, tasting his cum.

He groaned aloud and pictured sifting his long fingers into her silky hair as he guided her mouth around his shaft, urging her to take him deep and suck hard.

He mimicked the motion, fisting his cock and squeezing.

But it was picturing her smooth sex lips, flushed and swollen, his tongue licking up her juices and feeling the hot silky skin against his lips that did him in. He pumped, feeling the pressure build in his balls and his cock swell until his cum eased out the tip.

With a deep groan he gave himself over to the pleasure.

His cock exploded like a rifle going off. He groaned, watching jets of cum shoot out in front of him, the sensations making his knees weak and causing a sweat to break out over his body. He flattened sweaty palms against cool metal, bracing himself and savoring the pleasure.

When the contractions subsided, he expected his tension to ebb and blessed relief to wash over him.

Only it never happened.

His cock went to half-mast, but his tension remained.

He was nowhere near satisfied.

He glared down at the evidence of his frustration and stuffed himself back in his pants. If she knew how much power she had over him, it would jeopardize his mission.

His exceptional psychic power would do him no good against his lust for her. He needed either to satisfy it first or hide it from her.

How in the hell would he do either?

He had better come up with *some* plan, because of critical importance was first ascertaining her intentions. He couldn't forget that she was a descendant from the most malevolent and powerful psychic ever recorded.

Chapter Four

Jesse awoke to the sound of an engine purring and the smell of male, an earthy scent that sent heat pooling in her groin. She tried to lift her eyelids but they wouldn't budge. Her body felt equally powerless, like a dead weight.

She sensed that whatever vehicle transported her, it was descending.

And then a rush of memory returned.

The powerfully built man from the meeting was towering over her, his dark hair framing his unshaven face in thick waves.

She remembered his lips touching hers, his tongue gliding over her mouth, the incredible heat that ignited her body.

Her eyes popped wide with the next memory.

Shortly before she had passed out, he had called her Jezermiah.

She struggled to move but remained frozen. Directly above her was the ceiling of a high tech skimmer. She recognized the fancy light panels, music skids, and laser search system. Her peripheral vision finally locked onto a sweep of broad shoulders encased in a black cotton shirt. His hair fell over the back of his collar.

The gravitational pull grew stronger. The skimmer had to be in some kind of rocket ship that was descending to earth. At least she hoped it was earth.

The pressure in her ears mounted and her limbs tingled. Sensory touch returned to her body.

The craft stopped and the engine went still.

Silence for a beat until on its heels came the whine of gears. A ghostlike silence returned.

Her neck prickled with sensation and she could wriggle her toes, but she didn't dare move until she knew what was happening. She closed her eyes and waited.

A warm breeze glided over her skin, letting her know a door to the ship had opened, but still the silence was deafening, no sounds of life from any direction.

The soft rustle of fabric signaled that he had either turned in his seat or left it. She could feel his eyes on her. And he wasn't simply looking her way. His eyes were penetrating her, sliding over her skin in a purely sensual way. She felt him move closer, his strength and size robbing her of air. The incredible smell of him that sent her senses spinning filled her and made her sex quiver. She could feel a blush stain her cheeks. This man held a power over her that was unnatural.

She had to think. Do something.

If he was a PSI agent, she could well be facing her death.

"Jezermiah?" he murmured close to her ear, his warm breath washing over her.

The deep pitch of his voice startled her, but she didn't flinch. She could picture those full lips close to her skin.

It was now or never.

A swift right hook with her elbow caught him hard in the jaw and sent him reeling. His head cracked against the chrome gears.

"What the—"

Before he could make a lunge for her, she scurried to her feet and scrambled out the skimmer door with the sound of his muttered curses trailing behind. She made a run for the rocket's ramp and in minutes she was outside. But it took only a quick glance around to know that it wouldn't matter in which direction she ran. Damn! She ran anyway.

When she couldn't hear him behind her, she stopped and looked back. He was sitting there, legs dangling over the side of the rocket's ramp like he had all the time in the world. He twirled a toothpick between those sensuous lips, his jaw flexing with the motion.

Damn! She locked her hands onto her hips. Damn! What now? She glanced around at the endless prairie facing her from all directions. Not a mountain or tree in site. Absolute nothingness. If ever she was tempted to use her power over the wind it was now. But unless it was a matter of life or death she wouldn't. So far, she was still alive.

Her head snapped back to his. She could *feel* him laughing. Fury boiling over, she shot daggers at him with her gaze. He'd be sorry he ever took her. Maybe she *would* batter him with a hurricane, or whip him up in a small tornado. She half wondered if she could actually do that, having only experimented so far with gentle gusts of wind. She shot him an angry glare.

But when he stared back, a jolt of pure pleasure shocked and inflamed her, sending her off balance. She struggled to stave off the sensual heat building, sure now that he held some mysterious power over her. The temptation to exercise her psychic powers was almost too hard to resist, but caution won out.

She shook off the sexual heat filling her and stared back at him.

Metal winking in the distance behind the rocket caught her attention. She moved to the right and behind the ship a large compound came into view. A string of one-story adobe buildings with trees spotting its perimeter. She thought she saw the sun glinting off a water's surface.

She sharpened her focus. It was a pool. A large in-ground swimming pool surrounded by a wide patio.

She drew in a breath.

What was going on here?

It hardly looked like a military encampment, but why else would he bring her here? She glanced again at the endless prairie. What choice did she have? At least maybe she'd find a vehicle to steal.

She gave a last look at his relaxed pose along the ramp and then made a mad dash, arcing wide around the rocket and heading straight for the compound.

When she glanced back, he was nowhere in sight.

Within minutes, she was out of breath and quietly circling the compound. It was eerily silent. She approached a large carved double door. Would it be too much to ask that it be open? When she turned the brass knob, the heavy door swung ajar, and she stepped tentatively into a high-ceilinged tile foyer. Huge potted plants and peach and turquoise walls were bathed in sunlight by a large domed skylight. She could hear the gentle trickle of water gliding over stone.

She blinked in awe and stepped in farther.

A movement caught her eye. She tensed. Two hummingbirds flew out of a tree, one chasing the other and warbling in excitement.

She let out a breath, mentally berating herself for wasting time. She had to find a weapon fast and a vehicle to steal if she was going to escape. Escape how and to where she wasn't sure, but he was bound to come after her and she needed to be ready.

Chapter Five

Adam rubbed his tender jaw and smiled thinking about the image she made as she ran from him, her sweet backside barely covered by that scrap of lace and her limbs smooth, silky, and naked.

He had let her run. There was nowhere for her to go.

In the meantime he went back into the ship and started the skimmer. He drove toward the Rubic's, the luxurious complex of buildings designed to provide an atmosphere for maximum security and interrogation. It was here that he would eventually hypnotize her and test for brain activity in her right templar lobe.

Then he would question her about her family connections and determine where her loyalties lay.

He pulled into the underground garage and took the steps to the ground level.

After that he took his time as he entered the large sunlit kitchen, waiting for her to come to him. It wouldn't be long before she realized there was no real escape.

He filled the rice cooker and started it and then snapped on the stove. While he waited for it to reach optimal temperature he took a pound of salmon out of the preserver, rinsed it, and then dribbled a delicate buttered lemon dill sauce on top. Then he turned his attention to the vegetables, placing them on the smooth kondela chopping block.

As he chopped and sliced vegetables in perfect diagonals he pictured her wandering the complex, surprised by its opulence and warmth, examining the plush meeting rooms for clues, and puzzling over the individual bedrooms. Outside, tennis courts and pools dotted the back landscape and a large weight room, racquetball court, and hot tubs took up most of the underground level.

If he had to hole up here for weeks, he would get the truth out of her. It would be no hardship. And the Agency had given him no deadline for his return.

He felt himself relax for the first time in months.

* * * * *

Jesse was spittin' mad.

The only way out of here was in his skimmer and she needed a number code to activate it. When she found it in the garage she expected it to be triggered by his touch or a laser scan of his iris. If that were the case, she could have simply knocked him out, dragged him into it, started the damned thing, and then dumped him. The prairie had to lead somewhere. The earth *was* still round.

But she found it was activated with an old fashioned number pad. She'd have to torture him to get the code out of him.

She wanted to kick and maim something, badly.

This place was useless. More like a vacation spa. No means of communication to the outside world and no weapons of any kind. At least none that she could find.

Not that she'd really kill him. But he wouldn't know that.

After she had fully explored the compound, she settled on the only means of torture left in order for her to get the code out of him. With her plan in mind and the few tools necessary for the job, she followed the delicate smells coming from the west wing.

When she peeked into the kitchen, he was completely absorbed in pouring what looked like olive oil into a sauté pan. His sleeves were rolled up his muscled forearms and his big body towered over the stove, reinforcing her conviction that she couldn't physically overpower him despite her many defensive skills. He leaned closer, studied the oil, and then poured a drop more. He opened his black shirt at the neck and a few buttons down his chest. A light sheen of sweat dampened his wide forehead.

The same dark hair that covered his arms peppered his chest. She could almost smell him from where she stood. She blocked out the memory and watched as he adjusted the heat under the skillet several times before he looked satisfied.

A perfectionist.

He tossed in a small heap of vegetables and frowned. Then he adjusted the heat again and stirred with great concentration.

A control freak, too.

But, freak or not, the smells coming from the room were making her mouth water.

She took a quick scan of the inside and saw nothing untoward. Apparently his only immediate plans were to eat and she was starved. Her own plans could wait. She dropped her small bag of tools outside the door.

When she pushed through the swinging doors, he glanced up as though expecting her and let his heated gaze travel over her body. She had had enough sense to throw on some clothes. She would have preferred a pair of pants, but the only ones she found were far too large, so she settled for one of the less seductive sundresses she found in one of the closets.

His lips tipped up at one corner and without saying a word, he turned his attention back to his cooking.

It more than irritated her that the possibility she might attack him caused him no worry.

He glanced up from his stirring. "Hungry?"

Her eyes snapped to his. "You mean in addition to being furious, drugged, and held captive?"

He lifted a shoulder. "No, I was just wondering about your appetite."

Her mouth twisted. *And a comedian, too.*

She stormed in. But she didn't approach him. Not that she was afraid exactly, although she sensed danger being near him. It was just wise to keep her distance.

She took in the contents of the room. While the small sitting room was graced with comfortable chairs, the kitchen was all sleek lines of chrome and stainless steel. Marbled countertop, granite floor. No expense spared.

Whoever he was, he was important. And she was in trouble. She had no doubt now that he worked for the PSI Agency and that he suspected her identity.

But she had covered her tracks expertly. And there was no way he could force the truth out of her. Besides, she would have that code from him and be long gone before he could try.

First, she was going to eat.

"Care to join me?"

He carried two steaming dishes and laid them on the dining table that was set for two.

She regarded him suspiciously, taking her plate and moving clear down to the other end.

His eyes lit with amusement as she settled herself. What did he expect? That in between his kidnapping her and her torturing him they'd share a pleasant meal?

She glared at him.

He raised a long necked bottle. "Wine?"

"Are we celebrating something?" she spat.

He gave a husky laugh that made her breasts tingle.

"That would certainly be *my* wish." His lids lowered. "But I'm afraid I'm merely offering refreshment."

She ignored him and stabbed into her food. The fish flaked into tender pieces. When she took a bite, she couldn't suppress a groan of delight. It was seasoned to perfection. Even the feel of it sliding down her throat was irresistible. It seemed that within minutes her plate was half empty and her pangs of hunger replaced with delicious satisfaction.

When she looked up he was studying her with naked hunger.

She startled and the look vanished, replaced by a relaxed gaze. But the blood pumping to her sex told her she hadn't imagined it.

She took a little breath and finished quickly, anxious to get out of there.

"You're Tyre Leyton's great-granddaughter."

Her hand stopped mid-air. She looked up, determined to weather this. She couldn't deny knowing of him. Any history student would know he had been the leader of the last group of psychic overlords. They had used their paranormal ability to dominate the globe and control resources for their own greedy use.

Leyton himself, as the head, had centralized the world government, basing its headquarters in North America, and lived in splendor while the rest of the world's nations had to use profits from their GNP's to pay for such necessities as water. When he knew he and his army were about to lose to the rebels, he had ordered that the infrastructure of the entire North American continent be systematically destroyed. What had once been a prosperous unified global economy was brought to ruin during Tyre Leyton's reign.

No one hated him more than Jesse.

"So." She placed her fork down with care. "That's why you kidnapped me." She leaned back in the chair and folded her hands in her lap. "Well, I'm relieved. I thought perhaps you might be some renegade psychic trying to overthrow our small, soon to be prosperous, town. It's no secret that the pipeline will make Chinook valuable. A psychic gaining control of a small territory such as ours could lead to controlling the natural resources for which Alaska is noted." She pierced him with her gaze. "You are psychic, are you not?"

"Yes."

She was surprised by his quick admission.

"You haven't answered my question," he said.

She leaned in. "I didn't hear a question. It sounded like a statement." She flattened her palms on the table. "A false statement."

His eyes blazed into hers, trying to read her thoughts. She blocked them, an automatic response over which she had little control. It was one gift for which she was grateful.

His eyes narrowed. "There is no point denying it. What I need to determine is what you plan to do about it. Your inherited powers over the wind in such a vast, open, unobstructed country as Alaska could be enormous. You seem to have an expert understanding of what a powerful psychic could do by getting control of Chinook."

"So do you. Which means you must work for the PSI Agency."

"Right again."

His forthrightness puzzled her. "Well, you're wasting your time. While I'm sure your mission is worthy, you've got the wrong person."

"We've been looking for all three of you. For some time now."

Her throat constricted at the mention of her sisters. She blinked over at him, willing her heart to steady its beat. "Who?"

"Your sisters were located in Ohio and California."

She wanted to leap across the table and choke him. It was only knowing that by doing so she would confirm what he knew, that kept her seated. She could *not* let him know who she was.

"Three of them. Well, good for you. I hope you find them, because no more despicable a creature existed than Tyre Leyton. Course," she gave a shrug, "I'm not sure they should pay for the sins of the father and all that, but I'm sure the Agency knows what it's doing."

"That's what we intend to determine. There is little doubt that you are all level five psychics—"

She blew out a breath. "And how would you know that?"

"It would make sense, wouldn't it?"

"Not necessarily. If I remember my history, Tyre Leyton himself prohibited two psychics of equal power mating for fear they might procreate one more powerful than himself. And each generation after Leyton showed no psychic abilities whatsoever."

"Or, they chose not to exercise their abilities."

She balled up her napkin and threw it down. "That's the trouble with you psychics. You know everything." She shot up from the table. "If you were really smart, you'd make sure *you* didn't mate with another psychic, and then we wouldn't have to worry about any of you producing another Tyre Leyton."

He rose slowly from his chair. "Does that worry you?"

"What?"

He came at her with slow deliberate steps.

She backed up. "Why should it worry me? I'm no psychic." She licked her lips and glanced around for some escape. She had no reason to think he was going to kiss her, but she knew that he would.

His eyes dropped to her breasts. "You're trembling. Terrified that you'll produce the seed of your great-grandfather."

"Shut up!" she screamed. "He is not my great-grandfather." Her back thumped the wall. Before she could take a breath, he braced his hands beside her head, trapping her.

He leaned down, a whisper away, and murmured against her lips. "You don't know *what* would happen if two powerful psychics mated, but I have an idea." He tipped her chin up. "Pure pleasure."

She had no will to fight him. Too late she realized that she had let his low melodic voice hypnotize her. But when his lips settled over hers, rational thought fled. Only the hot burn in her belly mattered. And his lips *were* pure pleasure. Hot and smooth and wet.

He clamped her waist, pulling her against him as his tongue slid over her lips, teasing her mouth open. His erection, thick and hot between her thighs and pushing against her, made her gasp. Hot sensation sluiced through her belly, clear down to her toes. His tongue gained entrance, slipping along hers as he slid his arousal against her softness. A small helpless cry escaped her as need exploded in her sex and throbbed.

She was so pathetically weak. How could she do this? While her mind fought him, her body pressed forward, seeking him. Before she knew what was happening his hands slipped under her sundress and palmed her thighs, spreading her. Her breath caught. When she squirmed, his fingers slipped beneath her panties and explored. She strangled a moan when he slipped a finger up into her heat.

"You're soaked," he groaned. "You feel so silky, Jez." His thumb teased her clit, sending lightning licks of fire everywhere.

But the sweep of pleasure that shook her was not enough to block out him calling her by her grandmother's pet name.

She thrashed wildly, punching at him and fighting with all she had, worried that they'd gotten to her grandmother, too.

He stumbled back.

"That's what this is about," she railed. She looked around for anything that would serve as a weapon as she sidestepped him.

He was breathing heavily and his arousal filled his pants. She dragged her eyes away. He was so large in every way that she'd have to keep her wits about her if she was to escape him.

"You don't work for the Agency."

"I don't?" He blinked.

It all became clear. She was more worried now than ever. And what about her sisters? Had they fallen victim to handsome renegade psychics, too?

He dropped himself into a chair and raked both hands through his hair. "Look, it's hard to explain exactly what comes over me when I'm near you but..." His voice trailed off and he gave a laugh.

"I have to say," she began, stalling for time, "you may have been a good choice as far as looks go, but you're kind of stupid." She spotted a heavy brass lamp in the sitting room and inched her way toward it.

He frowned. "How's that?"

"If you wanted to seduce me, you didn't have to kidnap me, you could—"

"Seduce you?" he growled. Then he stood. "Look, while I admit I find you distracting, my primary mission."

"'Course, there is no way of knowing if your people's theory is even true, is there?"

"My people?"

She was within grabbing range of the lamp. All she'd need was for him to turn away from her, or to find a way to distract him. Damn, she was stupid. Of course she could distract him. He had just admitted as much.

"I mean, while I find you attractive," she continued in a husky purr, "there really is no guarantee that my mating with a powerful psychic would produce offspring of an even higher level."

He tipped his head. "That's what you think my mission is?" He got up from his chair and started toward her. "You think I'm a renegade psychic who planned to rape you?"

"I think it's pretty clear that you'd hardly need to force me." She unbuttoned her dress and let if fall to the floor.

Like a bug trapped in a light beam he stopped, still as stone, except for his eyes that roved over her body. She definitely had his attention.

"While your theory is flawed, I'm relieved you're not from the Agency. I'm sure they are hunting you, too. And while the idea of you fucking me is more than appealing," she said, lifting her T-shirt over her head and tossing it behind her, "I'm not likely to produce any offspring since you should have figured I'd be using birth control."

His mouth dropped and his eyes riveted on her nipples. They swelled and tightened to hard points. She groaned inwardly. The hot flush that crept up his neck made her shiver.

She hooked her fingers in the elastic of her panties and watched his face as she slid them off her hips. His gaze locked on the small dark thatch about to be uncovered. When she slid the lace down her thighs, she purposely bent forward, hiding her secrets from him, her breasts hanging like small pendulums before her. He craned his neck. She pivoted, giving him a view of her bottom and heard him groan.

She stepped out of her panties and straightened. He started for her, but she took a half step back before he could loom up in front of her. She needed to get him on his knees.

She spread her sex lips with two fingers and looked him straight in the eye. "Do you want to taste me first?"

He made a gurgling sound in his throat and dropped to his knees.

She picked up the brass lamp but then sighed when his tongue slid over her sex. He groaned, slipping his tongue up into her heat, clutching her thighs and spreading her wider. Her knees buckled. She had to get hold of herself before the pleasure swept her under. His thumbs slid over her clit.

She cracked the lamp over his head.

Chapter Six

When Adam came to he was sure he had been dreaming.

The last thing he remembered were Jezermiah's sweet pink lips, plump and glistening with arousal, and his tongue gliding over the silky hairless folds, tasting her and slipping up into her heat. He thought he would come by just tasting her. He grew hard as the tantalizing memory filled him.

Until his head started pounding. When his vision cleared, he saw that he was still in the kitchen area.

When he tried to move, he soon realized he was tied to a chair. Yanking hard on his restraints proved useless, and while his wrists were tied behind his back, each ankle was strapped to a chair leg. His chest was anchored to the chair's back.

He twisted around, but couldn't see her. Lifting up, he took the chair with him so that he was hopping in a circle. When he made a full ninety-degree turn he saw her. She was sitting on the couch, fully dressed, long legs crossed and swinging.

"It's about time you came to."

"I probably have a concussion," he growled. "That's the second time you've bashed my skull in less than two hours."

"Three hours. You've been out for a full sixty minutes," she quipped.

Despite her tone, he sensed a pang of guilt. He could sense a lot about her emotions that he bet she hid well from others.

"Untie me."

"Just as soon as you tell me the code that starts the skimmer."

"Forget it."

"Then I'll have to kill you."

He snorted. "With what?"

She jumped up. "With any number of things. How about a fork jammed into your eyeballs?"

He winced.

"A butcher knife would do fine for slicing off your balls."

He closed his eyes to *that* image.

"Or..." She stepped up close to him. "I could choke you with this rope." She wrapped it around her wrist and jerked.

But he wasn't paying attention. He was staring at her crotch as she stood before him. Now he didn't have to imagine. He knew what she looked like, what she smelled like, and how she tasted underneath those panties. He drew in a steadying breath.

If he was going to get himself out of this jam, he had to start thinking with the head that was above his waist.

He tipped his head up and looked at her. "So, which one is it going to be?"

She leaned down close. "Choking you." She gritted her teeth. "That would give me the most satisfaction."

He shrugged. "Suit yourself."

Before he could catch his breath, he felt the rough threads of a noose slipping around his neck.

"It's not going to work," he told her as she threw one end over a ceiling beam.

She gave it a tug and his head snapped up. "Tell me the code!"

When he didn't answer, she pulled it tighter, but it wasn't anywhere close to hurting him. For all her toughness, he knew she didn't have it in her.

"Look," he said, trying to reason with her. "Let's clear up a few things. I *am* a level five psychic, but I'm not a renegade. I'm a retired Commander with the PSI Agency and I'm convinced you're Jezermiah Cameron. My mission is to determine your level of psychic ability and your intentions during this reunification."

"Why should I believe you? And why should I care? Either way, you've kidnapped me and held me hostage. I just want to be left alone. I've hurt no one and have no *intentions* of causing anyone any trouble. Except you, if you don't let me out of here. Now tell me the code."

"Do you really believe if you mate with a psychic as powerful as yourself you'll create another Tyre Leyton?"

"I never said that."

"You thought it."

"You can't read my thoughts."

"All level fives can—"

"But I—"

He gave her an amused smile. "But you what? Blocked my thoughts?"

"No—"

"You know, you might just get the code out of me by using your abilities. You may be more powerful than I am."

"I'm not who you think I am." She walked over to the stove and secured the rope to its leg. "Besides, I'd rather torture you."

That, he believed.

She pulled on the rope and yanked gently. "All I have to do is stand on my tip toes, grab this rope, and let my weight drop and I could choke you."

"But you won't."

She glowered at him. "Why wouldn't I?"

"Because," he said, his voice gentle. "I don't believe you have it in you."

"That's quite a gamble you're taking." Her eyes met his, clear and steady.

"It's no gamble, Jezermiah. I know you. I've known you for a long time. It's just only now that we've met."

She drew in a soft breath. "What are you talking about?"

"We're fated. You and I."

She straightened, her expression clouded. "Fated for what?"

"To be together."

She blinked and then shook her head. "Fated!" She gave a snort. "I've allowed you to do it again. The way you hypnotize me so easily should prove that I'm no level five psychic."

"This isn't psychic energy, Jez, it's—"

"Stop it!" She clenched her small fists. "I just want..." She turned her back on him. "I just want to go home." Her head bent. "But now I have no home, since you've hunted me down."

"Jez—"

She whirled on him. "Stop calling me that," she choked, her eyes brimming with tears.

God, he wanted to hold her. He fought against his bonds. "Untie me, Jez. I can help you. You just have to trust me."

But she wasn't listening. She drifted away, mumbling something to herself. When she turned back to him, her eyes were brighter but still shimmering with moisture. She pursed her lips and studied him. "Yes," she murmured, brushing a tangle of hair off her face. "There's more than one way to torture a man."

Tension leaped in his loins at the way her lush lips lifted in a predatory smile. Her eyes dropped down to the growing bulge in his pants. She licked her lips and gave a little smile. "Oh, yes. This will definitely work."

He didn't like the sound of that.

"Let's see," she murmured to herself, pulling out more rope from the bag, and then dropping down beside him.

"What are you doing?"

She ignored him and walked behind the chair, her legs impossibly long in that short dress. He thought about how smooth and hot her thighs had felt against his palms. She was wrapping more rope around him and untying others, tugging and yanking and anchoring ends to corner posts and to one leg of the industrial stove. He was trying to figure out what she was up to when she tightened the rope over the beam forcing him to stand.

The chair fell away and he was tethered. Tied up like a wild stallion and readied to be broken. He stood with his legs braced shoulder width apart, unable to move them either forward or back, with his hands behind his back and his neck in a taut noose.

A sweat broke over his body. He wasn't sure how he felt about what she planned to do. Then again, he was probably letting his imagination run away with him.

She sauntered up to him and dropped her eyes down his body. "Yes, this will be perfect." She lifted her lashes. "Don't you think?"

He swallowed. "Perfect for what?"

She scraped her nails over his groin. He was wrong. He knew exactly what she planned to do to him, and he still wasn't sure how he felt abut it.

When she squeezed him through the heavy denim, he closed his eyes and groaned.

"Let's see." Her breath brushed his lips. "Where should I start?"

She released his cock. When he opened his eyes, she had stepped back and was studying his shoulders. She gave him a sultry grin. "First, I'd like to see if you're as big as you seem."

She plucked at the buttons on his shirt and drew aside the fabric. "Oh..." She glanced up at him and color rose to her cheeks. In a gesture that seemed purely spontaneous, she swept a tentative palm down his chest. He sucked in a breath with the contact of their skin. Her face flushed, fueling his arousal.

"I'd be careful about doing anything you'll be sorry for."

She bit her lip and then scraped her nail over his nipple. When he groaned, she looked surprised by his reaction and then did it again. This time he stifled the moan, but her hand looked so small compared to his muscled chest, her fingers so white against his dark hair that he was already tortured.

She seemed lost in her exploration, threading her fingers through the wiry hair and moving closer for a better look. Her breath fluttered through his chest hair. She smelled so good that he wanted to take a bite out of her. But she seemed not to notice, so intent was she on skimming her hands over every muscle, her concentration fierce, and with such exquisite care it was as though she were a sculptor molding the hard ridges with her palms. Her touch was killing him. He was hard as steel just thinking about the soft pads of her fingers moving down farther.

Standing on her toes, she reached up to push his shirt off his shoulders and then smoothed her palms over his bunched biceps, shaping them under her hands. She pressed her fingers into his muscles as though gauging his strength. She let out a little breath. If she had any ideas about overpowering him, she'd realize now that she was in over her head.

When she turned her attention back to his chest she hesitated. Her eyes dropped lower. As though compelled to touch him, she traced with her fingers the ripple of muscle along his stomach. He broke out in a sweat. *She'd have him begging before she got his pants down.*

She murmured to herself and then leaned a little closer, almost touching her forehead to his chest. When she breathed deeply, he had to strangle a moan. He didn't think anything could be more erotic than the thought that she was breathing in his scent. Then she licked his nipple and he jumped.

"Oh, you like that?" Her wet tongue sent a message straight to his groin and had him throbbing.

"I refuse to answer on the grounds —"

She stepped back, looking dazed. She gave her head a little shake as though gathering her wits and then frowned. "Is that right? We'll just see what tortures you and what doesn't."

He stifled a groan when she yanked on his fly button and unzipped his pants. "This won't lie." She pulled his pants down over his hips. He came bobbing out.

She drew in a breath. He swelled hideously large as she continued to stare at him, her eyes growing as large as saucers. The purpled vein that ran his length bulged and the head of his cock grew red and angry right before her eyes. His hairy balls pulled up tight. If anyone was being tortured, it was she.

She reached for him with a tentative touch and glided her fingertips smoothly over his stretched skin and then traced down his gnarled vein. His cock jumped. "You're beautiful," she breathed.

He choked back a laugh and then sucked air when she drew circles around the rim of his dick with one finger. He held himself so tight he could feel the chords along his neck bulging. The pressure built to unbearable proportions. When his seed wept out of the tiny slit, she touched her finger to it and smoothed the creamy liquid along his skin.

If strangling on his own lust was any indication, he'd never make it through this.

"Smooth," she whispered. "Not at all like the rest of you." She sighed. "I think I'd like to taste you."

He groaned, but his cock twitched in anticipation.

When she cupped his balls, he hissed in his breath.

"But not right now," she said, looking him straight in the eye while she cradled him, rolling the defenseless sac along her palms. When she dropped her hand, he didn't know whether he sighed in relief or disappointment.

She walked around to his back. He was definitely uncomfortable with that and held his breath until he could figure out what she planned next.

"This isn't going to work," she grumbled.

What the hell did that mean?

She stalked over to the kitchen and wrenched open drawers.

When she turned around, a medium sized carving knife gleamed in her hand. She started toward him.

In a purely instinctive move, he jerked on his bound wrists in an attempt to protect his balls. At the same time that he knew it was a meaningless threat.

Still, he kept a close eye on her. "What's that for?"

"I want to see more of you." She moved in back of him and slipped the knife under his collar. In one smooth movement, she slit the back of his shirt and then went to work on his sleeves. In minutes, scraps of his shirt littered the floor.

He stood stark naked before her, other than his pants that were stuck around his knees.

She made the same thorough examination of his back, tracing her palms over every chorded muscle until her small palms skimmed down his backside. He closed his eyes and almost gave it up.

"Not nearly so large here." He could hear the smile in her voice. "But definitely hard...and tight." When she squeezed one cheek, the breath left his lungs.

"You're a menace," he growled.

"Just give me the code and I'll end this torture."

Did he want that? He knew full well she intended to drive him to the brink and then stop until he gave her the damned code. But what she was doing felt so good he wanted it to last. And if he did give her the code, she'd run again and the Agency might not find her again for years.

He might not find her for years.

No way she'd get it out of him.

Warm flesh pressed against his back and hard nipples poked his skin. Oh God, if she stripped, he didn't know how he'd resist her. Her panties dropped at his ankles. He hoped the dress followed.

She moaned softly and rubbed her bare skin against him. "You smell delicious." She ran her lips and hands over his back, licking up his sweat, her tongue warm and wet as her bare tummy pressed into his backside. He could feel the soft tuft of hair tickling his skin.

She must have opened every last button of her dress.

He had to close himself off. He was a psychic, for God's sake, of the highest level. He could turn off his emotions with unusual ease. And he had to remember that her erotic words were lies anyway, meant to drive him crazy. He doubted she thought him delicious.

But he couldn't forget, either, how wet she was for him when he had kissed her.

Her hands skimmed around to his front, shaping the hard muscle of his thighs and then cupping his balls.

He hissed. "Cut it out, Jez."

"As soon as you give me what I want."

"How about if I give you what I want?" He cursed himself as soon as he said it. Any vulnerability she sensed would threaten what little control he had over her, but her tiny fingers felt so good fondling his balls. One hand moved farther below and gently kneaded the sensitive root of his cock. He buried the groan rumbling up his throat as she massaged and pressed beneath his balls clear back to his ass.

He swallowed hard, trying to hold back the seed building and filling him. But it was no use. It wept out the tip and dribbled along his length. He was so close to the edge he didn't dare let her know. Jesus, how could she not know? He was like a rocket ship about to launch.

That's what he'd do. Hold back until it was impossible and then relax suddenly. He would come before she realized what was happening. Two could play this game.

He tightened every muscle and could feel the sweat pour off his forehead.

"Oh," she sighed, moving one palm to his backside as she continued to massage his root with the other. "You are so hard, everywhere." She slid one palm down to the muscle roping the back of his thighs.

"It isn't working, Jez," he said in his most controlled tone. "You can stroke me for hours and I'm not giving it up."

She chuckled deep in her throat. "Oh, I don't think so…Commander."

When she ran a wet tongue along his spine and then dropped to her knees, he prayed to all the gods to deliver him. He'd been tortured before. Stretched along a rack once, his body burned another time and even carved up during his last capture, and he'd not given up anything.

But this. She was kissing the small of his back now and stroking his backside. Then her lips followed her hands. She bit him. Light stinging bites on his buttocks that drove him through the roof. He hissed under his breath.

"Hmmm…" Her lips hummed and vibrated as they traveled along his skin. His arousal throbbed painfully. "Still holding out, Commander?"

He didn't answer. But he was almost there. He relaxed every muscle in anticipation of the pure pleasure that would pump through him any second. He closed his eyes and shuddered as her tongue laved where she bit, waiting for the next erotic bite.

She jumped up. "That's enough."

"What the?" He balled his fists and wrenched against every restraint like some caged animal trying to get at her, his erection as hard as ever. "Stop this, Jez, do you hear me?"

She was standing just beyond his reach, eyes smiling and moving over every aroused piece of his flesh. "You look positively…dangerous like that. But then…" Her lips quirked. "You're all tied up."

"Not for long," he growled, twisting and heaving with a vengeance, feeling like he could level the entire building if he got loose.

She dropped to her knees and cupped his aching balls with one small palm. In half a second his traitorous cock was throbbing to attention. Stupid appendage, he raged at it, needing every ounce of anger to resist her.

She licked the underside of his dick with one tiny swipe of her tongue. He smothered a groan.

"Just how do you plan on escaping my tongue?"

"I've resisted torture by far more formidable foes than you."

She licked along his groin and then to his belly and traced along a thick scar. "So I see," she murmured, laving the ugly scar with a tenderness that killed him. Then her tongue swept down to his balls and her small hand clasped his rod. He stifled a string of curses and held himself tight, for all the good it would do. She suckled gently, drawing one ball and then the other into her hot mouth as her thumb swept up to his slit and smoothed his pre-cum all over his skin.

Jesus Christ! He couldn't give in to the pleasure, because she would just stop short until he gave her the code. He shut out the sound of her soft breathy moans as she suckled him and tried to estimate what the correlation coefficient would be of twenty-five trials with a standard deviation of 2.3.

"That's not going to work, Commander. And the answer is approximately .79." She lifted his balls and licked him beneath, clear down to his root.

God damned...fuck! His brain was exploding, his body vibrating with need. Her tongue licked and pressed and then worked its way up over his balls and over his rock hard cock. Then she took him into the hot cavern of her mouth.

Pure hot pleasure consumed him. He threw back his neck to suppress a groan as he felt the full press of her tongue sliding along his vein as she deep-throated him. He willed himself not to look down and watch what she was doing, but he couldn't help himself.

When he saw her dark head nestled against his groin and his cock buried inside her mouth he gave a violent jerk on his wrists, needing to sift his fingers through the soft waves of her hair. A shudder gripped him.

She drew slowly up and down his shaft, her tongue pressing too gently against his bulging vein. He was shaking. "Please, Jez," he groaned. She continued her slow, torturous pace. "Oh, God, please…" He was on fire, every nerve lit to a fevered pitch. Trickles of sweat dripped down his chest. He tried to thrust his hips, but she simply moved with him, allowing no friction to satisfy his driving need.

She curled her fingers beneath his balls and scraped lightly along his root, just enough to promise heaven but not enough to deliver. One hand cupped his ass, her fingers slipping between his crack and teasing him, driving him higher with no relief. It wouldn't matter where she stroked him, her touch was punishing.

"Stop it," he growled, even though he knew it would do no good. She had him exactly where she wanted him. Begging, pleading with her.

She stopped.

She blinked up at him, and dropped her hands by her side, her beautiful face inches from his cock. "Are you sure?"

He thrust his hips at her and thrashed in his bonds, wanting to mangle and destroy.

She jumped up and stepped back from him, watching, her mouth agape as he fought against the ropes.

She swallowed thickly.

"Get down on your hands and knees and finish me off. Now."

"No." She stepped back farther. "Not until you give me that code."

He railed against the ropes. For a minute they seemed to give. She looked startled and ran to the stove, bending over to adjust the knots. Her sweet bottom wriggled as she secured them. If he got free he'd fuck her so hard she wouldn't be able to walk for a week.

He wrenched with all his might at the rope while she struggled to tighten it, her lush bottom tilting up at him, torturing him beyond reason. He closed his mind to the thought that those lacey panties were at his feet. He could toss her skirt up and lick her from behind and then fuck her on all fours, pumping into her until she screamed and came over and over again. Until she thought she'd died.

While he growled and cursed, she glanced behind her, working quickly. The rope tightened.

She smiled. Then started toward him again.

"Do you know how sorry you'll be when I get free of these ropes?" he cursed at her. "I'll fuck you for days." He wrenched at the ropes securing his wrists, his body twisting, raw with rage. "I'll bite those luscious tits of yours until you're bleeding."

She blinked and stopped, too stricken to move. Good. Maybe if he scared the wits out of her she'd stop this, because he wasn't playing anymore. "If you don't get down on your knees and suck me off NOW, I'll spank you so hard you won't be able to sit for weeks. Now do it!"

She dropped gingerly and hesitated. "Do it," he growled.

She gave an anxious little breath and then licked delicately, torturously.

"Harder!"

Her tongue fluttered, teasing skin stretched so tight it burned.

"Jez, I'm warning you."

Her fingers plucked lightly at the small hairs on his balls.

"Suck me, damn it."

"Give me the code," she murmured softly.

He exploded with a string of expletives that he didn't even think he knew and that should have scared her to death, but she continued her relentless teasing. His body vibrated with need and rage all mixed together to create a relentless pounding lust.

And then the breath left his lungs. It was no use. He couldn't do it. He couldn't resist her sweet mouth and he couldn't make her do anything while he was tied up. And if he didn't come, he was sure he would die.

"Okay, God damn it, okay. I'll give you the code. Now suck me...hard, please."

She stroked his inner thighs. "The code?"

"Suck me."

She took him in her mouth and suckled gently.

"Harder."

She kept up a hot gentle pressure but no more and then slid a wet finger between the cheeks of his ass and barely rested the soft pad of one wet finger on his bottom hole.

"Yes," he breathed, pushing against her small finger.

Then all movement stopped.

"Okay," he ground through his teeth. "063—"

She pushed for entrance. He groaned deep in his throat when she sunk in to her first knuckle. A fierce shudder sliced through him. But still he was so primed that it wasn't enough.

"The rest," she mouthed, her tongue toying with his cock too lightly for satisfaction.

"4089," he breathed.

She gave a hot pull with her lips around his shaft that sent him to heaven. One more and he'd go off. He was sweating now and shaking so badly he thought he'd collapse.

"Two more," she snapped and then licked.

How the hell did she know that? But it made sense that she had figured it out. When she fooled around, the pad would have signaled an error every time she got to the ninth digit, letting her know that the code entered was incorrect.

"Get me to the edge, Jez, please, and I'll tell you."

She stopped and looked up at him. "How do I know you'll give me the right combination?"

"Please, Jez. I'm begging you." He thrust his hips at her. She looked him right in the eye and sunk deeper into his ass. He closed his eyes with the sweet feel of it, his cock bursting out of its skin. The pleasure seeping through his pores had every pulse point throbbing. She didn't move, all stimulation ceased. "You can trust me, Jez, please."

He looked at her, his eyes pleading while she stared up at him, her expression wary and her finger buried deep in his ass, her lips barely grazing his quivering dick.

She hesitated a moment and then seemed satisfied with his answer. She swallowed him whole, deep-throated him down to his root and suckled him. The pressure built swiftly, pounding up through him, his seed swelling and pushing. Oh, God, she was good. His body tightened, vibrated, reached.

She stopped. "Tell me," she demanded.

"67, damn it," he sputtered.

She squeezed his balls just short of pain, bringing his body to a screeching halt.

His body rebelled, lurched, fought for a release that couldn't come.

His head pounded.

He couldn't believe it. She was still kneeling before him, hand wrapped around his balls, but as far from him as she could get, looking a little stunned.

He couldn't speak, so paralyzed was he by the blinding loss of sensation. He struggled to draw air into his lungs.

"I'm—" he choked on his words, "—going to fucking throttle you when I get hold of you." His voice was a harsh rasp.

She finally released him and then with a startled gasp, jumped to her feet and ran out the door.

Chapter Seven

Jesse climbed into the skimmer, sucking in air from her dash to escape him. He was so strong he had pulled loose the stove leg. If it broke, the rope around his neck would come tumbling down. The rest would be easy.

She worked quickly, punching in the code, telling the skimmer to hurry and hoping the stove leg held.

Despite the fact that he had kidnapped her, she felt a little guilty for tormenting him the way she did and especially for stopping her torture before he reached satisfaction. The code bleeped. She tried to calm herself and concentrate as she punched in the numbers again. She glanced behind her, but there was no sign of him.

And even though he had callously drugged her, picturing his Adonis body shuddering to maintain control made her regret she hadn't used him for her own pleasure.

Watching those work-defined muscles flex and bunch in agony as she toyed with his sex, frustrating him beyond reason, was exciting. Even the scar that slashed across that hard belly was beautiful. The small burns that marred the sensitive skin inside his wrist and behind his ear called to her to soothe them with her lips. It was a warrior's body. And she had examined every gorgeous inch of it.

She sighed with disappointment. But not for long. Because for the third time now, she'd punched in the code he'd given her, and it didn't work.

Damn! She hit the console with the flat of her palm. Damn him.

She wanted to *murder* him. Instead, she spit out a long string of vulgar curses that graphically described all the things she'd like to do to him and then leveled a deadly kick to the console.

"Tsk, tsk, what a mouth," a low voice murmured behind her.

She whipped around to see him leaning against a garage post, his boulder-like arms crossed over that massive chest, his eyes heavy-lidded and smoldering. She held her breath, wishing now she hadn't stripped him, because one look at him had convinced her that he could break her in half with just a flick of his wrist.

She crossed her puny arms over her chest—a chest that couldn't even hold up a strapless top—and glared. "Well..." She moved her eyes over his body. "Took you long enough."

He dropped his arms. "That does it." He lunged for her.

Oh my God. She scrambled toward the back door, but he locked his hands onto her waist and dragged her back.

She thrashed wildly, kicking and flailing, trying to make contact anywhere she could reach and screaming vicious insults at him.

He got her in a vise grip that pinned her arms to her sides and flattened her back against the rock wall of his chest.

Snagging up one wrist, he twisted it behind her back and then clamped onto the other so hard she thought he'd snap her wrist.

"You make what I'm going to do to you so damned rewarding," he growled in her ear.

She heaved and pulled to no effect, then craned her neck to try to bite him.

He jerked his shoulder away. "Oh no, you don't. It's my turn to do the biting." He turned her roughly, pushing her ahead of him as he stomped back toward the compound.

"You're hurting me," she lashed out as she stumbled along.

"Am I now?"

"I think you broke my wrist."

He didn't answer, but after a minute he lightened his hold. Just enough that she could slip out of his grip if she waited for the right moment.

Her wrists were small and flexible. With just the right twist at the right time she could escape him.

But to where? She thought a moment. She could hide. The compound was big enough that at least it would buy her time.

He trudged her through the front door and up the long winding stairs to the second floor balcony.

"Where are you taking me?"

"To my own personal torture chamber."

She couldn't let him tie her up. She had to make her move before that.

They swept past several bedrooms until they got to the end of the hall where he pushed her into a lushly carpeted suite with a bed in its center that looked bigger than her entire bedroom at home. Off to one corner sat a sunken tub, the polished tile that surrounded it glinting in the sun that poured in through the circular convex skylights covering the ceiling. A low wall of ornate gaslights surrounded it. And above that, sheets of glass served as outside walls and showcased the wide expanse of the prairie.

She gawked.

"I'm going to enjoy this," he grumbled, dragging her into the room and stopping before the bed. His lips brushed her ear. "Picture yourself tied to that big bed, legs spread for me, pussy lips hot and glistening, begging to be fucked." His erection pressed into her backside and his scent surrounded her.

She gulped down a breath.

Then with a quick snap and twist, she slipped out of his hold, whirled around, and kneed him in the groin.

He doubled over, the breath leaving his lungs in a loud whoosh.

She dashed for the door and almost made it when he caught her ankle in a bone-crushing grip that sent her crashing to the floor, flat onto her stomach. He was on her in a flash, crawling up her body and anchoring her with his weight.

"Like I said, I'm going to fucking throttle you."

She didn't doubt it. After two concussions and an equal number of ball-breakings, she knew she had it coming.

She sighed in defeat, at least for now. There was nothing else she could do, and her body was limp with exhaustion. She cursed herself for being so stupid as to think she could best him in a physical struggle. She'd have to start using her head if she wanted to get out of this. She closed her eyes.

He was breathing hard as he lay on top of her. He had locked his hands with hers and stretched her arms out at her sides. His muscled legs entwined with hers and anchored them down. His chin rested at the top of her head.

She didn't move. And neither did he.

She listened to his breath slow to a steady rhythm. His body heat seeped through her skin, warming her and making her restless, but she kept still. Then she felt his heartbeat pick up until it pounded against her back.

"Jezermiah?"

She didn't answer.

"Are you alive?"

She almost smiled at the hint of real worry in his voice, but still she didn't answer.

A heavy pulse beat against her thigh. He groaned in her ear and rubbed up against her, his pants in contact with her bare legs and bottom, making her aware that her dress had hiked up to her waist. Her panties were still back on the kitchen floor.

She stifled a moan.

He moved her arms up over her head and locked her wrists together with one hand. With his free hand, he palmed her bottom.

The moan she buried bubbled up and spilled over as soon as his rough hands glided over her tender skin.

"I see you're alive," he breathed into her hair.

She ignored him, struggling to resist the feel of his calloused fingertips playing along her backside and his big hand kneading her plump flesh. She bit her lip to keep from crying out, but her sex swelled and throbbed, wetting shamelessly.

"You like this," he said, his voice thready with arousal.

She bit back a retort and held her breath.

He slid his fingers between her cheeks and stroked with a teasing touch. Lust, pure and unbridled, gripped her.

"Don't you?" he taunted.

She wouldn't answer. She couldn't let him know how much he excited her.

"So, that's how it's going to be," he whispered, sliding his lips over her forehead.

She turned from him and buried her face in the carpet. She would not give in to him.

He slid his fingers lower and fluttered them over her sex. "Mmm, wet." He slipped around her aroused flesh, coating himself with her juices. One long finger slipped up between her lips and into her heat. He sighed with satisfaction. "And hot." Against her will, her inner muscles clamped down, trapping him, holding him deep within her body.

"Oh yeah, you like this."

She shook her head, willing up some anger at what he was doing to her, but it wouldn't come.

With a slow agonizing stroke, he slid his wet finger out and slipped it up through her lips just short of her throbbing clit. He stroked the swollen tissue that surrounded the tiny kernel but didn't touch it.

She refused to squirm and give him any satisfaction, but she wanted desperately to tip her hips subtly and bring him in contact with that oh-so-tiny organ that held such pleasure. He threaded his fingers through her downy thatch instead, inflaming her, making her want to beg. He gently squeezed the fleshy folds protecting her clit, drawing a moan from her lips. Then he slid his thick thumb up her pussy.

"Oh," she breathed before she could stop herself, thankful that the carpet muffled her sigh of pleasure.

"I could fuck you now so easily," he murmured.

Her pulse jumped. He could.

His cock was a few quick movements away. Zip, release, and plunge and he'd be in her, impaled to the hilt. Except that he was so big, and she so tight, that it would take more than a stroke to stretch her. She shivered at the thought of him pushing into her, fucking her deep.

But for some reason that she couldn't fathom, she knew that he wouldn't do it. At least not now. It wasn't that she was reading his thoughts. He had them carefully blocked. She just knew that he didn't intend to do it now.

"Couldn't I?" he taunted.

She stayed mute, waiting, half hoping.

"But I won't." He gave an agonized groan and then slid his wet thumb up through her folds and probed her bottom.

Oh my God.

He pushed gently for entrance, his thumb so wet from her shameless arousal that he sank into her easily. She smothered a groan at the pleasure that swept over her. Her whole body came alive with the wicked sensation, every nerve lit and anxious. She blocked the thought of what she must look like with his thick finger buried in her bottom.

He bit her earlobe and began thrusting his hips against her, his breathing choppy, as aroused as she was by what he was doing.

She stifled a whimper and tried to stay still, but it was impossible. She tilted her bottom, thrusting against the penetration, letting the rough pad of his thumb stimulate all her sensitive tissue. He shuddered behind her and then slid a long finger up her cunt and massaged and pressed the sensitive pad where his fingers met.

Pleasure rocketed through her like nothing she had ever felt. Her womb contracted hard. She shivered and bucked, thrashing beneath him as he kept up his relentless thrusting and stroking.

"That's it," he groaned. "Oh God, yes." He bit her neck and then licked where he nipped.

At some point he had released her hands, but nothing mattered now but the white-hot pleasure stripping through her body. She gripped the carpet, her body vibrating with arousal, tightening, screaming for release. He slipped his thumb out, his cock bare now, and slipped it over her bottom cheeks, rubbing and teasing her. She stifled a cry of alarm, remembering how big he was.

And then he was pressing for entrance, groaning deep in his throat and probing her tight bottom hole, the pressure and pleasure mixing together to drive her to soaring heights.

"Open for me, baby."

She gave herself over to him and he pushed past her entrance into her bottom with a groan. She screamed with pleasure, yielding to him. He plunged into her, deep, burying to the hilt.

She exploded. First a powerful burst of pleasure that ripped through her, sweeping her under, and then wave after wave of it threading through her body and filling her with a bone-deep satisfaction that had her sobbing into the carpet. Every pulse point throbbed out in pleasure.

"Oh, fuck," he groaned. "Jesus fucking Christ." His big body shuddered around her. He was so deep, he felt like an earthquake erupting inside her as he pumped his seed into her.

If this wasn't heaven, it was close.

She collapsed under him and sighed.

"Jez?"

She couldn't answer him if she wanted to.

"Are you all right, Jez? Jesus. I never intended... Look at me."

It was the last thing she remembered before she drifted off into blissful unconsciousness.

Chapter Eight

The ghost of Tyre Leyton came to Jesse in the same way he always did. When she was most vulnerable, deep in REM sleep. He hoped to infect her with his evil.

Sometimes when her own thoughts turned dark and negative, she feared that he had succeeded, despite that her grandmother assured her that it would never happen as long as her heart was filled with love.

She had always wanted to believe her grandmother, but she had lived in fear of him always, afraid that if she let down her guard, she would succumb to him.

His voice, whisper soft, invaded her mind. You can never escape your destiny. You are my legacy, of my seed.

Jesse struggled to silence the sinister voice, but it was relentless. *In my power. Now, always, forever.*

No, she screamed, fighting against the darkness that gripped her, that surrounded her, that choked off her air.

Then she stopped struggling and concentrated on what her grandmother taught her. She drew in her thoughts, focused and reached for the light within. Images of her grandmother surfaced, her warm comforting smile, her voice. *It's all right, Jez. You're strong. Turn toward the light. Rid your heart of fear and let love in. You can do it.*

It was as though her grandmother was beside her.

And then Jesse was awake, blinking against the sunlight that bathed her, and surrounded by a familiar scent that comforted her pounding heart and engulfed her in a soothing warmth. Male warmth.

Her eyes popped wide.

She took in her ivory-drenched surroundings, his private torture chamber, the one in which last night he had sent her to heaven. She sighed.

Behind her that nemesis lay, spooning her body to his, his breathing deep and peaceful, his arms cradling her.

It was morning. While she still wore her sundress, she could feel that he was completely naked. His muscled stomach pressed against her bare backside and his sex, heavy and large but relaxed, nestled against her thighs.

Half of her wanted to stay like this forever, and the other half was still furious that he kept her captive.

Now was the time to slip away and hide.

She lifted his warm hand off her stomach and slowly rested it on his hip. His breathing remained steady. She nudged his leg off, slipping her own out from underneath. Rolling gently to the side of the bed, she attempted to slip her other arm out from under his, tugging just enough so as not to wake him.

Her eyes dropped down his body, over honed muscle and golden flesh that was covered everywhere with a light dusting of dark hair. The relaxed set of his face drew attention to his full lips and softened the menacing effect of his heavy beard growth. She swallowed any thoughts of running her hands down his body, annoyed with herself that he had such an effect on her. She pulled again at her arm, trapped under his neck. She frowned and leaned in close, lifting his thick hair just a fraction. A flash of metal winked at her. Handcuffs. Their wrists were locked together.

She wanted to beat him.

When she looked back at his face, he was fully alert and smiling. "You're not going anywhere." His eyes glinted with amusement.

She thrashed and flailed at him, punching at his arm but his big body didn't even budge. She wanted to beat him silly. "Where would I go, you idiot. I can't even get the skimm—"

"You'll hide." He propped himself on one elbow, pulling her down easily with the gesture and pressing his handsome face to hers. "And I want you close."

She shouldn't like the predatory sound to his voice, but she did.

"You raped me." She tipped her chin.

He reeled back, looking as though she had slapped him.

Good. He *should* feel guilty.

"Jez..." He tried to cup her chin. "Come on..."

She slapped down his hand.

His eyes turned hard. "You were moaning into the carpet last night—"

"Did you hear me moan 'yes'?"

His neck turned red and the pulse at his neck beat heavy, but he said nothing.

"Well?"

He pushed himself off the bed and stalked over to a desk in the corner. It did no good to resist his efforts, because he dragged her along as though she were a scarf trailing behind him. And kicking and biting had only produced temporary relief. But guilt, now *there* she had gotten a response.

She'd play that card until he agreed to release her.

He shuffled through a bottom drawer and pulled out another set of handcuffs.

"What are those for?"

Ignoring her, he lugged her over to a door that was along the same wall as the tub and then drew her through it into a gleaming gold and bronze bathroom. She stumbled in, taking in its contents. More skylights and mirrors surrounded her. Reflected back at her on all sides were the scarred rugged planes of his body. His thick penis, even in its relaxed state, looked wonderfully powerful.

Before she realized what he was doing, he snapped her other wrist with a handcuff and then ushered her into a large chamber with a bidet. He anchored the other end of the handcuff to a metal wall-bracket beside it. Then he uncuffed himself from her.

"Let me know when you're done." He slammed the door.

She supposed she should be grateful for the privacy, but it galled her that he kept her locked up.

When she was done, he handcuffed her to the sink so she could brush her teeth.

"We both smell of sex," he said. "We're taking a bath." He went through the whole locking and unlocking routine so that at no time was she unattached from either an immovable object or from him.

"*We* are?" She looked up from brushing and repeated his words, then spit out the paste and rinsed her mouth. "I hope that means we're taking turns bathing alone."

"Why should we?" He looked over the top of her head at her reflection in the mirror.

She wiped her mouth clean. "Because, it's the least you could do after last night."

He tensed and a large vein throbbed in his temple. "What about what you did to me?"

"You?" She feigned amazement. "You're comparing what I did to you with rape?"

His nostrils flared and she thought the vein would burst. Their gazes held. He looked ready to throttle her. For one terse moment she feared she had pushed him too far.

"I should have gone with my first instinct when you kneed me in the balls."

"And what was that?" she taunted, knowing full well that she didn't really want the answer, but it was too late.

"Spanking the hell out of you," he breathed.

"You wouldn't dare."

His eyes flared. "Just give me a reason," he gritted through his teeth.

She held her breath, sure that he meant it and willing her mouth to keep shut. She sensed that one more word out of her and he'd have her dress over her head and her bottom over his knee.

Their gazes locked in the mirror. Neither one of them blinked. She was dimly aware of the water running and acutely aware of how large his chest looked framed behind her. With his face unshaven and his hair falling to his shoulders, he looked more like a medieval warlord than a modern military commander. His neck muscles bulged with repressed temper.

Still, it was against her nature to back down. And she'd be damned if she would let him spank her.

She cleared her throat. "The last time you had your hands on my backside…things got out of control."

A muscle ticked in his jaw. She held her breath. For a fleeting moment she saw rage and pain and sadness all mix together in his expression. Then his gaze wavered.

With an abruptness that startled her, he snatched a towel off the rack and turned her roughly, patting droplets of water from her chin, and refusing to meet her gaze.

Without another word, he went through the locking routine and then dragged her out of the bathroom.

She breathed a small sigh of relief and watched in silence as he bent to turn on the tub faucets and then dribble scented oil under the spray, his tight buttocks almost impossible to resist. She leaned down to get a view of his balls hanging loosely between his thighs and fought the urge to reach out and cup him.

Then he straightened and turned her around. He wrapped her long hair in a twist and clipped it atop her head. Then he turned her back around and with a casual hand started unbuttoning her dress.

She grabbed his hands. "Please. At least let me take a bath by myself. You can lock all the doors. There's no way I could escape."

"You'd figure out something."

"But—"

"I'm not letting you out of my sight. Besides," he smirked. "I want to see more of you."

"So that's it. You want revenge." She tried to twist away from him but with barely an effort he pulled her back. She circled his wrists, her eyes pleading. "Only a petty man…a weak man, seeks revenge."

"Then I'm weak and petty." He drew aside her bodice and bared her nipples. She groaned at the way his eyes brightened at the sight of her. When he covered one small breast with his palm her nipple pebbled instantly. She closed her mind to the delicious feel of his skin against hers and tried to think.

Of course weak hadn't worked. The man had an ego the size of his cock. Guilt was her ticket.

She muffled a groan. He had bent his head and was blowing on her nipples and watching them pucker to arousal.

"I can't believe that after all you've done you would do this to me," she choked, forced tears filling her eyes.

"It's not going to work," he murmured, barely grazing one nipple with his teeth.

Her sex clamped down. Damn him.

"The last time I fell for your tears you followed it up by choking me." He squeezed just the tips of her nipples between two fingers.

Pure lust shuddered through her while she fought to keep her head straight.

Somewhere in her lust-laden brain it registered that she had gotten to him with those tears. 'Course, those had been real. No matter. She had tapped into his vulnerability and now she'd use it against him.

His lips closed around the tip of her nipple and suckled gently. She shivered as a rush of moisture settled between her legs. If this was how he planned to get his revenge, she might wait a bit before playing the vulnerable card.

He gently released her with a tiny lick. "Delicious."

She closed her eyes and thrust forward a little, anticipating the feel of his tongue on her other nipple. But the next thing she felt was her dress falling around her ankles.

"Oh, yeah. I like seeing more of you." He dropped to his knees. "What's this?" he said with feigned surprise, sliding his thumbs along her labia. "You're all wet."

She yanked on their handcuff and stepped aside. "You're an animal."

"Honey, you haven't seen animal yet." He slapped her bare backside and watched her jump.

She whirled around, ready with a retort until she looked down at his erection, full and thick, and all spontaneous thought abandoned her.

His gaze softened as though he could read her thoughts. When he reached up to thread his fingers through the soft tuft of her curls, she covered herself. He gave a soft chuckle. "We'll see how long that lasts."

Then he was dragging her into the tub with the strap of her dress hanging off their locked wrists. With a speed that alarmed her, he locked her other wrist to one of the gaslight posts that rimmed the perimeter of the tub and then did the same with the wrist that joined his. He flung her dress off to the side.

She could either sit on the tub's side, fully exposed with her hands anchored alongside her thighs or sit submerged up to her breasts with her arms stretched out to either side of her. With a sigh of surrender, she let herself slip into the water. She closed her eyes and let the bubbling water relax her, lifting one foot and resting it on the ledge so that one of the jets massaged her heel.

When she opened her eyes he was sitting across from her, sudsing his massive body, his eyes staring between her legs. She knew he couldn't see anything but swirling water, yet the flushed look on his face told her that he was drawing up the image of her pussy, fleeting though his glimpse had been.

His muscles flexed and rippled with a fury as he scrubbed across his chest and under his arms. He submerged himself and when he splashed up out of the water, he slicked his hair back with two hands while his gaze went back to her spread legs. He stood. The tip of his cock bobbed above the tub's waves, glistening with water and throbbing red. He started toward her, all one hundred eighty-five muscled pounds of him.

She dropped her leg, but he grabbed her ankle before she could close her thighs. He smelled glorious. Clean and male. And aroused.

Her heart leaped into her throat.

Leaning in close, he wedged his hips between her thighs, his breath washing over hers, a mixture of cinnamon and mint. He dropped her foot and braced his hands to either side of her on the tub's ledge. He was wet everywhere. Droplets caught on his chest and rivulets slid over and between his pecs. The urge to lick him was irresistible. A hot shiver slid down her spine.

"You *want* me to touch you, Jez."

She shook her head but didn't dare speak, afraid of what might come out.

"Liar." He slid one hand over her hip and down her thigh as his lips moved closer to hers, almost touching. She wanted to lick the water off his lips, too.

His palm hooked under her knee. "I could fuck you now so easily."

She jumped when the head of his cock glided along her cunt lips. *God, yes, please.*

"And you'd like it, wouldn't you?" His lips grazed hers. All she could do was whimper and thrust her hips. The blunt head of his cock slipped along her lips but couldn't enter her. She wanted to scream at him to tilt his hips back so she could impale herself on him, but she wouldn't give him the satisfaction.

"I'd go deep, bury myself to the hilt."

She stifled a groan.

He positioned himself between her swollen folds.

Instinctively, she jerked at her bound wrists, wanting to grab onto his shoulders. She almost cried out in frustration.

"I know you'd like that, Jez." He ran his tongue over her lips, exploring their shape and texture. Then he pressed forward.

The size and pressure of him was near heaven, soothing her ache to have him fill her as he stretched her beyond what she thought possible. She bit her lip to keep from crying out and begging him to fuck her hard. He wasn't having any easier time of it than her. He was shaking.

He grunted. "Yes, I could fuck you so easily." He pinched her nipples. "But I won't."

She choked on a breath.

He shoved away. "And this time I mean it."

She blinked in confusion, watching him senselessly squirt more liquid soap into his hands.

"Because the next time I do," he growled, his eyes burning into her, "it'll be because you *invite* me into your body." He rubbed his palms together with a vengeance. "And it won't be fucking."

It won't?

"It'll be making love, damn it." He turned his back on her and fooled with more bottles along the tub's ledge while she tried to catch her breath and understand what had just happened. She knew that he wanted her as much as she wanted him. She was swollen and aroused and tingling with need.

She wanted to pound out her frustration on his beautiful body.

When he turned around, his eyes, hot and mesmerizing, moved over her face and then down to the swell of her breasts.

"Let's see," he murmured. "Where should I start?"

"Start what?" she said in a breathless whisper, belatedly recognizing her own words to him when she began her torture.

"Cleaning you." His eyes smoldered as he knelt before her. "Every hollow, every curve, everywhere I can get my hands on...and fingers in."

She swallowed a breath. She knew he meant every word. Half of her *hoped* that he did. But the other half knew he meant only to torture her the way she did to him.

Her heart sighed.

If she were honest with herself, she would admit that it wasn't likely he was a renegade psychic trying to impregnate her. He would have raped her repeatedly already. She believed that he was a Commander with the Agency.

With a gentleness that surprised her, he picked up her foot and massaged it between his palms, separating the toes and running his fingers in between. He frowned and laid his hand against the pad of her foot.

"No bigger than my palm," he grumbled to himself as he slid his thumbs along each knuckle of her toe as though memorizing their shape.

She wondered if he'd give such attention to every part of her body.

When he took such care with her other foot, she laid her head back against the tub's ledge and sighed. His fingers were exquisite, circling her ankle and then tracing the muscles of her calf, kneading and stroking.

"Are you cleaning me or massaging me?" she breathed.

He simply grunted.

Her pulse picked up as his hands slid farther up her legs and stroked her knees. He applied more soap and smoothed it over her skin.

"So, Commander, do you believe I'm dangerous?"

He gave a snort. "Would I handcuff you if you weren't?"

She opened her eyes and for the first time answered him truthfully. "Yes."

His hands stopped and he looked at her as though trying to read her mind. A wet lock of hair fell over his forehead. She had such an urge to stroke her hand along the rough shadow of his jaw. Too bad her hands were bound.

"You're right. I would." He turned his attention to her other knee, sliding soap all around it. When his fingers strayed up her thigh, she drew in a breath.

He looked up. "But don't think getting my head bashed in and my balls broken didn't factor into it."

She could hear the smile in his voice. "You don't, do you?" she asked in all sincerity.

She sighed in disappointment when he dropped her leg and picked up the soap again.

"Don't what?"

"You don't think I'm dangerous to the Agency and its government."

He gave her hand the same deliberate attention that he did her foot. And for just a moment their hands clasped before he let go and began a slow massage of her forearm.

"I think you're a menace and I've said as much." He gave a long-suffering sigh. "But I think more a menace to me—" he looked up abruptly, "—and yourself." He washed her shoulder and collarbone and under her arm with a smooth gliding touch that carefully avoided her breasts.

"Thank you for believing that."

"That you're a menace?" His lips quirked.

She smiled at him.

He looked surprised, but then his frown returned. He started on her other arm. "I see another trick coming." He glanced at her.

"No tricks." She met his gaze, letting him read her thoughts. Suddenly she was weary of lying and wondered why.

She had been more or less lying her whole life. But now she only wanted the truth. "I *am* Tyre Leyton's great-granddaughter."

He dropped his hands and let out a breath. "Good."

"And I hate him."

His gaze warmed. "I know." He cupped her face and ran his thumbs along her cheekbones.

"And all I've ever wanted is to be left alone. To forget who I am and to ensure that no one else found out."

His hands stroked down her neck.

"And to protect my sisters." She let him feel all her worry over her sisters.

He gave a half smile. "If your sisters are anything like you, it's the guys they sent that I'm worried about."

"You know them?"

He nodded. "Your sisters are safe. You have nothing to worry about."

She wanted to believe him. She did. He was holding nothing back. What he told her was the truth.

Maybe he had been telling her the truth all along but she wouldn't open herself to listen.

Her grandmother's words echoed deep in her heart.

For the first time in so long she felt herself relax.

"Don't get too relaxed," he murmured, his gaze turning positively lecherous.

Chapter Nine

Jesse couldn't breathe. He was allowing her to see his desire, his passionate need to be joined with her, and she feared it was more than purely physical.

As soon as her fear surfaced, he gave an impatient grunt and tipped up her chin. "I won't seduce you. I'm not interested in your sexual response. I want all of you or nothing."

He stood, leaving her stunned, and with a casualness that belied his raging erection, he walked to the ledge that housed the bathing supplies.

He couldn't be serious. Every cell of her skin vibrated with arousal and with a need so powerful that it shook her. "Let me lick you," she choked, her eyes fixated on him.

His cock bobbed in response and the angry vein that ran the impossible length of him stood out in stark relief. She couldn't take her eyes off him. The pearly liquid of his arousal shimmered on the blunt tip.

Seemingly ignoring her, he grabbed up a small cloth and squirted peach colored lotion onto it. He came back and tipped her chin up, away from his erection. He looked at her a moment, his eyes hard, but even behind the dark depths she could sense his vulnerability.

He started at her chin, scrubbing her skin with tiny granules of scented apricot as he smoothed the lotion over her face with gentle strokes and swabbed the cloth back to her hairline.

"I meant what I said earlier." He dragged the terrycloth down the bridge of her nose and then dipped it in the water, turning her chin from side to side as he patted her face clean. She couldn't remember what he was referring to, but she didn't care. She studied his handsome face, relaxing into his touch and hoping that he wouldn't stop. But then his jaw tensed.

"We're both going to clean up and get dressed and then I'm going to call the Agency and have them clear you."

She sat up a bit. "You will?"

He gave a sigh and threaded his fingers through her scalp, his strong jaw softening a fraction. "There is no reason for me to run tests. It's obvious you're a high level psychic, but it wouldn't matter anyway. You're no danger to anyone and I can't see that you have any connection with the Continental Council."

"What council?"

He frowned. "It seems you're not the only one who thinks if psychics mate they'll produce super-psychics."

He soaped his hands and then caressed her neck. "Since you're not with the renegade council, you may be in danger of being hunted down by one, captured, and kept as a concubine, for the sole purpose of breeding."

If she had any sense she would have panicked at the knowledge of what he said, but he had slipped his hands past her collarbone and was sliding them over her breasts. With her arms spread out at her sides, he had full access, and she hoped he'd take advantage. "So the rumors are true?" she asked in as casual a tone as she could muster, not wanting to draw attention to how much he pleasured her for fear he would stop.

"Yes." He cupped her breasts, as though feeling their weight and then soaped his hands again. He lathered every inch of her, pinching and pulling on her nipples, his promise that he wouldn't seduce her hopefully forgotten.

When her nipples hardened to points, he rinsed her off and scraped lightly with his nail over the sensitive peaks. She smothered her moans, but her clit throbbed with each sharp flick. She thought she would come from that alone.

"I knew your nipples would be as red and dark as cherries," he murmured. "And they taste as sweet." She prayed he'd sample her again.

But he dropped his hands.

"Please." She squirmed along the ledge, desperate for his touch between her legs. "I'm aching. Just a little bit?"

His eyes grew stormy. She could see the battle he waged within himself. He was still as hard as steel. Her eyes dropped to his cock and she licked her lips.

He took a half step toward her, the tip of his cock almost touching her lips, but then he gave a disgruntled growl and dropped to his knees.

He suckled her nipples gently, causing her to spread her legs wider in response to her quickly swelling sex. Her arousal throbbed heavily and in perfect harmony with his lips. She moaned softly and rested her head back, completely surrendering to the feel of him.

He pulled her deep into his mouth, flicking his tongue over the tips, sending liquid fire though her veins and heating her body beyond endurance. Just when she thought she couldn't take anymore, he lifted his head and studied each nipple, tracing with his fingertip the edges of the areola with a reverence that startled her.

"So large and ripe for such diminutive breasts," he murmured, examining her meticulously.

She had never considered her small breasts seductive, but he was studying her as though he had never seen anything more beautiful. His obvious arousal and erotic words were torture.

"I don't think I'll ever get enough of them," he groaned.

He suckled gently, too gently. She spread her legs wider. "Harder," she breathed.

A low rumble of approval traveled up his throat. "Am I frustratingly gentle?" he asked, laving her nipple.

Before she could answer, he cupped her buttocks with both hands and squeezed.

She ignited. Every sensory nerve lit to a restless pitch. She wanted his hands everywhere.

"Everywhere?" he murmured against her nipple, his long silky hair caressing skin lit to bursting.

"Yes," she breathed, not caring that he could read her desires.

His fingers played along her bottom, teasing and stroking, one long finger sliding from the small of her back to between her cheeks, and then clear down to her sex and back. A dark shiver stole up her spine. He hesitated between her buttocks at the tiny bud of her dusky rose, stroking with the lightest touch, and then skittered away. She groaned in disappointment.

The head of his cock slipped along her sex, rubbing over her clit and circling it. It felt like it stood out in a sharp point from her labia. She bucked against him, starving for the friction that would bring her to climax.

"Tell me where you want me to touch you."

"Everywhere," she begged, yanking on her wrists, needing to grab him. Unlock my hands, please." She thrust herself at him. When he glanced into the water at her writhing hips, a smile curved his lips.

He didn't answer, but instead slid a finger up into her cunt. Her breath stopped with the quick sweep of pleasure.

"Look at me." He knelt back on his heels, his finger still impaled in her, his huge body tense with arousal. "I want you to watch me feel every inch of you."

She closed her eyes and groaned.

"Open them, Jez."

She bit her lip and opened her eyes, meeting his gaze, her eyes pleading with him to touch her. His thumb grazed her clit for just a second before slipping away. Her clit throbbed violently, just short of release. She closed her eyes and moaned.

"Keep them open," he demanded.

She lifted her lashes, determined this time to hold his gaze, despite that her body vibrated with lust.

His finger slid out and back to her buttocks and probed her bottom. "Oh…" She sucked in a breath.

"Keep your eyes open while I slide into you," he said, his eyes burning with arousal as he slicked her juices around her tight hole.

"I'm trying." She shuddered when he pushed his finger in one knuckle deep and then stopped.

"Oh, my God." Her body clamped down hard against the erotic sensation as though not sure whether to rebel or relax with the penetration, but so alive with the pleasure. Her clit swelled harder than she'd ever imagined it could.

"I…" she choked, "didn't know how much I'd liked that."

He smiled in approval and then rubbed his thumb over her clit. Her hips rocketed off the ledge.

"I think you'd like to be fucked both places at once, wouldn't you?" he taunted, his eyes bright with desire.

She gasped, unable to answer, as he eased a little farther into her bottom and then made circles around her clit.

"Wouldn't you?"

"I…" Her body melted and then shook, quivering with desire, but she held his gaze.

His eyes smoldered. "Answer me, Jez, and don't lie to me."

"Yes," she choked, feeling the flush burn her cheeks but unable to keep the vision of being penetrated from both ends out of her mind.

"Or…" He moved close and whispered in her ear, "…three ways." He licked her earlobe.

When she gasped in response he smiled against her hair.

"Who would you like fucking you?" he growled. "A few of those muscle-bound gorillas who hovered around you before that meeting?"

"What?" she choked. "No."

83

"You're lying." He slid his finger deeper causing pleasured, needy sounds erupting from her throat. His thumb continued its relentless gentle stroking.

"I can't…"

"Tell me, Jez." He slid his finger smoothly out and then slipped back, deep into her bottom.

She couldn't think. He began a gentle rhythmic thrusting. She could only feel and want. Need overwhelmed her. She spread her legs wider, not caring about the image she made as she bucked against his hand, yanking at her restraints.

He barely grazed her clit now and his finger slid out and stopped.

"That's enough."

The breath left her lungs.

"I already know you want me sexually, and I'm not interested."

Oh, my God. She wanted to kill him. Was he crazy?

She thrashed and screamed at him, "Then at least release me so I can satisfy myself!"

He stroked one long finger over her cheek. "I *will* be releasing you," he said, his eyes moving over her, studying her expression. "It's what you want, isn't it?"

She couldn't answer him, couldn't think at all. She was gasping for breath, her mind a fog of lust.

He started talking again, but only half of what he said reached her brain. She so badly needed him to be inside her. What did he say about her having to invite him into her body?

He turned his back on her and gathered up some of the oil. She watched his buttocks flex and tighten as he moved.

He took a heavy breath. "The rumors about PSI agents hunting down psychics and killing them are exaggerated by the renegades. Unless they are plotting with the new council to overthrow the government, they are free to live their lives as they are."

"I see." She gave a quiet sigh, no longer wanting him to release her.

He came back to her. "Look at me, Jez." Her eyes met his. "When I release you, you had better not run or hide from me, or you'll be sorry."

"What do you mean? Why would I do that now?"

"I don't know." He trailed a finger down her throat. "*You* probably wouldn't even know why you did it. But I'm not leaving until I'm sure you're safe. And I don't feel like getting my head bashed in again."

Leaving? The thought filled her with panic. "I don't want you to leave."

"Why?" He cupped her chin, his eyes searching her face, intense and burning into her thoughts.

"Why?" She swallowed. She didn't know, other than she wanted him desperately. The need to be filled by him overwhelmed her.

"Please…Adam."

His gaze softened when she called him by name.

"You know what I want," she pleaded softly.

"I know more than you know yourself." He leaned in close, his eyes open, and brushed his lips with hers. "And I know what you *need*. Don't I? Even if you don't." His tongue flicked over her lips.

"Yes," she breathed, touching the tip of her tongue to his and reaching for more. He ran his tongue along her lips, tracing and exploring their shape, molding them together.

"Yes, what?" he growled, sucking on her bottom lip and then trailing his tongue along her jaw line and biting with tiny nips that took her breath away.

"Yes, whatever you say, Adam."

He grazed the tender skin along her neck with his teeth. "If you think I'll settle for half of you, you're crazy." He suckled gently on the delicate pulse that throbbed erratically under his skillful mouth.

He lifted her to sit on the tub's ledge. His eyes dropped to the tiny rivulets of water that settled on the downy hair at the juncture of her legs.

He soaped his hands and smoothed his palms over her stomach and then lower, tangling his fingers in her soft curls. He spread her legs wide, his dark eyes glittering like polished stones.

Arousal flooded her as she watched his jaw flex and go rigid at the sight of her, so flushed and swelled, so ready for him. Her sex was splayed open by desire, inviting to be fucked. Surely he'd succumb to her now?

He smoothed his palms down along her inner thighs and watched her sex throb under the heat of his gaze.

"Maybe I should soap my cock and clean you thoroughly," he murmured.

"Yes, please, Adam."

He trailed his fingertips along her swollen lips and leaned in close and studied her. Her clit throbbed, aching for his tongue. When he touched her with the pad of one soapy finger, she cried out. And then his fingers were everywhere, slipping up her pussy and thrusting, sliding over her labia, rubbing the sides of her clit.

"Do you think you're clean enough?" he murmured, his eyes liquid with desire.

"No." She arched her hips into his hands as every finger continued in motion along her swollen lips. He pinched her clit.

She gasped and shuddered.

"I can't forget your other hole. The one in which I *raped* you last night, right, Jez?"

"Yes," she breathed. "I mean..."

"Look at me." His eyes were hard. "Shall I clean you thoroughly there, too?"

She nodded.

"Ah…" A smile curved his lips as his finger slid between her buttocks. "Yes, you'd most definitely like being fucked from both ends at the same time, wouldn't you?" He probed her bottom with his finger and she shuddered violently. "Answer me, Jez. Wouldn't you?"

She was drowning in sensation. "Yes, anything, please."

"Open for me," he growled.

She tried to relax into his hand but she was strung so tight she was shaking.

He splashed her pussy with water and then his mouth was on her, his tongue flicking along her clit and then sliding along her lips. She screamed with the pleasure of his tongue sweeping over her, laving every layer of her before he returned to her hardened bud. His finger sunk deep into her bottom. She sobbed.

When he suckled her clit harder, she exploded around his lips and his finger, throbbing with the exquisite pleasure as wave after wave of contractions gripped her in a sexual heat that was torture and that seemed to go on forever. Every muscle turned to liquid fire, everything centered at her cunt and then burst out to every nerve in her body.

When she finally collapsed, hanging limp in her restraints, he jumped up and unlocked her wrists. She fell into his arms.

"Jez," he murmured, taking her into his arms. She wrapped her legs around his waist, and then he carried her out of the tub. He ran his lips over her forehead and murmured non-sensical words she didn't understand.

Then she was lying along the big bed and he was toweling her off.

He rolled her onto the large terry towel and patted her back and buttocks dry. She stretched languorously, enjoying a deep contentment that filled her clear down to her toes. She sighed and almost drifted off to sleep.

His large hands stroked and kneaded her shoulders, then drifted to where her wrists had been locked. He pressed his lips where tender skin had met cold metal and licked.

Then he kissed the nape of her neck with featherlike kisses that trailed along her hairline. Her blissful state made her forget that he hadn't reached satisfaction until she felt the evidence of it pressed against her thigh.

"Sleep," he murmured, rising from the bed.

She flipped over and watched him grab a towel for himself from the neatly piled stack alongside the tub. He was still bone hard. His muscles flexed and rippled as he rubbed the towel down his powerful body.

"What about you?" she asked.

He looked up and scowled. "What about me?"

"Come here," she said softly. "I'll take care of you."

He dropped the towel onto the carpet and flung open the doors of a large closet. After he grabbed a pair of sweat shorts off a shelf, he shoved his legs into them and hiked them up. She was sure that the elastic waist was a welcome relief. There was no way he could get that impressive erection zipped up.

She dragged her eyes away and looked at his face. He was turned away from her. "Come over here, Adam."

He looked over at her, his eyes a mixture of impatience and regret. "I told you. I'm not interested in sex. I want more."

He turned from her and riffled through a cabinet full of dresses.

"More of what?" What did he expect from her? That in little more than twenty-four hours of being kidnapped, she'd receive some revelation that they were meant for each other? Or that she would fall in love with him?

He came over to her and laid a white sundress on the bed. "This should fit." He placed satin panties beside it.

"Whose are those?"

"Jenna's. She's a female agent built like you only shorter. They should do fine."

"Sounds like you know this Jenna intimately."

"I do," he said, meeting her gaze but offering nothing more.

A stab of jealously pricked her. "Well I'm not wearing another woman's panties." She flung them aside and picked up the dress.

"Suit yourself." He shrugged and turned from her. "I'm going out by the pool. There's body lotion and perfume on the dressing table if you care to use it." He headed toward the door.

"All Jenna's, I suppose?" she called after him.

He slammed the bedroom door behind him.

Chapter Ten

Adam was stretched out along the chaise lounge talking to Shannon Reidel when Jezermiah finally came out to join him. The virginal white sundress he gave her clung to her curves like water. Why had he chosen that dress? He must have some masochistic tendency of which he was unaware.

And it was just his luck that she refused to wear Jenna's panties, because he had finally made some headway getting his erection under control and now he was not going to be able to get out of his mind that she was naked beneath.

He could tell she was still in her little snit about his relationship with Jenna. Good. If she hadn't closed off her psychic abilities all these years, she'd *know* they were destined for each other.

It was killing him not to join with her. His loins ached with a need far greater than sexual. Although that was killing him, too.

She eyed him warily as she slid onto the lounge beside him. He ignored her while he spoke to Shannon, telling her that Jezermiah had no connection with the New Continental Council of renegade psychics.

"So, you've found she's no danger to the government at all?" Shannon asked.

"No, she's a royal pain in the ass, but we can't keep her on our watch list for that reason."

Shannon chuckled. "She sounds interesting."

Jezermiah was scowling at him and craning her neck, trying to see Shannon's face on the tiny screen.

"Right," he said into the cellufile, adjusting his earpiece so he was sure Jezermiah couldn't pick up anything. "Tell Jenna I'll talk to her about it soon."

"Jenna?" Shannon asked. "What are you talking about?"

Jezermiah's eyes burned into him.

He wondered what it would take to get her really riled. He turned away from her, onto his side, and concentrated on the call. "As soon as you give me the word, I'll be back," he told Shannon.

"That's not necessary, Adam. You can leave whenever you're ready. The Agency is grateful for the time you've given us."

"Right. I'm ready to leave now, but I'll wait until you give me the okay."

Shannon chuckled.

"Agh! What the—" He was drenched from his chest down to his feet and Jezermiah was standing before him with an empty bucket. "I'll call you back, Shannon." Luckily his communication devices were waterproof. He snapped his case shut. "What was that for?"

"Everything!" She flung the bucket down. "You drug me, kidnap me, accuse me of the most heinous acts, then ravish me and now you're leaving?"

He hid his pleasure at hearing that he had gone from raping her to ravishing her. He lifted a shoulder. "What do you want from me?"

"What do I want?" She balled her fists. "What do *I* want? I'll tell you what I want." She took a breath. "What about protecting me? You're the one who said I'm probably in danger of being captured by that council of lunatics. What about that?"

He swung his legs over the side and went nose to nose with her. "*I'm* the one who needs protection. From you."

She scowled back at him, steam coming from her ears, but said nothing.

He pushed up off the lounge. "I'm getting out of these wet clothes."

"No you're not. We're in the middle of a fight and you're not leaving." She swung her legs around just as he was rounding her seat and tripped him. Before he knew what was happening he was falling headfirst into the pool. When he came splashing above the surface she was looking at him, stunned.

"That does it," he growled.

She backed away. "It was an accident."

"I'll bet." He heaved himself up over the side and started toward her. "I may have drugged and kidnapped you, but I'm sick of being bashed in the head, kneed in my balls, and now kicked into a pool."

"I didn't kick you," she stammered, glancing around for an escape.

"Like I said, I should have gone with my instincts the first time you maimed me."

Her mouth dropped and her eyes flew to his hands that he was flexing against his thighs. "You wouldn't da—"

"Oh yeah," he growled, "say it. Please, just say it once. Tell me that I *wouldn't dare*."

She made a dash for the hedges surrounding the pool and crawled underneath. He stepped back and then made a running leap for the other side. When he landed she was a few yards ahead of him and making a run for the nearest out building. He gained on her in seconds. With a sweep of his arm he snatched her up and threw her over his shoulder.

"I'm going to enjoy— Agh!" She bit him. He dragged her off his shoulder and whipped her around so fast he was sitting with her over his knee before she could scream. He pulled her skirt up and made a gag out of it, tying it around her mouth so she couldn't bite him. She growled and punched at him as he feasted his eyes on her silky white bottom bucking and squirming over his knees. His cock swelled in record speed.

Before she could punch him again, he pressed his forearm against her back while he grabbed both her wrists and wrapped his one hand around them, anchoring them together at her back. Then he spanked her bottom hard, leveling stinging slaps that had her jumping on his lap.

"That's for knocking me unconscious. Twice." The sound of her lush flesh smarting under his palm was immeasurably satisfying. She flailed, kicking her legs and growling what sounded like a string of wicked curses. He twisted his one leg over both of hers to keep her still.

"And these—" he slapped her again, five quick vicious spanks right in a row, "—are for my family jewels that might never recover."

She was choking and snarling so loud he was almost worried he had gagged her too tight. When he looked at her she had twisted around and was shooting daggers from her eyes. There was going to be hell to pay when he finally let her up, but for now spanking her senseless was much too satisfying for him to resist.

"And this—" he smacked her with the full force of his palm, covering her fleshy mounds completely, one and then the other, "—is for biting me, I can't remember how many times."

She yanked her neck back and arched against him to no avail. He had her anchored solid, belly pressed right over his erection.

"And these—" he smoothed his palm over the satiny pink flesh, enjoying the heat that rose from her skin and feeling his cock throb with each wriggle of her delicious bottom, "—are for wanting those men at the meeting to all fuck you at once." For that he leveled a string of short smacking spanks that had her flesh flushing a deep red.

He was hard as granite now, and he wanted her more than ever. While he stroked the smooth rounded flesh her muffled curses turned to tiny moans. He slipped his fingers between her thighs and groaned when he met soft wet flesh. She shivered beneath his hand.

Cursing himself, he quickly untied her gag, expecting her to let loose a blast of expletives that even he'd never heard. He let her roll gently onto the grass beside him.

She pushed her hair off her face. "How can you say that?" He offered no resistance when she punched at his arm with a fury. "I never," she choked, "said that I wanted any of those men. You said it!" She slapped at him, with both hands now, and then sobbed.

His heart sank. "Jezermiah..." He reached for her. She came willingly, and let him take her into his arms and settle her onto his lap. "Don't cry." He smoothed tangles of hair from off her face. "I'm sorry." He lifted her skirt and ran his palms over her tender bottom. He could still feel the heat rise from her sensitive skin. She whimpered against his chest. "I don't want to fight with you," he murmured. "You just make me so crazy." He stroked the smarting flesh of her bottom.

"I won't be able to sit for weeks," she sniffed.

He cupped her bottom and felt the heat against his palms.

And then she licked him. Flat on his nipple and then trailed her tongue along his muscles as though tasting him. She sighed against him and snuggled in closer.

He had no will to resist her. He loved her. For now he would take whatever she had to offer.

She turned her face up to his. "I want you to come inside me." She slipped off his lap and lay back on her elbows along the soft cushion of grass. She slid her dress up to her waist and spread her legs. "I'm... I'm inviting you into my body, Adam," she said almost shyly.

Her pussy was glistening red, inviting him all on its own, the puffy lips so swollen her clit all but disappeared.

"Please, Adam," she pleaded.

He went to her in a move as natural as breathing and eased her back, laying himself against her length. He cradled her face, smoothing her hair back and running his lips along her brows.

"Things will never be the same once I enter you."

"What things?"

His tongue fluttered along her eyelids while he eased the blunt head of his cock between her soft plump lips. The feel of her was killing him. "Everything." He drew her knees up and eased in slowly, wanting to savor every inch. He groaned with the feel of her heat surrounding him.

She softened even more, opening to him in every way, her lithe body melting into his, molding to his strength.

"Please, Adam." She stroked down the bunched muscles of his chest, pulled tight with the need to control himself. "Let go, Adam, please."

"You don't understand, Jez." He hissed in a breath as he slid in deep. The tip of his cock settled against her womb. He trembled with the need to control himself as he slipped out slowly.

"You fill me completely, Adam." She smoothed her hands down his back and then to his buttocks, urging him back in. "Move. Let me feel your power."

"Oh God," he choked and thrust up into her, hard, hitting her womb then rearing back for another powerful stroke. He couldn't stop himself.

"Adam," she screamed. Her body tightened and then gripped him both within and without. As he continued to thrust with fast powerful strokes, her pussy clutched him deep, refusing to let him go, the pressure and the friction driving him higher. She scratched down his back, drawing blood and sobbing with each powerful contraction as her orgasm consumed them both. And then he was pumping his seed into her in heavy pounding bursts.

The prairie let loose with a rush of wind that swept the landscape and swirled around them like a small tornado and in seconds they were plunged into darkness. The roar of the wind was so great in their ears that it mimicked a siren, blocking out all other stimuli.

And then as quick as it came, it calmed. The sky brightened and the wind became a gentle breeze that caressed them as they lay, limbs tangled together, hearts beating in unison, with his seed buried deep in her womb.

Soon after, gusts of wind kicked up as though nudging them to emerge from their sensual haze.

Still, he didn't want to slip out of her.

She clutched his buttocks. "Stay, please."

He looked into eyes liquid with love, even if she herself was unaware.

"Are we still alive?" she said, her eyes blinking with uncertainty.

He smiled against her lips. "Barely," he murmured. "I think we might be in heaven."

Her eyes glistened with tears. "I think so, too."

The rains pounded his back. "Let's go inside."

He lifted her and soon they were back in the bedroom and he was drying her off.

She grabbed his wrist. "What happened out there, Adam?" she asked, her expression filled with both apprehension and wonder.

He framed her face in his hands. "What do you think happened, Jez?"

"I…" She cleared her throat. "I think we might have moved heaven and earth."

He rubbed his thumbs under her eyes. "Go on."

"I felt a psychic shift. As though we had fulfilled some destiny. It happened when you spilled your seed in me, Adam."

He smiled. "Maybe we did. Maybe we've realized our own destiny in each other."

"Do you believe that?" She circled his wrists.

"Yes, love." He pressed his lips to hers. "Yes, I do."

She stood on her tiptoes and kissed him back. "I do, too." She brushed her lips over his. "I'm not afraid anymore, Adam," she said, tears filling her eyes. "I think I understand now."

He traced her lips with his thumb. "You understand what, love?"

"That love is more powerful that evil." She kissed his thumb. "With the love I have in my heart...for you, my great-grandfather's evil thoughts can't reach me."

His heart filled. "Yes." He kissed her with all the love he felt. "Yes, there's no room for hate in a heart filled with love."

"That's what my grandmother always said."

"She was right."

"But she also told me to be careful who I gave my heart to."

"She didn't want you to give your heart to a man who didn't love you, Jez. But I love you. You believe that, don't you?"

She smiled. "Yes. As much as I believe now that we're meant to be together. And I'm not afraid to have your child." Her eyes grew wide. "Adam, I think that's what happened out there. I think we might have conceived a child."

"That's what I think happened. We might have conceived a very special child. But not because the child will be a psychic. But because it will have been conceived in love."

Her eyes grew wider in wonder.

He turned her toward the large picture windows. "Look."

A wind so fierce that it rocked the smaller outbuildings had captured the prairie. And the clouds seemed to be warring for space. Had there been any trees, they would have been uprooted. The hiss of the wind tunneling through every corridor and bending around every corner grew louder, its power staggering.

Adam circled her waist from behind as they watched quietly the awesome spectacle nature played out right before their eyes.

He pressed his lips to her hair. "I love you, Jez. I know you don't understand that, but I've always loved you. It's just that it took me so long to find you."

She sighed. "I love it when you call me Jez. And I want to believe you. I'm trying, Adam. From this point on I'm leaving Jesse behind. Thank you, Adam."

"My pleasure, Jez." He nibbled along her neck. "God, has it been my pleasure."

They held each other tight. Tight enough to last a lifetime...and beyond.

About the author:

Kathryn Anne Dubois lives the demanding life of a mother of five, a wife of 30+ years, and a public school art teacher. What better reason to escape into the delicious fantasy world of writing romantica.

Reviewer Lani Roberts of *Affair de Coeur Magazine* has this to say of Kathryn. "Kathryn Anne Dubois makes her debut...with such sexual intensity that the readers will definitely cry for more."

Kathryn was first published in 1999 with Virgin Publishing's *Black Lace Line* whose publisher's claim "only the most arousing fiction makes it into a Black Lace - erotica at the cutting edge written by women for women" and later with Red Sage's *Secrets* and still writes for both publications. She is pleased to have joined the wonderful authors of Ellora's Cave.

Kathryn has been an active member of Romance Writers of America since 1998 and lives in the greater Philadelphia area.

Kathryn welcomes mail from readers. You can write to her c/o Ellora's Cave Publishing at 1337 Commerce Drive, Suite 13, Stow OH 44224.

Also by Kathryn Anne Dubois:

A Man's Desire
Perfectly Incompatible

Rayne Dance

Mlyn Hurn

Chapter One

"It was a dark and stormy night."

Rayne threw the mystery novel across the room. It was too damned hot to be inside reading; especially since power usage was still so closely monitored since the end of the psychic war. Walking back to where her book had landed, Rayne picked up the maligned text carefully. Books were an expensive commodity these days, as was just about everything, unless you happened to be gainfully employed and non-psychic. Going over to her front door, she looked outside through the screen.

"Bullshit! I'd give just about anything if it was a stormy anything."

Rayne walked outside and over to where her well had been successfully drilled a few years ago. She was luckier than many of the small farms around her. Her plants were still growing healthily, which was primarily due to her daily watering schedules. The buckets she filled twice a day and toted sometimes half a mile, took an hour to fill some days. By the time she finished filling them, the sun would be low enough in the sky for her to begin watering.

Finally, she had enough water to begin. Picking up two of the buckets, Rayne started the slow walk to the most distant of her precious plants. There was a watering can at different points along the path where she could fill them to water several rows and avoid carrying the buckets as far each time. Beginning with the first row, Rayne wondered how her sisters were getting along. That was one of the things about watering her delicate herbal plants and floras with a bucket—it gave her lots of free time to think.

The year was 2150. Since his assumption of power in 2048, Tyre Leyton had ruled with an iron "psychic" fist. He had established a system of overlords, who ruled over large cities, or regions. These overlords followed Leyton's laws, which were passed by his selected legislators. The psychic overlords that the rebels finally defeated had destroyed what was once a unified world economy, using their paranormal ability to dominate the globe and control resources for their own greedy use. While the top overlords centralized the world government in the North American continent and lived in splendor, the rest of the world's nations had to use profits from their GNP to pay for such necessities as water.

The overlords had systematically destroyed as much infrastructure of the North American continent as they could when they knew they were about to lose to the rebels. Since the peace accord, most of the world had been striving to rebuild the heaviest damaged areas during the Final War of 2100. Rayne worried about her two sisters when her hands were busy, leaving her mind free to worry. While she was unaware of her sisters' exact locations other than which state each lived in, it was probably wisest for their safety.

Moving on to the next row, Rayne realized that she had not heard from either of her sisters for over a year. She couldn't help but resent the fact that they had to be separated for their protection. And sometimes she wondered if living in such isolation was worth the supposed safety it provided.

Rayne had finished the second row and now needed more water. It was getting darker and soon there would be no light at all. She hated watering in the dark. It seemed like she was always taking a wrong step and slipping in the shallow mud. Many times she returned home covered in mud. She resumed the watering as quickly as possible, reminding herself to focus on the plants, not her family or friends.

Of course, she missed her grandparents and often wished she could return to be with them once again. She didn't, though, because to do so could expose Maile and herself to detection by the government's police force designed exclusively to investigate, track and, when necessary, remove psychic citizens. Maile had sensed the three young girls' powers early on and secretly trained them. But she had come upon them once practicing a ritual that went back so far no one was completely sure of its origin. It took great concentration, and it was assumed that only equal psychics could truly accomplish such psychic connections successfully. Rarely was there more than one psychic child born into a family. But with the girls' history of direct psychic lineage, one could only guess at their true powers.

Rayne shook her head, hating to remember the fear in her grandmother's face when she had found them that day. Along with the fear came the pain of being forced to leave her grandparents forever. Her sisters had seemed to understand better, or they were just better at concealing their pain at leaving the only home they had ever known. Unfortunately, she didn't know exactly where either one was but sometimes the urge to find them was almost irresistible.

* * * * *

Rayne was dead tired as she made her way back toward her house. She still would have to make something to eat for her menagerie of pets. From the look of the dry earth, she might have to water during the night once again. Just the thought of that made her groan out loud.

"Good evening."

Rayne would have jumped out of her skin if she could. The deep masculine voice shocked and surprised her, coming from her front porch as it had. Obviously a visitor had made himself comfortable waiting for her. Abruptly, she stopped a few feet from the steps.

"Who are you? What are you doing here?" Rayne snapped at the unseen stranger. It was pretty much unheard of for newcomers to move into the area. Therefore, newcomers—strangers—were usually viewed with suspicion. Almost everyone farmed land and some raised animals as well. A stranger in the area stuck out like a sore thumb and word spread quickly about them.

"When you saw no one was home you should have left!" she accused him with her next breath. Her heart was racing, especially since she couldn't see him. It took several deep breaths before she calmed enough to "turn on" her psychic abilities. Despite the darkness, she had already guessed he was alone.

Suddenly there was the strike of a match and it flared brightly in the cooling darkness. Rayne blinked quickly, trying to focus on him in the small flicker of light. As she watched, he lit a pipe and took several long draws on it. The sweet redolent scent wafted through the air toward her. Smoking of any kind was pretty much wiped out these days. There were still kids who thought it was fun to smoke marijuana just to try it. But pipe smoking had become something only the very wealthy could afford. Tobacco had to be imported from South America, and since the war, prices had continued to skyrocket.

The flare from the match also served to momentarily highlight the stranger's face. He glanced in her direction and the man's startling hazel-colored eyes struck Rayne as quite unusual. His face looked sculpted and tanned. He came to his feet and was highlighted from the light behind him, inside the house. There was no missing his broad shoulders, tapering to narrow waist and hips. Something about this man was setting alarms off in her head, her psychic consciousness and her stomach. She couldn't deny that butterflies were beating like crazy and she still had not yet seen the man clearly. In the light, he might be downright irresistible—

Rayne stumbled at the first step of her porch. When she could get a better look at her visitor, he would also be able to see her more clearly. Tonight she had seemed to be particularly klutzy. She felt like one big mud pie.

The stranger crossed towards her quickly, extending his hand to her. Rayne pulled her hand away from the wooden handle bar, not completely sure that touching him would be a wise idea. She wasn't sure whether her reticence came from a desire not to get him muddy, or was it something deeper and more elemental that was sending warning signals to her brain. Her grandmother had told her once that some people could sense a psychic just by touching them. Maybe she could buy herself some thinking time by sending him into the small living room and she'd sneak around back, rinse off and then dart upstairs to do a decent clean up. Showing him her muddy hands, she spoke again.

"Sorry, I'm all muddy. If you want to go in…wait! Who are you and why are you here?" she added quickly, belatedly realizing that she was being much too accepting. Living in the small, easy-going rural area was definitely affecting her level of caution and usual alertness.

"I am Sean McDougal. I've heard nothing but compliments about your farming techniques and how you seem to be able to grow the healthiest plants in spite of the drought. I wanted to meet the lady with the green thumb."

"My thumbs are normal and why are you interested?" Rayne asked him promptly. Everything he had said was true. All the farms around her had come to see what she was doing differently. Her neighbor, the Jackson's oldest son, had even come several times to help her water since he'd first visited with his father.

"I just purchased the Scott farm."

"Oh," Rayne answered quickly. "My neighbor's son had mentioned last month that the place had finally sold. If you want to go in and sit down, I'll join you in a few minutes. And if you wouldn't mind going into the kitchen first and flipping on the outdoor light I would appreciate it. Thanks," she added before taking off around the side of the house.

* * * * *

Sean watched the woman scamper away into the darkness before he went inside to follow her instructions. Flipping on the outside light, he could hear water running. Unable to resist, he quietly moved out the back door, following the noise. As he came upon the pool of light, he felt like he had been gut punched. Standing under a running outdoor shower, a young woman clad only in a white, armless T-shirt and cotton panties stood, getting completely drenched to the skin. To the side he saw the outline of jeans and what looked to be another shirt tossed aside.

His eyes moved over her body slowly. He knew looking at her was only going to raise her barriers even more once she saw him. But there was no way in hell he could turn away from the soaking wet woman in front of him. As he stared, her arms lifted and her hands sleeked her long, waist-length hair back from her face. This lifted her breasts beneath the wet and clinging shirt, highlighting her hard nipples. Those breasts looked the perfect size for his hands. And her nipples promised to tease his tongue once he captured the taut bud in his mouth.

He could still leave silently. She had not yet seen him or sensed that he was even there. That did surprise him since she was supposed to be psychic—

It was too late a moment later. She was now facing him and her eyes had opened slowly. Taking a moment to focus, there was no effort on her part yet to cover her body. Sean, being male, took advantage and looked down at the apex of her thighs, concealed only by the thin, cotton fabric—now wet and nearly see-through. Expecting to see a lush, black forest or even a trimmed bushy garden, Sean was surprised to see flesh and the indentation of—

Abruptly Rayne turned away, turning off the water. She walked the few steps and picked up her clothes. Sean could see the tension in her face and opened his mouth to apologize.

"No, please, Mr. McDougal. Don't say anything. I think you should leave, though." Rayne took a step past him, not lifting her eyes to meet his.

"I apologize. I heard the water and I didn't think—"

"It's all right. Please, just go, though!"

Sean nodded slowly, reluctantly starting for his truck. "I'd like a chance to talk with you—"

Rayne shook her head. "Please go!"

Sean decided that retreat would be best at this point. He had obviously embarrassed her, and to continue might only serve to alienate her. The last thing he needed was anything that would hinder his final investigation for the Psychic Sensory Investigations Agency. Walking around her house to where he'd parked his vehicle, he admitted that he was grateful to finally be getting out. He was sick and tired of using his psychic ability to track innocent people down, and possibly destroy the life they and their families had made.

Driving back toward the large farming concern he'd purchased, Sean knew that he was possibly luckier than his fellow agents were. Thanks to his father's foresight and cleverness with money and investments, he had money to purchase land and start a new life...completely divorced from the Agency. In the early years following the war, he believed that the Agency and its policing agents were needed to track remaining psychics still loyal to the Leyton legislature and its overlords.

Unfortunately, some of the agents Sean had run across during his time with the Agency didn't quite agree with the views of the new government administration plan for tolerance. The goal, these days, was to identify and track psychics. The hope was to prevent the past from recurring and show that all people can live together peacefully.

One of the greatest problems was that some people still thought all psychics were evil and that they wanted to rule over all non-psychics. The pervading belief was that psychics could read anyone's mind, which naturally leads to fear. Sean had been taught almost from his first conscious thought to master his powers so he had complete control, not the powers. After college he had been looking for some excitement and danger, and ended up crossing paths with a PSI agent, Trevor Thomas, who had then recruited him.

His recruiter was now a department head of the Agency and working hard to get programs to educate about psychics and what kinds of talents and abilities they can have. Trevor believed that only through education could society achieve healing as a people. With education would come understanding, acceptance and tolerance, and hopefully would lead to friendship. When Sean had told Trevor he was leaving, he'd been offered several interesting management-level positions. Sean refused because even though it had been the excitement that had drawn him in the first place, he was tired of the subterfuge and delving into people's pasts. The last few years everyone he'd investigated had been harmless.

"Harmless" for psychics meant the individual was a level three or less. Tyre Leyton had been a five, and most of the overlords had been recorded, or speculated to be level four. Sean had tested to a level four when he joined the Agency, but since he was working with them he was perceived not to be a threat. And over the last few years, the remaining psychics from Leyton's time were living peacefully with the new government in power and were closely monitored. Many were aging or their grandchildren suffered from a chemical dependency to the drugs some of the overlords had used to enhance their powers.

Sean had been instrumental in bringing down the largest known band of psychic holdouts to date. Several of the men he had become friends with over the years through the Agency had infiltrated the band until they could gather enough information to know the location of them all and finally arrest them for re-integration into society. If it appeared after several years of conditioning therapy the person could not be safely reintroduced into the public, a permanent incarceration would occur.

Chapter Two

Sean stopped thinking about the past as he turned down the gravel road that ended at his farm. Pulling the truck to the side of the house, he turned off the ignition. As he climbed from the cab of the truck, he could hear the barking of the two dogs he had gotten as a bonus with the purchase of the farm.

A moment later the two large multi-colored, mixed breed dogs were there to greet him. Squatting down, Sean gave each of them a few pats and rubs.

"Keep that up and they'll be putty in your hands, Sean."

Sean stood and saw his sister, Colleen, standing on the wrap-around porch of the house. She had her arms crossed but they were resting on her big belly. Her thick auburn hair had been cut short since they'd moved here, making it easier for her to care for. Her green eyes were usually smiling and she wasn't afraid of the sun, as evidenced by the freckles sprinkling her cheeks and forearms. Sean's hair was several shades darker than Colleen's and his skin tanned easily. Whenever they were together, people always guessed they were siblings.

"Shouldn't you be sitting down somewhere with your feet in the air?" Sean asked as he walked toward the front of the house to join her. As he started up the front porch steps, another voice answered him.

"I believe it was that position which got her into—"

"Bob!" Colleen admonished her laughing husband, ignoring the grin on her brother's face. Pretending she was not blushing, she sat on the porch swing beside him. As she adjusted into a position of comfort, she could hear her younger brother joining her husband in the laughter. "Keep this up much longer and the two of you will be cooking your own meals."

Bob stopped immediately. "I'm sorry, darling. Have I told you how lovely you look today?"

Colleen ignored her husband's belated attempt to smooth things over as she replied, "No, but you had best continue to tell me several more times today to make this feeble attempt at sucking up work."

Sean laughed and sat down on the top step. The dogs lay down near enough hopefully to get an occasional pat or rub. As he relaxed and started to enjoy the fact that he was a farmer, his sister interrupted his thoughts.

Colleen spoke softly. "How did your little trip work out for you tonight?"

Sean frowned as he turned to glare at his sister. "Who told you about my visit to the neighbor's?"

"I did," Bob answered sheepishly. "This woman should be working for the police. She could interrogate anyone."

Sean laughed and shook his head. "Just you, Bob. And you sound like you knew all along things would not go as I had planned."

Colleen shrugged. "Call it a woman thing, if you insist. But I was pretty sure that you couldn't just walk up to Rayne and get her to tell you her deepest secrets. Why should she in the first place? She has all the 'gentlemen farmers' knocked on their collective asses by how well her small farm is doing. Did she laugh in your face when you asked for her secret recipe?"

Sean glared at his sister. "Let's just say that I'll need to try again."

"What happened?" Bob added.

Sean knew that his brother-in-law was curious to know why the lone lady farmer was the talk of the town. The gratitude Colleen and Bob felt that Sean had hired him to work as his foreman here was unnecessary in his opinion. Bob had worked on different farms and ranches since his teen years. The last fifteen had been as manager or foreman, and since coming here he'd expressed his desire to make this place the most successful in the area. Between this place and the tiny concern bearing the name of "Green Gardens" there was really no accurate basis for any comparisons.

His trip to "Green Gardens" had only come about because he had received a visit from a neighbor — a fellow rancher and farmer — and his son. Upon his retirement, which his superiors had not wanted to accept, he had shared his plans. "One last assignment" was how they had put it. A rumor put a great-grandchild of Tyre Leyton in the area of his new home. The report had only recently been filed and they needed it checked out. Reluctantly Sean had agreed. This evening he had planned on filing his report through the secure uplink his computer still maintained with the Agency. In spite of his observances and subtle conversations, he had not found anyone that had required further investigation.

Yet this afternoon, walking Ralph Tandy and his son back to their truck, Bob had struck up a conversation about a particular kind of fertilizer, so he had deliberately held back and soon he was strolling more slowly with Billy, Ralph's teenaged son.

The young man was in high school and obviously worked out, so Sean had asked if he was participating in sports. It had seemed like a safe topic. The sad look that covered his face told Sean he'd made a mistake. Quickly, as the kid was shaking his head, Sean asked him something else.

"What do you do with your free time?"

Billy's grin had flashed so quickly Sean wasn't sure he'd seen it. "I've been helping Ms. Waters lately."

"Helping her with what, Billy?"

Billy had stopped walking, glancing toward his father. He grinned at Sean. "Just around her place. She's alone there and I thought she might appreciate a helping hand."

Sean had looked at the kid's face and he had known that Billy was keeping all of this from his father. "She's an older lady and you're helping her out," he had offered, thinking that teen boys must be getting nicer. When he was seventeen, helping elderly women would have been nonexistent in his scheme of things.

There had been no mistaking Billy's grin as he winked at Sean. "She's twenty-five and I'm hoping to help myself into her hot little shorts."

Sean had tried to hide his surprise, but he'd known he'd failed as Billy's grin widened. "I've heard older women are the best! You don't have any of the bullshit girls my age want to hand out. I imagine a few more times of helping her carry water and so on will have her ready to strip naked and fuck in the garden!"

"Hey! Billy! We need to get going."

Sitting on the porch now there wasn't a single doubt in his mind that Ms. Waters had the hottest body he'd seen in quite some time. As he'd stared at her firm full breasts and rounded ass revealed by wet knit material, he could see exactly why Billy was falling all over himself to help the lady. He easily replaced the scenario that had been replaying in his head that starred Billy banging some older trollop. It was now his naked body joining her in the cold water, and his hands running eagerly over her wet flesh, shoving clothes out of his way.

"Sean!"

"What? Sorry, Colleen. I didn't hear you."

"I'm aware of that. Do you want me to reheat your dinner? If not, I'm going to bed so I can get an early start for tomorrow."

Sean paused for a moment to ponder his sister's words, but then decided he couldn't have missed too much. "Go to bed, Colleen. I can forage for myself, and thanks."

He sat quietly thinking about the beautiful Rayne Waters. His attraction was powerful, yet he still knew that he would check a little closer before he could explore anything at all with the seductive siren he'd observed tonight.

* * * * *

Sean came down the broad staircase reluctantly. He was dressed in a suit to satisfy his sister's demands. It didn't make any sense why Colleen was insisting on all of them dressing up for dinner tonight. He paused for a moment at the foot of the stairs as he heard voices coming from the living room. Since moving in here, the only time Colleen had made them use the living room before had been when their parents had come for a visit.

Stepping into the room a moment later, he understood his sister's odd behavior. The woman he had seen nearly naked and who had starred all night long in one after another of his erotic dreams was now seated on the sofa his parents had insisted on buying him during their visit. Her black silky hair was caught up into a haphazard knot, leaving tendrils of hair across her neck and ears. As she turned to see what her hostess was looking at, Sean realized she was wearing a pale pink dress. The cloth was cotton, and probably not considered sexy by most. Obviously they had not seen the soft material draping over this lady's curves.

"Oh, good! Here's my brother now, Rayne." Colleen walked toward Sean and linked her arm with his. "He never seems to remember what time supper is."

Sean kept his eyes glued to his guest as she slowly turned. There was not the surprise in her eyes that he had expected. Perhaps his sister had only kept him in the dark about their guest.

"Hello, Ms. Waters," Sean spoke softly. He watched as her eyes looked away from his gaze as she spoke.

"Good evening, Mr. MacDougal. I accepted your sister's invitation to save you from coming back to my place."

Sean started to offer his hand but she had already turned back toward his sister. He let his hand fall to his side as he listened to her speaking to Colleen.

"Thank you again for your kind request."

Sean watched as the raven-haired woman resumed her seat on his sofa, smiling as Bob joked about his wife's cooking. He had wanted to touch her hand, he realized with a jolt of surprise. Deciding he needed a drink, he turned toward the drinks cabinet in the living room.

"Would anyone care for a refill?" he asked as he poured himself a shot of bourbon. Pausing, he considered tossing that one back and refilling his glass. It only took a moment for him to conclude he needed all of his faculties this evening.

Colleen called out to him from across the room. "No thank you, Sean. Rayne and I are having tea."

Before he could turn away, his brother-in-law was at his side. "Pour me one like that, Sean. I have a feeling this is going to be a long evening."

Sean frowned and glanced at Bob while he poured the requested drink. Passing it to him, he asked softly, "What makes you say that?"

Bob took a quick drink before he spoke. "Don't take this the wrong way, Sean. I love Colleen and I never...well, hardly ever, look at another woman. But sitting across from that woman is going to be tough! She is so fucking hot!"

Sean stared at his brother-in-law in disbelief. Bob fell into that classification of the "never stray" kind of husband. It was totally out of character for him to even make a comment like that. Looking at Bob, with his slightly thinning brown hair, Sean guessed that women would probably still find him attractive. Quickly, he opted to skip confessing how he had seen their dinner guest last night.

"She is pretty," he muttered as he picked his glass up to finally take a sip.

"Ack!"

Sean grinned at Bob's response to hearing Sean's words. The look in his brother-in-law's eyes spoke volumes, which was reinforced by his next words. "Pretty! You are either insane, Sean, or you've gone blind."

"Bob! What are you two doing over there?"

Sean watched as his brother-in-law grimaced behind the napkin he used to wipe his mouth a moment before he answered his wife.

"Just getting a drink, honey."

Sean followed Bob, but his gaze was focused on Rayne. She was even more beautiful when seen in good lighting. The dress she wore really did more to conceal than reveal her sensuous figure. Granted, he was comparing it to last night, which wasn't fair to the dress. He walked over and stood at the far end of the sofa where Rayne was seated. As he watched her talking with his sister, he concentrated on trying to perceive as much as possible about her.

The idea that psychics could read minds was only true in some cases. What he did was to open all his senses, focusing on the subject. Channeling all of his energies into his powers, he opened himself to receive whatever output possible. Over the years, Sean had learned that he usually got what he wanted within a few seconds from most people. It took him a moment to realize that the only input he received was coming from Colleen and Bob! Turning his eyes to rest only on his guest, he did something he rarely did...channel all of his concentration and focus on Rayne.

Once, several years back, he and a friend through the Agency went on a camping weekend. After too many beers, his friend, who was a level three psychic, suggested they try their abilities out on one another. Sean had long suspected that his power was greater than level four, but had disguised and not used it for so long that he was stunned to discover that his friend was able to block his efforts. He was equally surprised that he blocked all the tricks his friend had up his sleeve as well. In the cold light of morning, they decided to keep this secret from the Agency.

An alarm sounding drew his attention abruptly back to the present. He saw that Colleen was getting up.

"Dinner is ready."

Rayne quickly set her drink down. "Let me help you, Colleen."

Colleen quickly shook her head negatively. She wiggled her fingers at her husband instead. "Bob will help me. You stay put and we'll call you both when we get everything on the table."

* * * * *

Rayne shifted uneasily on the sofa and picked up her glass. Hurriedly, she took a sip and then another. Suddenly her throat felt dry and seemed to be closing off. She didn't want to do anything else stupid in front of this man. While his eyes had been devouring her last night, she had seen him clearly. His stone-chiseled features, warm hazel eyes and sun-streaked reddish brown hair had struck her immediately with intent, deep and overwhelming desire. The rush of emotion had left her feeling raw and vulnerable. Her reaction had been knee-jerk when she'd asked him a moment later to leave. If she'd been completely honest with herself, she would have admitted that was the last thing she wanted.

This morning, as she first heard Colleen's dinner invitation, her gut reaction had been, "yes!" Then she'd be able to see the handsome man who had sent her normally logical and sensible brain into limbo while her body took over. Last night she'd slept barely one solid hour. Each time she awoke it was with the impression of this man's face in her head. Her heart would be racing and she was completely aware of the fierce need she felt deep inside herself. The last time, at dawn, the erotic dream had still been alive in her mind and easily entered her consciousness.

In the dream, as the water coursed down over her head and shoulders, she had lifted her hands to rub sensually over her breasts. The hard nipples had jutted eagerly in her palms as she pressed and then massaged her big tits. She'd shivered and opened her eyes. Like slow motion, Rayne watched his eyes move down and back up her wet body, thinly veined by the scraps of cotton.

Walking toward her, the handsome man had jerked his shirt off and tossed it aside. Her heart jerked wildly as he stepped under the water with her. One of them took a step forward, or was it his hand touching her arm? A second later their wet bodies pressed tightly together. Wet mouths met and slid against each other. The meeting of their tongues was not a gentle, questing exploration. Hot, fierce and demanding, Sean's tongue battled with Rayne's. With Rayne caressing his shoulders and neck, Sean cupped his large hands beneath her breasts.

Her groans and her body pressing into his grasp had signaled her eagerness. She had barely noticed when his one hand dropped down and cupped her mound possessively. Rayne eagerly welcomed the fingers that eased under the cotton and massaged her clit. There was no stopping him nor did she want to, as first one, and then two fingers slid easily into her slippery pussy. The curling and pressing of his fingers denoted his level of experience as he had controlled and mastered her motions.

There had been no thought other than acceptance as her body jerked forward into his body the first time. And the contractions and spasms of her cunt around his fingers a few seconds later were unmistakable. Limp and clinging to his shoulders, she'd not said a word as he moved her toward the house. But he wasn't taking her inside. Instead, he had pressed her flat against the side of the house. Standing almost immobile, Rayne had savored the feel of the shivers dancing along her nerve endings while his fingers were no longer resting dormant within her body. The stimulation of her clit had seemed almost too much as she heard dimly the sound of his zipper sliding down.

In her dream, Rayne had lifted her thigh to give him more access to her body. But he was already pushing her tiny panties aside. The thrust of his cock into her body had forced the air from her lungs. Gasping and feeling dizzy, Rayne had wrapped her arms around Sean's neck and held on. Sean's hands were lifting both her thighs as he impaled her with his staff. His last jab had sent another cycle of orgasms through her completely spent body. The only things keeping them upright were his strong, muscular thighs.

As the sky turned pink, Rayne knew the wetness between her thighs had only been her body's juices. Sitting on the side of the bed, she'd reluctantly acknowledged that it quite easily could have been his cum leaking out of her right now. Never before had she felt such intense reactions, asleep or awake. The intensity frightened her more than the fact that even though it was only a dream, she'd not given any thought to the fact he was a stranger, unknown, and had totally forgotten about using a condom!

Rayne sipped her tea eagerly, needing to cool herself and calm her emotions. A flush stained her cheeks, though, as she recalled what was in the pocket of her dress right now. During the heat of the afternoon, she'd gone into town and purchased, for the first time ever…condoms! She'd been so embarrassed, not really knowing what kind to buy. Still, none of that had stopped her from completing the purchase and putting one in each pocket of her dress. Telling herself she was being foolish, Rayne had walked the one-mile path between their properties.

* * * * *

"I am sorry for last night."

Rayne looked up into Sean's hazel-colored eyes. The desire she'd felt last night, and all through the daylight hours today, came rushing through her once again. Her breath caught in her chest as she realized how strong it was with him so close. He had walked silently to stand less than three feet from the sofa, directly in front of her.

"My mother would wonder what happened to the little gentleman she raised."

Rayne had to smile at his words. She didn't doubt his sincerity. But this self-deprecating humor only heightened her attraction. A moment later, without warning, her body reacted to the image that popped into her consciousness. It was from her dreams. Sean had pushed her back against the wall. His hand curled around the leg she lifted, pulling it higher. Rayne wrapped her hands around his neck and then felt the thrust of his cock splitting her flesh.

It was crazy, but she jumped and her hand jerked, as she seemed to feel the thrust of his cock into her cunt. It was as if her body had truly felt the impact. Tea spilled and Sean acted immediately by offering her his napkin. Taking it, she wiped her hand and then blotted the spot on her dress.

Still looking at the spot, Sean's finger entered her field of vision. She looked up, not sure what he was doing. "What?"

"You missed a spot. I'd offer to dab all you want…" his voice trailed away as he moved his finger a little closer.

Rayne glanced down and saw the large tea spot on the bodice of her dress. If she asked him to dab, his hand would be directly over her nipple. Immediately she regretted her last minute decision to skip underwear. Her nipples were definitely making their presence known, especially the one beneath the wet spot. Heat washed over her cheeks as she realized Sean must have been aware of their arousal when he first offered his napkin. Pulling the fabric away from her skin, she tried to press the wetness out. The napkin was too damp, making it worse.

"Let me," Sean whispered a moment later.

Rayne looked up and saw that he had another napkin, this one pristine. Ignoring that conscientious and cautious voice in her head, she let her body's desire act for her. She nodded her head and lowered her hands. It would have been better to let him take hold of the fabric and duplicate her motions. Instead, the fabric flattened once again across her full breast and peaked nipple. Pushing back the logic telling her to take the napkin, she nodded her head in agreement once more.

* * * * *

Sean had been watching Rayne closely. Her second nod fired his desire, which was barely held in check as it was. The thought of his sister returning was the only thing preventing him from seeking a kiss from her full lips. Each lick of her tongue sent his temperature a degree higher. But he did ignore his mother's voice telling him to pick the fabric up and away from her skin. That would be the logical and smart way to do it. He held the napkin flat to his palm and pressed his hand lightly over her breast and nipple. Slipping his hand a little lower, his hand curved around the globe. It was impossible to resist the lure of lifting the breast and just holding it for a moment. The sound of her breath catching forced his eyes upward.

Rayne's eyes were closed and her lips parted. A moment later, her tongue licked across her lower lip. Sean's cock responded promptly and he couldn't resist closing his hand in an unmistakable squeeze, followed by a gentle massage.

"Oh my God."

Rayne's cry told him her reactions to his touch were mirroring his. He shifted his hand, allowing the napkin to fall to the floor. This time as he cupped her breast he felt her hard nipple poking in his palm. Massaging her flesh, he wiggled his hand side to side. This still wasn't enough. His hand moved lower and he stimulated her tender bud further by rubbing his fingers back and forth across the distended peak. His cry drowned out hers.

"Yes!" Rayne whispered.

"God! You feel so sweet, Rayne. I want to suck this nipple into my mouth. Can you feel me drawing the bud between my lips? Suckling you deep inside before I flick my tongue over and all around this sweet morsel. Damn it! I want to carry you upstairs and take you on my bed right now."

Rayne slowly lifted her heavy eyelids. Desire and arousal were raging inside her, demanding attention and satiation. All she had to do was say, "yes." Even a simple nod of her head would probably be enough. Just nod her head and she would experience what she was sure would be pure rapture in his embrace. Her head dipped downward, nodding her agreement.

"Dinner's ready! You can pour the wine, Sean."

* * * * *

The table was quite large, but Colleen had arranged the four place settings at just one end, two on each side. Sean was next to Rayne and he held her chair for her to be seated. As she sat down, Rayne took several long, deep breaths to try and cool her ardor down. She'd never felt anything like the fire burning through her belly a few minutes ago in the living room. If Colleen's voice hadn't interrupted them, Rayne had no doubt she'd be upstairs ripping Sean's clothes off him right now.

Shivers chased one another up and down her spine. It was probably the excess adrenaline. She was shocked that she could be so easily seduced by this stranger's touch. It didn't matter that technically he was no longer unfamiliar to her. And she wanted to get even more familiar with him! Breathing deeply, she called on her usually well-disciplined control to take over and get her through this evening. Lying to herself, she wished she'd never met Sean MacDougal.

Chapter Three

Sean had looked down at Rayne for a few moments before he turned to do as his sister had requested. He immediately noticed the way her dress was now clinging to her breast and distended nipple. Without thinking it through, he took the napkin she had started to open and placed it to drape down over her shoulder. Looking up he saw that Colleen and Bob were both staring at him. Acting nonchalant, he shrugged his shoulders.

"Do you have an extra napkin, Colleen? I was a klutz and caused Rayne's tea to spill on her dress. Dinner smells delicious!"

Sean stepped over to the wine, opening it easily. He then moved around the table, pouring a generous glass of wine for each of them. As they began eating, conversation seemed a little easier. As host, he went out of his way to keep everyone's glass filled. He tried not to stare, but his gaze seemed to keep returning to Rayne's profile.

Her skin was lightly tanned and there was a soft flush on her cheeks. Thick eyelashes looked almost too long to be real, but the fact that he could see no eye shadow or lipstick caused him to assume that everything was natural. Her lips were full and each time she opened her mouth to take a bite his thoughts kept wandering down erotic avenues. Last night his dreams had all involved her luscious breasts and those long legs. But now, watching her mouth as she ate, or replied to his sister's unending questions, he knew that tonight it was going to be her lips starring in his dreams. Imagining the taste of her mouth, the softness of her lips and even how her mouth might feel around his—

"Sean!"

He looked over at his sister who was glaring back at him. Grinning he reached out and took a sip of his wine. "Sorry, sis. I was getting ready to tell Rayne that I had just learned about the festival that is held once a year. It sounds like a lot of fun."

Sean shrugged, having been caught daydreaming among company. He felt like a guilty kid, unable to respond to his sister since he had not been listening to the dinner table conversation, as a polite host would probably do. The simple truth was that he was more interested in looking at Rayne than he was in idle, superficial chatter. His gaze drifted down to where the napkin he'd tucked in earlier still concealed her breast. Falling for his surveillance subject wasn't something he'd ever done before. Abruptly he stopped eating, mid-bite.

What the hell! No way was he "falling" for any woman. He didn't have time for that in his life now. He was a man who had a plan for his life, and was determined to keep to the plan. Now that his life was becoming his own once again, order and peace was something he wanted. Women were expected now and then, but a certain type of single woman was not a good idea. Some women seemed to automatically know the rules, and others like Rayne...she was different. He didn't want to be deterred or deflected from what he'd set as his course for his future life.

Setting his fork down, Sean finished his glass of wine in a single gulp. Bob's voice penetrated his consciousness a moment later.

"That's no way to treat wine this good! Not to mention what it costs for a bottle these days either."

Colleen laughed softly. "That's true, Bob. So few good wineries survived the war. We're lucky that our family's cellars had been dug centuries ago and that they stored away a certain amount each year."

"I meant to comment on how good the wine was tonight. Were you thinking of restarting wine production with the land here? I understand before the war this was all very good for grape vine growth," Rayne said softly, in between bites.

Sean shook his head, forcing himself to focus on the conversation. "For now I'll leave the wine growing to my father and younger brothers. I'm not sure I'm cut out for that kind of life." Standing, he moved around the table, refilling everyone's glass. He noticed that Rayne had taken barely a sip or two from her glass. Taking his seat, he turned to smile at her. "Are you not much of a wine drinker?"

Rayne shook her head negatively. "I'm not much of a drinker of any kind. There was never any around as I grew up, and when I left home...well, I was never big on the rebellion thing."

Colleen laughed softly. "That was me as well, Rayne. My siblings did plenty of rebelling for my parents, with Sean leading the pack usually. Were you an only child, Rayne?"

"No, I have two sisters."

Sean was sure she started to say more, but something had made her stop. As he watched her, she resumed eating slowly. It was then he realized that even though his sister had been asking probing questions most of the evening, Rayne had managed to divulge very little facts about herself. Frowning, he concentrated on eating for a moment as he thought. Perhaps she was interested in him and was applying the old adage about men and mysterious women. More likely, he acknowledged with a fair amount of disappointment, was that she had probably figured out he had worked for the Agency. If that were true, he should move forward quickly before she disappeared.

*****

Rayne walked along the dark path slowly. She had excused herself as soon as she felt was polite after dinner. It had taken a firm determination to refuse a ride home, insisting that she wanted to walk the shortcut back to her place. Throughout the delicious meal she'd had the distinct feeling that Sean MacDougal was watching nearly every move she made. It embarrassed her, considering what had occurred before dinner. Just remembering how aroused she'd been with only his hand upon her breast was disturbing her usually placid, quiet life. Pausing for a moment, she closed her eyes. All too easily could she recall every scent, touch and emotion she'd felt as his hand caressed her breast.

Opening her eyes again she continued the walk toward her home. Her head was telling her it was just sexual need. Like all the hierarchy of human needs, the sexual one required occasional attention. This feeling was nothing more than the basic need for…

"Damn it!"

She'd stubbed her toe. Stupidly she'd worn open-toed sandals, showing off that she had taken extra time to paint her toenails that afternoon. Just another example in her mind of how foolish and childish she was behaving. Looking up at the sky, she raised her hands, palms upwards and fingers outstretched. All she needed was some rain so she wouldn't have to keep up this nightly watering ritual every day.

Rayne lowered her hands to her sides. That was the problem, she decided. Lack of rain. That was causing her to be up at night, watering her precious plants. She wasn't getting enough sleep and that is why she was acting so strangely! That had to be the explanation for all the unusual feelings and desires.

"That's it! Whew! At least now I know why I've been so nervous and jittery. I'd be having the same reactions around any male. It's sex, pure and simple," she said out loud, as if voicing the words would make the thoughts and feelings more concrete in her head.

Rayne continued walking until she reached the last turn before home. From here, late at night and if you stayed perfectly still, you could hear the sound of the ocean waves lapping the sandy shores. Many times she wished she had sought out a place closer to the water, but funny things tended to happen when she was around open water. It was better to be here, safe and growing her garden of interesting things. Maile had recommended the girls avoid places they might easily stand out and be identified as being different. In this small, sleepy community Rayne was sure she was safe.

Turning reluctantly, she walked the last couple hundred feet to her place. Coming around to the front, she was stopped abruptly.

"Hi ya, Rayne! I thought I'd come over and help you water tonight. Wow! Don't you look beautiful tonight!" Billy's voice ended on a note of amazement.

Rayne smiled at the young, virile and muscular teenager. She'd been aware of his infatuation almost from the very beginning. For a while she'd argued with herself about accepting his help, but sometimes she was too tired so she'd accept. She worked hard at keeping everything friendly and casual between them. Often she'd make remarks about his age and the differences separating their lives. Once, though, he'd gotten a little too poetic, writing a song about lover's strife.

"Hi, Billy! That is awfully sweet of you. Don't you have school tomorrow?"

"That's no problem. I could always bunk down on your sofa and hop a ride with one of my friends at the end of the lane."

Rayne knew her eyes must have popped wide open at his words. Sleep on her sofa? That was the last thing she needed right now—a lovesick teen in her living room. Damn it all, she thought quietly. Now what?

"Hello, Billy!"

Rayne and Billy both spun around at the deep voice speaking from the end of her porch. Breathing deeply, Rayne couldn't decide if she was angry that he'd followed her or relieved that he was here to deal with the problem of Billy. She ignored the little voice in her head whispering that after the teen left she could end up with an even more difficult situation to handle. Her heart started pounding as she saw that Sean had changed into jeans earlier and removed his shirt at some point while following her. At some point she would have to deal with the fact that she'd not heard him once the entire time, which was more than just a little unnerving.

"Isn't this nice, sweetheart!" Sean smiled at Rayne as he came up beside her. Casually, as if he did it all the time, he wrapped his arm around her waist and pulled her close to his side. "With Billy here to help me, we'll have this watering done in no time flat. Then we can get to bed early tonight. You haven't been getting enough beauty sleep lately, most of which is my fault."

Rayne couldn't believe what was coming out of the man's mouth! In just a few words he had claimed they were sleeping together and made it sound like it had been going on for some time now. The reputation she'd worked so hard on of staying apart from the people around here, beyond friendship, was blown. Men! She thought disgustedly and looked up at Sean, glaring fiercely.

"Great idea, Billy! I see you've already drawn most of the water, so this shouldn't take too long at all." Sean turned her easily toward him and kissed her full on the mouth. "You go on in and take a shower, babe. I'll be in as soon as we get done here."

Rayne watched as Sean good-naturedly patted Billy on the back, indicating for him to proceed. Ignoring her glare, Sean grinned back at her and then had the audacity to even wink! Disgusted, Rayne turned and stomped into her small house. Inside she threw a few pillows in disgust before she realized that one of them, either Sean or Billy, would end up watering the farthest corner of her small field. Scurrying around for her sneakers, she put them on and ran out of the house.

Running down the rutted path, she found the two men were working their way toward the back, rather than toward the house. Immediately she could tell that Billy was bowing to the Alpha male. What was it about this man? She was sure Billy would be angry and truculent, at least! Her ego was a little bruised as she watched them joking around, unaware of her approach at first. She grabbed one of the buckets of water and started toward the back.

"Hey! I thought you were going to get ready for bed."

Rayne didn't turn at Sean's words. She didn't want him to see her vulnerability, on any level. The need to protect herself was running high inside her at the moment. "I'm not tired, so I'll do the back rows myself. I know them better and there's less chance of me crushing anything in the dark."

She took off down the narrow lane as quickly as her feet would carry her without actually running. At the last row, she filled the long spouted can from one of the pre-filled buckets of water. Taking a moment to thank her earlier oversight in leaving a partially filled bucket, she quickly watered all the delicate plants that were partially shielded by the windbreaks she'd constructed. This was the only plant that was growing in her field that was so rare most people thought it was extinct. But with careful tending, she had encouraged the small cutting she'd stolen to grow into about twenty healthy plants. With time, she could probably have grown enough for it to be reintroduced, but she didn't want that to happen.

Finally, she finished and replaced the barriers. Turning, she saw that Sean was standing a few feet away, watching her. Picking the watering can back up, she moved around him. Since her rows were narrow it left only enough space for one person, not two. Her body pressed against him and he took advantage of the moment to grab the can from her hand.

"I sent Billy on home. There are really only a few more rows to do. That kid is fast."

Rayne moved on down the row, aware that Sean was watering the plants she'd not done in her rush to reach the others first. She filled the other can that Sean must have left when he'd followed her with the last of the water in her bucket. Quickly she moved into the next row, working carefully, but with speed. Dawdling tonight didn't seem like a good idea. A few feet along she heard Sean begin the row in front of hers.

"I imagine you aren't used to this old-fashioned way of doing things," Rayne spoke quietly, surprising herself by speaking at all. Part of her head was convinced the best idea was to say nothing, while the rest of her body was reminding her about that very human need she'd been thinking about during the walk home. No doubt about it—sex with Sean McDougal would be pretty amazing. The sight of his naked chest, in the moonlight, was enough to get any woman's engine racing. And hers had been primed since the first time she saw him. All day long she'd been fighting thoughts of him, or thinking about him. Reminding him of how different they were had worked with Billy, so why shouldn't it work in this case as well?

* * * * *

"There is nothing wrong with doing things an older way if it works. From what I've heard in town, you seem to have more than the proverbial green thumb. Rumor has it this land was worthless for growing anything until you took over for back taxes." Sean spoke softly, hoping that by revealing what he knew she might open up to him. They had certainly made a connection earlier before dinner. He'd followed her after she refused a ride, only because he was worried about her walking alone at night. But she'd obviously done fine, except when she'd stubbed her toe the one time. He'd nearly revealed himself then to offer his help.

"I've done nothing special."

Sean watched while Rayne finished her row and they walked back to the beginning together. Picking up the other bucket, he topped off his can, and added some more water to hers. "Not much more to do," he murmured softly.

"You can leave if you want," Rayne spoke quickly.

Sean turned his head and lifted one eyebrow as he met her gaze. "It goes more quickly with two."

"I know, but I can manage this easily. I figured you'd want to get back home and to bed."

131

Sean grinned and shook his head. "Actually, I'm not at all sleepy tonight. This should help tire me out some. Maybe I'm just feeling wired or something. It's possible something got me all stirred up earlier in the evening."

Rayne's watering can slipped from her fingers. Water splashed up onto her dress and legs. She quickly picked it up without another word and started dousing the plants. She'd only done two when Sean's hand came out and took hold of her wrist.

"Slow down, Rayne. Drowning them won't help."

"Damn, I wasn't thinking," she muttered and resumed her task once he'd released his grasp upon her slender arm.

Sean watched her quietly for a few moments and then continued as well. After he'd gone a few steps he heard Rayne speak again.

"If you hadn't chased off Billy, I'd have all the help I needed. He probably won't be coming back at all after your caveman display at the house."

Sean grinned in the darkness. He had wondered if she was going to comment on that or just let it slide. Without stopping his work, he replied, "Billy wasn't helping you altruistically. That randy young boy had just one thought on his mind and it involved getting into your panties."

"I knew that, but I enjoyed having some help once in awhile. I could handle a seventeen-year-old boy. Besides, there are no 'panties' for him to be getting into."

Sean shook his head and scoffed doubtfully. "What's that supposed to mean?"

"I'm not wearing any!"

Sean's watering can slipped from his fingers as he heard her words. He spun around and looked at Rayne, his eyes lowering immediately to her waist and below. When he lifted his gaze to hers, she looked away from his hurriedly. He was sure she was wishing she'd kept her mouth shut just now. And he rather wished that she had not informed him because now all he could think about was her sitting at his dinner table without her panties on! God! If possible, he wanted her even more now. Deliberately he picked up the can and finished the row. Without waiting for Rayne, he walked back and refilled. As he began the last row, he was aware that Rayne had nearly finished hers.

He held his tongue until she finished and was passing him. He knew his voice sounded harsh as he spoke quickly. "I hope to God you didn't talk like that around that young puppy. With the slightest encouragement, a kid that age is like dry tinder."

"I am not stupid, Sean. I could have handled Billy. Now he won't be stopping by to help anymore. I'll let you finish since you have been so eager. Good night," Rayne said sharply, turning quickly. She muttered back over her shoulder, "And thanks."

Sean watched her until she was swallowed by the darkness of the night. Illogically he thought that it had sounded nice, hearing her call him by name. Up until that point, it had seemed as if she were avoiding any direct notice of him. Almost as if by not speaking his name, she could avoid giving him form and substance, or a place in her life. With a jolt of surprise, Sean acknowledged that she was going to have to get used to the fact that he was definitely in her life from now on. He knew then that no matter what he discovered about her, their lives were going to be intertwined for some time to come.

Chapter Four

As she stomped back to her house, Rayne told herself to go inside, turn off the lights and lock all the doors and windows. That would be the safest thing to do at this point. She didn't need complications in her life. Her life was comfortable, despite the hard work. Why should she let turmoil in? Hell! She was inviting it in!

Sitting down on her front steps, she slowly began taking her sneakers off. In a moment she'd take them around back and wash the mud off. Even though she could think of other things she'd rather do, it was better to do some things now to save more work later. A smile curled her lips upward as she recalled the many times their grandmother had tried to get her and her sisters to clean up after themselves. They were always more interested in hearing about the past and testing their psychic powers. Grandpa had disapproved of using any psychic power to help with their day-to-day lives.

Rayne had never longed to return to the days when the psychics ruled as overlords. The world was a much better place, according to Maile, since the rebels had overthrown the psychic government. But with her grandmother's warnings echoing in her head, she never forgot to hide her psychic abilities from everyone. One never knew who might report someone to the government as a possible psychic. They could arrive on one's doorstep or at a place of work and whisk him or her away with a psych search warrant. Sometimes people never returned.

Lowering her head, she covered her face with her hands. Dear God, it must have been terrible for people — psychics — right after the war. Their grandmother might have scared them too much with her stories, but she'd wanted the girls to be prepared. In the end, it hadn't mattered because the sisters had been forced to leave their home much too early as it was.

"You look worn out."

Rayne lifted her head and saw Sean walking toward her. He was still shirtless and he now had some mud on his boots and jeans. "I'm fine. I waited to offer you the use of the outdoor shower to rinse the mud off, if you want."

Sean sat down beside her before she could move, putting his hand on her forearm to restrain her when she did start to get up. "Seems to me the only reason I'd want to wash the mud off now would be if I were going inside. If I'm walking back to my place, then I might as well wait."

It was the way he lifted that one eyebrow, she decided. That one simple little action seemed to be the answer she needed. Or maybe it was just hearing him say the words out loud. In that moment, she knew there was nothing in the world she wanted more than for him to come inside. The grip on her arm had relaxed and she stood up.

"Then I think we both should wash the mud off."

She didn't wait but started around toward the back of the house. If Sean was interested, then she guessed he'd follow her to the shower. Hoping that he had come after her, she didn't look back as she pulled her dress up and over her head. She reached her hand out to pull the chain cord that would release the water. A larger, more tanned hand covered hers a moment later. She felt the heat behind her a second before the chilly water came crashing down over her body.

"Ooh!"

One hand encircled her waist, pulling her back against him. Immediately, she felt his hard cock pressing insistently against her butt. There was no way she could stop the wiggle of her hips pressing and rubbing across his flesh. She felt his lips against the side of her neck as he kissed his way to her ear lobe, which he paused to nibble for a few seconds.

"I want you so much right now that there is no way that cold water is going to cool me off."

Sean's deep, husky voice sent shivers through her body. The hand around her waist moved down over her flat belly and cupped her mound. He slipped two fingers into her cleft and rubbed lightly.

* * * * *

"I should apologize for last night, but I can't. I've never seen any woman look as beautiful or desirable as you did with your clothes dripping and clinging to you." His mouth moved to the side of her neck, kissing and then sucking on her skin. One part of him wanted to mark her as his woman and he didn't give a damn if it was macho, chauvinistic or caveman at the moment. All he wanted to do was to show the world that she belonged to him—she slept in his bed and it was his children she would bear!

The primitive thought shook him to his core. He'd never really thought of himself as getting married or having children. That was something he would leave to his siblings. They could worry about carrying on the family name. But right now, it was Rayne he wanted to see pregnant, her belly swollen with his child. His hips jerked forward, grinding against her soft ass at the vision of a tiny black-haired child suckling at her breast.

God! He'd never thought a women breastfeeding was erotic. The image in his head of Rayne tenderly holding his child while it nursed eagerly upon her breast was making him harder by the instant. His fingers moved more and wiggled between her soft, completely shaven pussy. He wanted to give her pleasure. The need to arouse and satisfy was strong and driving.

"I want to be inside you, Rayne, but I don't have a condom. Let me pleasure you with my mouth and fingers tonight."

Rayne turned in his arms. "I have one in the pocket of my dress."

Sean pulled her close and kissed her mouth hard. He stepped away and grabbed the soft fabric, looking for a pocket.

Upended, the pockets disclosed the packages she'd tucked inside. He managed to catch one but the other fell to the grass. Fumbling for a second only, he turned back toward her. His breath caught in his chest as he looked at her wet, naked body. She had slicked her hair back off her face and was standing with her arms down. In that instant, his heart seemed to skip a beat. Shaking his head, he stepped back to her.

"Do you want to go over to the grass?" he asked her softly.

Rayne shook her head. "No. I want you to take me standing up, against the house. That's how it was in my dreams last night. Please."

Sean's head jerked once, in agreement. He was kissing her a second later, savoring her lips before delving more deeply with his tongue. His hands skimmed over her skin, feeling the heat only partly cooled from the water. One second he cupped and massaged a breast, the next he was stroking her thigh or slipping in between to sample the secret sweets awaiting him.

When or how he did things to her became a jumble in his hurried rush to be inside her. Finally, his hands were lifting her upwards and pressing her against the house. And then he thrust into her body, hard and fast.

"Uhh," Rayne grunted as his body slammed against her.

Sean paused, though it wasn't easy to hold back his desire just then. "Are you okay, honey?"

Rayne nodded. "I'm fine...please...go on."

"Yes!"

Sean started thrusting faster, shorter strokes. He was stunned by how tight and hot it felt to be inside her. Damn! It felt so good he wished they were lying down so he could make it last longer. Doing it this way was hard and awkward...but he had been taught by his mama to please a lady. Although he was sure she had not considered this when she was talking about pleasing.

"Ooh!" Rayne cried out once, and then again, with her voice an octave higher. "Ooh...oh my God!"

Sean felt her climax even as she spoke. He tried to hold back but it was too much for the first time. Holding her tightly, he thrust quickly to his orgasm. Over and over he shot his come into the condom protecting their bodies. The regret that swamped his senses was intense and shook him deeply. He pushed the thoughts and feelings away as his body quieted and he relaxed his tight grip upon Rayne's body. Slowly, she slid down and he stepped back once she was steady on her feet. He wanted to say something, but he wasn't sure what was the right thing to say right now. This had never happened before. Women he'd had sex with before had been from work, or acquaintances whom he'd known for a while.

Rayne stepped away from him. As he watched her, she walked over to where he'd dropped her dress. She didn't pick the dress up. Instead, as he watched her pretty ass jiggling a little, she picked up the other condom package that had fallen from her pocket. Still without saying a word, she started walking back toward the front of the house. When she had gone about ten feet, she looked back to where he seemed to be glued in place. The smile on her face jolted him instantly, arousing him again—to his surprise.

"I have more inside, but I don't want to waste any." She wiggled the package in her fingers, almost like a wave toward him, and then kept on walking.

Sean MacDougal was no dummy, nor did he need to be told twice. Grabbing his jeans, he took off after her.

* * * * *

Rayne was standing by the bed when Sean rushed in a few seconds later. From the single light she'd turned on, the bed was dimly lit and she could see the scattered condoms across the bed from where she'd tried to decide which to take earlier. Suddenly she felt her cheeks heating in embarrassment as she recalled how bold she'd been acting since she'd met this man.

Like yesterday, never before had she showered with just her camisole and panties on. And certainly she'd never done it with anyone in shouting distance. Her behavior with this man around was inexplicable. Maybe he was making her go insane? That might explain her crazy actions—nervous, jittery and skittish like a wild mare. Just like a mare around a stallion, was her next thought.

She saw Sean toss his jeans into the corner and walk toward her. He looked so strong and good that she shivered in reaction. How or why he was affecting her like this didn't make any sense. Eagerly she went into his arms, kissing him hotly. She copied his motions and slipped her tongue into his mouth. When one of his hands cupped her breast, she groaned softly. Soon they were stretched out across the bed, lying on top of the prophylactic packages.

"That's quite a rainbow collection," Sean whispered as he picked one up.

"I didn't know what to buy, so I got the assortment." The words came out in a rush as she caught her breath. "It was the first time."

Sean lifted his mouth from kissing his way toward her right nipple. "I'm glad you thought ahead. A modern man is never sure whether he will be presumed to be too forward if he has one, or thoughtless if he doesn't."

Rayne giggled at his honesty. It made no sense why she felt comfortable with him. The same as it was inexplicable the way his warm breath flowing across her damp skin aroused her so deeply. Or the way that he had so easily invaded her dreams and they scarcely knew each other.

Suddenly, she remembered her grandmother telling her once that psychic women needed to be very careful with whom they fell in love with. The old woman refused to say why, just that her granddaughters needed to be cautious about whom they gave their hearts to. Rayne lifted her hand and caressed the side of Sean's face, trailing her index finger slowly across his lower lip. He surprised her when he opened his mouth and sucked her finger inside. She wanted to look away but she couldn't. After a few seconds, Sean's hand pulled her finger away.

"That's how it feels to be inside you, only a hundred times better. Hotter, tighter and sweeter." He sucked her finger back into his mouth, sucking in a quick rhythm. When he let her finger slip free, he smiled at her. "Of course, there is another way I can show you how pleasurable making love with you is."

Rayne held her breath as Sean lowered his head until his mouth hovered above her breast. His breath blew over the hard tip, raising goose bumps in the surrounding sensitive flesh. When his tongue licked around her nipple, it was like a child's tongue eagerly circling an ice cream cone. Rayne could feel her nipple getting harder and tighter, the skin puckering more with each second. When his mouth finally opened and suckled her nipple gently, she cried out softly. As he sucked and tugged with his tongue and mouth, Rayne felt the resulting pull deep inside. It felt like a string was attached to her pussy and each resultant lick or suck sent shards of excitement straight to her groin.

"Sean!" she moaned his name, lifting her hand to curve around the back of his head. "Yes! I want you inside me again!"

Sean pushed up against her hand a few seconds later, but tugged her nipple still enclosed in his mouth with him. Finally he released it with a loud, wet squelching noise. His fingers had slipped down and were working magic between her wet pussy folds. As he pressed and then wiggled his index finger around her clit, Sean pressed kisses from one nipple to the other.

Rayne could feel her body tensing, needing…with each touch of his mouth or fingers, heightening her arousal. Sweating and writhing upon her bed, she began pulling at his shoulders, his arms, and finally trying to push his hand from between her thighs. But he resisted her completely.

"I want you, Sean." She paused to lick her lips. "I want you inside me."

Sean smiled down at her, but shook his head slowly. As she stared up at him, he slipped two fingers inside her channel. She could feel them wiggling around, searching for—

"Oh God!"

Rayne cried out as he found her G-spot, pressing and massaging the area with his fingers. She closed her eyes, but just as quickly opened them as his rhythm changed. Every time she felt herself almost reaching the pinnacle, Sean switched how he was touching her. Or he alternated the way he massaged deep inside her. She knew she was crying when she dug her fingernails into his skin, demanding release.

"Soon, my sweet. Let go...stop fighting me and just flow with the feelings. You are trying to anticipate my moves. Just let your breath flow with the feelings."

His words soaked into her brain. She couldn't do what he wanted. To let go like he wanted might possibly release the power inside her. Fear of being discovered had governed her life for so many years. How could she relax her guard? She barely knew this man. Could she trust him?

Torn between her emotions, her body's demands and the chaotic thoughts in her head, she was startled to feel Sean's hands on her thighs. Opening her eyes she saw that he was moving down her body—

"No!" she moaned hoarsely, her voice cracking. She reached down with one hand and threaded her fingers in his hair. Pulling a little, she tried to pull him away.

"Hush, sweetheart. Shh."

Rayne told her hands to push him away...or was it pull? Then it didn't matter. His mouth was on her flesh and his tongue was making a magical spell. She swallowed once, getting ready to tell him to stop. That was her plan. Then she felt his fingers deep inside her once again, all while his tongue was deepening the thrall which held her. One deep breath and then she'd tell him—

"God! Oh my God! Sean!"

Her climax slammed through her body like a sledgehammer. There were no more thoughts that made any sense. Everything was sensations, feelings and emotions. Her body shivered and jerked rhythmically. Nothing had ever been this overwhelming. Not even when she discharged psychic energy. One moment she was still in control, but then with just one deep, relaxing breath her body took over.

Chapter Five

Sean moved slowly away from Rayne's body. Something had just happened that he had never experienced before. The problem was that he was not sure what it was. The air around them had suddenly felt charged with electricity. His own senses had been so heightened that he had very nearly lost his control as he witnessed Rayne finally orgasm without restraint. He couldn't be sure. Still, he thought he'd heard the clap of thunder.

Looking down at her face, Sean thought she looked so peaceful. She could be the poster child for relaxed right now. But he couldn't shake the feeling that what had just happened was not out of the ordinary. Even more than that, he realized in surprise that he wanted it to happen again and again. He wasn't used to being this aroused on more than just the physical level with a woman. Perhaps he should just leave —

"Sean."

He turned his head slightly and saw that her eyes were open and watching him. For a moment he wondered how long he'd been lost in his thoughts. That certainly didn't fit into the realm of proper bedroom etiquette at all. A woman usually expected all of the man's attention, based on his past experiences.

"Sorry." He stopped as the usual phrases he normally referred to women he'd known in the past didn't seem at all appropriate. "Is something wrong?"

Rayne shook her head. "Aren't you going to…you know?"

Sean smiled and lifted one hand to smooth an errant strand of hair back from her face. "I wasn't sure if you'd fallen asleep. You looked so peaceful that I hesitated to interrupt."

"I wasn't asleep." She paused and shifted around a little. A second later she pulled a crinkled condom package from beneath her. "Still have enough to go around." Grinning she held the prophylactic up with her fingers.

Sean reached out and took the packet from her. "Just what all did you want me to work my way around?"

"Me?"

He paused before answering, having heard the catch in her throat despite the boldness of her reply. Lightly, he pressed his lips to her forehead, the bridge of her nose, and lastly her chin, completely skipping her lips. From there he kissed her right cheekbone, and then the left. Moving a little on the bed, he kissed her breastbone. Another light kiss and he was between her breasts.

"You know, if I kiss you all the way around that could open up some interesting…positions."

Even in the dim light Sean could see the bright flush staining her cheeks. Perhaps it was too soon to explore some avenues. Kissing her parted lips, his tongue caressed its way inside and explored the softness within. His hands began caressing her body, from her breast to her thighs and back up. As far as he was concerned, he was ready and about as hard as he'd ever been. But he wanted to arouse Rayne once again. Often he'd satisfy a woman first, and then enter her cunt, to come inside her tight, wet body. With Rayne, though, he wanted her to climax with him inside of her. He also wanted her to come as hard as she had earlier.

It didn't take long once he shifted one hand between her thighs. While his fingers began to entice and seduce her, his mouth lowered to capture her nipple once again. Soon he matched the sucking motion to that of his fingers until her hips were writhing and her legs scissoring restlessly. He sensed she was nearing her peak so he quickly grabbed a packet and ripped it open.

Rayne's hands lifted to help. "Can I do that?"

Sean shook his head quickly. "Not this time, Rayne. I don't have that much control." He gently pushed her down and moved above her. She was already moving her legs apart, lifting one leg. He paused and positioned her legs, prompting her gently with his words. "That's it, my sweet. Ready?"

He waited until she nodded in agreement and then he eased forward, instead of thrusting. Moving slowly, he pushed forward until he was fully embedded in her hot channel. Bracing with his arms, his hips began moving. With measured strokes he went in and out. He had the thought that he would draw this out as long as possible, but that was before Rayne's orgasm began. As before she seemed surprised, but he felt the beginning muscle contractions, soon strengthening and quickening. Each one of her muscles seemed to be grabbing and sucking on his cock all of a sudden. The air around them felt alive with electricity again.

"Oh God!" Rayne cried loudly, her arms and legs wrapping around his body, trying to hold him close.

There was no holding out any longer for him, though. With a single shout of release, Sean's hips jerked in and out of her body, with much quicker strokes. He felt her body beneath him, around him, and he was in heaven. Above them he thought he heard the thunder crack through the skies once again. As he released his seed, everything charged with static electricity. When he looked at her, there was an aura surrounding her. His hips jerked forward again for the last time.

Sean leaned down and kissed Rayne's mouth. Her lips were curved upward in a gentle smile. A sudden surge of pride filled him. He had satisfied this incredibly beautiful woman. In truth, while pleasuring a woman had always been a priority for him, feeling that it was the most important part of lovemaking was a shock to him. He started to shift away, but her legs tightened around his hips.

"I'm too heavy," Sean protested quietly. "I don't want to crush you."

The grin on her face made his chest swell. "What a way to go, huh?"

Sean laughed and when she lowered her legs he moved off of her body. "Shall we get under the covers?" he asked softly.

* * * * *

Rayne nodded and moved reluctantly. Quietly she swept the remaining packets together, and set them in the drawer beside the bed. When she glanced up, Sean was removing the used condom. Quickly she turned away, wondering how a person handled things like this. Before she could think about it seriously, Sean flipped the covers back. He climbed into her bed as if he'd done it a thousand times before. Her breath caught in her chest at seeing his broad shoulders and tanned skin against her white sheets with the tiny pink roses. Her eyes lifted and saw his head resting on the bright pink pillow she'd chosen as accent color for the bed. Hurriedly she got under the covers as well.

Lying beside him, with the sheet tucked under her arms, she folded her hands. Reality was hitting her hard in the face at the moment. What was supposed to happen now? Idle chatter? Could she possibly sleep in a bed with a man she hardly knew? Suddenly she wished she had discussed this kind of thing with her sisters, or another woman. But she'd been living on her own for so long that the subject had never before come up. So now what? She chewed her lower lip as she pondered.

Slowly, she started circling her thumbs around one another. Going one way about ten times, and then stopping and reversing direction. After her fifth change of direction, Sean's hand covered hers, stopping the restless movement.

"What's wrong?"

Rayne didn't turn to look at him. "Nothing is wrong. Why should anything be wrong? I'm fine."

"Do you want me to leave?"

It shocked her that he had so easily gotten to the hub of her dilemma, which unsettled her deeply. It should have made her feel relieved that he was bringing the subject up so she didn't have to, right? But it wasn't relief she felt. God! Had he brought it up because he really wanted to leave, but wanted to leave it to her to make the final decision? Was he wishing that he could skip out and never see her again? This was making her crazier than she normally was!

"Is that what you want to do? Uhm…is that what you usually do…in situations like this?" She spoke softly, hated the unsteadiness in her voice and hesitation.

Immediately the bed shifted beside her. A moment later Sean was pressed to her side and his hand was turning her face toward his. The anger on his face gave her another unexpected surprise. God! This was turning into a night full of unexpected emotions and happenings.

"Let's get a few things straight, Ms. Waters."

Rayne heard the affronted tone in his voice. She wasn't sure if she was supposed to reply, but then it became a moot point as he continued.

"Number one—this is a first for me. I have never, got that, never had sex with a woman I've only just met. Not even in my wilder days. That isn't me. Understand?"

Rayne nodded, but Sean wasn't really waiting for her acknowledgment as he continued.

"Second—if you don't want me to spend the night just say so, damn it! You don't have to handle me with kid gloves. I've got a tough skin."

Silence followed his words. Rayne waited for at least a minute for him to go on, but he didn't. Finally she spoke up. "Third?"

"Third? What makes you think there's a third?"

Rayne shrugged her shoulders. "I just assumed from the way you were going that there had to be a number three."

"All right! Third—don't ever twiddle your thumbs after we've made love. If I bored you, or I didn't measure up to your expectations, then just tell me to my face, lady! Don't sugar coat it, sweetheart, or play bored. I won't act like your boy toy that leaves your bed immediately after he's performed his tricks." He turned away and laid down, flat on his back. "And if you chew your lower lip, I'm going to kiss you every time."

Rayne felt her mind reeling under all those telling revelations. Obviously this confident and assured man was feeling some of the same things she had. It certainly made her feel better to know she wasn't the only one feeling like a fish out of water here. She started to twirl her thumbs again, but stopped abruptly, separating her hands and placing them palms down on the sheet covering her stomach. Her lower lip crept between her teeth unconsciously before she realized it, but stopped that quickly as well. She wasn't stopping because of Sean, though. And she'd tell him that, in a minute.

"You shouldn't be using the pink pillow," she said a moment later. The minute the words left her lips, she knew how stupid they would sound. Beside her, she heard Sean chuckle softly.

"Pink isn't my best color? Is that what you're saying? Or are you one of those people who think redheads shouldn't wear pink or red?"

Rayne couldn't stop the laughter that bubbled out. Giggling, she sat up, holding the sheet in place. "You don't have red hair, but Colleen does. She'd look beautiful in any color. And I only said that because I didn't know what else to say at this point."

Sean sat up beside her, reaching behind her back and exchanging her sage green pillow for his pink one. "How's that?"

"Better," she told him softly, intensely aware of his masculinity suddenly. "I've never done this before, either, so I really didn't know what I was supposed to do. My grandmother didn't cover this, so if there was a proper etiquette-way to handle it, I never learned it. I know I screwed up the whole condom thing. Oh, and the chewing my lip thing would make number four."

Sean smiled at her, reaching out to casually push her hair back. His fingers brushed her shoulders and she felt the frissons of desire course through her again. "You won't hear any complaints from me. I thought you handled it quite well."

"Thanks, I guess. This was a first for me too, and I didn't know...anyway, I always chew my lip or twiddle my thumbs when I'm nervous and don't know what to do, or say. I wasn't bored. I couldn't be bored. It was amazing."

Sean grinned and lay back down, this time with his hands behind his head. Rayne looked at him over her shoulder and decided that he looked the epitome of a satisfied male, on several levels. She wasn't angry and a moment later scooted back down in the bed as well. Taking a deep breath, she ended up yawning.

"I'm getting rather sleepy myself. Do you want me to go, or stay?" Sean asked.

Rayne pondered for a moment, yawning again as she did so. "You can stay, please. Uhm, I do have a question, though."

"What is it?"

"If you stay, do you think you'll want to do it again? Tonight, I mean."

Sean grinned, but he didn't answer her right away. Instead, he tossed the covers back and went over to turn off the single light. Despite the darkness, he still made his way to her bed without bumping into anything or stubbing his toe once. As he climbed back into bed, he shifted around and rearranged his pillows.

"If you insist, I could probably manage to do it again tonight. But I am rather tired as well, so if you could wait until morning—"

Rayne punched his arm.

Sean cuddled up close to her warm body. "Besides, there is nothing like morning sex. All warm, relaxed and still drowsy. Now go to sleep, Rayne. I'll wake you if anything important comes up."

Rayne fell asleep with her head pillowed on his chest, cradled in his arm.

Chapter Six

Dawn was just lighting the sky as Sean approached the front porch of his house. As he walked along, idly he'd kick at rocks. This was pretty much the last place he wanted to be right now. But discretion had told him to get back home before his sister was up to begin cooking breakfast. He also wanted to be cleaned up and ready to face the day before Bob, or any of the workers, started their morning chores.

"Look what that mangy cat dragged home."

Sean's head jerked upward. In spite of the dim light, he could see Bob seated on the porch. Trying to think quickly, he opted for delay tactics.

"What makes you say that?"

"Perhaps it's those scratch marks."

"Damn!" Sean realized that he'd forgotten to slip his shirt on before he reached the house, but he'd been too lost in his thoughts to remember. "So you didn't know that I'd left the house last night?"

"Nope, and I doubt Colleen does either. But you should probably get cleaned up before she comes down. I got the impression that she is quite fond of your new 'friend' even though she doesn't know her well yet. She might have a hard time choosing loyalty to her brother, if you should screw this up."

Sean pulled his shirt on, buttoning it up halfway. Walking up the steps, he paused to lean against the post. "What makes you think there is something for me to 'screw up,' as you put it?"

Bob grinned at his brother-in-law. "Hmm, from what Colleen has told me, and since I've known you, you have never had a long-term relationship with a woman. Granted, you may be suffering from temporary impairment of your senses, but Rayne is the kind of woman a man commits to. Don't get me wrong here, Sean. I love Colleen with every fiber of my being, and I love her more every day we're together. Still, I'm not dead. I can understand the attraction."

Sean couldn't explain his reluctance to discuss Rayne, or his relationship with her, with anyone. He knew Bob only had his best interest at heart, but that didn't change the strange feelings he'd been experiencing since he'd first seen her. It was more than just being physically drawn to her. There were things beneath the surface beyond his last job for the Agency to check her out. Last night he'd felt more than arousal and satiation. In fact, his feelings were deeper than any he'd ever experienced before, and he was angry that he was feeling anything at all.

Hell! All he'd wanted was to leave the Agency and enjoy his life in quiet, without danger and intrigue waiting around every corner. From their advance check, everything had indicated that even if Rayne had some psychic power, it wasn't a great deal. Most psychics used their powers to further their financial gain whenever possible. Seeing the modest house, and the miniscule farming concern, it was obvious she wasn't bettering herself in any way other than the old-fashioned way—hard work. So his involvement, if that is what it was, couldn't be construed as anything else.

Sean stopped as he realized he wasn't making any sense. Was it possible that she had robbed him of logical thought? Maybe she was a modern Delilah and she could steal his "strength" by having sex with him.

"Aren't you two the early birds? What in the world are you both doing up at this hour?"

Both men rushed to answer her at the same time, but then Sean gestured for Bob to answer first.

"You were so restless, honey, that I just surrendered and got up."

"Just restless, I guess."

Colleen looked at him for another second before she nodded once and crossed the porch to take the chair beside her husband. She folded her hands atop her belly. "We had planned that conference call for tonight at nine. I assume you'll be around for it."

Sean absent-mindedly nodded his head in agreement. The word "night" had him imagining another night in Rayne's bed. How he'd get through the day without seeing her was beginning to loom as a major problem. He knew he was acting as randy as a virgin bridegroom on his honeymoon. It didn't matter what else was going on, where they were or how much money they'd spent—all he really wanted was to be in bed, with his new wife.

"I'm going to shower. We've got a lot to get done today."

"And the call?" Colleen asked again with determination, evident by the tone in her voice.

"I will do my best to be around for the big call with the rest of the family." Sean held his hand up in the traditional Boy Scout honor signal before turning toward the door. As he ran upstairs, he heard Colleen expressing her doubts to her husband.

"I'd better work on a good excuse for why Sean couldn't be home for the call."

"Don't fret, love. Sean will do his best..."

* * * * *

Later that day, when Sean was so distracted he almost caught his hand in the blades of the machine he and Bob had been working on, he excused himself and went into his office to do the never-ending paperwork. He didn't get anything accomplished because his attention kept wandering. All he had to do was close his eyes to recall every second of last night with Rayne. Each touch, caress and kiss was reexamined throughout the afternoon as he sat alone, staring at the computer screen.

Somehow he made it through dinner and excused himself to go back to his office again. He sat there until Colleen and Bob joined him for the call with the rest of the family. It surprised him that during the entire call his thoughts were focused more on a woman he hardly knew instead of on the lively family discussion. Once the call ended, Colleen and Bob informed him that they were going to bed early.

A few minutes later he wandered out to the front porch and sat down. As he propped his booted feet on the porch railing, he thought that the night was still warm and he couldn't help but wonder if Rayne was watering now. Glancing at his watch, he saw that it was still a few minutes until ten, which was the time she told him that she usually started.

If he drove to her place, he would be there in about seven minutes. His boots hit the wood a second later and he was jogging to the truck. The keys were in it and he was driving almost too damned fast toward Rayne's about a minute after he'd finished the thought.

* * * * *

Rayne looked up as the truck lights started up the short gravel road to her place. Even though she wasn't expecting anyone, there was no doubt in her mind whose truck it was. She turned her attention back to the old-fashioned water pump, continuing to fill her assortment of buckets. A minute later, a pair of boots came into her peripheral vision. Without looking up she spoke softly.

"Hello, Sean."

"I came to help you water. With the two of us, it won't take as long."

"That is true, but you don't have to help me. I assume you came over for sex." As the words left her lips, they didn't sound as uncaring and casual as they had when she'd practiced being nonchalant and light-hearted. She didn't want to reveal how deeply her emotions were running already for this man. Caring for him would be to break all of the rules. It would be risky and she was not a risk taker. Maybe her sisters could do it, but she wasn't strong enough to cope with the circumstances. That's why she kept separate from others, to keep her heart safe and whole.

Years earlier, when it came time for her to leave home, she had asked her grandmother if she could have an old trunk in the attic. As expected, Maile had nodded her head, never asking which trunk or if it held anything. Nestled deep inside were some very old keepsakes. The most valuable, in her opinion, was the diary she'd found buried at the bottom of the trunk. The diary had belonged to her great-grandmother and contained facts that Rayne doubted had been recorded anywhere else.

Suddenly, her thoughts were interrupted as Sean grabbed her forearms and pulled her up as he stood. Facing him, she could see the anger on his face. "I'm sorry if my honesty offends you, but I thought if that's what you came for…" she paused and shrugged her shoulders, "…then we could go on in and do it before I water. After you leave, I'll come back out and finish."

For a minute, Sean didn't reply. Rayne could see that he was struggling to control his anger. Knowing that keeping her mouth shut probably would have been the wisest choice she went on talking.

"I just mean that I don't expect you to help water before we have sex. That is too much, it's almost like having you pay me for sex."

"Shut up, damn it! Good God, woman, do you have a death wish or something?" Sean relaxed the hold on her arms, slowly releasing them completely.

Rayne could see he was breathing rapidly. She was lucky, realizing belatedly, that he had not struck out at her. She guessed he had every right to be angry. Basically she'd accused him of treating her like a prostitute, except instead of money the payment for sex was work. Not that she'd ever think he would have to do that. He was too damned good looking for that.

"I guess I should apologize," she spoke quickly, rushing the words. "I didn't think about it from your point of view. I didn't mean to insult you. Gosh, Sean, anyone looking at you would know that you didn't have to pay for sex, or bribe a woman either. I mean…well, you are probably the best looking man I've ever seen. And, well, to be honest, I just wasn't sure what would happen after last night. Nothing was said about seeing each other again. All day long I kept thinking…anyway, that's what I came up with…that perhaps if you came back, it would only be to have sex."

Sean's hands grabbed her shoulders. "Shut up, Rayne," he muttered a second before his mouth covered hers.

While his mouth and tongue mastered hers, his hands began roving her body. When his hands discovered her unbound breasts beneath the thin cotton T-shirt, she felt his groan rumble in his chest. She moved her hands down his chest and did something she'd wanted to do since the first night she saw him. One of her still-wet hands cupped his manhood, pressed demandingly against the zipper of his jeans. His groan was even louder that time, but when she began to stroke and squeeze his hard cock, he suddenly moved away from her.

"What's wrong?" Rayne asked quickly. "What did I do wrong?"

Sean shook his head at her, and ran one slightly shaking hand through his hair. "You did nothing wrong, Rayne. But if you'd continued for much longer, I'd have taken you right here in the mud."

Rayne felt the warm feeling inside her start to grow and brighten, like a small candle. She couldn't stop the grin that curved her lips. For the first time she felt power as a woman, a sexual being. She was very fit and strong, as a human being, but she'd never had any confidence in her appearance or her womanly wiles.

"Okay," she forced the words out, her stomach in a jumble. "I'll start over. Hello. Nice evening, isn't it?"

Sean grinned at her words. "Yeah. There is still some warmth from the day, but cooling off enough to be comfortable sleeping weather." He moved over to the water pump and began filling another bucket. Without looking at her, he went on. "I didn't get much sleep last night."

"Me either," Rayne told him softly, preparing another bucket to be filled. "I've never shared a bed before." Immediately as the words were said she realized how naïve that made her sound. It was true, but that didn't mean she wanted to shout it from the rooftops. Hurriedly she added, "Except for my sisters. We shared a bed growing up, at different times."

The last bucket was done and Sean picked up two of them. He started walking down the row, leaving one every other row. Rayne grabbed two herself, the water sloshing slightly as she hurried to reach the next two rows. Sean met her and told her to start the watering and he'd take the buckets down the line. Nodding her head, she started with the first row. Near the end of the second row, Sean was starting on the third. It took even less time tonight.

Nearing the last row, Rayne quickly moved to it, skipping two in between. "I'll do this last one, if you don't mind. If you get done before me, I'll meet you at the house." Turning quickly, she saw the odd look Sean gave her before he followed her directions.

Behind the protective netting, Rayne used the small flashlight she kept in a plastic box to check her precious plants for damage, insects or anything else. They all looked very healthy, though, and she was soon walking back up the lane. She could see that Sean was seated on the porch swing, looking quite relaxed and at home. For a moment she let her thoughts wander about the two of them living here, in her small house. But logic soon took over. With the huge white house on his property he'd have no reason to ever consider her place as anything but a shed at best, or an outhouse at worst.

As she took the first step, Sean patted the empty seat beside him. "Join me?"

Rayne nodded and sat down while he stopped swinging for a moment. Once she was seated, he began the gentle motion again. It was easy to close her eyes and let her body relax. All around were the gentle sounds of the night and the soft wind barely moving the leaves of the bushes and trees. Behind her she felt the warmth of his arm, which he had lifted back up after patting the seat. It was so easy to let her head ease back and rest against his arm. She couldn't remember the last time she'd felt this relaxed and peaceful...actually it was not since she'd left her grandmother.

"Do you sit out here often, Rayne?"

She nodded her head without thinking that he might not be able to see in the darkness. Then she remembered she was leaning back on his arm. She lifted her head. "I'm sorry to lean back like that. I just...I don't know. It felt right."

Sean smiled and she could see the flash of his white teeth for a moment. She turned her face forward again, looking out at the dark sky. "To be honest, Rayne, I was getting ready to gently nudge you into moving over and resting your head here."

Rayne watched as he patted an area on his upper chest, near his shoulder. "I would, but I think I stink, from working all day and then again tonight."

"Here I was thinking I would be the one. We could go back and use that shower of yours."

"Are you thinking about using my shower and leaving? Or did you have something else in mind?"

Sean stood and pulled her up beside him. "I'll be willing to do anything else you have in mind, pretty lady."

They walked around the house to the shower. Rayne paused, not completely sure how to continue...gracefully. She kicked her sneakers off, leaning over to tug the muddy socks off. When she looked back up she gasped in surprise. So much for going slowly...Sean was already stripped to his shorts and watching her.

Her words slipped out without thinking.

"Oh my!"

And her eyes seemed to be fixated on his aroused cock.

Sean came closer. "You know, that is the first time anyone has ever said that when they've seen me nearly naked."

"Have there been a lot of 'anyones' in your life, Sean?"

Sean was unsnapping her jeans and beginning to push them down over her hips. His fingers caught under the elastic of her panties and dragged them along as well. Her T-shirt, which had been tucked in, was long and fell to the top of her thighs. She slid her hands to the bottom edge, starting to pull the shirt up. Sean's hands stopped her.

"Not yet," he whispered to her softly. "I have a little fantasy, if you don't mind."

Rayne shook her head, aroused and a little scared. Then she realized that she trusted him not to hurt her, no matter what might happen. He would never lose control and harm her in any way. She couldn't explain how she knew this, but it seemed instinctual, this trust in him. When Sean shifted her toward the shower, she went with him. He reached out and turned on the water.

"Eek!" Rayne cried out as the cold water rained down over them. As she became wetter, she lifted her hands and slicked her hair back, off her face.

"God! You are so beautiful, Rayne!"

She heard Sean's voice a second before his hands cupped her breasts. Her nipples were hard points jabbing into his palms, covered only by the thin white cotton. His hands massaged and rubbed her full breasts. His voice was hoarse as he spoke.

"This is my fantasy. Seeing you that first night…and now! That night I hardly slept for the erotic dreams I kept having—all of them starring you." Sean lifted his hands to her face. His thumbs gently rubbed across her cheeks. He moved them up and slicked her hair back once again. "Tell me, Rayne, did you dream of me? Or was that first time all my emotion?"

His honesty in revealing his emotions surprised her. She couldn't hold her own words back. "I dreamed of you, Sean. You took me outside, up against the house. We were both soaking wet."

"Like this?"

"Yes, except that...you didn't wear a condom." She stumbled over the words, surprised that she had allowed that detail to creep out.

Sean groaned at her revelation. "Rayne! I wanted to feel your flesh against mine, but the risks these days are too great. Please believe me when I say that I've always been very careful. I would never do anything that might put you at risk."

Rayne nodded her head. She could tell him how she felt, about her inexperience. Instead of speaking her emotions, she moved her hands down his back, slipping under the elastic band of his shorts. She curled her fingers into the tight muscles of his ass for a moment before continuing their downward movement, dragging his shorts with them. Freeing his cock, she let the shorts fall on their own accord. Her hands curled around his hard rod, exploring his flesh while the water still rained down over them.

Sean reached his hand toward her, managing only a few light strokes across her lips before she stepped away.

"Turn the water off, Sean," Rayne asked him quietly. She didn't wait for him, but walked away, over to the small patch of grass. Dropping onto the grass, she duplicated his earlier motion. Except instead of wood, she patted the soft green carpet.

He shut the shower off, walking the short distance. Looking up at him, Rayne appreciated his masculine differences. Obviously he had left his shorts behind before crossing over to her. She could see his doubt before he spoke.

"Maybe we should go inside, sweetheart. It might not be a safe time of the month for you."

Rayne shook her head negatively while she pulled him down beside her. Once he was down, she pushed him until he lay supine, on his back. His surprise was evident on his face as she straddled his thighs. Her hands explored his chest, pausing to tease and toy with his hard nipples. Slowly she worked her way down, past his waist. Scooting farther down, she took his hard manhood into her grasp. One hand didn't circle his shaft as she stroked upwards. Her other hand lightly stroked his smooth, shaven groin area.

She looked up as she spoke. "Why did you shave?"

Sean grinned up at her. "I used to shave all over, when I swam all the time. But feeling how wonderful it was last night…well, I couldn't help but think about what it might be like if we were both smooth."

Rayne smiled, not knowing what to say. "Thank you" seemed trite. Instead she shifted off his legs for a moment, rearranging her body. He moved his legs to give her better access. Rayne started to stroke and caress his cock with her hands. It was obvious that she was eager, but inexperienced. Sean sat up suddenly and lifted Rayne's face. Kissing her lips, he smiled gently.

"I'll show you what to do, but I don't expect this."

"I know. Somehow I knew that you would not, but I want to please you as you did for me last night. I would like to share what I felt when you touched me. I'm sorry I don't know more and have more experience."

Chapter Seven

Sometimes in life you know a life-altering event is about to take place. Or you know what just happened has changed you forever. Sean knew it right then, as Rayne confessed her lack of experience and her desire to please him. He was in love. Head over heels, crazy in love with this woman he hardly knew. It was too late to pull back, even if he wanted to do that. He didn't want to pull away from Rayne. From this point on he wanted to live his life with Rayne.

Unable to speak for the knot in his throat, Sean directed Rayne's movements with his hands at first. But soon he didn't need to do anything but lie back and accept the onslaught her inexperienced hands were wreaking upon his senses. One minute her hands were caressing his cock, hand over hand. Then she shifted her attention to his balls, pulling, lightly squeezing. When she lowered her head and he felt her wet hair sweep across his thighs, he groaned loudly.

Her breath whispered across his flesh a moment before he felt her soft lips against his cock. As her mouth opened, Sean forced his head upward so he could watch. He saw Rayne lick her tongue around the ridge of soft flesh, pausing to flick at the joining of skin on the underside. As her mouth opened farther, Sean watched as she took the head of his cock in her hands. A few seconds passed, or maybe it was longer, before the wet heat of her mouth enclosed him. He fell back to the grass, the vision of her giving him pleasure burned in his head.

After that Sean lost track of every little thing she did, but she was constantly busy and moving from one area to another. Kissing, touching, squeezing, stroking until he thought he would go crazy. He was so hard he thought he was going to explode any moment when he felt her move even lower and begin to play with his sac and balls. When she began to use her mouth, he shouted into the quiet night.

"No more, love! I can't take anymore."

Rayne nodded and moved her body quickly to straddle his hips. He realized that she was going to take him inside her. His hands grabbed her waist, stopping her movement.

"We can't, darling. It's too risky, isn't it?"

Rayne shook her head from. "I'm sure it's safe. Please, come inside me this time. Let me feel your flesh in mine. I want to know your essence remains inside me, even after you have left."

Sean shook his head negatively but his hands were already assisting her. Slowly he eased her body down. The sensations were incredible as he felt his cock spreading, separating and finally pushing past her puffy pussy lips. She was already quite wet, and her flesh enclosed him quickly, completely. Once she was completely astride him, Sean lifted his hands to her breasts. The shirt was already drying.

"Take your shirt off for me, Rayne, please. I want to watch your pretty breasts bounce. Will you do that for me?"

Rayne nodded and pulled the shirt off, tossing it aside. She slid her hands forward to brace on his chest while she moved her hips. A groan escaped her lips.

Rayne followed his directions and he watched her body move and react. He flexed his hips and saw the surprise on her face. Her breasts bounced and jiggled as she moved faster. He slid one finger between her wet lips until he found her clit. Using what he'd learned about her body and responses from the night before, he stimulated her quickly. Her orgasm came slowly, building from deep inside. Sean could feel her tensing, squeezing him tightly. But when she finally came, it caught him by surprise.

The air around them seemed to spark with electricity. As her flesh began its spasmodic contractions, Sean could hold back no more. He let his climax wash through him. Except this time, the electricity seemed to be going through him, not just in the air around him. Above them in the skies, he was sure he heard the clap of thunder several times. The air felt heavy with moisture, like it wanted desperately to rain.

Sean realized he was experiencing his climax on more levels than ever before. This was much more than just the physical release. It was as if his body was a part of the earth for a moment. As he dropped his last barrier, he seemed to flow into Rayne's body and they were one person and yet still part of the earth. Over and over, his body jerked in response to the onslaught of physical, emotional and—could it be—psychic reactions?

He was finally aware of Rayne collapsing upon his chest, lying on him like a limp noodle. She mirrored his own feelings right then as he closed his eyes. If he didn't move, he could still feel the fine tremors deep inside her body. At that moment, Sean knew nothing had ever felt that good in his whole life. Breathing deeply, he listened to the rhythmic flow of Rayne's inhalations and exhalations. A second later he was sound asleep.

* * * * *

Rayne awoke alone in her bed the following morning. She could tell it was late by the amount of sun streaming through her windows. Damn! She'd missed her morning watering. Rushing around, she pulled on a cotton dress and ran outside without any shoes.

Outside, she crossed the open lawn area to the pump. Grabbing the first bucket, she was surprised to see it was still wet inside. It didn't seem possible that it had rained last night and she had not heard it. She always knew when it rained, even if she was sound asleep. Stepping carefully because of her bare feet, she walked to the first row. She didn't need to bend down to see that they had already been watered that morning. Turning suddenly, she stumbled down the lane to the last row. Moving the protective windbreaks, she looked in and saw that even her special plants had been watered.

Her legs gave way beneath her and Rayne collapsed onto the ground. She knew in that moment that she was in love with Sean. He had never told her how he felt, and it didn't matter. Without words he had shown how much he cared for her. By watering for her, he had demonstrated that he was willing to care for what she cared about. Did she need to know anything else about him? Through one act he had shown her that he was a good man. He had undoubtedly been as tired as she, if not more. Two more times last night, after stumbling into her bed, Sean had proven how much stamina he had by making love to her. Thinking about it now, she grinned. What a stud muffin!

Taking a deep breath, she rubbed her fingers over her cheeks to wipe away the tears. Suddenly there was a deep need inside her to see him. She wouldn't have to speak to him, but she had to see him, even if from a distance. Jumping to her feet, she walked briskly back to the house. If she cleaned up quickly, she could take the rear pasture path and be over there in an hour. Once she was at his house, then she'd worry about a good excuse for why she was showing up without an invitation.

"Good morning, Miss Waters. I'm glad to have caught you."

Rayne froze in her tracks. A man was standing on her lawn. Parked a short distance away was a modern skimmer, sleek and bright red, which always seemed a better fit for the old world, rather than the destroyed world that now remained following the rebellion. Many people still used vehicles from long ago, in spite of the dependence on fossil fuels.

Her gaze traveled over the tall, slender man. He had blond hair and was quite tanned, but she couldn't see his eyes because of the reflective style sunglasses he was wearing. His clothing screamed money and affluence. Rayne realized she hadn't seen someone dressed this finely since…she'd never seen anyone with clothes, or a skimmer, so expensive. All of her senses went into overdrive right then. She didn't know his name, or why he was here, but she knew that he was trouble. Closing her eyes for a moment, she gathered all of her thoughts and emotions into one place in her mind. Sean's name screamed through her consciousness. God, she wished he were here right now.

"Yes, I'm Rayne Waters. Are you lost?"

The blond man chuckled softly but took a couple of steps in her direction. He stopped when she backed up. "No, I'm not lost. I was hoping we could talk, if you have the time. Actually, I'm feeling pretty parched." The man stopped for a moment, rubbing his throat. "Could I get something cold to drink?"

Rayne had been raised to be polite to everyone, even though she was feeling uneasy. She nodded her head. "Sure. You can sit on the porch swing while I get it ready."

* * * * *

In her small kitchen, Rayne began preparing a tray of iced tea. Hearing her grandmother's voice in her head, she even set out a few of the cookies she had made yesterday. She had planned on offering them to Sean, if he had come to call last evening. As she stirred the tea, she couldn't stop the smile that curled her lips upward. He certainly had come to call! Yes, sirree! Even though it wouldn't have met her grandmother's strict standards for a gentleman caller, Rayne had no complaints.

Still, she wished she'd had more time this morning to have taken a shower and put more clothes on. No one, or at least hardly anyone, ever came to visit in the middle of the morning. Most people around here were hard at work, trying to get their morning chores done. This was the kind of life that never really changed, no matter what might be going on in the world. Sure, there had at one time been lots of experimental hydroponics studies being conducted on modern farm sites. But since the rebellion, so many things had returned to the simpler way of doing things. Life was more elemental, on many levels.

Rayne finally picked the tray up and started toward the living room and the front porch. Just inside the living room, though, she stopped abruptly. "Ooh!" she gasped and lost her grip on the tray. Everything teetered for a moment and then came crashing back on her. Glasses fell, cookies dropped, china broke in the abrupt accident. Rayne was suddenly wet with tea. Taking a step was the wrong thing to do, though. Her shoeless foot came down on wet, slippery wood and then found a piece of broken glass. In less than a minute, she was on the floor.

The blond-haired man was still standing by her sofa, where he had been looking at the few photos she had on the wall and end tables. He had not heard her entrance, but took a step forward now.

Outside her open front door Rayne heard tires squealing, quickly followed by the slamming of a door. "Rayne! Damn it all! Rayne! Where are you?"

Rayne looked up from her bloody foot and saw Sean leaping up the front steps of her porch. A second later the screen door banged open and he raced through it. She saw his eyes go from her, to the area around her and then to the man in the room. As his attention returned to her, Rayne tried to smile.

"I'm fine. I just had an accident and I fell."

* * * * *

It had been only a few hours since he'd left Rayne. He had been working the first two hours or so, but then upon his return to the house, Bob had been seated on the wide verandah, listening to the man who had come to sell him…damn! What had the guy been selling again? He'd been listening to the guy for twenty minutes and he hadn't remembered a thing the man had said.

Hopefully, Bob, who looked like he was paying attention, had gotten the gist of what he'd need to know for an informed decision. Right then he realized once again just how lucky he was to have Bob working with him here!

"I'm sure you can see how this would benefit a place this size, Mr. MacDougal."

Bob nodded his head. "I think this could definitely make a difference. What do you think, Sean?"

Sean turned his head and saw that both men and Colleen were watching him and obviously waiting for his answer. He opened his mouth to reply when suddenly his mind had filled with Rayne's voice screaming his name. Shaking his head, he looked around, but she hadn't been anywhere that he could see. That proved that he had not physically heard her voice, but rather it had a psychic sound reverberating in his brain. Hurriedly, he jumped to his feet and ran down the steps, looking in the direction of her place. Nowhere did he see Rayne, which was proof that it was not his ears that heard her voice.

Turning back toward the porch, the sudden need to see her was overwhelming, literally swamping all of his senses. He couldn't stay here. The compulsion to see her was too great. Pausing to shout at Bob, he turned abruptly.

"I trust your decision, Bob. I'll be back as soon as I can." Two seconds later he was running towards his truck.

The trip to Rayne's, that had taken seven minutes yesterday, had only taken him four today. Luckily the sheriff and his deputies hadn't been around as he careened down the gravel lane to her property. He slammed on the brakes as he saw the bright, new-looking skimmer. This was the first one he'd seen since he'd left New Frisco. Seeing one at her house didn't do a single thing to allay his concerns.

Running up the porch steps, he didn't know what he expected to find. He only knew that his gut feeling demanded he rush over. Unbidden had come the thought that he was her knight rushing to her rescue, but he pushed it away quickly. Throwing open her front screen door, the scene inside her living room wasn't what he'd expected, but then he hadn't really stopped to consider anything before charging over to her house.

* * * * *

Sean took a step toward Rayne, trying to take in the scene before him, and just what the hell was going on here!

"Grrrr!"

"Wroof! Wrooof!"

"Mmrrreeooowwww!"

The room was suddenly full of animals, the likes of which he'd never seen in his life. Two of them looked like dogs, but they were bigger than his large working dogs. And from the sounds they were making, they were in protective mode. Sean didn't move as he looked at the four-foot tall dogs. He wasn't sure that he liked the idea of such powerful animals around Rayne. She might not be able to fend them off if they decided to attack her.

"Are you all right, Rayne?"

Rayne smiled up at him. "I'm okay, but I probably need a Band-Aid on my foot."

The blond man moved forward and Sean turned to look at him. Something about the man's expensive clothing and perfect haircut set his teeth on edge. He didn't know this guy, but already he didn't like him.

"It's my fault, I'm afraid. Miss Waters was getting us something to drink and didn't hear me in here looking at her photographs. I didn't mean to startle you, Miss Waters." He pulled a pristine white handkerchief from his pocket and started forward to offer it to Rayne. After just two steps he stopped as the dogs began growling again.

"It's all right. Sean, what brought you over here?"

Sean ignored Rayne for a moment, glaring at the other man. "Who the hell are you and what are you doing here?"

"My name is Anton DeVeau. I just stopped by to discuss something with Miss Waters. I'm sorry for having caused you such distress. Is there anything I can do to help?"

"We're fine. Maybe you should come back some other time, though."

"Thank you for the offer—"

Sean and Rayne spoke at the same time, but her voice faded away first. Sean was glad when the stranger excused himself and left quickly. Sean followed him to the door, waiting until the sleek skimmer had traveled cleanly over the gravel, barely disturbing the dust. Something about the blond man set his psychic senses on alert. Mentally he noted to call into the Agency's base in New Frisco. Turning, he found that Rayne had wrapped the white handkerchief around her foot. The dogs were concentrating on eating the cookies and lapping up the tea.

"I didn't know you had...dogs?"

Rayne smiled. "I like pets. And they usually stay outside until I call them in. I didn't do that because you...well, they like to sleep with me. I didn't want to push the Alpha male issue. If you'll pick up the glass, then I'll get up with your help. Oh, thank you for watering for me this morning."

Sean crossed the room and squatted down slowly, still feeling leery of the dogs. Luckily the glass hadn't shattered and was only in just a few big pieces. He placed them on the silver tray. Shifting, he set the tray to the side.

"Grrrmmmmeeeeooooooaaaaaarrrrrrrrr."

Sean spun back at the odd sound, but the dogs were now seated complacently. He looked at Rayne. "What is that?"

"Another pet," she said, smiling. "I have several. Could you help me up? I think my foot will be fine if I just put some gauze on it."

Sean followed her into the bathroom, watching for a moment before he spoke. "Why don't you take a quick shower and then I'll run you into the hospital? We can wrap a towel around it."

Rayne looked back at Sean, over her shoulder. "Are you telling me indirectly that I stink?"

"Good God! Of course not, honey. I'm worried about your foot. It's obvious you've been out in the dirt without your shoes on, and now you've cut your foot. If nothing else we should go in and update your Tetanus booster."

"Okay, but please go to the kitchen and bring me one of those towels. I don't want to mess up one of the bathroom towels."

Sean was back in about four minutes, pausing to wipe up the remaining tea and set the glass fragments and tea tray back on the counter. The dogs merely watched him, but as he entered the kitchen, he thought he saw the tail of another animal disappearing around a corner. Somehow he knew the story about her pets would be an interesting one. Everything about Rayne was proving to be out of the ordinary and quite intriguing.

In the bathroom, he sat on the closed toilet, watching her dim reflection through the full-length shower door. He watched her washing her hair, rinsing it, and then as he saw her picking the bottle up again, he spoke.

"Come on, Rayne. You don't need to wash it twice, or condition your hair. I feel we have a more pressing need."

She turned suddenly and leaned her face close to the door. Then she stuck her tongue out, before returning to her shower. Still, she merely finished washing her body, which turned out to be a rather erotic show as well. As the door opened, her hand came out and grabbed for a towel. She held it in front of her, wrapping it around her body, but then had to slide it around to tuck the ends for security.

Sean grinned. "Sit down and let me wrap this towel around your foot before we have blood everywhere. Stay put." He added a moment later, "I'll go grab something for you to wear."

Chapter Eight

Rayne was sitting on her front porch with her foot elevated. She had refused to move in with him. Colleen didn't need more stress in her life right now. Her stubbornness had surprised Sean, but he had let it drop. What he wouldn't listen to was her tackling the watering.

"Just wait until I get back. Surely you can do that."

"I'm missing one whole watering, though."

Sean turned his eyes from the road toward Rayne for a second. She could feel his emotions even though she was looking out the window of the truck cab. Lifting the soft drink in the large cup, she sipped it slowly. Sean had bought them lunch for the ride back home. That was when he had told her he wanted to stay, but he had to hurry home and change clothes. Tonight was a meeting of local business owners, and of all nights, this one included dinner and he'd agreed to give a short talk. He would have sent Bob, but Colleen had reminded him three times yesterday and twice this morning after his return that they had Lamaze class tonight. It was the longer one, with the video and tour.

"All right," Rayne told him quietly a few moments later. "I'll wait for you."

"Promise?"

Rayne turned to look at him, surprised that he seemed to know her that well. "Yes, I promise."

Sean grinned at her. "No toes, fingers, legs and eyes crossed, right?"

She couldn't resist him, even though she hadn't gotten her way.

It was nine o'clock now, which was the time she liked to start filling the buckets. She couldn't remember how many times she wished she'd spent the extra money she'd gotten on an irrigation system, even if hadn't covered the whole area. And it hadn't become a problem until she'd received the warning to be wary of people poking around. The PSI agents had gotten a tip a couple of months ago. That was when she had had to resort to conventional watering methods. No more "rain dancing" until the commotion settled down once again.

As a very young child, she had discovered her powers over water. She could move it, as in making waves in her bathtub while nothing moved. When she was five, she made waves appear suddenly in a completely placid lake when there wasn't a breath of wind. At age eight she got to see the ocean for the first time, and the last as far as her grandmother was concerned. It was a very wet group that piled back into the old car for the trip home.

It was only after they had to leave their grandmother did Rayne begin studying other things, among them casting spells and Native American lore regarding the making of rain. At age thirteen, she brought a light sprinkle, and it only covered a really small area. But at eighteen, there was a spectacular thunderstorm, with lightning galore. She soon discovered the big storms were easy; it was getting the rain to fall in a small isolated area that was hard. Only after listening to a friend from near her grandparents' farm complaining about the rainstorm that seemed to be traveling across the whole breadth of the country did she realize that while it might be fun, her powers definitely had consequences.

Thus it was when the drought started a few months earlier, Rayne had thrown caution to the wind, and started "making rain." When she was in town one day, she heard people complaining about how the weather station couldn't explain some unusual cloud patterns. Combined with the warning about the PSI agents, Rayne stopped her nightly dancing in her field.

With immeasurable displeasure, she began the backbreaking work of hand watering.

"Do rain…do rain…do rain!"

Rayne turned her head to look at the brilliantly colored parrot perched on the bar she made for him so he had a good view on the porch. "Hush, Homer." Looking at the sky, she pleaded for either help with the bird or patience for her in dealing with the recalcitrant parrot. "Why is that the only thing he wants to say anymore?" A moment later she turned to the parrot. For a second she questioned in her mind whether or not the damned bird was grinning at her. "If you get me in trouble, Homer, I won't be the only one who gets screwed!"

Homer merely shifted his claws on the perch, and then bent his head to scratch with his beak. "Do rain…do rain."

Rayne shook her head, leaning it back on the cushion of the chair. "Shut up, Homer. I'm not letting a damned parrot talk me into doing anything!"

"Grrrrrmmmeeeeeeoooooofff."

A second later she felt the brush of the soft fur against her leg. The swish of a tail batted back and forth, barely missing her drink resting on the table. "Hey, Mohan! You are going to knock something over with that tail of yours."

"Cccchhhhhuuuuffff…ccchhuuuffff."

Rayne looked down at the animal anxious for her attention all of a sudden. For a moment she closed her eyes and offered up a prayer that Mohan had decided to stay away from the commotion that morning. Most people didn't react too well with a one hundred and fifteen pound Amur tiger. Well, technically Mohan wasn't pure tiger anymore. Shortly after she had settled here, she had gone to the nearest animal shelter, hoping to bring home some sweet pets to love. What she had found were the two puppies that now resembled small horses, an obnoxious parrot and an animal that wasn't identifiable—by sight anyway.

Looking into the small, white-and-black-striped cat's history, she had discovered that nearby had been a government facility before the war. Rumors had gone around about testing, using animals and so on. But at the end of the war, it was shut down, except for a minimal maintenance crew. After the animals all died, it was closed permanently. Mohan was now full-size and was probably the result of crossbreeding a cat and a Siberian tiger.

Rayne was always careful around her, because no matter how house-trained an animal might be, a person couldn't erase millions of years of instinctive behaviors. She'd never seen Mohan show the slightest interest in hunting anything. If something smaller came into her vicinity, she was usually the more timid at the unexpected meeting. And luckily, all of her menagerie seemed to be amicable. The only trouble was Homer, who up until he'd adopted his newest phrase, had been particularly fond of phrases he'd learned at his previous owner's place of business, a strip club.

"Ccchhhuuuffff!"

Rayne rubbed Mohan's head as she rested it on her leg. She'd gotten used to the unusual sound, which she had learned was typical of tigers when greeting their caretakers. Whenever she looked into those sad, pale blue eyes though, she couldn't help but wonder at what terrible things they must have done to some of the animals at the research center.

Glancing back into the house through the window, she saw that it was almost ten. Sean had thought he'd be back here around nine thirty at the latest. She knew he would be exhausted by the time he did get here, and she hated the thought of him having to water before he could sleep. She was tired, so she was damned sure that he had to be exhausted. Since he'd gotten up earlier, he'd had even less sleep last night.

As she scratched behind the big cat's ears, she mused out loud, "If it did rain, it would have to be for at least thirty minutes to do any good. A downpour would only run off with the dry ground. Where as a nice, slow and gentle rain would have enough time to soak in and not cause any flash floods lower in the deeper sections of the valley."

Rayne stood slowly, pushing the big cat away. It wouldn't be easy to do, but if she were careful with her foot, and worked quickly, she could be done before Sean got there. He probably wouldn't believe her if she said she'd done the watering, but perhaps she could say that Billy had shown up. That way Sean could get the rest he needed, if he chose to do it here. One part of her brain told her that it was the fact that he had spent the last two nights here that was the real cause of their lack of sleep. Still, Rayne sensed that if he wasn't here she would spend the night tossing and turning.

"Quite the conundrum," she murmured as she walked unsteadily down the steps. To concentrate the rainfall, she'd have to get into the middle of the field. Usually she didn't care if the rain fell outside the growing field, but if the roof was soaked, or the grass wet, Sean would definitely be suspicious.

* * * * *

Progress was slow as Rayne walked, or rather hobbled into the field. To the man watching her from a well hidden spot a few hundred yards away, it was obvious the cut she'd sustained that morning must have been deeper than he had originally thought. Anton DeVeau lowered the specially equipped night-vision binoculars for a moment. There had been a moment this morning, looking at the photographs on the woman's living room wall, that he had gotten a distinct flash that told him Rayne was the psychic he'd been searching for this last year.

Anton was a direct descendant of the overlord Marcel DeVeau. Marcel had been a close friend of Tyre Leyton. Approximately fifteen months earlier, Anton had gone to Paris to close up his grandmother's home following her death. He had been astonished to find a personal diary that, even though it was not signed anywhere, had become obvious to Anton as he read through the old pages that the author was his grandfather. He was surprised to learn that his grandfather had been assigned a special task, which unfortunately was interrupted by the rebellion and the subsequent overthrow of the psychic regime.

The diary had revealed the story of a woman who had caught Tyre's attention in the year 2065. Because of association with Tyre, whether she was a natural psychic or not was never questioned. As time went on, Marcel wrote in the diary that the woman became known as Tyrea, adopting the name of her master when she became his recognized concubine. By this time, Tyre had been in power for seventeen years. A law had been passed which prohibited two psychics of equal power mating, due to the circumstances that they might then procreate. It was unknown if that child would have greater power than the parent, and Tyre's government didn't want to find out.

Four years later, 2069, Marcel noted that suddenly Tyrea had left without word to anyone. Anton read that his grandfather had been surprised by the depth of anger Tyre expressed at being deserted by the woman. Marcel wrote that he had long suspected that Tyre felt much more for the woman than one usually saw between a master and his concubine. He suspected his sire's anger hid an aching heart. Tyre searched for the woman for several years, but as the rebellious outbreaks grew in frequency and depth, his attention was pulled away from matters of the heart. Then in the year 2100, only nine months to be exact, Tyre had given Marcel a task. Marcel was to do everything in his power to find Tyrea.

In the diary, Marcel recorded his arguments with Tyre over what he considered a waste of his precious time when the rebels were almost knocking on the palace doors. That was when Tyre had revealed the truth to his friend, and swore him to secrecy. Tyrea had been pregnant when she disappeared years earlier. Tyre had learned that she had died shortly after giving birth, but a child had survived. Marcel argued that he could be of much more use here, but his ruler had been insistent, finally revealing the truth. Tyrea had been a natural psychic. He did not know what level, but he suspected it was high, considering the concern Tyre was now expressing.

Anton read between the lines that Tyre had feared a son had been born, who could possibly defeat him by being a much stronger psychic. Marcel had noted all of his findings as he began his search, but the end had come too soon. Marcel had been in Paris, briefly visiting his wife, when word of defeat reached them. The diary ended with Marcel writing that he had not succeeded in his final task for his sire, but hopefully he would die nobly, thus honoring Tyre with his death.

Anton lifted the binoculars once again, focusing them on where he had last seen the beautiful woman. He had not been unaware of her beauty when he had finally met her. In the sunlight, she had been tanned, healthy looking and damned sexy. His immediate reaction to the woman's beauty surprised him still. He had been so devoted to rebuilding a strong psychic presence in the world for so long, that he had ignored a personal life for himself. Something about Rayne was making him have all kinds of personal, erotic thoughts.

Like that thin cotton dress she'd had on that morning. He could tell that she'd been naked beneath it by the way the sunlight had shown through the lightweight material. Standing in her living room, he had entertained thoughts of taking her on the floor. Anton didn't regard himself as a Neanderthal, but he was fully aware of his own attractiveness to women. There had been no doubt that a woman, living in the middle of nowhere, would welcome the attentions of someone like himself into her lonely existence, even for just a few hours.

The arrival of the other man had taken him by surprise. His surveillance had been completed a month ago, but then he had been required at the Center to discuss what he had found. No one acted without discussing their actions with the New Psychic Council and obtaining approval. The presence of this man, Sean something, had surprised him. The brawny teenager he'd seen from time to time had not worried him in the least. The minute Sean had burst into the living room, Anton had felt the change. With all of his psychic focus on discovering Rayne's identity, he had given no attention to the other man.

It unnerved him to think that the other man might have truly been a psychic, and in his temporary rapture with Rayne, he had missed the opportunity to psychically assess him. Telling himself to forget the past and concentrate on his assignment, he focused the binoculars on the porch. Scanning the length of the porch, he didn't see her so he shifted his gaze toward the lawn in front of the house. Still not finding her, he wondered if she had decided to water the field after all. Starting at the front row, he began scanning the rows. He located her standing in the middle of the field.

"What the fuck?"

The binoculars revealed that the woman was twisting and turning, with her hands raised skyward. Granted, she wasn't moving smoothly, or evenly, but he guessed she was dancing. Why the hell would she be dancing in the field at—he glanced at his watch—almost ten at night? Before he could formulate any further thoughts concerning Rayne, there was a loud clap of thunder overhead. Less than a second later, rain was pouring down on his head.

Cursing loudly, Anton fumbled to get the binoculars back to his eyes. Quickly he relocated Rayne. She was standing in the same spot, clapping her hands while the rain soaked her clothing. Her joy in the gentle rain drenching her, and her plants, was unmistakable. Logically, her happiness at having rain would make sense—after all, she was a farmer. Watching her, Anton lowered the night-vision binoculars to reveal her clinging clothes. Beneath the wet cotton dress, he easily saw the way her breasts were defined with taut nipples. Moving them down more, he lingered at her hips and thighs, enjoying how the material was caught between her legs as she moved back into the lane. From behind, her ass was perfect and heart-shaped.

The appearance of bright lights shining up Rayne's gravel road blinded him and he dropped the binoculars. Quickly he moved back under cover so the lights couldn't highlight him watching Rayne. He considered waiting until the lights left again, but he didn't like getting wet, and sitting here with water filling his expensive shoes wasn't his idea of fun. It was an easy decision to head back toward the small town and visit the local bar. Maybe there he could find out what had changed since his last visit.

Chapter Nine

Sean slammed the door of his truck. He couldn't believe what he was seeing. At dinner he'd had a glass of wine, and before he'd had a whiskey from the cash bar. Surely that wasn't enough liquor to make him hallucinate, was it? In college, he drank a hell of a lot more at fraternity parties. Looking up at the sky, he verified that he was standing where he could see stars, and clear skies. Still, about thirty yards away, he could see that it was raining on Rayne's field. The same field that he had been thinking about speeding up a way to water it more quickly. When the field went fallow, he was going to have irrigation and watering installed.

Seeing it raining in front of him, and not on him, was mindboggling. In his family, back in the early 1960's, an aunt had lived in Florida. A favorite story passed along from her was that she'd seen several times where it rained on one side of the street, and not another. No one had ever really believed her story back then. And to be perfectly honest, he had always assumed it was an old lady's daydream. Then he saw Rayne walking towards him, out of the field.His breath caught in his throat as he saw how beautiful she looked soaking wet. The rain obviously wasn't bothering her in the least. In fact, he could see that she was smiling. Something about her screamed erotic and sensual, but it seemed to be more than just the clinging dress to her body. These feelings were much deeper, more elemental than simple lust. She was part of the rain, even part of the nature that surrounded them.

Sean knew this woman was getting under his skin. When he wasn't with her he was thinking about her. The most alarming thing was the way he was thinking and planning in his future, including her in his plans and dreams. He was assuming she would be in his life, now, tomorrow and next year.

When he had decided to retire and settle down, marriage was not part of the picture. Women, plural, was what he had planned on, perhaps making up for the solitary life he'd led during his years working as an agent. Rayne was more than unexpected...she was a shock to his physical, emotional and psychological well-being. Yet every time he thought of her, he felt something inside him awaken and move through him. Perhaps he was imagining this as well, but when he was with Rayne it seemed as if his psychic power was enhanced, or purified in some way he couldn't explain. His mind, though, kept shying away from acknowledging what was happening.

"You're early. I didn't think you'd be here for another hour or so."

Rayne's words didn't make a lot of sense just then, so lost in his thoughts had he been until her voice disturbed him. "So much for resting your foot and you following the doctor's orders. Did you think you'd start watering without me? Good thing it started to rain, huh?"

* * * * *

Rayne wasn't sure if he was being sarcastic or not. Unfortunately, she'd stopped focusing once she saw his lights start up the gravel road. She could feel the rain lessening as she walked toward Sean, and it stopped when he crossed the lawn to meet her on the soft grass.

"Too bad it didn't last longer. I guess it was just a fluke."

"Let's go inside and get you dry. The ground looks damp enough to hold until morning. I'll water before I head back to my place." Sean moved before Rayne could react and swung her off her feet and into his arms.

"I can walk," she protested as he walked up the steps.

"And you'll walk even better tomorrow, once you've rested and elevated your foot." He walked to the bedroom, setting her on her feet. Without waiting for her to do anything other than take a deep breath, Sean was pulling her wet dress up and over her head. The wet dress hung over his arm as he walked to the bathroom. Less than a minute later he was back with a towel. "Start drying and hop on the bed. I'll get some more dressings and change that bandage now."

Arguing would be useless, so she sat on the bed, holding the towel in front of her. Pulling her hair forward, she started drying it with one end of the terry cloth. As Sean came back in, she spoke to him. "Maybe I should just take a pair of scissors and cut all this stuff off right now. It certainly would save time, not to mention water."

Sean sat down on the edge of the bed, lifted her foot and placed it on his thigh. He began unwrapping the old dressing, but didn't reply. Rayne watched as he tenderly took care of her foot. She was a little miffed that he had not immediately told her that her hair was too lovely to be cut or something like that. All her life people had made comments about her hair. There was also a niggling voice inside her head telling her she was being foolish and reminding her that she didn't play games like this, with people. She prided herself on being straight and honest.

"So, do you think I should cut it, Sean?" she prompted a moment later, watching as he finished applying the stretch netting to hold the dressing in place.

Sean looked up slowly. "I think you should do whatever you want. It is your hair."

Rayne had not expected him to say something so politically correct. It irritated her following her own silly word play. "You don't like long hair?"

Sean smiled at this point. He tossed the used dressing into the small trashcan, and then gathered the remaining things together. "I like long hair, and I think your long hair is beautiful." He turned and walked into the bathroom.

As he came back into the bedroom, Rayne's towel hit him in the chest. He grinned and picked the towel back up. "Should I ask why you threw the towel?" He set the towel on the bed, and then walked over to a chair in the corner of the small bedroom. Sitting down, after removing his suit jacket, he began unbuttoning his shirt. His skinny, western style tie already hung around his neck. When his shirt was hanging loose, he pulled his boots off before standing and dropping his dress pants. Soon he was naked and began walking back toward the bed.

Rayne frowned at Sean as he neared the bed. She wasn't immune to how sexy he looked naked. The fact that he was getting into her bed was still surprising to her. The whole sex and relationship thing, if that is what this was, was confusing to her. The movies she had seen, along with the old tapes of television shows, were all she knew of male and female relationships. Despite the confidence she felt in her powers, and her body strength, this part was unknown territory.

"I'm not sure why I threw it, but I'm sorry for being so childish. I thought all men preferred long hair."

Sean grinned as he climbed into the bed beside Rayne. "I think your hair is beautiful long, but I have no doubt that it is difficult to take care of. I am equally sure that you would look fantastic with shorter hair. I think this was one of those 'no-win' situations that women like to get men into."

His accuracy was grating, and technically they barely knew each other. His logic was perfect, which didn't help her frustration either. Just what she had thought she would accomplish with this nonsense, she had no idea. In all honesty, since she had met Sean, she wasn't altogether sure of anything. The feeling of drowning seemed to be a near-constant state for her when he was close to her. Yet when he was not around, her ability to focus on anything except him was definitely impaired. Her insecurities felt overwhelming suddenly, and she felt the need to lash out again.

"You know, since I didn't need help with watering, there really wasn't a need for you to…uhm…" Her voice trailed away as she ran out of temper. It was kind of funny in a way. The words had sounded a whole lot better in her head than they did spoken. If he was in her bed just for sex, did she really want to know it?

Sean interrupted her thoughts as he finished her sentence. "Sleep over?"

Rayne nodded her head slowly. She felt completely at sea with her emotions and thoughts rising and falling like angry waves in a storm. Her life was calm and peaceful. It was nice, quiet and nothing bothered her. Deliberately she kept her success at growing things at a low level, getting by and not drawing attention to herself or what she was doing here. Until Sean stepped into her life. If only he had not come over that evening—

If only she had not asked him to turn on the light. Maybe she should have waited until he was gone. Perhaps it was that he saw her when she was tired, and letting herself become elemental with the water that first time. Stopping her dreams of him might have been helpful too—

"Nickel for your thoughts."

Rayne turned and saw that Sean was now sitting upright beside her in the bed. Without consciously thinking, or planning it, she looked deeply into his eyes and for the first time really tried to read his thoughts. As a child, she had been very good at this psychic game. In fact, with practice, she had developed the ability to put suggestive thoughts into certain types of subjects' minds.

* * * * *

Sean could see that something was bothering Rayne tonight, and it went a lot deeper than the fact it had rained, or that he had left her alone for a meeting. Looking into her violet colored eyes, he knew instantly what she was going to do. On the one hand, he had hoped the Agency had been wrong about Rayne. The next instant he was angry that he had not been able to see her psychic powers until now. There was no disguising the look on her face as she stared into his eyes. She was delving into his mind.

In that split second, he made a decision. Only with time would he know if it was right or wrong, or the depth to which it would affect their lives. He made no effort to block her as she began weaving her way into his thoughts. As she began to delve more deeply, looking into his memories, he fought off the need to block her. It was instinctive to fight such probing, but perhaps she had to do this to trust him.

It was a risk, of course. What she would learn in the next few minutes could cause her to turn from him in anger and fear. There was an equal chance that she would see this gesture of his as a sign of his trustworthiness. By opening his mind to her, he was showing her she had no reason to fear him. He wanted her to see that even though his initial reasons for seeking her out had been nefarious, from now on his goals were to protect her. There were no doubts in his mind that she might betray the government and turn to the psychic renegades. Sean hoped she would believe his thoughts and deepest emotions by seeing them in their rawest form, and without any words to hide behind.

He was surprised by her reaction, which came less than a minute after she started. She moved so fast he didn't have time to grab her either. Like a flash of lightning, she hopped out of the bed and across the room. Sean stopped to pull on his jeans before following her.

* * * * *

Sean stopped on the front porch. Rayne was standing on the grass, looking out across her small planting. The moon was no longer full, but it still gave off enough light to reveal how beautiful she looked naked, her dark hair trailing down her back. Slowly he walked down the steps and crossed the lawn. He was a few feet away from her when she spoke.

"I never saw you coming, Sean."

"What are you talking about, honey? Why don't we go back inside? We can talk about anything you want. I'll answer any questions you have."

The short, staccato laugh Rayne answered him with didn't ease his worries in the least. He took a deep breath before he spoke to her again.

"I didn't hide anything from you. If you want to look again, I won't block you. I'm an open book for you to read."

"What if I say I'm bored and I don't want to read anymore?" Rayne questioned softly, glancing over her shoulder at him.

Sean didn't want to admit how much that possibility would hurt him. But he also didn't think she meant it. "I don't believe you. I think you want to know as much about me as I want to know about you."

Rayne shook her head negatively, and Sean watched the black silk sweep back and forth across her back. God! He thought without pause, she was the sexiest and most beautiful woman he'd ever known. And she seemed to be doing it without knowing or caring.

"Are you going to arrest me? Charge me with some kind of espionage or treason thing?"

"Of course not, Rayne. You aren't guilty of those things."

Rayne turned slowly to look at him. "What am I guilty of then? Why send a PSI agent after me? I have almost no contact with anyone. I live quietly and abide by the rules set up by the new government following the rebellion. Who am I to draw the attention of the Agency?"

"I am no longer with the Agency. I retired. I volunteered, sort of, to check you out." Sean knew the minute the words were spoken he should have kept his mouth shut, or picked different words.

"Have you 'checked me out' adequately for a full report to the Agency? Is there anything else about me you need to know? Have you been rifling through my drawers while I slept? Walking through my brain while I dreamed? Damn you!"

Rayne turned away from him once again and began walking toward her open field. "So, now what happens? Do you make a report on me and then I have to put up with someone checking on me all the time? Is this what happens for the rest of my life? Do you get some kind of special reward for having located certain psychics?"

Sean followed her to the edge of the lawn, where the grass gave way to her plants. "There is no reward, damn it! I haven't made any reports yet. The truth is that you blocked me so well I was beginning to think they were wrong. I still don't think you could be any relationship to Leyton, no matter what the informant had to say."

* * * * *

Rayne froze in her tracks. He had just spoken the name she had hoped and prayed to never hear in conjunction with her sisters or herself. Hearing Sean say the bastard's name made it sound much worse than when she had considered possible reactions and consequences. If he knew the truth, she knew he would undoubtedly turn from her in disgust. Who wouldn't? Her great-grandfather had been the cause for the hardship and destruction of so many lives. Why would anyone want to be around her?

"Oh my God!" she spun around, wincing from the pain. "What about my sisters?" She stopped abruptly as she sadly realized that she had no way to contact them, to warn them!

Sean grabbed her upper arms, stopping her movement. "It's too late, Rayne. I waited in making contact with you. Since I was already so close to you and my cover was in existence, I delayed enough to give the others time to investigate."

"Damn it, Sean!"

"No, Rayne! You don't want to do anything to draw more attention. I can make discreet inquiries in the morning. I'll contact the others and see what they've found out in the morning. I know you are innocent and have no intentions of any wrong-doings."

Rayne heard his words but she wasn't sure that she could believe him. And how could he speak for the Agency? He was retired, so why should they do what he recommended? They would most likely send someone else to check her out—

Her blood ran cold as she remembered her visitor from earlier. Something about the man had set off alarm bells. Falling had distracted her.

"Rayne, listen to me, sweetheart. I will convince the Agency that you are not a threat, and will not be one in the future. There is nothing to worry about. I promise you."

She voiced her doubts. "Why will they listen to you, Sean? What can you possibly say to convince them that I am 'harmless,' so to speak?"

Sean pulled her into his arms, hugging her so close she could feel his heart pounding through his chest. His warmth seeped into her body, heating her from the inside out, like a slowly glowing coil of fire. "Because I am going to marry you, Rayne! That is why they will believe me!"

Chapter Ten

The sun had been up for more than an hour before Rayne shoved the quilt off her stiff body. Sitting on the swing all night hadn't helped her feel better emotionally, or physically. Hearing Sean state he was going to marry her last night had obviously shocked him as much as it had her. She had seen his surprise the minute the words were spoken. Still he had not taken them back, despite the three opportunities Rayne gave him before he finally left last night.

Inside the house, she dressed in shorts, T-shirt and sneakers. Pausing only to grab an apple, she was back outside a few minutes later, beginning to fill buckets once again with water. If she hurried, she could be done before it got too hot. Then she could spend the rest of the day thinking and worrying. Maybe she could even take a nap!

"Good morning."

The voice startled her since she had been so wrapped up in her thoughts she had not heard anyone approaching. Looking up, she saw that it was indeed who she thought it was.

"Oh, uhm...hello Mr. uhm...I am sorry, but I've forgotten your name."

"Anton DeVeau, *mademoiselle*. You were rather stressed yesterday. I am glad to see that you have recovered completely?"

Rayne heard the questioning inflection at the end of his nice speech and nodded her head. "Ah, Mr. DeVeau, now I remember. Thank you. It wasn't too bad a cut after all. Everyone is fully recovered."

"Everyone?"

Rayne smiled, shrugging her shoulders. "The dogs, and others, have also recovered nicely. Sorry about the muck up and all. I never did hear why you had come to see me."

"Ahh, yes, I see. Your animals—a most interesting collection you have, Ms. Waters."

"Thank you, Mr. DeVeau. We're a family and we make the best of it." Rayne stood up and looked at the stylishly dressed man. His city polish certainly made her feel like the country bumpkin, but then she was happy being here so she didn't feel in the least bit intimidated by him. "I need to get busy, so what was it you wanted?"

"A straight forward woman! How refreshing!" Anton DeVeau took his pristine white handkerchief out, mopping his forehead. "I was hoping we could go inside and discuss this."

"Normally we could, but I need to get busy with watering. That is the thing about farming, neither plants, or animals, wait for us. I need to get this done before the sun gets much higher." Rayne picked up two of the buckets. "If you want, you can tag along with me, or wait on the porch. But if you follow me, pick up two of the buckets. No need to waste two good hands, is what my grandmother used to say."

Anton followed her down the lane, setting the buckets where she directed. Changing her usual plans, she started watering at the front today. She was halfway down the row when DeVeau drew her attention once again.

"I understood that your family was not farming stock, at all."

Rayne paused and her senses seemed to go into overdrive. Slowly, she began walking back toward the man. Letting her mind begin to work its psychic magic, she continued to water the plants but started to look inside DeVeau's thoughts. Reaching the end of the row, Rayne moved around him to start the next line. Idly, trying not to draw attention, she brushed her hand over his shoulder.

"Sorry, but you had a dragonfly on your shoulder."

Rayne's feet stumbled over one another as she realized this man was psychic. When she touched him, she got a direct link to his power. He was blocking her and trying to read her mind. The shock stiffened her back and she dropped the watering can. Why the hell were two men with apparently equal psychic powers showing up on her doorstep? More importantly, if Sean was a PSI agent, then what was Anton DeVeau?

Anton's hand grabbed her arm. "I think we should go inside right now, Rayne."

Rayne walked beside him, wondering if she could break his grip. With her foot injured she would be off balance, and that could make her blows less accurate. She might not get a second chance.

As they reached the porch steps, Anton pulled a small, but very effective laser gun from his inner jacket pocket. "Don't try anything fancy. I am a lot stronger than you, and I believe that in spite of your little show last night, you are not as powerful as the others believe you to be. Tyre Leyton may have been a level five psychic, but I doubt your great-grandmother was of equal power."

* * * * *

Inside the house, Anton pushed Rayne down onto the small sofa. He crossed to sit in the chair, which faced the sofa but had its back to the door. There was no fear in him about being interrupted. Before coming over here, he had stopped to make sure that Sean MacDougal and his men would be quite busy all day repairing the sudden leak in the main irrigation line, not to mention the broken fence which was allowing his prize cattle access to the main road. Smiling, he let his gaze travel over Rayne.

"I believe I made the right choice in choosing you over your sisters." He settled back into the chair, crossing one leg over the other, appearing the epitome of casual. His smile turned into a grin when he saw how tense Rayne became when he mentioned her sisters. "The others really wanted me to seek out Jezermiah, but somehow I knew you would be the most...malleable. Yes, malleable is the perfect word. The fact that you hand-water plants and take in strays told me everything I needed to know about you."

"What do you want? I don't have any money. I make just enough to feed the animals and myself. I don't own any jewelry worth anything."

"True. I've been through all of your accounts and those of your sisters. The council was convinced that either fire or wind would be the best choice. More powerful, more destructive, were how they put it. And on the one hand I can agree that the destructive force of either is astronomical. Still, I kept coming back to good old water."

Rayne shifted on the sofa. "I won't help the psychics regain power. I won't help overthrow the government. My…" She swallowed hard. "Tyre Leyton was a bad man. He was very evil, and I think he was even insane at the end. Even if he were still alive, I would not have had anything to do with him. And I don't want anything to do with the psychics who thought he was a great leader."

"I wondered how much you knew about your past. How long have you known about your true familial history and no longer believed in the fabrication created by your grandmother?"

"Don't call my grandmother a liar, damn it! Secondly, I am not going to do whatever it is you want me to do. You might as well leave because nothing you say will change my mind."

"Getting upset won't make any difference, Rayne. And you will do exactly what I want, or I will take one of your sisters in your place."

Anton watched the color drain from her face. Finally she believed that he was serious about this. This was going better than he had anticipated, and the side effects, or "perks" as he'd started to consider them, were much better than he would have thought possible. Rayne was a beautiful woman and having her share his bed was not going to be the hardship he had been expecting. Eventually, once he assumed his rightful position, he might even let her be his concubine, just as her great-grandmother had done for Tyre Leyton. Together, Rayne and he would bring forth a new generation of super-psychics, which no one would ever be able to overthrow again.

"What do you want from me? There really is nothing I could do that would be of any help to you. You might not see it at the moment, but I am rather useless."

Anton laughed softly as she spoke. He stood when she finished and began walking around the room. "For what I have in mind, no special talents are required. All you have to do is lay back and take it."

Her surprised gasp told him that she understood him this time. He turned from the pictures on the wall he had been looking at. "I believe you will be able to do the job. In fact, now that we've met, I'm actually looking forward to my task. You are more beautiful than I expected. Spending a few hours a day between your thighs won't be the onerous task I was dreading. This way the council won't have to listen to me complaining all the time."

"You didn't come all this way just to...sleep with a psychic." Rayne shifted uneasily on the sofa. "You aren't that unattractive that you must resort to forcing a woman to share your bed."

Anton turned sharply to look at her. Slowly the angry look faded. "Nice try, my dear. But making me angry won't change a thing. What I want isn't a bedmate. What I want from you are children."

"No!"

"Oh, yes, my dear. As many children as possible, in fact. Our children will rule the earth. Surely that is inspiration enough! You will be mother to a new world. A world of powerful psychics, with lesser psychics and humans serving us. Can you say honestly that such a powerful position doesn't excite you?"

* * * * *

Rayne realized that Anton DeVeau was insane. There could be no other explanation for such wild imaginings. Ever since she had discovered the truth of her family history, through her great-grandmother's diary, she had not wanted to think about where she had come from. Her life began with her grandmother, Maile, and her grandfather. Before that, nothing mattered. She had powers that she had been taught from her first breath to keep secret, and not reveal. Suddenly her life was unraveling and it appeared there truly was nothing she could do about it.

Breeding little psychics with this man was a nightmare of an idea. It was as crazy as this man was. And one that she could not allow either of her sisters to face. In that fact, this man was correct. When she looked at him, he no longer looked in the least bit attractive. Foremost in her mind was concern for her sisters, and Sean. It didn't seem at all fair that she was losing him. Not that she had ever really had him, but sitting on her sofa while the crazy man walked around, she realized that she loved Sean MacDougal. He'd gotten past her fences and around her walls. God! She wished he were here right now —

Abruptly she stopped that thought. She didn't want to take the chance that Anton might take a peek at her thoughts and be alerted. Her fear that he might harm Sean shocked her. It was hard to think at all, between her fear for Jezermiah, Carmella and now Sean. How could she protect them? Killing herself would only turn his attention toward her sisters, and she wasn't a quitter. She stopped thinking as she realized Anton was speaking again.

"We will take these photos with us, the ones of your grandmother as a child. And the one you have of Tyrea when she was younger. They will all prove archival when it comes time to record our royal history. Our children will appreciate knowing where they came from, of course."

Rayne felt her stomach cramp, hearing him talk so nonchalantly about the future and children. She'd never give birth to a child of his. But the truth was hard to face that she might not have a choice. He could force himself on her and impregnate her against her will. From the sound of the council, there already existed a network that would be working toward these goals. Finding help once they left here could very well be impossible.

When her stomach cramped again, Rayne stood. Anton turned immediately to look at her. "I'm hungry. I sometimes get low blood sugar. I'm going to make myself something to eat."

Anton nodded once. "Good idea. After that we will go to bed and get started on business. I'm looking forward to sampling your treasures. From what I've seen so far, you have a great body. I've always been a tit man, and you have some pretty fine boobs from what I've seen so far."

His coarse words were like a slap across her face. It reminded her of what she was up against, alone. Taking a deep breath, she forced herself to calm down. "Have a seat and I'll make us something to eat then."

"Don't bother trying to run, Rayne. I could easily catch you. My skimmer is close by."

"Don't worry. I believe what you've said, and I don't want my sisters to be hurt. I won't run, I promise. Just sit down and I'll get busy in the kitchen."

Anton nodded and moved over to the sofa. He sat down, putting the gun on the empty sofa seat beside him. Rayne turned and walked into the small kitchen. Quietly she began preparing a large meal. Pausing partway through the preparations, she went back into the living room, offering Anton a glass of sherry. She went to the pantry, and put the food just inside the door, leaving the door open a few inches.

In the living room, she found Anton lounging on her sofa, with the gun still beside him. "The food will be ready in about ten minutes. I need a shower to clean up first."

Anton nodded, his eyes watching as she walked down the short hallway. In the bathroom, Rayne quickly stripped her clothes off. Stepping into the shower, she slid the door closed.

Turning on the water, she began scrubbing her skin, wanting to remove Anton's presence, if that was even possible. Rinsing her hair, she then turned off the water. Opening her eyes, she shrieked as she saw that Anton was standing in the bathroom door, watching her. In horror, she wondered how long he'd been there. It made her feel sick inside to realize he had seen her like this. Worse though, she now saw that she had to open the fogged door to get her towel.

He was smirking as she slid the door open, reaching for the towel. He was holding it so she had to open it all the way. Shame filled her as he saw her naked body, and she had no way to hide.

"A shaved pussy! Now that is something I was not anticipating, Rayne. You are just full of surprises, eh?" He chuckled as she jerked the towel away from him, wrapping it around her body. "There I was admiring your big boobies bouncing and jiggling while you are washing your hair, and all the while the best treat was still to come."

Rayne pushed past him, but not fast enough, because he still managed to briefly cup her ass. Hurriedly she ran into her bedroom, and heard him enter the room a few seconds later. If this plan didn't work…quickly she stopped her thoughts, not wanting to betray herself too early.

"Put on something sexy," Anton told her a moment later. "I'd like to see you wearing something hot while we eat. Not that I need to work up my desire. I'm already hard and horny for you. I can't wait to plant my meat in your shaved cunt. A few rounds of hide the sausage, as my naughty German uncle used to say, and you'll be nicely fucked, and much more malleable."

Rayne shuddered at his coarse words. Perhaps the sherry had done its work better than she might have hoped. "I don't have anything sexy."

"Sure you do, all women have sexy clothes." He walked over to her closet. A few seconds later, he pulled out a white, wrinkled, cotton waist-length top and short skirt. She hadn't worn it since moving here, and it was too tight. "Wear this, and

197

skip the bra and panties. I'm going back out for another glass of sherry. Come out when you are dressed." He walked to the bedroom door and then turned to look over his shoulder. "Put your hair up as well."

Rayne pulled the small top on, which strained across her chest, and ended only two inches below the full underside of her breasts. The skirt fit a little better, but it was still too tight. Putting her wet hair into a topknot pulled the shirt up, and she had to tug it back down before going back out.

"I'll bring the food out here," she told Anton on her way to the kitchen.

Chapter Eleven

"God damn it all! What the hell is going on here, Bob? I can't believe this shit! We just get the irrigation pipes fixed and now someone calls and says my prize bull is heading toward town! This is unreal. I think this goes beyond normal happenstance and things going wrong."

"It does seem strange, Sean. But Colleen took the call. They said there was a hole in the fence." Bob paused, taking out his handkerchief and wiping off his forehead. "Even Colleen said she thought it seemed too weird. She tried the main phone lines, which connect the barns and outlying buildings. When the phone didn't work, she walked outside and found the lines had been cut—and in two places. I could see wear and tear, but not twice on the same phone line."

Sean rubbed the bridge of his nose. He could feel a headache coming on and didn't think it was going to get much better anytime soon. Last night had been pretty much a sleepless one, and his thoughts kept returning to Rayne. There was no doubt that he'd not handled the whole situation very well. Blurting out he was going to marry her had to rank near the top of the ten most stupid things to say to a woman you'd met just a couple of days earlier. The truth was that nothing about their time together could be called normal.

All morning he'd felt the need to see Rayne, and talk things over with her. First he would apologize, and then he would tell her that everything was going to be fine. Last night he'd put a call through to Shannon Riedel, the Agency Director. After giving a verbal report on Rayne, he asked for her to run a check on the man at her place yesterday. He was relieved to hear that her sisters were both fine.

"I'm confused, Bob. If the phone line is dead, how did Colleen hear about the fence?"

"The call came in over the radio. Then she called me on my cell phone. I was planning on taking Bill with me to catch the bull, and I've already got Jack and Johnnie working on the fence."

Sean nodded, wondering if it was safe to take off for Rayne's now or not.

"We'll be fine if you want to work in the office, or maybe go check on something, or someone else."

Sean turned slowly from his perusal of his land to look at his brother-in-law. He smiled ruefully as he saw Bob's grin. "I'll take my cellular phone. Call me if you need any help. I think I'll grab a quick shower and then drive over."

Bob started the engine of his truck as Bill climbed in beside him. "That sounds like a good idea. You might want to snitch a few flowers from Colleen's garden as well."

"Get out of here!" Sean told his brother-in-law with a grin.

* * * * *

Twenty minutes later he was halfway down the gravel lane to Rayne's when he saw the skimmer pulled to the side. A sick feeling came over him and he gunned the engine, speeding the last one hundred yards to the house. The truck skidded as he slammed on the brakes. He saw Rayne sitting on the grass, surrounded by her menagerie. Since she was facing her field, he couldn't see her face. As he came closer, she still didn't turn around to look at him.

"Rayne? Are you all right, sweetheart?"

The dogs had come to alert positions, moving behind her, facing him. They weren't growling, but he could tell that all of them were on edge. "Rayne?"

The dogs moved, preventing him from coming any closer than six feet. There was another animal, but he couldn't tell what it was from this position. "Honey, please call the dogs off. I need to talk to you."

"Sit!" Rayne commanded the dogs.

Sean came quickly around the side but stopped abruptly as he saw the huge animal with its head on her lap. He'd never seen one of them outside a zoo but he was sure he was looking at a white tiger. Most disturbing was the blood on Rayne's white top and skirt, and it was also on her arms and the animal's coat. Within a second he was down on one knee beside her.

"Rayne? Are you hurt? Where did all this blood come from?"

She didn't look at him as she answered, which only served to heighten his fear.

"I'm sorry, Sean. I was going to contact the sheriff soon. I had to do it. I didn't have any other options. I had to protect my sisters, the world."

Sean knew something awful must have happened. Why in the world would Rayne be thinking about the world, or how anything she might do actually have a worldwide effect? "Your sisters? Are they here? Has something happened to them?"

"No, Sean. He chose me because he knew I would give in to his demands. But I wasn't going to let him touch me. I couldn't bear the thought of him..." Her voice broke and she sobbed soundlessly.

Sean knew she'd feel better if she broke down and started to cry. This tenseness and self-control didn't seem at all natural, or healthy, following a crisis. His second thought was what the hell the crisis was? And foremost, what "him" was she talking about? Could that Anton guy have come back? There hadn't been information on him yet when he'd last checked in at the Agency.

"Rayne, honey, I need you to focus and tell me what is wrong. What happened? I passed DeVeau's skimmer on the gravel road. Is he here? Where is he now?"

Rayne took a deep breath, but it seemed to rattle in her chest as she exhaled. "He's on the sofa...or I guess, part of him is still on the sofa."

"Shit!"

Sean took off running for the house. He vaulted up the front steps and almost pulled the screen door off its hinges. Whatever he'd thought he might find, it couldn't have prepared him for what he did find. There was a lot of blood, and Anton DeVeau, or rather part of him, was on the sofa. One glance told him the man was dead so his first call on his cell phone was to the Agency.

"Agent 0010," he told the operator. "Special Red Alert call to security. Code three-three-alpha-two." He waited while his call was immediately patched through to Shannon. "I need an emergency clean up out here, Shannon."

"What happened, Sean? I had just received the information you had requested and was going to have my assistant fax it to your home. DeVeau is the grandson of Marcel DeVeau. He was an overlord closely tied to Tyre Leyton. Our Paris branch has been tracking increased psychic activity throughout Europe and the African continent. Anton was sighted in Paris, following his grandmother's death. He obtained a number of items from a lock box at her bank. Unfortunately, he seemed to have gone back underground shortly after that. Rumor has associated him several times with the Psychic Continental Council, but nothing definite could be found."

"Well, you don't have to worry about him anymore, Shannon. The Paris branch can mark him off their watch list."

"Damn! You mean he has shown up there? Does this mean the sisters are aligned with the council? You know what that would mean."

Sean didn't need to be reminded of what the directive from the Agency had been. If proof had been discovered showing the subject was indeed linked to the council, he had been sanctioned to eliminate the threat. After meeting Rayne, the thought of losing her had nagged at him for a short time. All doubts were dispersed after she'd come to his home for dinner. And the more time he'd spent with her, the more he knew there was no way that Rayne would ever associate herself with the psychics who had formed the council.

"There is no connection whatsoever, Shannon. I am a hundred percent certain of it. You know me, and I've hunted and investigated a lot of psychics for the Agency. Rayne would be happy as a hermit, living with her menagerie of weird animals."

Sean was immediately aware of the heavy pause before Shannon answered him.

"Rayne, is it?"

Sean was sure she was smiling, despite her words. "Yeah, it's Rayne. I plan on marrying her, Shannon. You always told me some woman would knock me on my ass one day. I've met her."

"Ha! Now this woman I look forward to meeting. I'll let all the women on my staff know you have lost your bachelor status. I'd better send out for more Kleenex."

"Yeah, right. Anyway, I really need a clean up out here fast. I'm going to take Rayne to my place, and then I'll be back here to wait for the crew to arrive. It is a level three job, by the way."

"All right, Sean. I'll await your report and send the crew. Don't forget to send me my wedding invitation!"

"I'll send the report tomorrow, through the encoded channel. And if you can't make the wedding, I'll expect one hell of a big gift."

"You bet, you dog! Thanks for taking this last job, Sean. I owe you one."

"Clean this up for me, Shannon, and we are square. I'll be in touch."

* * * * *

It was nearly three in the morning the next day before Sean finally got back home. His first stop was his bedroom for a shower. It was more than twelve hours since he had carefully encouraged Rayne to help him pen up the "tiger-cat." He tied up the dogs, giving them plenty of food and water. The only pet that went with them to his place was Homer.

Colleen had immediately taken charge of Rayne, taking her away within a few minutes of their arrival. Sean put Homer in his gilded cage on the front porch. He gave him some food and fresh water before going to find Bob and let him know that he must go back to Rayne's and wasn't sure what time he'd return. The crew had arrived within thirty minutes of his return. It never failed to amaze him how quickly they could get somewhere.

He had pretty much stayed out of their way, other than directions on making sure certain things would have to be cleaned to a near-normal state. Sean had been determined to make this the least traumatic to Rayne as possible. About two hours after the crew had arrived two other men had arrived with a large truck. Once he had signed some forms, the two men had departed to transport DeVeau's skimmer. Already there was a crew working on his hotel room and erasing his presence there.

Twice while the cleaners worked, he had gone out and watered Rayne's field. Using his computerized communication device, he had connected with the wireless remote to the Agency's database. He had searched and finally discovered what Rayne's secret plant was that she kept hidden at the rear of the field. They would definitely have to discuss the safety of growing this little flower, he decided with a wry smile.

Remembering how he had described Rayne to Shannon, he wondered how they would make a life together. With a deep sigh, he acknowledged that if she preferred to live at her house, then that is what they would do. That would eliminate the need for Bob and Colleen to build the small house they had planned to start a few months after the baby came. His sister and brother-in-law could stay in his huge, nearly perfect house and he would stay with Rayne.

Of course, there were a lot of improvements he could make at Rayne's place. And if he made them slowly, he was pretty sure he could talk her into accepting them. First, would be irrigation installation. Next, he'd see about making sure the house was sound. It probably needed a new roof. The shed she used needed a lot of work, and the truck he had seen looked like it came from the previous millennia rather than the past decade or so.

The whole time he spent watering Rayne's plants, his thoughts roamed freely over just about everything except DeVeau and the way the man had been mauled to death. He doubted the big cat was normally like that, but he'd have to talk to Rayne first before its future could be determined. She might raise a stink about it, but if the animal was turning predatory then neither she nor her other pets would be safe around it.

Walking from the shower into his bedroom now, he consciously told himself to stop thinking about the past, or what he'd seen today. Focus on just now, he told himself silently while he idly dried his hair with the towel. He stopped in front of his dresser to comb his hair before applying some after-shave lotion. His thoughts on Rayne, he considered going to the guest room tonight, or just calling it a night and going to sleep.

* * * * *

Rayne watched Sean as he combed his hair in front of the dresser mirror. She was quite sure that he had not yet realized that she had snuck into his room and climbed into his bed while he was still in the shower. Admiring his muscular back and tight, hard buns, she knew she was in love with him. It really had nothing to do with his attractive body. The scales had tipped when he had taken charge today.

She had no doubt there would be lots of questions to answer, and his anger to deal with when he learned of Anton's plans. But it had been rather nice to be taken care of today. The shock of killing a man had pretty much worn off by early evening. She was by no means a callous person, but it had been a matter of survival. If she had left her home with Anton, the opportunity to thwart his crazy plans might never have come again. Today, they had been alone in her house.

She had carried the food on a tray to the living room, and Anton had eaten lustily. He had complimented her cooking abilities.

"I am surprised to find that you can cook."

"My grandmother taught me when I was quite young. Living alone gives one lots of opportunities to improve."

Anton had smiled at her. "Well, you won't have any of these daily drudgeries once we get to Paris. My family is quite wealthy and we will have servants to take care of these things." He had dabbed at his mouth before continuing. "In fact, all you will have to do is breed and breastfeed. I should imagine one child every two years would be best. I'll admit, my dear, I am quite looking forward to breeding you. Of course, you lack culture and education, but these faults can be corrected. The thought of plowing your belly was rather depressing, until I saw you. I'll enjoy fucking you several times a day until you are pregnant."

Rayne had shivered in disgust at his coarse words. His confidence had cemented her decision. If she didn't want to end up living her life on this man's terms, the time for action was now. Standing when they were finished, she had told him to stay seated.

"I'll just set these in the sink. I have some nice liqueur for after dinner, if you would like."

"That sounds good. I doubt it will be as good as I am used to, but it will probably help relax you."

Rayne had nodded and taken the tray into the kitchen. Turning on the water of the sink, she had let it drown out the soft clicking noise she made with her tongue. The pantry door then opened and Mohan had walked toward her silently. Holding the tiger's gaze, she had paused to pray for forgiveness. Softly, her words distinct as she had practiced, she directed the wild animal that lurked below the surface of the domesticated cat.

"Mohan, intruder," she lifted her hand to point, and then gave the command. "Kill, Mohan!"

She had run out the back door, unable to listen to the sounds. Exhausted and stunned, she had collapsed onto the lawn, covering her ears with her hands. How long before the dogs came, followed by a blood-covered Mohan, she had no idea. Cradling the big cat's head on her lap, she had spoken softly, trying to soothe its frazzled nervous nature. Her guilt was massive. There was every chance Mohan might have to be put down after this. Once she'd gotten the taste of the kill, it might be impossible to keep her as a pet.

At one point, she had lowered her head to rest on the cat's bloody coat. Had she done the right thing by risking her beloved pet's life to save her own? She had murdered a man in cold blood, even if it had not been by her own hand. She would have to decide whether she was going to call the sheriff or take a chance and bury Anton's body. And she would have to get rid of his skimmer as well. Even though she had not seen it, she was sure it was parked only a short distance away. Also he might have rented a room in town. What if someone there raised an alarm and started inquiries? Or perhaps the council Anton had mentioned would send someone to find him.

When Sean had shown up, she hadn't known whether to be relieved or fearful. But then he had taken over and relieved her of any decisions. He had brought a change of clothing out, and then together they had gone around to the outdoor shower. As directed, she had gotten under the spray with her clothes on, and then removed them. Mohan had wandered back with them and even stood under the spray without any kind of fuss.

Colleen had made a fuss over her, but not asked any questions. She had taken a few aspirins along with a glass of milk. The sound of the door shutting on Sean's truck had awakened her. Quietly she had walked the short distance to the room Colleen had discreetly pointed out when she gave her a brief tour. Inside the room, she had heard the shower running and sat on Sean's bed to wait for him.

* * * * *

"I'll answer your questions now, if you want."

"What the fuck!" Sean spun around in surprise. He had no idea that he wasn't alone in the room. Ever since he had met Rayne he'd had reason to doubt his own psychic abilities. Shaking his head slowly, he walked over to the bed. "I don't have any paper with me at the moment, Rayne."

She smiled and shifted up onto her knees on the bed. "We could go down to your office if you'd prefer."

"The only thing I prefer right now is my pillow and sleep." He stopped as he saw that Rayne was wearing the top to the silk pajamas his mother had given him last Christmas. "I think you forgot the bottom half of that outfit." He sat down on the far side of the bed.

Rayne shook her head. "I didn't forget. Colleen only gave me the top. I think your sister has matchmaking on her mind."

Sean considered the lighthearted tone in her voice for a moment, and then he stood back up. He tugged the comforter and sheet down on his side of the bed. "Maybe." He pulled on the blankets until Rayne got up so he could pull her side of the bed down as well. Without another word, he got into bed and pulled up the covers. He put his hands behind his head as he leaned back on the pillows.

Rayne stood and watched him for a few seconds before she spoke. "You object?"

"Nope. I am rather in favor of the idea myself. How do you feel about it?"

Rayne slipped under the covers, turning on her side to look at him. "I'm not opposed, but I don't want you to think that what happened today influenced me."

Sean rolled over onto his side to face Rayne. The room was only very dimly lit by the faintest of lights coming from the bathroom. "You may think it is too early, but I love you, Rayne. What happened last night and today didn't change my feelings."

"It is too soon for us to be sure, but I think I feel the same way."

"Just think?"

"I'm pretty sure, Sean. Today's events have changed things, or they will. I could end up in jail."

Sean shook his head negatively. "No, you aren't going to jail. We will have to be careful about your kitty cat, though." He paused to shake his finger at her.

Rayne nodded and leaned forward to grab hold of his finger. She pulled it toward her, closing her mouth around it. Sucking on it for a moment or too, she then smiled. "I feel very guilty about it all. I didn't do this without provocation. Mohan never would have attacked without my giving the signal."

"I wasn't planning on going over all of this until morning, but I am curious about one thing. I didn't know you had a tiger living with you, by the way." He paused to give her his mildest glare. "How did you end up with a tiger named Mohan?"

"It's a long story."

"Go on, honey. There is no place else on Earth I'd rather be."

"White tigers are very rare any more. Very few in the zoos and captivity survived the war, and on average in the wild, only one in ten thousand are born white. No white tigers in the wild were found after the 1950's in fact, and the wild species, which is really just a sub-species of the Bengal tiger, only survived in captivity due to inbreeding and crossbreeding programs."

"They are albinos then?"

Rayne shook her head. "Not at all. The white tigers, which survived until present times, are the result of the breeding programs using inbred and crossbred mixes of the Bengal and the Siberian tiger. An albino would have pink eyes, and there had been only one recorded instance of true albino tigers, Sean. In Cooch Behar, which we know as West Bengal, in India, two albino cubs were shot in 1922."

Rayne paused to shift slightly on the bed. "The white tiger has pale blue eyes, a mottled grayish-pink nose and is white with the dark stripes that can vary from black to a chocolate brown color. White tigers are born only to parents who both carry the recessive gene for the white coloring."

"What about the Siberian tigers I remember hearing about in history?"

"Actually, Sean, no wild white tigers have ever been reported in either the former region of Siberia, or anywhere else in the world, except the one found in Rewa. The Siberian White Tiger that existed in zoos were all cross-bred production."

Sean reached his hand out and captured a lock of Rayne's hair. Slowly he wound it around his finger. "You are a fount of information, my love, but how did you end up with something that is obviously on the endangered species list and should be in one of the few remaining zoos?"

"At the beginning of the twenty-first century, the tiger Species Survival Program reinforced its stand against the breeding of the white tiger in captivity. The white tiger is a freak of nature, and obviously cannot survive in the wild. But the popularity of the animal made it a money-maker for zoos, which was the same for the propagation of black leopards, white lions and king cheetahs. They are all phenotypic aberrations and bred solely because they are 'crowd pleasers.' Sorry, I know I keep rambling."

"It is understandable. Go on, honey."

"There was a government research compound near here. After the war, funding was cut. I'm sure you get the idea. My Mohan was the result of some kind of weird breeding program and was waiting for—"

"And you being the soft-hearted woman you are just couldn't let that happen, huh?"

"She only weighed twenty pounds when I first got her," Rayne replied quickly, defending herself.

Sean lightly tapped Rayne's forehead. "Rescuer of animals, grower of strange plants and what else should I know about you?"

"You know more about me than I know about you. I know your sister…"

"And Bob, as well," Sean added with a smile. "I come from a big family so it's better that you don't meet them all at once."

"Hmm. So, what happens now? Tomorrow do we go on as if nothing happened? What if someone starts asking questions about him?"

Sean kissed Rayne to stop her from asking more. "Shh." Slowly he made love to her lips, easing them apart before he finally caressed her tongue with his. "You taste so sweet."

"Toothpaste," Rayne told him quietly.

Laughing out loud, he shook his head. In that moment, he knew. Rayne was the woman he undeniably wanted to spend the rest of his life with; psychic headaches and all that would probably come their way. Sean guessed he should wait, but he couldn't. "I love you. Please marry me, Rayne."

"What if I go to prison? I don't think you would be happy with a monthly conjugal visit."

Sean shook his head. "You aren't going to any kind of jail. I called the Agency and everything has been taken care of. Your place looks like it did the day I met you."

"What if someone comes looking for him?"

Sean pressed his finger to her lips. "It's all over. I'll need some details, but that can wait until tomorrow. You don't have to marry me as part of the plan."

"You told your boss you were going to marry me though, didn't you? It's part of my 'parole' and marriage is how I will be observed in the future. Since I'm a psychic, right?"

"If you are repulsed by the idea, I'm sure we can work something out."

Rayne stared into his eyes for a long time, and he started to wonder if she was going to turn him down. Then he jerked in surprise as her hand grasped his cock. As her soft hand began massaging and pulling on his hardness, he groaned softly. Dimly he was aware of her scooting toward him, but her hand didn't pause or slow down.

"I probably will have some issues I'll have to work out once my state of shock goes away, Sean. But right now," she gave a firm, unmistakable yank on his shaft. "Put this to good use, and we'll worry about tomorrow later."

"My pleasure, my love," he told her with a smile, rolling her onto her back. "I got the watering done before I came back here, so we can sleep in."

"Uhnh," Rayne groaned as Sean thrust into her body. "Thank you, my love, but I could have made it rain."

"What the…?"

Sean paused in between strokes of his cock in and out of Rayne's wet pussy. Make it rain? Had she really said she would make it rain?

Rayne's hands pulled his head toward her, meeting his gaze. "Yeah, that's what the lady said, mister. Now, do your husbandly duty and we'll talk about rain and waves and tiger tails later." She kissed his lips hard, punctuating her meaning.

As Sean got back to the business at hand, he heard a squawk from a far corner of his room.

"Do your duty! Do your duty! Do your duty!"

Life certainly would never be dull with Rayne in his life!

About the author:

Mlyn is a 47-year-old woman living in Indiana, USA. She worked as a Registered Nurse for 23 years in Pediatrics. Reading Barbara Cartland and Harlequin romance novels in high school spurred her to start writing. She did technical writing for her employers until she started writing erotica four years ago. She began her own website for people to view her stories. Mlyn is single and lives with her cranky cat Georgia, who she named after her favorite artist for inspiration, Georgia O'Keeffe.

Mlyn Hurn welcomes mail from readers. You can write to her c/o Ellora's Cave Publishing at P.O. Box 787, Hudson, Ohio 44236-0787.

Also by Mlyn Hurn:

Blood Dreams
Burning Desires
Family and Promises
Family Secrets
His Dance Lessons
Medieval Mischief
Rebel Slave
Submissive Passion
Things That Go Bump In The Night 3

Fyrebrand

Lora Leigh

Dedication

To the wonderful ladies and family at EDBM. Pat, Barb, Tigg, Beth, Momma Sue, Stacey, Punque and Lue Anne. You encouraged me, supported me, and nagged endlessly. You were friends when times were good and you held me up when times were bad. You always took time to explain what I didn't understand, and to read what you didn't always like. And through it all, you taught me to accept the stories that were a part of me. Thank you.

Chapter One

He touched her gently. Too gently. Carmella strained beneath Torren's tender strokes, forcing back the aggression rising inside her as her desire rose. His long, dark brown hair caressed her arms, creating a curtain of rough silk around his head while his tongue laved her hard nipple and his mouth suckled the eager point gently.

His hands, work-calloused and large, moved over her body with sensual knowledge, but with restraint. He was holding back, just as he always did. Her head tossed on the pillow as she bit her lip to keep from crying out in frustration.

"Adrenaline overload," he whispered against her breast, moving lower, his lips like a stroking flame over her skin. "Relax, Carmella."

His voice was thick and husky with lust as he nipped at the flesh of her abdomen, traveling closer to the center of the heat spreading through her body. But there was something more. A vein of knowledge she couldn't quite grasp...almost amusement. As though he knew the needs tormenting her and refused to ease them.

Her fingers clenched in the blankets of the bed beneath her as she fought for control. She could handle it, she assured herself, she always had before.

"Carmella." She opened her eyes, staring down at him as he paused over the pulsing mound of her cunt.

God, he was so rugged, so handsome. The angles of his face were an artist's dream. High cheekbones, the sharp slash of his nose, the stubborn chin. The male sensuality in the curve of his lips combined with the sun-darkened tone of his flesh gave him a brooding, intense look.

"Are you going to fuck me or talk to me all night?" She restrained the urge to bite him. Why did she always want to bite, to claw? The desperate throb of an almost violent lust surged through her veins.

Torren's lips quirked into a small smile. Too knowing. What knowledge did he possess that she didn't? And why couldn't she sift through the myriad psychic impulses to make sense of it?

"Eventually, I'll fuck you." His hand slid up her thigh, parting her legs further as the long strands of hair caressed her flesh.

Carmella shivered. She loved the feel of the silken strands on her skin.

"What do you mean, eventually?" She panted as she tried to tamp down the heated urges flowing through her.

She wanted to fight. Wanted to force him to restrain her, to plow inside her with every hard, throbbing inch of his thick cock. She trembled at the thought, allowing the image to flow through her mind as she whimpered in growing hunger.

"Damn, you're hot enough to burn me alive." His fingers skimmed the saturated curls between her thighs.

Her vagina pulsed, spilling the thick juices of her need from its gripping tunnel.

"Torren, stop teasing me." She wanted to scream, to demand that he give her the agonizing pleasure/pain her body was craving.

God, what was wrong with her? She needed him, loved him as she had never loved anyone. Torren fulfilled her. Soothed her. But nothing seemed to touch that dark core of lust growing steadily in her body.

Torren moved between her thighs, his eyes narrowed as he watched her. Hard, muscular legs spread hers; the broad head of his cock kissed the swollen lips of her pussy. Carmella shuddered, her hands fisting in the blankets as flames nearly erupted over her body. No. No. She couldn't let that happen.

She bit her lip, feeling the wide head of Torren's erection part the wet curves of her cunt. Her body was taut. She fought the flames and the agonizing pleasure as he began to stretch the delicate tissue of her vagina.

"Torren." Her strangled gasp was a plea. God, she couldn't be begging for something she knew she could never control. And she would never be able to stop her response to what she needed so desperately.

"It's okay, love." He sheltered her, coming over her as his hips worked his cock deeper insider her in smooth, shallow thrusts. "Hold onto me, Carmella," he whispered at her ear. "It's okay."

But it wasn't okay. The scream trapped in her throat was one of frustration and fury. The heat building through her body was too dangerous to ever relinquish control of.

"Hold onto me," he whispered again a second before his cock surged inside her, hard and deep.

She couldn't stop the keening cry that escaped. Couldn't halt the desperate spasm of her vagina around the thick, hot shaft impaling her. It was so good. Not what she needed, but so damned good.

His hair flowed around them, smelling of man and cleaning soap, damp and cool against her hot skin as he began to fuck her with a steady driving rhythm. Carmella arched her neck, her fingers tightening around the blankets gripped between them as dark lust surged through her body. Oh God. Her skin was heating, her blood flaming. Torren's cock stroked, caressed, tormenting sensitive, aching, nerve endings to a point of pleasure she could barely stand. She had to come soon. She had to.

"Now," she begged desperately as she fought the erupting power threatening to release. "Please, Torren. Please, now."

He slammed home. His arms tightened beneath her shoulders, his knees digging into the mattress as he began to fuck her hard and fast, pushing her close to the edge, so close...

Carmella couldn't contain her cry as the orgasm, lighter than she would have preferred, swept through her body, tightening it with pleasure. The desperate edge of hunger dulled as she heard Torren growl out his own release, the hot pulse of his semen emptying into her vagina as he tightened in her arms.

Breathing rough, her skin still prickling as heat raced beneath it, she tried to relax in his arms. She didn't want him to know how close to the edge she was coming. Couldn't face his realization of the perversions that tormented her.

"Okay now?" His lips caressed her cheek. A loving, gentle touch that brought tears to her eyes.

"Fine," she lied. She hated lying to him. Hated the needs that tormented her.

Torren moved to her side lazily, pulling her into his arms as he cuddled her close.

"Sleep, baby," he whispered. "Tomorrow's another day."

The reflective tone of his voice bothered her, but the fight to hold back the violence rising inside her took all her concentration now. She nodded against his chest, but she knew sleep would be a long time coming.

* * * * *

We can't wait much longer. Torren sent his thought to the man who waited miles from their location, pacing his rooms furiously.

Dammit, Torren. I'm moving as fast as I can. He could hear Ryder's lust pulsing in his voice. The connection he allowed the other man as he made love to Carmella had been strong. Ryder had sensed in every pore of his body the nearly uncontrolled needs sweeping through her.

Move faster, Torren suggested darkly. She nearly lost control tonight, Ryder. We can't afford to allow her to do that until you are with her.

A bleak pause followed his words.

Head to the beach house tomorrow. I'll have the Hummer waiting outside the east end of New Cincinnati. I'll cover her from here.

It was a risky plan. Torren stared down at Carmella, knowing she didn't sleep as she pretended to. Her muscles were taut, small goose bumps raised along her flesh as she fought the power coursing through her. He had to save her. He had to protect her. He kissed her head softly, enjoying the feel of her silken, fiery-colored hair against his lips.

She was a Fyrebrand. But even more than that, she was a blood link to the greatest psychic monster ever created. Her power was deep, strong. The psychic ability to spark and generate fire from thin air; to destroy, if need be, with flames hotter than any man could create, pulsed within her small body. And she was slowly losing control.

I love her, Ryder. But he knew and accepted that she would never be his alone. There was no jealousy, no anger in that thought. He had known for years that she belonged not just to him, but to Ryder as well.

I'll take care of her, Torren. The unspoken emotion lingered in Ryder's thought, as did the surge of dark, intense lust. He would complete the circle Carmella needed. He would complete them all.

Torren tightened his grip on her, holding her close, regretting the coming separation, but looking forward to the reunion. Carmella wasn't the only one restraining her lust, her darker desires. Torren was as well.

A smile crossed his lips. One he was glad Carmella couldn't see. Anticipation rolled through his body, thickening his cock, heating his blood. His hands smoothed over her back.

"You aren't asleep," he growled at her ear as he lifted her thigh over his, pushing his erection against the wet curves of her cunt.

Heat awaited him. A gripping, milking pleasure he needed one last time before he left her to Ryder's care. He rolled to his back, pulling her with him as she gasped in pleasure.

She impaled herself on the thick shaft, her back arching as she cried out at the pleasure he brought her. She surrounded him with fire, a lava-hot intensity he was more than willing to lose himself in.

"Ride me, Carmella." He gripped her hips as her small hands braced on his chest and she began to rise and fall along the hard length of flesh spearing into her. He gritted his teeth, his hips meeting her downward glide as he fought to take her easy, gently.

She cried out above him, her hips moving faster, harder, her pussy gripping him like a silken, slick fist. Torren gritted his teeth. His cock throbbed, ached to spew its hot release into the tight depths of her vagina.

His hands tightened on her hips, pushing her to ride him, to stroke the tight clasp of her pussy over his cock repeatedly. She was crying above him, her nails biting at the flesh of his chest, stroking his lust higher.

"Fuck me," he ordered her, his voice tight, nearly desperate. "All of me, Carmella."

He arched his hips, driving every hard inch inside her as she began to shudder convulsively, her cunt rippling along his shaft as her orgasm tightened her body. He thrust inside her again, hard, heavy, and then once more before he erupted inside her, groaning in pleasure, holding back the regret. It was much less than he wanted, but he knew soon—very soon—it would be everything the three of them needed.

Chapter Two
Two Weeks Later

Carmella was wearing black. Ryder could only shake his head at this as he followed her in his astral form, staying between her and her pursuers, throwing the hounds off every chance he got and generally protecting the finely curved ass as it raced through the underbrush in the hills above New Cincinnati, Ohio.

She was dressed in the color of night from head to toe, form fitting, and snug. It was the color of mystery, of secrets. It was his color—and hers as well, it appeared. Her clothes hid nothing from his eager, astral gaze, though, and made his cock throb hard and demandingly in his physical body still sheltered in the inn back along the edges of town.

He kept up with her easily, drawing on Torren's added powers, as his astral form traveled farther away from his physical body than he was entirely comfortable with.

He sent her pursuers up and around the mountain with the false form of a young woman fleeing. As they moved, Carmella was forced to change her direction, opting instead for a path that led down the mountain to the safety of the inn she had been staying at in town.

She had gotten careless in her search for her commander and lover, Torren Graves, whom she believed had been captured by PSI, the Psychic Sensory Investigations unit of the new government, the week before. Her ties to Torren were strong, but her focus was faltering severely. If it weren't, she would have already been well aware of the fact that he wasn't in the prison she was watching so hard. She would have caught on instantly to the plan they had set in motion more than a month before. And the damned group of vigilantes would have never managed to surprise her as they had.

The coordination it had taken to draw everything together that night would terrify the director of the PSI if she ever realized he had managed to do it. There were things he kept from everyone, the true scope of his abilities being one of them.

The world wasn't ready to acknowledge that such powerful psychics were once again in the government.

He followed the woman, catching a glimpse of her expression as she glanced back at the lights that scoured the mountainside, a frown on her heart-shaped face as she realized the hounds had somehow lost her scent when they shouldn't have and were moving up the mountain, rather than on her heels.

He stilled his grin. She knew it wasn't logical. Carmella would never trust what wasn't logical. He had a hell of a fight ahead of him because his attraction for her, the rioting hunger that rose inside him, would never make sense to her.

He watched as those long, exquisite legs jumped a low boulder, her body hovering in the air for a long second before she hit the ground running again. Amazing. She twisted around the hulking forms of shadowed trees, avoiding more than one trap set to catch the unwary. She couldn't see them on the cloudless night, and he couldn't sense a flow of psychic power, though he knew he should have.

The power it would have taken to send out the "feelers" to detect the upcoming obstacles should have been near impossible for him to shield. Instead, he had only to worry about hiding her physical form. He should have been hard pressed to keep her safe. The fact that he wasn't had a twinge of excitement running through his veins. She was strong. Damned strong. It would make for a very interesting relationship.

You have obstacles moving along the street at the point she'll enter. Torren relayed the information to him telepathically. Ryder could also feel his anticipation. He had been separated from Carmella for over a week now, giving Ryder time to accustom Carmella's unconscious mind to his presence, thereby assuring the conscious part of her that he could be worth the risk of trusting. Not that he expected it to be easy, though. Ryder sent a burst of power to the fleeing woman's left, giving the impression of a pursuer's light flickering in the underbrush. She shifted to the right, though he saw her hesitate. She was getting more suspicious now. She sensed no one there, saw only the light, and he knew she was starting to suspect she was being led along the path.

Carmella burst into the rubble-choked alley, bracing her hands on the concrete dune that stood in her way and flipping over it like an ethereal shadow. Then she stopped, hidden on the other side as he felt the tendrils of her power reaching out to him.

Avoiding them wasn't hard. She was trying to be cautious; to be certain there was no chance of touching the senses of the hounds still baying in the hills above her. But she also knew she was being watched.

Ryder shook his head and pulled back. He had her close enough to safety now and was fairly certain she would now find her own way to the Inn several blocks over. This had been his main objective, other than getting her ass away from the lynch mob that had detected her outside the prison grounds hours before.

I'm pulling back, he informed Torren. Cover my retreat.

The surge of power it took to return to his own body could be detected and tracked by another psychic, even one without astral power. He felt Torren providing the cover he needed as he forced himself to return from the astral plane and back to the physical.

Ryder opened his eyes the moment his psychic presence slammed back into the flesh and blood form. He drew in a deep breath as he fought the exhaustion that invariably came with such extreme use of his powers.

Ryder's lips quirked. He had been watching her for a week now as she searched the city for Torren. She was struggling with her own senses, the knowledge that her commander wasn't where she had been told he was. She was fighting herself so strongly that she refused to see the truth. Had refused to accept it even at the time Torren had offered it to her. The offer was rescinded now. Ryder would demand where Torren could not.

It wasn't going to be easy, leading her through her own fears, breaking her control. The grip she had on her own heightening desires was even tighter than the control she used psychically. Even more importantly, it was drawing away from the control she needed to focus and contain those powers.

Torren had been aware all along of Carmella's destiny. As a minor talent, his gift for seeing the potential of the future had been strong where Carmella and Ryder were concerned. He knew what had to be done, and he knew his part in it. The hard part would be convincing Carmella.

She's on her way back in, Torren informed him as he continued to follow Carmella. *She's suspicious.*

We didn't expect it to be easy. Ryder closed his eyes as he fought to still the anticipation of what was coming.

She's frightened, Ryder…

Bullshit, Ryder responded with an edge of amusement. She's pissed and she's getting careless. You aren't where you're supposed to be. She can't just kick ass and be done with it.

If there was one thing he had learned from Carmella's dreams, it was that the dominant, hard-edged side of her would cause complications in matters requiring a long degree of patience. She was quickly losing control rather than being able to wait and watch for the best opportunity to strike. It was going to get her killed.

Yeah. Torren's amused admiration of those qualities filtered through the mind connection easily. *That girl sure does look good kickin' ass, though, Ryder. It's a fine sight to see.*

Ryder snorted. Perhaps he would have seen it by now if his old buddy had been a bit more forthcoming when they had separated as a team years ago. Ryder had always wondered why Torren had sent him to join the group preparing to rebuild the government and the country, rather than both of them heading there.

The other man was an amazing tactician. As a seer, which was one of Torren's main psychic powers, he had the ability to glimpse what was coming and to know how to work toward it, or away from it. Rather than taking the job of working within that new government himself, though, he had sent Ryder.

PSI had been created to draw in those psychics with enough power to aid the rebuilding. It was also created to investigate and neutralize rebel psychics, and those intent on creating another demonic leadership such as Tyre's had been.

Carmella was under investigation not just because of the strength of her powers, but because of her connection to Tyre. The bloodline, which ran thick and strong, took her back to the two most powerful psychics the world had ever known—Tyre and the Tyrea.

That left her two choices now. She could submit to testing. If it was learned she could bond and be controlled by a disarming psychic whose only powers were that of neutralizing hers, or an absorber, who could soak it in, then she would live in relative peace. Or she could accept the drug the government had created that would control and eventually destroy her power. Otherwise, her freedom and possibly her life were at stake.

We'll save her. Torren's mental voice was as strong as Ryder's resolve.

You should have told me sooner. Ryder couldn't keep the edge of anger from his thought at the future Torren had not told him was coming.

Would you have left? Would you have done the work you have done? Would you have put in place the ties to this new government that will ultimately save her? Torren's questions were valid ones, and yet still that spark of jealousy remained.

Torren had found her, guided her, had been her lover for more than a year now while Ryder did the job he had been sent to do. During that time, his dreams had been in turmoil as his own lesser "seer" abilities had taunted him with her images while giving no clue to her whereabouts. Only after Torren had provided the necessary link had Ryder been able to slip into her unconscious mind and see the woman that had tormented him. A woman whose very life was now held in the balance of a government that was more than wary of any blood link back to the monster who had destroyed it once before.

The rewards will be worth it. Torren wasn't the least compassionate in his feelings toward Ryder's jealousy. Not that Ryder had expected him to be. I'll watch her while you sleep. Better get some rest, because she won't be as easy to conquer as you want to believe she will be.

Ryder didn't doubt that in the least.

Chapter Three

Carmella wasn't stupid. She knew she was being followed through her flight along the outer boundaries of New Cincinnati. She knew an astral watcher followed her, pushed her pursuers away from her and made a wide path of safety as she fought to escape the mob that had come upon her on the hill across from the prison.

Psychics were able to detect others of their kind, and were constantly on guard for them. But detecting those non-psychics, who had been taught to shield their thoughts, trained for years to hunt their fellow man and lived with the anticipation of the hunt, was harder. Especially when all her senses were concentrated elsewhere.

She needed Torren out of that prison—if he was there. She needed him out. She couldn't leave the area until she knew for certain he was safe. How the hell PSI had managed to capture him was a mystery to Carmella. She had known his obsession for that blonde-haired little witch of the new governor's would lead to nothing but trouble. But had he listened to her? Hell, no. Now there he was, drugged, trapped in the hellhole, unable to free himself or to help her free him. It was pissing her off. And it made no sense.

The blonde wasn't even his type. Delicate, fragile women had never appealed to him. Perhaps, it was Carmella's own jealousies that had her convinced of that. Her own pain as he had drawn away from her. He had been an anchor, a lifeline to the often tempestuous, nearly out-of-control emotions that could overtake her. He could draw her back with his passion, his gentleness. Even when she longed for something wilder, an intangible *something* she couldn't define or make sense of, Torren had eased her.

She moved quickly through the decades-old rubble and shadowed nightlife of New Cincinnati as she made her way back to the inn she was staying at. Finally, order was being established within the country. Lawlessness, lynch mobs and the desperation of a nation, she prayed, would slowly ease as the citizens replaced their nightly terrors with full stomachs and work-weary bodies.

Exhaustion clamored at her now. She was looking forward to a hot meal and the bed that awaited her. She moved carefully through the waste-filled alleys, making certain to stay within the shadows, to pull a close shield around the powerful abilities that could fairly hum with their strength if she wasn't careful.

Strangers were rare in the streets of New Cincinnati after dark. The lynch mobs knew who their locals were, made a point of it. Strangers were automatically distrusted, imprisoned, subjected to horrors she didn't want to relive for fear of never sleeping. She knew well the danger that awaited her if she was caught. It made the fact that she was being "watched" all the more worrisome.

She entered the torch-lit main room of the inn, ignoring the curious looks of the inhabitants as she stared around the bar. The inn had once been one of the many office buildings that sat outside the main thoroughfare of the city a century before. It was one of the few left standing.

The large central room held a multitude of tables and weary strangers to the city. Some she knew were psychics, some were bounty hunters, others were just killers.

She strode quickly through the long room, ignoring the distrustful, lecherous gazes of the men and the brooding, wary looks of the women as she made her way to a small, empty table in one corner.

She didn't like so many people watching her. The air felt thick with their emotions, the danger that surrounded many of them. It increased the nervous energy plaguing her now.

You need to center yourself. Otherwise, a PSI spy will pick up on you instantly. Torren's mental voice was cool, commanding.

Where the fuck are you? She was careful to keep her head lowered, her expression clear as he established the link that had been broken for over a week.

I'm not really sure I can tell you. There was a thread of amusement there that she knew she should worry about, but she was just too damned tired.

This isn't helping me any, Torren, she told him fiercely.

She was alone in this now. She was confident enough of her abilities to survive, but she missed Torren. Missed his support, his touch and the knowledge that there was someone to lean on.

I'm sending someone to help you, Carmella. His information had her holding her breath in surprise. *He'll be there soon. I want you to be waiting when he makes contact.*

There was something lingering in his thoughts that she couldn't quite put her finger on. Almost as though he didn't trust whomever he was sending.

Oh, I trust him well enough. There was a bit too much amusement in the thought.

And he's supposed to help me how? Irritation was crawling through her body. Dammit, she didn't like waiting around like this.

Stop, you're bleeding power! The command bordered on anger. Dammit, Carmella, you're losing control. Pull it in.

She tightened her jaw, doing just that. But it was damned hard. Her frustration level was becoming dangerously volatile.

You need to rest. I'm safe for now, he assured her. Get dinner, then fucking go to bed and sleep. You're too damned tired to keep stretching yourself like this.

And whose fault is that? She snarled silently, furiously. If you had kept your ass with me instead of sniffing some civilian honey pot I wouldn't be here now, would I, Torren?

It infuriated her. He was her lover, professed to love her, yet he had disappeared after nearly being caught trying to get close to the governor's daughter. A tempting, sensuous blonde who had drawn his gaze more than once during the speech the governor had given that day.

Sniffing some civilian honeypot? Mocking amusement accompanied Torren's thought. I never just sniff, Carmella. You should know that. Now be a good girl, stop being so jealous and get your dinner and some rest. You're wearing me down with all that frustration and weariness dragging at you. It's tiring.

Carmella clenched her teeth but refrained from growling as the waitress set a mug of beer in front of her.

"Dinner?" The slight woman's bored air pricked at Carmella's anger.

She glanced at the lighted menu display over the bar and sighed. It hadn't changed in days. Cabbage, potatoes, and boiled chicken with vegetables. Hell, it beat some meals she had been forced to eat.

"Dinner," she sighed, rubbing her brow. Torren was right; she was too damned tired for this.

The waitress nodded, moving away quickly as Carmella allowed her gaze to roam around the room in disinterest until the woman returned with her food. She ate quickly, efficiently. It was energy, nothing more, and as tired as she was she would need that energy just to pull her ass up the stairs to her room. As she pushed the plate back and picked up the mug of beer waiting beside it, she felt her senses hum in sudden awareness. She was being watched.

She could feel eyes on her, someone studying her, not astrally, but with such a physical presence it was disconcerting. The room was dim; especially the corners, but she found the offender easily enough.

Good God, he was a dangerous one. Carmella met his gaze for long seconds, her brow lifting mockingly as his look touched on her breasts pushing against the snug confines of her black top before meeting her gaze once again. His lips quirked in answering sarcasm.

He wasn't classically handsome. His features were too rough, too savage, for such a description. His thick, shoulder-length blonde hair was pulled back from his forehead and restrained at the nape of his neck. Like her, he was dressed in black with a light leather overcoat that fell to his knees. Her eyes narrowed. The man was packing more than just muscle under that coat.

He was easily six two, with broad shoulders. She bet his stomach was flat and rippled with strength, his arms would be strong, his thighs powerful. Her vagina clenched at the thought. Staying power. He looked strong enough to have it, if he wanted it.

She sneered at herself. She hadn't met a man yet that could still the fires that raged in her body. It didn't keep her from aching, though. And the man watching her lit a flame in her womb that threatened to burn out of control. She could feel her body crackling with desire. Singeing with guilt. She was furious with Torren, yet was lusting after another man herself.

She pushed her fingers tiredly through her short red-gold hair, breaking away from his gaze quickly. Hell, she was so damned tired she knew she wasn't up to a fucking, no matter how good it could get, even if she was so inclined. But it didn't keep her from wanting.

Carmella pulled the price of her meal from her snug pants pocket as she rose to her feet and made her way to the second floor of the inn. The room she had taken had once been a small office suite. The entrance had a frayed, aging couch and single chair but was otherwise bare. It was the shower she needed right now, though. The dust and grime of a day spent hiding in trees and along the rough ground had done little for her disposition this evening.

Long minutes later she stood beneath the tepid, surprisingly fresh flow of water. This wasn't river water as she was used to. It was clean and sweet-smelling, with just a mild touch of chlorine. Evidently the city's water station was working ahead of schedule.

She didn't expect hot water, but was mildly surprised that even the chill had been knocked off it. She leaned against the rough shower wall, letting the lukewarm stream course over her after washing her hair and her body quickly, enjoying the rare pleasure of being totally clean.

The soothing spray of the water eased some of her tired muscles and relaxed her marginally. Minutes later, the rationed flow of water began to slow, and Carmella turned the taps off with a sigh of regret before stepping out of the shower stall.

With no more than a coarse towel wrapped around her body she moved through the central room and entered her bedroom.

She barely kept from betraying her awareness that she was being watched the moment she stepped into the room. It was the same presence that had followed her through the woods earlier, eerily similar to the sensation of the stranger's eyes that had watched her in the bar.

Who was he and what the hell did he want?

She had no doubt the presence was male. Who he was became the greater question, though. And why was he watching her?

Chapter Four

Carmella flipped the towel from her body, dropping it carelessly on the chair beside the bed as she feigned ignorance of the presence. She kept the shields around her own powers carefully in place, hiding her knowledge of the watcher as well as the strength of her psychic talents.

Bad girl. The amused chiding in Torren's voice at her display had her fighting a grin. *You always were a bit of an exhibitionist, weren't you, baby?* His arousal filled the connecting thought.

It surprised her, the dark undercurrents flowing through the connection. There was no jealousy, as she would have expected, only heat, approval. Arousal.

Naked, she moved to the bed, lying back on the soft mattress as she stared up at the ceiling.

Feels like the bastard from the bar earlier, she mused, knowing Torren was listening closely. He's powerful, whoever he is.

There was no answer forthcoming, as though he too were considering the uninvited visitor.

For a second, as her gaze had connected with the stranger, she had sensed a power in him, a hidden well of strength that aroused her curiosity and more.

He made you horny, Torren accused her with a thread of laughter. Be honest, Carmella, he made you wet.

She sent him the impression of her silent snort. It's not like you've been of any use to me lately. Too busy chasing after blonde bimbos.

Blonde bimbos can be a nice diversion. But I didn't fuck her, baby. I just wasn't fucking you.

She didn't like his tone, or the information. It hurt to realize his desire for her was fading. She hadn't expected that. But then again, she hadn't expected to be hit so quickly with her own lust for another man. She hastily censored her thoughts from the man who had been her lover, unwilling that he would know the innermost part of her longings. Longings she had never shared with anyone.

She had gotten close several times. Torren had nearly brought her to the release she needed once or twice when his fury with her had overwhelmed his consideration. But close didn't count except in battle.

The stranger at the bar had been powerful. Physically, at least, with a glimmer of carnal knowledge glowing in the blue eyes that had watched her across the room. Tall, strong, and if he was by chance psychic, then that physical power could be greater than normal. Enough to hold her down. Enough to thrust inside her with a strength and power that could ultimately push her over the edge. Maybe.

She sighed softly. She had never gone over the edge, so she had no idea what it would take to push her there. At five feet six, with a willowy slender body, she just didn't seem to inspire mindless lust in men. Torren seemed to want to protect her, rather than fuck her mindlessly. Not that the soft kisses and gentle touches weren't nice at times, but her sexual fantasies little resembled the touches she had received.

Her lips quirked. How surprised he would be to know the sexual fantasies that tormented her body. They were raw, carnal images that came from hearing the rough, sexually explicit descriptions of the acts she had overheard men talking of throughout her life. That and the words from the nearly ancient novels of another time.

She had found the cache of books years before in the hidden basement of a nearly demolished home. Paperbacks so close to falling apart she feared reading them. But once the words had leapt from the front page, she had been ensnared, helplessly caught. She had been as fascinated then as she was now with the excitement of being watched by a presence so strong it could slip past the psychic barriers she had placed around the room.

She had a job to do tomorrow. Wherever the hell Torren was hidden she had to find him so they could get the hell out of there before she was detected by the PSI agents that must surely be looking for her. But that was tomorrow and this was tonight.

Until then, she could play with her psychic Peeping Tom just a little bit. The surge of excitement at the thought of that sent the blood racing through her veins in excitement.

Watch me, she thought, thinking of the watcher as she opened her thoughts to Torren once again. Knowing her lover was "seeing" mentally what she was doing—feeling her arousal—brought a keen edge of excitement to her lust.

Damn. This is a dangerous game you're playing, little girl, he warned her, but his thought was filled with heated desire.

Enjoy it. She hid her grin from whoever watched. Let me enjoy it.

She closed her eyes, bringing to her mind the image of one of the rougher passages she had re-read not long before.

Her body was sizzling with lust, and though she could have slept while the watcher moved about the room, there was no way she could sleep with the fires of arousal burning in the depths of her pussy the way they were. She would give the bastard something to watch, to wonder about, and give herself the relief she needed to help her rest.

Damn, Carmella. Torren's curse was one of frustration rather than shock or disgust as the image filled her head.

She settled herself comfortably on the nearly flattened pillow, her hands rising to her already swollen breasts. She drew in a hard breath as her fingers smoothed over the distended peaks. Heat flared through her body, piercing her womb at the touch. She could feel her pussy creaming, soaking the red-gold curls between her thighs as she built the image of the written scene in her mind.

Her thumb and forefinger gripped her distended nipple, and she couldn't hold back a moan as she pinched it lightly. Then harder. Oh, that was good. Pleasure sang through her bloodstream, pounding through her body.

In her mind's eye it was the stranger from the bar touching her. Holding her captive against a wall, his powerful body blanketing hers, holding her still as she struggled to escape him. She would have to fight him. Fight to win. She didn't want a man she knew she could best; she wanted one strong enough to take her down and fuck her mindlessly even as she screamed out in fury.

Fuck! Torren's fierce, lascivious thought only made her hotter. He was seeing the image she was creating, images she had hidden before.

Torren had been uncomfortable during the few months he had been her lover, when he glimpsed the rioting needs that tormented her body. He was a strong alpha psychic, but he had no desire to assert the darker side of his passions. At least, not with her. She had a feeling the stranger who had watched her earlier would have no such problem.

She bit her lip, forcing back her moan of need as she twisted the hard point of her nipple. Her other hand smoothed over the flat plane of her stomach until it tucked between her thighs. She was wet; so slick and creamy her juices matted the curls that shielded her cunt.

She could feel Torren, still connected with her, watching her, his own arousal sizzling between them now in ways it had only threatened to before. But it was the stranger she saw. His hands touching her, tormenting her.

She imagined him holding her easily as she fought him, his hard body pressing her into the wall, his fingers twisting the tender flesh of her nipple as the fingers of his other hand took possession of her pussy. She arched away from the touch, but he followed her, his fingers sliding easily through the soaked slit to the clenching entrance below.

He wouldn't allow her satisfaction to come easily. She wouldn't submit to him without first testing him, pushing him past his own limits of control. And there lay her greatest desire...and her greatest fear.

He would have to take her control with the loss of his own. She didn't want a man able to maintain his own power, his own desires as she lost hers. She would want him to overpower her because he had no choice. Because his lust for her would be greater than his need to control his own power, physical or psychic. There were few psychics alive with the honor she required that would allow a lifetime of control to vanish for lust alone. But she could dream. And she could imagine such a thing occurring. And imagine she did.

* * * * *

Ryder allowed his astral body to move closer to the bed, for the first time in his life afflicted with such lust, such overwhelming desire, that he could feel it even now, separated from his physical body. His psychic form felt every bit as sensitive, as heated as he would have been if he were physically standing by the bed watching her.

She was a hot little package. Her skin was smooth, creamy, with no betraying blemishes of disease or sickness. Her breasts were full, her stomach flat but by no means undernourished. Her legs were strong, rounded and slowly spreading to accommodate her slender hand as she caressed her wet cunt.

It wasn't the first time he had watched a woman masturbate, unaware he was in the room with her, but he'd be damned if it wasn't the most arousing. What was it about Carmella Dansford that tempted his control? And tempt it she did—in a number of ways that surprised Ryder.

As an alpha psychic, there was a part of him—a darkness he had kept hidden most of his life. It was one of the main reasons for the control he had built up over his lifetime. That darkness made him wary, and the desires it produced often made him wonder at his own sense of honor. Until now, no woman had ever strained that honor or the control he valued so highly. He was almost tempted to return to his physical body and wait until morning to contact her. That would have been the wisest course. But lust was never wise, and Ryder was filled with that blistering, foolish emotion in ways he never had been with another woman.

She was laid out before him, ripe and flushed, her breathing hard and deep as she pulled roughly at a hard, reddened nipple, while her fingers worked slowly through the swollen slit of her pussy. She was so fucking wet that the red-gold curls of her cunt glistened with the moisture that saturated them.

Torren, son of a bitch, she's killing me. It was only with the help of Torren's mental shield that he was able to hide his identity from her. He had no doubt she knew he was there.

The woman was a damned banquet of carnal delight. Her breasts would fit his hands perfectly, and he'd be damned if he didn't want to be the one twisting that perfect, hard nipple. He wouldn't allow her to smother her cries, though. He wanted to hear her screaming with the pleasure and erotic pain he could give her.

Her eyes were closed, her teeth clamped over her lower lip as she held back her cries. Her hips undulated against her fingers as she stroked the hot, wet flesh of her cunt. What was she thinking? What was she imagining? The need to know was driving him insane.

Cover me. I'm going in, he ordered Torren, unable to bear the thought that the other man was experiencing whatever fantasy she had conjured and that he alone was left to merely watch the results. He wanted to see the images filling her imagination—needed to know the key to Carmella's passions. To do that, he would have to slip past the physical and enter her amazingly complicated mind.

Damn, she might be more than either of us can handle, Ryder. Torren's thought was a morass of lust, affection and anticipation.

He felt the added strength Torren sent to him as he stepped closer. Entering her mind undetected wouldn't be nearly as easy as entering her room had been. Her blocks were strong; her mind would be even stronger. But there was always a crack, a weak point. Ryder knew well there was no such thing as an impenetrable mind.

Chapter Five

God help him. Ryder sent out the silent prayer after finding the weak spot in Carmella's defenses and slipping into the shadows of her daydream. She would be the death of him — and her, if he wasn't careful. Because when he got hold of her he was going to fuck her until he killed them both.

She was imagining him. It was the most amazing sight, seeing himself holding her against the wall, his hands rough, his hips pressed against that pretty ass as he held her in place. And she was fighting him tooth and nail. Fighting as her image of Torren wavered around them.

"Say no," the shadowy Ryder ordered. "When you say no, I'll let you go."

Ryder wondered if he actually got his hands on her, if he could let her go should she actually say no.

"Go to hell." Her curse echoed in the confines of the dream she had built within her mind.

"Wrong answer," the dream Ryder taunted.

His hand moved from between her thighs to deliver a stinging slap to the well-rounded curve of her buttock. Ryder watched her flinch, heard her cry out. Son of a bitch, it was her daydream and it couldn't have hit his own fantasies much closer.

He watched as she struggled, kicking back, her head tossing as she tried to slam it into her dream lover's face. The male vision only chuckled, then smacked her again a second before his fingers delved into the cleft of her ass and slid to the area of her pussy.

It was wet. Ryder knew she was dripping wet without seeing it. The dream Ryder hummed his appreciation of what he found as the woman bucked in his arms.

He forced her legs apart then, his powerful thighs flexing. She screamed in outrage, cursing him as his body bent, his cock lining up between her thighs. Ryder had a second to glimpse the penetration of her cunt.

He stood back, watching as the pair fucked furiously. The dream Ryder was hard-pressed to keep his cock inside her as she fought him, but somehow he managed. She tossed and writhed, then whimpered as she came. The orgasm was light, her body pulsing for more. Behind her, her lover stiffened, driving his erection inside her one last time as he obviously spent himself as well.

She was nowhere near satisfied, despite her orgasm. She needed more, yet seemed too tired, too frustrated to bring herself to peak once more. He hid in the shadows of her mind as he felt the exhaustion sweeping over her. Sleep would come soon.

He had slipped into her mind while she was occupied with her own needs, but her subconscious would be used to him now.

Her mind darkened—images, memories, flickering about the mists that began to fill her subconscious. He stood back, waiting, knowing that when sleep took over another part of her would awaken. It was this part of her he longed to see.

The little fantasy he had glimpsed had intrigued him, giving him more than one clue into Carmella's sexuality. But he needed more. He didn't expect what came to him.

He saw the pages of a book, then the images jumping to life on the tapestry of her subconscious. He watched in surprise and lust at the twisting figures that began to fill her mind. In each, the female was in a position of submission, two males, out of control and consumed with lust, filling her. He was going to explode with his own arousal, Ryder thought heatedly. The female images were Carmella, the males' misty forms were his and Torren's. And they were willing to force her compliance. She was starving for raw, carnal sex. To submit, to be taken. Not raped, but forced to relinquish her own control to a man—or men—strong enough to take it. Someone stronger, more powerful than she.

She fought in each sequence of events. Struggled against the males' greater strength only to eventually accept the spears of hard, eager cocks ready to take her. But even in the midst of the lust, he saw something more. In each one Carmella's dream lovers, though out of control, never truly hurt her. The voices were rough, though tender; commanding, but not unkind. And after possessing whichever part of her body one of the shadowed shapes managed to penetrate, they praised her.

The tight fit of her small pussy, the heat of her ass, the grip of her mouth or the stroke of her tongue—each image, each fantasy, was different. And here was the key to the woman.

He eased back from her then, aware he was close to the edge of his own control and moving closer toward the vilest act a psychic could participate in. Taking her in this vulnerable time of her greatest need. And he could. He could weave his astral force into one of the shadowed male shapes and give her what she fantasized about. Without her consent. Without her own conscious realization that it was, indeed, what she wanted.

He forced himself through the small break in her barrier that he had found. He repaired it quickly, reinforced it to keep her safe then returned to his own body.

Ryder sighed deeply as he looked away. He stared up at the ceiling, contemplating his options. He liked to consider himself practical—kind in many respects. He worked for the new government because he knew the laws being put in place were for the protection of everyone—psychics and non-psychics alike. Laws that would be set up as unbreakable for the protection of everyone. Laws that, if in place now, would assure his instant punishment.

She won't be easy, he told Torren, amazed at the sense of gentleness he was suddenly feeling toward her.

She knew I was there when she took that little fantasy trip. She's strong. She's losing her defenses. Torren's tone was concerned. *She's too tired.*

Can you shield her until she awakens? That could be a complication. If she were that tired, then her powers would be easily detected by the PSI searching for emanations of psychic strength that weren't contained by the government-issued restrainers created for civilian psychics, or the unique signal of a tested PSI member.

As always. Torren's softer emotions for the girl filled his thoughts. He was worried, aroused, eager. But her protection was uppermost. As it always had been, even before she had come into Torren's life.

Ryder shook his head as he remembered his first contact with Torren right before receiving the file on Carmella from the PSI director. The future he had predicted had made little sense until he received the file and saw the woman who had occupied his fantasies for years. The same woman PSI was now contemplating extreme measures against because of her link to the past.

Fyrebrands were elemental psychics. The creation of that particular psychic talent had been artificial. Tyre had been extremely adept in the elemental powers, as had his wife, the Tyrea. They had been the most powerful and had easily taken positions of leadership. Since then, every advanced elemental discovered had been found to trace back to Tyre. The man had impregnated more women than those recording it at the time could keep track of. But his mate had been Leila, the Tyrea. The birth of her daughter had been discovered, as had the efforts taken to hide her as the war had started to turn the tide in favor of those fighting to destroy the merciless psychics who had taken power.

Where the child had gone wasn't learned until after her death. But it was reported that she, too, had given birth. That direct bloodline of the two most powerful psychics was suspected to run in Carmella's veins. If it did, then her life hung in the balance if it was ever discovered.

Chapter Six

The next evening the stranger returned. Carmella watched as he entered the inn, his gaze catching hers immediately as he stopped at the bar once again.

Who is he? She knew Torren was in her mind, watching her, keeping track of her movements, but he hadn't yet offered to reveal his location.

She hadn't even bothered returning to the prison. She knew she wouldn't find him there. Whatever game he was playing would have to be endured until he was satisfied. She had learned that a long time ago. It didn't mean she had to like it.

The day had been a fucking washout, Carmella thought as she sat with the back of her chair braced against the wall. She had scoured the city, wondering where Torren was, and having nothing but the conversations he kept up in her head to go by. But she never sensed a strengthening in the mental link. She was starting to think he was nowhere near the city.

She glanced broodingly at the stranger who made no effort to hide his interest in her. She finished off the shot of whisky she had ordered after her meal, refusing to redirect her gaze.

Her dreams the night before had been filled with him. Stark, vivid, lust-filled dreams that left her aching, her pussy wet, her breasts sensitive. She had never had such a reaction to a man. Had never been so certain that one could stem the rising fury of need that sometimes grew inside her, tormenting her body and her mind before she found a way to push it back.

Several times throughout the day she had been forced to tamp down the overriding lust. It grew in her, like a shadow of fury that threatened to rage out of control.

She rolled the small shot glass on its end, her fingers gripping it lightly as her gaze returned to the blond-haired, blue-eyed temptation that stalked her dreams, and now her evenings. Why was he just watching her? If he was Torren's friend, why hadn't he made contact yet?

I'm sure he'll let you know eventually. Amusement whispered through her mind.

Is he the one you contacted? She knew Torren could easily detect her anger. It grated on her that he refused to tell her where he was, yet trusted another instead.

And if I don't know where I am? he asked her, his voice silky, almost...deceptive. And he didn't say if he knew the guy or not.

I won't know if it's him until he gives you the information I gave him.

She sighed tiredly. *Why am I getting the feeling you're setting me up, Torren?*

She couldn't ignore it any longer. He wasn't where he was supposed to be. His telepathy wasn't cut off. If PSI had him, he wouldn't have a chance of linking with her mentally. Which meant PSI didn't have him. But neither was he helping her find him. Her frustration level, high to begin with, was only growing daily.

Have I ever hurt you, Carmella? She couldn't ignore the affection he felt for her. The truth of his loyalty to her. It was all there. Just as it had always been.

No. She pushed her fingers restlessly through her hair, glancing back at the stranger.

I won't start now.

Torren wouldn't, but what about the stranger? She had to do something soon. She was becoming too frustrated, too near to losing her control. And this unknown man wasn't helping. He made her hot. Too damned hot and in all the wrong ways.

Carmella sighed tiredly. Her temper was fraying at the edges. Ever since the first glimpse of that man the night before, she had been tormented with images of him rising over her, taking her, his hard cock driving into her repeatedly. The muscles of her cunt clenched as she fought to pull her thoughts back.

His lips quirked in wicked humor, a dark blond brow arching faintly in question as his gaze stayed on hers. Damn, he looked too sexy — too male. And clean. Son of a bitch if the man didn't look clean. There were few in the bar that could claim that distinction, even herself.

The stranger was dressed completely in black. Black boots, jeans, shirt and leather overcoat. He looked as tough as rawhide and too tempting for his own good.

The dark clothing seemed to only further accentuate his almost white-blond hair and wicked blue eyes. His dark skin, the sardonic quirk of his lips, the well-trimmed dark gold beard and mustache all combined to make him look like a pirate. A marauder. A sexy, untamed male.

She kept her gaze on him as she stood up from her chair and began to work her way to the bar, ignoring the heated pace of her heartbeat that seemed to echo in the depths of her pussy. What was it about this man — a stranger — that affected her as no other had?

She moved through the crowded room, ignoring murmured invitations from various men as she passed, keeping her gaze on the stranger until she slid between him and the bar stool beside him.

Neither budged. Her breasts were pressed tightly against his chest as he stared down at her broodingly, the heat of his body whipping through her nipples where they pressed against the cool expanse of his leather overcoat.

"Bartender, whisky," she gave her order as she fought to keep from panting.

As the bartender moved to fill the order she felt a wide palm at her hip. It was steady, moving no further, cupping the curve of her body with a heated caress. She raised her eyes to him.

"Who the fuck are you?" she hissed low enough that only he heard her words.

She felt like ramming her knee into the intriguing bulge between his thighs when his sensual lips tilted in a mocking smile, his hooded eyes glimmering with lustful purpose.

His head lowered, moving next to hers, his lips whispering against the sensitive lobe of her ear as he whispered, "Your most erotic fantasy." His voice was dark, deep, a sensual rasp over her senses that sent her clit throbbing, her heart pounding. "Are you going to say no?"

Carmella's eyes widened as the memory of her fantasy the night before surged through her mind.

Say no and I'll let you go. It was her fantasy. Or was it?

He moved back slowly, his expression erotically intense, his lips parted just enough to make the sensual male curve a temptation she could barely deny. At her hip, his fingers flexed, stroked, his fingertips inching beneath the snug hem of her shirt at the waistband of her pants.

She flinched at the stroke of pure sensation as his fingertips smoothed against her bare flesh. Calloused. Warm. Creating an erogenous zone where none should exist.

Psychic. She knew he was, but she couldn't sense any emanations of power at all. Carmella had a sensitive awareness for those psychic waves, yet she could detect nothing.

"I'll do better than that," she whispered at his ear, licking her lips, allowing the tip of her tongue to barely glance the strong line of his earlobe. "If you want it, big boy, you have to take it. Think you can?"

Before he could reply she collected her shot glass, threw back the hard liquor and moved away from him. She glanced back to see him watching her, his head lowered, his gaze brooding. The look sent an arc of pure arousal pulsing through her body and a sudden, overriding image of him doing just as she had dared him to do.

Oh, bad girl. Torren was laughing at her as she swept from the room. A challenge like that would be hard for a man to refuse. *You just gave him permission to force you, Carmella.*

Only if he's man enough. She hadn't yet found a man who could overpower her. Psychic or not.

Torren was quiet for long, intense moments.

You might get more than you bargained for. His thought was heavy with warning, and a small, thrilling spark of lust she had always felt he kept carefully hidden.

You had your chance. She threw the door open to the small suite of rooms. *You wanted a bimbo, honey, instead.*

The door bounced on the inner wall then swung forward again. Carmella caught it and slammed it closed before clenching her fists and fighting for control. She could feel the anger, the throttled desire and frustration building inside her. She needed a good fight but there was none available. No, she needed a good fight and a hard fuck. She trembled at the thought, the muscles of her pussy rippling.

"Where are you?" she growled as she stalked to the dingy window of the room, looking out into the darkened street with a sense of helpless rage. "I'm tired of this game, Torren." The sound of her own voice was a comfort for her, even though it wasn't needed for him to hear her.

If only it were a game, Carmella. His lingering regret washed through, and a frown creased her brow as she felt it. *I wish it were no more than a game. Then you would find ease and I would find peace.*

She laid her head against the pane of glass, ignoring her reflection as well as the regret that lay heavy in her heart.

Yeah, she agreed silently. *If only it were a game.*

Chapter Seven

The knock came on the main door to the suite the next morning, just after a quick breakfast of bacon and toast purchased from the restaurant downstairs. She came to her feet slowly, sending out a cautious mental feeler for any signs of aggression outside the wood panel.

She sensed Torren then, slipping into her mind, watching cautiously.

Can you tell who it is? she asked suspiciously.

I don't feel danger. No sign of aggression. The knock came again.

Gripping the heavy blaster pistol strapped to her side, she moved slowly to the door. She lifted the long weapon from its holster, keeping it at shoulder level as she quickly turned the door knob and threw it open. She moved to the side of the frame and brought the weapon to bear on a more than impressive chest.

She breathed out deeply as she stared at the visitor smirking down at her.

"What the fuck do you want?" The instant antagonism was followed by a hard pulse of moisture between her thighs.

Without waiting for an invitation, he placed his hand on the door and pushed past her, stepping into the room.

The aggressive arrogant move had her forcibly tamping down the power that sparked inside her. She could feel her stomach tightening, heat flaring in the depths of it. He lifted a brow mockingly as he passed her.

She quickly holstered the blaster as she moved back into the room, slamming the door behind her. Fury surged hard and fast through her veins as she fought the overwhelming response as the man turned to face her.

Her senses were going crazy, impressions tumbling in on her, a confused jumble of fear and knowledge. And danger. She could feel it licking over her flesh like a lover's caress.

This is your doing, she accused Torren furiously. *I know this is your doing. You can't hide it, you son of a bitch. What are you up to?*

You don't know any such thing. Settle down, Carmella. See what he wants. Torren's demanding presence did little to still the sudden confusion running rife through her.

Her eyes narrowed on the stranger as his gaze flickered to her heaving breasts beneath the snug fit of her black top. Her nipples peaked, and her senses fractured beneath the lust in his eyes when they rose back to hers.

"I would think what I want would be obvious by now." His blue eyes were sparkling with laughter as he watched her.

Carmella snarled. Arrogance strengthened every line of his face and glittered in his eyes.

"Well, let's pretend it's not," she suggested sarcastically. "Who the hell are you and what are you doing stalking me?"

He crossed his arms over the black shirt he wore, causing the material to stretch over the bulging muscles of his arms. Strong, thick muscles. She gave herself a mental shake as she felt Torren's amusement.

If this is your little buddy, Torren, I'll roast you when I find you, she promised him silently.

"I imagine Torren's been in contact with you by now," the stranger suggested softly. "He sent me to bring you to him. I'm Ryder."

Carmella stilled. He didn't say Torren had sent him to help her find him, but to take her to him.

Torren? Does he know where you are?

It's possible. She could hear the mental shrug in his voice. *If it's really Ryder, then anything is possible.*

And how the hell am I supposed to know? She watched the other man carefully as she mentally thought of all the ways she could kill Torren. Slowly.

Ryder watched her mockingly as she fought for answers, his demon's blue eyes tracking each curve of her body until he returned to her face. When he saw her gaze, a confident, sensual smile crossed his expression. She could see the male superiority in his gaze, the complete assurance that she would do as he wanted.

The aggressive arrogance in his attitude had her forcibly tamping down the power that sparked inside her. She could feel her stomach tightening, heat flaring in the depths of it. He lifted a brow mockingly.

Carmella. Torren's warning thought drew her attention from the other man. *You're bleeding power again. Rein it in.*

She breathed in deeply. The amount of psychic static her powers generated would bring any and every PSI agent within a ten-mile radius running if she weren't careful.

"My shield covers you," Ryder told her as his lips quirked in amusement. "Go ahead and get mad. I'm sure I can handle it."

He wore arrogant superiority as easily as he wore the faded black jeans. His voice resonated with it, sparking something inside her that she tried to convince herself was anger alone. But she knew better. And she knew Torren would as well.

Son of a bitch, she didn't need her lover trampling through her mind right now. It was strange as hell to lust after another man while the man she had fucked more than once looked on. But it was also discomfortingly arousing. It added an edge she didn't want to look deeply into.

"And how the hell am I supposed to be sure Torren even knows you?" She propped her hands on her hips as she watched him distrustfully.

"Because I just said he did." He shrugged his wide shoulders, his arms still crossed over his muscular chest as he watched her, almost laughing at her.

"Oh, and I'm just going to accept that," she assured him, thickening the mockery in her voice. "I don't think so, big boy."

He chuckled, a low, rough sound that caused her cunt to clench heatedly.

"Torren told you I was coming, Carmella. He's with you now. The code was simply Ryder. Or, ride her. I rather liked the idea of the latter."

You didn't, she hissed silently, furiously.

Oh come on, Carmella, I'm sure he misunderstood. But she heard the laughter in his voice. The knowledge that he most likely had done just that.

Ride her! She hoped her snarl conveyed itself across the mental channel. Ride her! I should let him while you watch, you sick bastard.

The surge of lust that speared her mind shocked her. The thought of it aroused him almost as much as it did her.

"I don't know you, and Torren never mentioned you to me," she assured him softly as her hand lowered to palm the butt of the pistol. "Try again. Get the code right this time."

"You didn't have a code with Torren, but you slept with him," he growled, a glimmer of possessive anger sparkling in his gaze. "Now you'll sleep with me."

Damn, he sounds kinda pissed over it. Carmella ignored Torren's amusement at the other man as she stilled. She belonged to no one but herself, yet this man acted as though he had somehow claimed her for his own. A claiming she had no say in. She didn't think so.

"Torren doesn't acknowledge you," she informed him softly. "And you have no rights to me. Period."

"Yes, he has acknowledged me." His eyes narrowed on her expression. "As a matter of fact, he's rather amused right now, I believe."

"Prove it," she challenged him, her senses flaring, anticipation spreading through her body. She could force the fight she needed so damned bad, then she could talk reasonably. She would show him first, though, that she wouldn't be mocked. She wouldn't be ordered. Not unless he could do what no man had before.

"I can give you what he couldn't, Carmella," he told her softly. "I can make you submit."

Her eyes widened as she felt her face pale. "I don't know what you're talking about."

"Don't you?" he asked her softly. "I think you do, baby. And I think you're dying to find out if I can."

You expect me to just follow this bastard? she snorted silently to Torren. What does he do, buy his arrogance wholesale?

Torren's answering amusement wasn't much help.

Carmella watched Ryder as she stilled the pulse of arousal and fury churning through her system. Emotion only clouded her mind, and as desperately as she needed to find Torren, she would be damned if she would just accept and follow anyone.

Unfortunately, Torren was doing little to help her. He was neither agreeing nor disagreeing with anything Ryder was saying. His amusement whispered through her mind, as though he enjoyed the confrontation playing out before him.

"And I think you're a bit too damned arrogant," she growled. "I want to find Torren, not fuck." She forced the lie through her teeth as she faced him. "You aren't saying anything to convince me you can help me with that."

"That's your pride talking," he said softly. "You already know Torren sent me. And trust me, I can find him. But not without boundaries. I lead. You follow. It's that simple."

Nothing was that simple. Carmella could sense the hidden currents flowing from him, the dominance that was as much a part of him as the blue of his eyes, or the brilliant white of his hair.

She breathed in deeply, fighting for patience as she stared across the room at him. He was too forceful. Too dominating. She could feel her body tensing, the urge to fight swelling within her. He made her want things she knew would never truly exist, and it terrified her.

She pushed her fingers restlessly through her hair as she fought to think logically. Okay, Torren had sent him...

I wouldn't send anyone that couldn't do the job right, Carmella. His thought was suddenly strong, pulsing. He's saying all the right words, but I don't know for sure.

His suddenly cool demeanor worried her.

Then how the hell am I supposed to know? she snapped silently.

There was no answer forthcoming.

"Standing here looking at you isn't a hardship, but it's not getting us any closer to Torren either," Ryder smirked. "Are you ready to ride or not?"

The blatant sexuality of the question had her hackles rising instantly.

"Excuse me?" She could feel her power pulsing, energizing.

The grin that tilted his lips did little to ease her mind. It was pure sexuality, unapologetic, richly sensual.

"I'm ready to leave now. Get your things and let's go."

He expected her to just follow him? To mindlessly accept that he could be trusted?

"I don't think so." She braced her body, watching him carefully. "I don't just follow anyone, Ryder. Not even on Torren's command. Which he hasn't given me, by the way. It's not going to be that easy."

Challenge? she asked Torren.

There was a long, thoughtful silence. *It's the only way to know for sure. I know how he fights. But the challenge you put out last night might get you more than you're bargaining for.*

Her responses leaped in a betraying surge of arousal at the thought. She smiled slowly, watching Ryder's gaze darken at the movement.

"Torren's a smart bastard." She shrugged her shoulders negligently. "But I'm not exactly stupid. You haven't yet proved you can lead and until you do, you'll have no loyalty from me." He was cocky enough, Carmella gave him that. If arrogance and superiority equaled strength, then he'd have it licked. But they didn't. They often equaled a too-large ego and too little power.

Carmella smirked in Ryder's direction.

His gaze became hooded, sweeping slowly over her body as she stood facing him. She kept her body loose, prepared to jump. She wouldn't let him surprise her.

"Who said anything about wanting your loyalty?" he murmured, the blue of his eyes deepening. "The strongest rules *and* rides. Are you sure you can handle that?" The sexual connotations had her brow rising slowly.

Her lips quirked at the challenge. "Think you're man enough?"

"Oh baby." He grinned then, and there was no hiding the heat of lust that flared in his gaze. "I know I am."

Chapter Eight

Overconfidence had been many a man's downfall when it came to her, Carmella assured herself. She had faced off against more than one, and only Torren had ever beaten her. And even then, Carmella felt it was closer to a draw than an actual loss on her side.

As she placed her pistol and assorted knives out of the way, her eyes narrowed on him. Balancing herself carefully, she allowed the shields around her powers to drop. She felt Torren reaching out across whatever distance separated them, his own power shielding the room, covering them from PSI detection.

Instantly the room hummed, crackling with energy as the force of her elemental power began to grow within her. She would fight him with everything she had and she would show him who would rule and who would ride. She snorted silently, watching him carefully as he flexed the powerful muscles beneath his shirt and watched her with a smug quirk to his lips.

"I'm giving you one chance, Carmella," he said softly. "We can do this the easy way."

"Can you tell me where Torren is located?" she demanded as she let her arms rest at her sides, her fingers flexing as energy traveled through them.

He sighed, shaking his head mockingly. "Sorry."

She shrugged in return, allowing a smile to tilt her lips. "Then I guess we'll have to fight it out, won't we?"

"Carmella, if I take you down I'll fuck you." He almost shocked her with his explicit words. "It won't be nice, or easy, and it sure as hell won't be the least bit romantic. I'll plow as deep inside your pussy as I can. And it won't stop there."

Carmella tried to still the surge of lust that swept through her womb. She had never been taken down, dominated, fucked until she screamed. She had fantasized about it. Had dreamed of it. But it had never happened. She shook her head slowly.

Well, he's confident anyway. Torren's thought was too amused to suit her.

Shut up and let me concentrate, she told him absently.

With a threat like that you'll lose for the hell of it, Torren quipped as Carmella tried to push him from her mind.

"Promises, promises," she sighed mockingly as his gaze flickered to the beaded tips of her nipples beneath her snug top. "You're such a tease, Ryder."

Ryder chuckled softly as his gaze returned to hers. "Taking you down will be a pleasure, Carmella."

She licked her lips slowly, sensually. "Are you going to talk me to death, big boy, or actually make a move?"

He made his move with a speed she didn't expect, leaping for her in an effort to enclose her in his arms.

He was fast. She had to give him credit for it. And, son of a bitch, if he wasn't powerful. Static filled the room, flipping around her as she spun out of reach, ducking and twisting to the side as he grasped for her. At the last minute, she extended her leg in a kick that had him cursing as it glanced his shin. Power filled her.

He hadn't come at her with a psychic blow, but depended on physical strength instead. As she flipped around to face him she sent a surge of static in his direction. Crackling mid-air like an invisible whip, the arc of energy should have struck him across his chest, putting him down for several long moments.

Instead it fizzled out against an invisible barrier inches from his body. Her eyes narrowed. Someone had to be providing Ryder with his own amplifying powers. "Call off the guard dog," she snarled. "Fight me alone or don't fight me at all."

"Did I say I was going to play fair, Carmella?" he asked her gently as he glided around to the other side of the room. "Your powers are elemental. Fire, if I remember correctly, with a few lesser talents thrown in. Do you think I'd drop my guard?"

She lifted her lip in a sneer. Anger surged through her, but the lust pounded just beneath her skin.

"You aren't defenseless," she accused him softly as she worked her way to the center of the room, watching him carefully.

"Neither are you, baby." He grinned. "Come on, Carmella, burn me. I dare you."

She laughed softly. "Come and get me, Ryder." She spread her arms wide. "If you can."

She sensed the attack coming. A whip of dead space. It nearly terrified her. She dropped to the floor, sending a surge of fire in the direction it came from as she processed immediately whether to jump or roll. She jumped, clearing the disarming shock with less than an inch to spare as she threw a blast of deadly flames at Ryder's head.

She heard him laugh as she hit the floor and rolled to safety before coming to a crouch, watching him carefully. The son of a bitch wasn't even singed. He stood casually against the wall, once again protecting his back. She narrowed her eyes at the implied weakness.

She jumped to the side as another arc of disarming power flew toward her. Flames met it, outlining its strength and width as she rolled across the floor and sent a fireball as big as his head toward him at the same time.

He jumped out of the way, aiming again.

"You're getting old." She jumped the whip of power that would effectively still her own for up to hours at a time. "Damned disarming shit. Figures you'd be a passive. Maybe *I'll* get to ride *you*." She threw a blade of static at his side, forcing him to glide further into the room as she rolled away from yet another disarming beam. "Dammit, don't you know how to do anything else? This is getting boring."

She jumped the next beam, timing the jump and her position. She threw a wall of flames, turned in mid-air and aimed a kick at his tall body. Her foot connected with his shoulder, throwing him off balance as she landed on her feet and attacked.

A quick kick to his stomach interrupted the next disarming force. A fist to his eye got the next one. She managed to land a strike to his kidneys, but even with the flames spreading around them, he caught on quickly.

She couldn't halt her cry when a blazing force of power collided with her head. Not his hand, but power. Pure, unadulterated psy-energy that threw her halfway across the room and left her shaking her head to clear her mind as she jumped to her feet.

Flames shot through the room, a shield around her, as several similar forms of flames flared in different areas. She kicked out as she passed him, only to have him catch her ankle and twist.

Recovering, Carmella flipped, intending to catch his jaw with the other foot but only glancing a blow off his shoulder as a dagger shaft of pain sliced through her arch.

"Bastard," she growled as the disarming force sizzled along her foot. Any higher and she would have been down.

He attacked then. His leg swept under her feet as they touched the floor, taking them out as she twisted at the last moment, catching her weight on her hands and flipping away from him. At the same time, she sent a charge of static electricity at what she hoped was his undefended back.

"Son of a bitch!" His curse had her smiling in triumph as she crouched, holding her weight on her knee, the other leg stretched out for balance and strength, her fingers touching the floor as she instantly assessed a point of attack.

She moved as he turned, giving her a chance at his broad back. Coming to her feet in a surge of power, she aimed for it as she anticipated the expected move for him to turn and protect it.

Sheer surprise shot through her as his arms suddenly surrounded her. Flames licked over her body, then extinguished as he chuckled.

A strangled scream escaped her throat as she felt him absorbing the power she was releasing, drawing it into his own body rather than being burned by the fiery waves.

She struggled against his hold, kicking back, slamming her head into his shoulder as he lifted her off her feet, his arms tightening around hers as he kept them clamped to her sides. Chuckling in victory, he lowered his head, his lips grazing her ear.

"Winner rules *and* rides," he growled. "My rules are I ride you."

Chapter Nine

The naked lust in his voice seared her cunt. She couldn't escape his hold. No matter how she fought, wiggled or kicked back, he never faltered. She had never—not in her entire life— been so effectively overpowered. The feeling of helplessness, of utter submission, did nothing to stem the raging lust the fight had brought on. It made it worse.

"Bastard," she snarled, barely able to push the word past her lips as she fought for breath.

Flames built beneath her skin, but a second later sizzled out as the effects of a mental psychic blast suddenly paralyzed her. Her muscles went lax, despite the fury overwhelming her.

Damned psychic disarmer. She fought the numbing effects of the mental blast, determined she wouldn't give in. Not this easily. Damned cheat.

He grinned down at her as his hold shifted, one arm going behind her legs as he cradled her against his chest. She couldn't halt the shiver that raced through her body, had no way to tighten her muscles, steel her will against his effect on her. The force of the mental disarming relaxed every bone and muscle in her body while paralyzing the ability to move or to use the psychic abilities she possessed.

Disarmers were rare, but incredibly powerful.

"Now now, Carmella." He smiled down at her softly as he dropped her lightly on her bed and began undressing. "You made the rules, darling. I intend to fulfill them."

She could feel her breasts swelling as she struggled against the paralysis, willing strength back to her limbs so she could fight him, struggle, rip the clothes from his body. A fury of lust was rising inside her; where it came from she wasn't certain. But she wanted to test this man, tempt him, make him as wild for her as she was becoming for him.

"God, you're beautiful." His husky voice surprised her as he knelt, straddling her knees, his hard body rippling with muscle, the length and width of his cock causing her eyes to widen in surprise...in a tingle of feminine fear. "Tell you what. I'll make a deal with you. When I strip these pants off you, if you're not just as fucking wet as I am hard, then I'll let you be. Otherwise, you're mine, Carmella."

Torren, she whispered his name, torn between emotion and lust. She could feel him watching her, wanting her. He was aroused, his carnal excitement reaching out to her with surprising strength.

Her womb pulsed, her cunt igniting in a surge of need that left her breathless. She could feel her breasts throbbing as the nipples became tighter, harder, anticipating his touch to her body.

Her gaze flickered to the strength of his erection and she couldn't hold back a moan at the thought of him working it inside her, stretching her, possessing her. The thick root was as darkly fleshed as the rest of his body, as though he tanned in the nude. Heavily veined, the plum-shaped head throbbed erotically.

"Are you wet, Carma?" he asked softly as his hands went to the stretchy waistband of her form-fitting pants. "I bet you are. What do you think?"

She couldn't breathe, that was what she thought. His knuckles rasped against the flesh of her stomach as he began to ease the pants down her legs. She was defenseless. Unable to tighten against the excruciating pleasure of his touch, she could only lay there, feeling the shudders of pleasure work over her body as he undressed her.

Torren! The mental scream was desperate.

It's okay, baby. He won't hurt you. Despite the gentleness in his tone Carmella knew he was watching, feeling, knowing every word spoken, every touch.

She should be ashamed. Mortification should be searing her soul. Instead, her body responded with a blaze of heat that rocked her to her core.

Ryder's gaze became hooded, dark with hunger, as he stared down at her pussy. She thought he would speak, but he drew in a ragged breath instead as he moved to undress her. Her boots were unlaced and jerked from her feet along with the thick socks she wore beneath them. He pulled her pants quickly from her ankles, then moved to her upper body and worked the snug tank top over her head and arms, leaving her spread out before him.

"You're wet." He made it sound like an accusation, but his voice was hoarse with his own desire as he spread her thighs and moved between them once again.

Carmella was panting now. She could feel her juices flowing through her vagina, hot and slick, preparing her for him.

Torren. She felt lost, desperate. The pleasure searing over her body was terrifying her.

She felt him there, within her mind, sharing her pleasure in a way he never had before. The edge it gave to her own lust was razor sharp.

"I could take you now and you would love it." His hands smoothed up the outside of her thighs to her waist. "Are you tight, Carmella? Will I have to work my cock inside you or will it penetrate easily?"

She growled in desperation. She wished he would just do it. She didn't care how he achieved the penetration as long as he penetrated her.

"I bet you're as tight as a fist," he whispered as he leaned closer, his lips caressing hers. "I bet I have to work every inch inside you."

Oh yes. She shivered in anticipation as she watched him closely, slowly feeling the effects of the disarming beginning to ease. If he didn't hurry and start she was going to do it for him.

One hand moved caressingly along her side before cupping her breast slowly. His long fingers cupped the swollen mound before his thumb and forefinger moved to grip the nipple between them. Lightly. Oh God, she didn't want lightly. Carmella whimpered, the blood surging hard and fast through her veins as she fought to keep from begging.

"How do you like it, Carmella?" He licked her lips slowly, the heat of his tongue, the sensuous pleasure in the moist caress driving her insane. "Slow and easy, or hard and fast?" His fingers tightened on her nipple, pulling at it gently, working the flesh as sharp spears of pleasure drove into her womb.

She was within a second of having complete control of her body when he suddenly moved. She screamed out in anger as he flipped her to her stomach. Laughing—damn him—he was laughing as she began to struggle against him.

Carmella bucked, writhing beneath his harder, stronger body as she fought him. She was powerless. The touch of his skin, the very nature of his powers holding her own back, locking them inside her as they mixed with the surging lust screaming through her body.

"Say no, damn you." He nipped her ear as his legs tightened at her thighs, holding her still as she thrashed against him. "Say it, Carma. Now."

His cock nudged between her thighs, sliding in the thick cream her body had produced to ease his path.

She fought him as he tucked one hand beneath her, lifting her hips, holding them still as his cock kissed the entrance to her pussy.

"Do it," she nearly screamed. The heat of lust was driving her insane. Having him hold her despite her struggles, determined to take her, was nearly more than she could bear.

He chuckled, controlling her easily as she felt the head of his cock work into the entrance of her clenching cunt. Oh God. He was so big, so hot. She tightened as though to push him out, hearing his breath catch as her muscles clenched around the tip of the invader.

Her hand tightened in the blankets beneath her as she fought to find purchase against the mattress with her feet. She'd be damned if she would make it easy for him. She nearly bucked him from her for an agonizing second.

"Oh, that wasn't nice, Carma." His voice was strained. A second later he delivered a stinging smack to her rear.

Carmella stilled, whimpering at the dominant, forceful blow. Heat flared on the cheek of her ass, traveling directly to the building fire in her cunt. She stilled, panting, feeling the cream easing from her vagina as excitement blazed through her body. She had never known anything so damned hot. She had never felt so helpless and yet so feminine.

He wasn't trying to take anything she wasn't willing to give. Rather, he was taking her. Period.

His hand landed on her undefended ass again and she could only back into it, crying out as moisture covered her body and wave after wave of pleasure/pain streaked through.

He held her easily, the erotic spanking making her insane as she felt her flesh heat. From one rounded cheek to the other, his hand slapped with firm pressure that had her screaming in need.

"God, you look so pretty. Your sweet ass flushed and red." His voice was thick, filled with a dark male arousal that had her pussy creaming further.

"Do it," she cried out, shaking, needing the feel of his cock stretching her, invading her, more than she needed air to breathe.

"My rules," he whispered again, though his voice was strained, rough with his own lusts. He wasn't unaffected, his own control was stretching its limits, she thought deliriously. "God, you feel good, Carmella."

He held her hips as the head of his erection worked its way farther inside her heated pussy. She felt the muscles protesting, parting, little darts of sensual pain ravaging her system.

"Raise up." He pulled back on her hips with one hand as the other locked in her hair.

She wanted to scream out at the explicit dominance of the move as he moved her to the position he wanted her in. She was on her hands and knees, kneeling before him, her head arched back, her eyes widening in surprise at the erotic thrill of the forbidden.

She could feel Torren now. Ghostly fingers stroking her nipples as his excitement flared inside her. Oh God, it was too good.

He's taking you, Carmella, he whispered silently, erotically. *I can feel every sensation in your body. You love it. You love having him fucking you like this. Holding you down. Don't you?*

Carmella whimpered, dazed, confused by the overriding sensations building inside her as Torren made her more than aware of how much he liked the psychic voyeurism.

At the same time, Ryder pushed deeper into the quivering depths of her cunt, the width of his cock searing in the pleasure/pain of the penetration. She was so wet, so slick for him, she could hear the soft sounds of her flesh sucking him in, protesting any retreat.

"Ryder." Her back arched as the pressure on her hair intensified, drawing her back farther. "What the hell are you waiting for?"

"You." His voice was a hard growl as the short thrusts of his penis lodged him deeper inside her.

She was so full, stretched as tightly around him as a fist and glorying in each stroke of sensual heat it built in her body. She was shaking, whimpering, unable to protest anything he would want of her.

"Do you feel Torren, Carmella? Can you sense how much he likes feeling you get fucked? Getting taken?" Ryder's harsh words were followed by an abrupt powerful thrust of his hips that sent his cock burying into the very depths of her pussy.

"Yes," she screamed out in awareness, in ecstasy. It was too damned good. Too much.

She was impaled, empowered. She moaned weakly as she felt and heard both men cry out a second before Ryder lost control. His hand left her hair as both hands gripped her hips and his cock began to thrust hard and steady inside her gripping cunt.

She cried out, tortured, tormented by a pleasure that was more than she could have imagined.

She was helpless in the grip of Ryder's lust, her needs and Torren's pleasure. For the first time in Carmella's life a man had managed to best her. She felt small, helpless, feminine and in such heat she feared she would burn them all in the conflagration.

The muscles of her pussy clenched around Ryder's thrusting erection, aware of the fact that the act itself should have been humiliating, considering her lover was experiencing each sensation through his psychic connection to her.

"Yes," Ryder hissed behind her as she began to back into his thrusts, demanding more.

His hand smacked her rear again. Then again. Lost in the pleasure, in the forceful domination of the act, she could only cry out, pushing closer, demanding more.

"God, you're beautiful, Carmella." His voice was rough, almost broken. "And so fucking hot you're burning me alive."

And she didn't care. If the flames of who and what she was engulfed them all, she would have no regrets. At least, not if the building, pulsing knot of sensation in her womb was allowed freedom first.

Mindless, exacting, the pleasure built inside her with an intensity she could have never expected. Her clit was pulsing, swelling, even as her womb began to shudder with the shock of heated intensity flaring through her. She whimpered, losing herself and fighting to hold onto her sanity.

When the explosion came she knew in that one blinding instant she would never be the same. Her eyes widened as she heard Ryder encouraging her in the release. It erupted in her womb, then tightened and exploded in her pussy as she fought to hold back the flames building beneath her flesh.

Hard pulses of rapture shook her, threatening her mind and the last dregs of control as she flew apart beneath the rapid, forceful strokes inside her vagina.

She heard Ryder cry out, was aware of the hot, hot blasts of his semen deep inside her clutching cunt. She moaned instinctively though she knew she was dying, flying, coming apart in ways she could have never imagined as the pleasure disintegrated every cell in her body.

Carmella could only tremble in reaction as she felt Ryder ease her to the bed. Hard, warm arms wrapped around her, a broad chest cushioning her as her eyes closed in exhaustion so complete she didn't even think to fight it.

"Don't let me go." She shivered as she felt him pull the blanket over her.

"Never." She heard the whisper but wasn't certain if it was real or her imagination.

But his arms didn't let her go. His chest didn't move except for the soft rise and fall of his breathing. The hard body sheltering her didn't budge. She could sleep. For once in her life, Carmella felt safe.

* * * * *

Ryder felt her slide into unconsciousness as she lay in his arms like warm, firm silk. Her hair flowed over his arm, her head rested against his chest. He breathed in deeply, tired, drained from the forceful release he had experienced inside her tight pussy.

Had he ever known pleasure that intense? Had another woman touched him so completely, so effectively, as this one did? He understood Torren's warnings then. The ones that cautioned him that dominating Carmella, mastering her and her powers, wouldn't be easy because her innocence, her needs, would sink into him so completely.

She had loved the thrill of the fight. Had relished being helpless in his arms, unable to escape. She had blazed as she felt Torren experiencing the act through their link. The added pleasure, the taste of the forbidden, had almost stolen her control. Almost, but not quite. He hadn't yet taken that last measure of strength she possessed.

I told you it wouldn't be easy. Torren's thought reflected his own regret. *You'll have to be harder on her.*

Ryder snorted. *Why did I get the shit job, Torren? I have to piss her off so you can soothe her?*

It didn't bother him that this woman would belong, eventually, to both of them. What did bother him was that he would be the one to hurt her.

She'll forgive you. She'll forgive us both in the end. It's the only way to prove you can master her, Ryder. She has to know it. She knows I can't do it alone. It wouldn't have done me any good to try. The job was always yours.

Chapter Ten

Carmella had never felt the "morning after" blitz of nerves and self-consciousness. She was usually out of bed long before any partner who dared to share it, and in control of herself. Show no weakness. She had been taught that rule early in life.

When she awoke hours later, wrapped in Ryder's arms, his heat and strength enveloping her, the subsequent emotions that followed held her still, silent, as she fought to make sense of them.

Ryder's legs were tangled with hers, one hard thigh pushed high between them. Her head was pillowed on his chest, one arm draped over his waist. It felt too right, too comfortable. And yet she felt hopelessly ensnared.

Torren was silent for now. She had gone to sleep with Ryder's arms wrapped around her and Torren's psychic energy soothing her. The unusual ménage had left her uncomfortable in the face of the once-again changing relationship with Torren. It left her feeling as though she were drowning when it came to Ryder, though.

Carmella wasn't a fool. She knew next to nothing about Ryder and she wasn't about to trust her life to this man just because the sex was great. And the sex *was* great. God, was it good. Thrilling, dominant, everything she had fantasized over for years. But that didn't mean she had to lose her head. And damn, Torren wasn't making this any easier on her.

"I can hear you thinking. You're going at it a mile a minute." Ryder's deep, warm voice stirred her senses. It was a caress, a stroke of longing over emotions she had fought for so many years.

The large, graceful hands that stroked over her back stirred more than just her senses. She could feel the arousal heightening. It was unfamiliar, confusing. She didn't like being affected so easily.

"Read thoughts too, do you?" Carmella moved to roll from his embrace, but his arms tightened around her as he pulled her beneath him, bracing himself on one arm as he rose to stare down at her.

"I can hear the static," Ryder whispered, his lips lowering to hers. "Let's see if I can give you something else to worry about."

His blue eyes glittered in stark, sensual arousal. Carmella felt her breath catch in her throat as the soft mat of his close-cropped beard caressed her cheek a second before he shifted yet again and his lips covered hers.

It wasn't a hard, dominant kiss. Carmella trembled, her fingers clenched on his shoulders as his lips whispered over hers. Stroking, encouraging, asking permission in this, rather than taking.

Confusion swamped her as she stared up at Ryder. He watched her curiously, his expression tender, a glimmer of humor, of heat in his eyes as his lips nudged against hers, parting them for the soft lick of his tongue.

Her heart was racing, emotions and confusion overwhelming her senses as he touched her so gently.

"You taste good, Carmella," he whispered against her lips, the caress firing nerve endings she didn't know she had.

His lips nudged against hers again, his beard rasping pleasantly against her skin, a warm roughened caress that had her shivering in response, fighting to breathe. Her gaze was locked by his, held mesmerized, ensnared by the brilliance of his desire, the warmth in his gaze.

Carmella could feel a whimper gathering in her throat and fought it back as his tongue licked against the seam of her lips once more. It was hot, heated silk and tempting desire. She couldn't deny the need to taste any longer.

Mouth watering, heart hammering, she touched her tongue to his. Her breath slammed in her chest as he stroked it, his gaze never leaving hers. Sensation speared through Carmella's body with the force of a tidal wave, leaving her shaking in the aftermath. Her womb clenched, her pussy ached. And still he stroked, nudged, teased her with those perfect, sensual lips.

Carmella fought the need to devour the taste of his mouth. The gentle, delicate stroking of her lips was too good to let go of. She had known only a few kisses, and never one like this. It was like ambrosia of the senses.

And Ryder wasn't unaffected either. His cheeks had turned a dull red, his eyes darkening, his breathing rough and heavy as his hands flexed, one in her hair, the other against her waist.

"Damn, you're sweet." Ryder broke the kiss, resting his forehead against hers as his chest rose and fell, hard and fast. "I could eat your lips like candy, Carmella."

"More." She couldn't resist the temptation.

She reached up, tangling her hands in the long strands of his thick hair as she tilted her head.

"More?" He licked at her lips as she nudged against his—close, but not what she needed.

"Ryder. Please." She arched closer as his palm stroked from her waist to her thigh and back again, and yet he still wasn't kissing her, wasn't satisfying the building need she had for his slow hunger.

"Please what?" he whispered against her lips, staring into her eyes as she fought to keep them open.

She tried to get closer to the teasing temptation of the kiss, but he only moved back, always just a breath from the touch she needed.

"Tell me what you want, Carmella."

What did she want? She didn't know. She wanted the sweet languor that had drifted through her senses at the tenderness he had given her moments ago.

"The kiss," she answered, hungry for more. "Please kiss me like that again. Soft. Like you mean it."

Ryder paused, a glimmer of surprise in his eyes a second before heat replaced it. His head lowered, his lips nuzzling against hers, and Carmella flinched from the pleasure.

She couldn't hold back the whimper now. She couldn't still the overpowering, unfamiliar need rising in her chest like a greedy beast gasping in desperation for more.

The sweet ache traveled to her swollen breasts, her hard, inflamed nipples. It washed beneath her flesh, across her abdomen, then down to strike ruthlessly at her tender clit, her weeping pussy. Carmella twisted against him, reveling in the soft stroke of his lips and tongue as her eyes closed, too heavy, too caught in the web of arousal he was spinning around her.

"Yes, baby," he soothed, his voice hoarse, his own control sounding strained. "Feel how good it is, Carmella. How good it can be. You're burning me alive."

Carmella could feel the tautness of his body against her, the fine film of perspiration that gathered along his flesh. The knowledge that it was affecting him as greatly as it was her made the intensity deepen, strengthen.

Emotion swelled inside her. Blistering, frightening, as he cradled her body closer to his own, the light mat of dark blond hair on his chest rasping her tender breasts.

"I need more, baby," he growled, his breath panting from his chest. "Let me have you. Let me in, darlin'."

She lifted her eyelids, staring up at him as he watched her with drowsy sensuality. He was asking her? Had anyone ever asked her?

Carmella couldn't hold back her cry as her lips parted for him. What came next shocked her senses, tightened every cell in her body. His tongue pressed into her slowly, stroking over hers as his head tilted, his lips covering hers with tortured restraint.

Heat enveloped her; so sensual, so evocative, she could only tremble against the sensations moving through her. Ryder seemed no less helpless in the grip of the flood of pleasure. His body was tense, tight, as he fought the carnal demands to experience the almost innocent sweetness of the caress.

The hunger raged just beneath the surface, though. The inferno of demand was only stoked higher, hotter as they fought their bodies' demands to ease the building arousal in exchange for the agonizingly gentle caress of lips upon lips, tongues stroking, learning, tasting.

Chapter Eleven

The silky warmth of Ryder's beard caressed her cheek as his head tilted again, deepening the kiss further. Carmella's nipples were roughened by his chest hair, sending flares of sensation rioting through her body. It was the most erotic, most sensual act she had ever known in her life.

"Ambrosia," he whispered as his lips slid from hers, his beard rasping her skin as his lips trailed across her cheek, along her neck.

His hand wasn't still either. It cupped her breast, his thumb and forefinger catching a nipple firmly between them as Carmella arched into the touch. She couldn't process the complete sensory overload that gripped her body. Pleasure, hot and sweet, twisted through her womb, making her pussy weep in need.

"Ryder." She sighed his name. Needed to hear it, needed to know it was real. She fought to hold back her agonized pleas as the sensual ache built between her thighs.

"Carmella," he answered her, his tone wicked as his head lowered to lick a thrusting nipple.

Carmella jerked against him, drawing in a shattered breath as the pleasure curled around the tip before streaking to her sensitive womb and causing it to spasm with the strength of the sensation.

Before she could recover he enveloped the hard peak in the heated cavern of his mouth before his lips closed around it, drawing on it with a lazy hunger that had her hands clenching tightly in the hair close to his scalp as she fought to hold onto sanity.

She trembled, shuddered from the force of the pleasure, as she fought to sort through the emotions tormenting her now.

"This is killing me." She twisted against him as he suckled at her breast, his tongue laving it, curling around it as though her nipple was a favorite sweet treat.

"Will you die happy then?" he asked her lazily as he began to kiss a path down her perspiration-slick stomach toward the moist ache between her thighs. The heated throb there was a physical pain. The muscles of her cunt clenched in hunger as the building sensation in her clit drove her higher toward the mindless pursuit of release.

"I'll die happy," she moaned weakly as he moved down her body, parting her thighs, his fingers sifting through the tiny, desire-soaked curls that covered the mound of her cunt. "Just let me come."

"Not yet." He licked into her belly button, murmuring his appreciation of her as his lips continued their path of discovery to her aching pussy. "I want to taste you this time, Carmella. All of you."

A second after he spoke his tongue swiped through the slit of her pussy with a caress so destructive she nearly exploded. His tongue rasped the swelling pearl of her clit, sending sparks of sensation tearing through her body.

"God, Ryder." Her hips arched, her hands moving from his hair to tangle in the blankets of the bed. God forbid that in her pleasure she should pull his head away from her with her desperate grip.

It was so damned good. His tongue worked its way slowly along the soaked slit, probing, teasing, drawing yet more of the frothing cream from her pussy. Her body was tight, her flesh tingling as he ate at the tender curves of her cunt, making her insane for more. Making her insane to come. She could feel the inferno building in her womb, through her pussy, her clit. She writhed beneath his careful strokes, fighting to draw him closer to the little bud tormenting her with its need.

"Stop teasing me," she panted as he skirted around her clit once again and moved lower to lick at the juices spilling from her vagina. "I can't stand it, Ryder."

"You're so good, Carmella. So sweet and hot." He was breathing hard, fast, his voice rough with his own arousal. "I could eat this sweet pussy all day long."

She cried out as his tongue dipped into the well of her cunt, thrusting deep and hard inside her, the gentle rasp of his beard adding to the erotic sensations with an intensity that left her breathless.

He caressed her pussy as he had her lips. Smoothing over the inner folds, his tongue licking, flicking at the hungry mouth of her vagina as he tormented her into mindless lust.

Then he licked up again, circling her clit, coming closer to the swollen bead but never really giving her the relief she needed. Then his mouth covered it as he suckled it between his lips, his tongue rasping, hot, fiery strokes that destroyed her.

Her orgasm tore through her with the strength of a hurricane. Velvet waves of sensation flooded her entire being, tightening her body further, forcing a shocked scream past her lips.

Before she could recover, before the last violent vibration of release could ease, Ryder was rising between her thighs, coming over her, his lips covering hers as his cock began to ease into the tight tunnel of her cunt.

She tasted her juices on his lips. It was tangy, with just a hint of an earthy musk as his tongue speared deep into her mouth, his erection working inside her pussy.

He filled her slowly, pausing as he settled into the cradle of her thighs, the head of his cock pressing deep and hard into the very depths of her cunt. Carmella shuddered at the pleasure, the need rising inside her once again. His gentle lovemaking was more than she could bear. Never had she known such depths of arousal, such deep, all-consuming pleasure as what she felt now.

"I can't wait," he whispered, his voice rough, his lips moving over hers with an edge of desperation. "Now, Carma, I can't wait any longer."

And he took her. Carmella cried out as his cock retreated then pushed back in a hard, soul-destroying stroke. His hands gripped her thighs, raising them, pushing her legs back to open her further for his invasion as he began to fuck her with an almost mindless rhythm.

He stretched her, filled her. Each stroke was a lash of shattering pleasure inside her pussy, deep in her womb until she was begging, pleading, needing him harder, faster, needing the release building inside her with a desperation that terrified her.

Ryder was groaning into her neck now, biting her sensually, before licking over the small mark, kissing it, driving her insane with the added touch. His body flexed, bowed, his muscles rippling beneath her hands as she gripped his shoulders, holding on as he rode her through the driving need for release.

When it came, Carmella swore she was dying. Her eyes flew open, widened, her breath halting in her throat a second before a low, tremulous wail issued from her.

"Yes, Carma," he groaned. "Come around me, baby. Come for me, Carma…"

His harsh male cry joined her in the symphony of rapture. Carmella felt him tighten, his cock jerking, his hot seed spilling inside the depths of her vagina in heated spurts. And still he thrust, stroked, driving her through her orgasm as she cried out his name.

The aftermath came slowly. Shocks of pleasure echoed through Carmella's body as Ryder collapsed beside her, drawing her against his moist chest as he too fought for breath, for recovery. It was a unique feeling for her. A sense of security, of warmth, and one she wanted to hold onto for a long time to come.

And Carmella fought for understanding. Because she knew, deep in her soul, that when she lost Ryder—and she would lose him—it would destroy a part of her. He completed her. Fulfilled her. How would she ever be able to accept less again?

Chapter Twelve

I was less then? Torren. Amusement crackled in the intrusive thought as Carmella heard his voice echo through her head, answering to her last thought. He had been amazingly silent as Ryder had taken her, yet she was aware now that he had been experiencing each second of it.

I'll find you soon. She didn't tell Ryder she had made contact. For a moment she wondered if he knew how close Torren was to her thoughts at all times.

Follow Ryder. The command was harsh, uncompromising. *He'll find me. You have to do this his way, Carmella.*

Dammit, Torren. What are you getting me into? She cursed silently. *He knew you were there last night. He knows you shared it.*

Of course he does. She felt his soft sigh. *There are things you don't know, Carmella. Just be careful. Do as Ryder tells you.*

She snorted silently. She didn't think so.

"I have to shower." Carmella tried to pull herself from Ryder's arms. She needed to escape his touch so she could make sense of her own confusion, her own fears.

Something wasn't right here. Something wasn't making sense and she hated her own suspicions worse than anything, because she had a very bad feeling Torren knew a hell of a lot more than he was saying.

"Do you think I don't know he contacted you just now, Carmella?" Ryder asked her softly, his voice almost menacing. "I can feel his energy all around you. You don't have to hide it."

Confusion filled her as he watched her. His gaze speared into her, accusing and harsh.

"I don't know you. If you're who you're supposed to be, then we'll reach Torren with no problems," she whispered. "I can't just trust…"

"Don't know me?" he snarled. "If you don't know me, damn you, it's because you refuse to look."

He pushed himself from the bed, turning his back on her; displaying the most delectable male ass she had ever laid eyes on. Smooth, firm, curved so temptingly it made her hands itch to cup it. Damn. How had she missed seeing his backside? It was a fucking work of art.

"Stop staring at my ass like that." His voice was a rough, angry growl.

"Why?" She laid back on the bed, a flare of regret rushing through her as he dragged his pants up his well-muscled legs. "It's damned fine looking."

"Get a shower." He didn't comment on her appreciation of his male form. "I'll go back to my room and shower. I'll meet you back here so we can head for Torren's location."

She frowned at that, raising up on her elbows as she watched him.

"Then you do know where he is?" Which meant Torren knew the location as well. "He's not with PSI, is he?"

He paused, the muscles of his back tightening at the question as he turned from her.

"PSI hasn't taken him. Yet."

Silence stretched between them for long, tense moments. Carmella rose slowly from the bed, watching Ryder carefully.

"Where is he and how long has he been there?"

"He's several days from here, but getting there won't be easy, Carmella. You have to trust me. Implicitly."

Carmella picked up the towel she had thrown across a chair the night before and wrapped it slowly around her naked, sensitive body.

"Trust you, huh?" she asked him softly as he turned to meet her gaze. "And how am I supposed to do that? You've given me very little reason to do so."

His expression was somber, quiet. "I've given you more than I've ever given anyone else, Carmella."

She drew in a deep, hard breath. There was something about the way he said it, the regretful tone of his voice, a glimmer of longing in his eyes that threw her off balance, made her want to trust him. Made her want to give him everything, anything he needed.

She looked away from him, fighting her needs, what she saw as his needs.

"I'm sorry," she whispered finally, shaking her head. "Trust isn't just given…"

"Spare me, Carmella." He jerked his shirt on, then his boots, lacing them quickly. "We can't wait around here any longer. We leave tonight. Get ready to go."

"Ryder." She stopped him as he reached the door.

He paused, turning to her slowly. His expression was hard, fierce, his eyes glittering with suppressed anger.

"Did you know where Torren was all along?" she asked him, hating the suspicion forming in her mind.

His lips twisted in amused mockery. "I know many things, Carmella. If you would take the time to learn how to look, so would you."

He stalked from the room and, seconds later, she heard the door slam with an abrupt, sharp sound. She winced, getting the feeling he was a bit too restrained in the way he closed the door.

* * * * *

Ryder stalked down the short distance between his room and Carmella's, slamming his own door viciously behind him. Son of a bitch, this was more complicated than he had wanted it to be. He hadn't wanted to get this close to her this fast. Hell, he hadn't wanted to get this close to her period.

He shook his head at his own ignorance.

I told you she wasn't the trusting type. Torren growled the dark thought. *Dammit, of course she's suspicious.*

She had the chance to bond with me, Torren, he snarled silently. *While I took her, she could have opened up.*

It grated that she hadn't. That she had fought the final acceptance of her heart. Without it, he would never regain her trust once she learned his deception. And yet he knew that the moment she opened herself to him, she would know the lies. It was a double-edged sword and one that left him a little pissed off.

She had the same chance with me many times, Ryder. It will come when it's meant to.

Ryder could sense Torren's frustration, his impatience. The end of this debacle was nearing and he knew they both looked forward to its conclusion.

Dammit, I never thought I'd end up sharing the woman I loved, and not regretting it, Ryder finally groused silently. *Damned good thing it's you, Torren. I'd have to kill anyone else.*

Yeah. Same goes. Torren's mocking laughter had Ryder's lips kicking up in a grin.

They were both possessive bastards. They always had been. It amazed him that the thought of sharing Carmella didn't fill him with fury. But, he had known Torren was a part of her from the first touch he had made to her mind. She loved him, yet the love was incomplete. That had changed when she awoke in Ryder's arms. As though her heart, her woman's soul, had been waiting for the last piece of the puzzle to be complete. It was strange as hell.

Hurry and get her here. Torren was running out of patience. *Our time's running out and Reidel has already contacted me twice for an update. The third time she'll start making demands.*

Reidel was likely already doing so.

We'll leave within an hour or so, Ryder promised as he headed to the shower. *I want to get this completed as quickly as possible.* Carmella's frustration only fed his, made his sexual hunger for her darker, more intense.

I'll be waiting for you. Torren's impatience was beginning to affect him now. Between him and Carmella, Ryder's own emotions surged hotter, more volatile than before.

Ryder felt the psychic tie disconnect and he sighed wearily as he stepped in the shower and turned the lukewarm water on full blast. Son of a bitch, if life wasn't getting too damned complicated.

Chapter Thirteen

"Where are we headed?" Carmella closed the door to the fairly new land and water Hummer.

The new motors, created just before the fall of the psychic government fifty years before, were powered by energy-rich sun crystals. Discovered deep within the earth's surface, the crystals, once exposed to the sun for several years, trapped a reusable solar power within the many faceted chambers they held.

The cloudy gray crystals, once energized, were nearly as clear and perfect as diamonds. The discovery had rocked the energy-poor world at the time. Fossil fuels were nearly exhausted, and only the most powerful of the citizens could afford the minute amount of electricity being generated.

"We're headed south," Ryder told her quietly as he engaged the motor and pulled away from the inn. "We'll cross the river outside town and head into West Virginia. I want to stick fairly close to the coast, though it will make the trip longer than it would be going straight through."

"And we'll end up where?" she asked him patiently.

His hands tightened on the steering wheel as he glanced at her.

"Figure it out," he finally suggested with a shrug of his shoulders.

Carmella sighed heavily as she sat back in her seat. Men amazed her. He acted like a betrayed lover. What the hell did he want? She thought only women pouted when the commitment thing became an issue. And it wasn't like she actually balked at. She just wasn't willing to trusting the man without proof. Good sex did not always mean a good relationship. But, damn, if it wasn't really good sex.

"Reading minds isn't one of my talents, Ryder." Though she admitted it would sure as hell come in handy right now.

"Reading me could be," he told her, his voice clipped, cool. "If you wanted to."

She glanced at him a bit mockingly. "I can imagine the perverted things that run through your head," she grunted. "I don't need to be a mind reader for that one."

She watched his lips thin and shook her head in irritation. He was worse than a damned female virgin looking for commitment. What the hell was wrong with him? She didn't need another man complicating her life, making her question herself on a daily basis. Torren did just fine with that, and she didn't have to tolerate him as a lover anymore to boot.

Not that she had to tolerate Ryder exactly. Her cunt ached at the thought of his penetration, his thick, heavily veined cock working inside her, stretching her, filling her.

She barely controlled the shiver of arousal that would have shuddered over her body.

"Get ready." Ryder's voice was cool as he headed the Hummer out of town. "We'll be crossing the river at the old shipping docks just after dark. It could get hairy."

As he spoke, he touched one of the controls on the dash, activating the virtual screen on the windshield that was used in place of headlights. Instantly, a colorized, crisp view was reflected back at them. The windows at the side of the door darkened further, enclosing them within a cocoon of intimacy that had Carmella instantly wary.

She had been similarly enclosed in vehicles before. With Torren, and on occasion, other men they worked with. She never felt the hot, anticipatory surge of arousal that flushed her body now, though.

Carmella stared at the view screen in front of them, showing the silent streets. There were few lights as the land slowly darkened, but the heat and motion detector on the screen easily picked out the bodies lurking in what would have otherwise been shadows.

The night folk were getting ready to move in—the vigilantes, the psychic rebels, the predators of the fallen city. What had once been a thriving, profitable area had been turned into a rubble-filled hellhole.

The rebuilding had begun in what was considered the upper portion. There, the more affluent citizens had managed to keep themselves protected with guards, heavy iron fences and attack dogs. Now, the upper district was watched with jealousy and fury. Once again the less privileged were losing out to those who were protecting themselves with the added help.

The best food went to their markets. Markets that the lesser citizens were not allowed entrance to. The scraps, the decayed portions left days later, were then shipped to the downtown district. It was this lack of equality that had first given the psychic government a hold on the land. A promise to keep the land equal. To use their gifts to stop corruption and crime. It had bred the worst wars the world had ever known.

"Why aren't you using the old bridge?" she asked as the Hummer turned along one of the broken streets and bumped its way toward the old docks.

Ryder glanced over at her as he maneuvered between the collapsing buildings and deeply pitted path that had once been a wide, well-paved road.

"A heavily armed, well-equipped Hummer traveling over that bridge would be hard to miss," he told her quietly. "The bridges are watched by both PSI agents and vigilante forces, especially at night. I want to avoid as many as possible."

"There's no way to hide a damned tank, Ryder," she said. "And you're heading into one of the worst areas imaginable. West Virginia won't be easy to get through undetected."

"We'll be well protected." He didn't sound unduly concerned. "After we pass through West Virginia the going will be easier. Many of the lower states are building back faster than they are in the north. Same can be said for parts of the west. Evidently, the pioneer spirit is still alive and well."

That didn't surprise Carmella in the least. She remembered her grandmother's tales of the areas he was talking about. Strong, determined men and women would rebuild. She'd heard that in the south the psychic witch-hunts had ended decades before because most of the citizens had natural talent. Enough that they didn't outright kill unless it was needed.

"Many of Tyre's followers were said to have headed for the Keys," she said then, whispering the dreaded name as she fought the fear in her chest. "They never found Tyre's body, did they? Or the Tyrea's?"

"No. They thought the Tyrea still lived after the government fell. But no one was certain."

The Tyrea was said to have possessed the powers of all the elements. Fire, wind and rain. She had been the most feared of the psychics, and rumor was that she had also been the one who finally turned the tide in the last bitter wars.

"Do you think he's still alive?" It was her greatest fear, that he lived.

"No, I don't think he is," Ryder finally breathed out. "He was just a man, Carmella. An extra-ordinary man. A man driven insane by the manipulations to his brain. Like the rest of them, he couldn't control the fallout."

"And what of those who are his descendants?" she asked him, praying her voice was even, that the fears that filled her were hidden.

"I don't know." He glanced at her, his look intent. "There were over two hundred of the bastards to begin with. Before they were taken out, there were ten times that many. Who knows what happened or the repercussions that came of it? According to tests later, the children of the original group had no insanity, merely a lust for power. Those who didn't become rebels were marked for death by their brothers and their fathers."

The last decade of the wars had been horrendous.

"Those of Tyre's line are automatically killed, even now," she pointed out.

He sighed wearily. "That wouldn't benefit the new government in any way," he said softly. "Too many of us, especially the stronger psychics, can make that link. We can only pray that one day the horror will ease, and somehow, we'll find a middle ground again."

Carmella stared at the view screen, knowing full night would have fallen, the darkness obscuring the desperation of a land torn apart. Her grandmother had warned her, in those days before she split her apart from the two sisters Carmella had idolized. They were each of the Tyre. To survive, they would have to be separated.

She hadn't seen her sisters since she was ten. She had lost her grandmother, and she couldn't even remember her parents.

"We're moving into the dock area," Ryder warned her. "After we cross the river it should be pretty smooth."

The river was a mess. It moved with a strong current, though it was said to be much lower now than it had been more than a hundred years previously. Below the surface the possibility of disaster waited. Washouts from farther upriver had collected all manner of debris. Broken bridges, the hulking remains of sunken ships and a shattered society lay in wait.

They moved into the water slowly as Ryder activated the marine propeller at the back of the vehicle, and the airtight locks on the motor and doors. Artificial air began to instantly pump into the small confines as the Hummer became a mini motorboat moving into the murky depths of the less than secure Ohio River.

Chapter Fourteen

"Are you ever going to stop pouting?" Carmella asked him hours later as the vehicle sped across the deserted, fairly intact highway Ryder had chosen as their route to wherever the hell they were going.

She turned in her seat watching his brooding expression. It was really rather cute, she thought. He was trying not to actually pout, but his expression was one of pure male offended ego. The lowered brows, the narrowed set of his eyelids, the firm line of his mouth. He wasn't pleased with her. He had been upset ever since the confrontation at her room in the inn.

"I do not pout, Carmella." He flicked a glance at her out of the corner of his eyes as he navigated the vehicle using the virtual screen in front of him. "I'm concentrating."

She looked at the dash. The impressive display showed radar tracking, speed, and a small directional map with part of the course laid out.

"Concentrating on what?" She unclipped the belt that strapped across her shoulders and waist so she could lean more comfortably against the door and watch him. "Looks like the vehicle does most of the work."

Ryder grunted. "They cost enough. They should."

Carmella frowned at a sudden thought. "How did you manage to get a state of the art Hummer and still keep the skin on your back?" she asked him suspiciously. "Takes a lot of cash to acquire one of these babies."

"I had the funds. I wanted it." He shrugged easily.

"Why would you want it?" She didn't like the suspicions rising in her mind. "Why would you need it? Why not a smaller one?"

"You're a very suspicious woman, Carmella." A small smile tilted his lips. She felt her womb clench in response to the look of complete male confidence. It was too sexy by far.

"I'm still alive because of it." She was betting he could write the book on how to be an aggravating psychic male.

"Possibly." His smile flashed in the dim light of the vehicle. "If you want answers you're going to have to do better than that, though."

"You know, Ryder, you betray me and I won't be a happy person." She felt the need to warn him of this. "The last son of a bitch who tried to sell me out to a PSI agent is rotting somewhere in hell. I don't think you want to join him."

Actually, he was most likely nursing more than one burn scar, but she felt a tough attitude starting out might be important with Ryder.

He smiled again as he glanced at her. The rakish, devil-may-care grin immediately set her hackles up.

"I'm a disarmer, baby, and an absorber," he reminded her. "And a damned good one. Better make sure you do it right the first time you try, because if you don't, it's your ass that will pay the price."

She frowned with what she hoped was fierce severity. "What does that mean?"

"It means I'll set your ass on fire if you even attempt anything so asinine towards me again. A little harmless tussle is one thing. You try to blindside me and I'll take it seriously."

"Excuse me?" She blinked incredulously. "A harmless tussle? Is that what you call it? If you hadn't cheated with that shield someone was helping you keep around you I would have fried your ass."

"Uh huh," he agreed lazily as he flipped one of the many buttons on the middle of the steering wheel before taking his hands off it to stretch in indulgent unconcern. "You convince yourself of that, darlin', if you have to. But I know better."

"What do you mean by that?" She crossed her arms beneath her breasts, ignoring the heavy lidded look he gave the full mounds, as well as the way her nipples hardened and peaked for his appraisal.

"It means we both know better," he growled. "Take your shirt off."

She blinked at him in surprise. She felt her body tense, tighten, at the darker tone of his voice, the sexual intensity that filled it. She glanced at the display on the virtual screen. The vehicle was evidently on some sort of autopilot, because his hands were busy loosening his pants rather than steering.

Carmella was aware of the fact that somewhere along the line the subject had been diverted, but with the heat building in her cunt and the arousal clawing at her womb, she decided to tackle it later. Now, alone in the vehicle, darkness surrounded them and the time to enjoy the hard body in the seat across from her was too much to resist. She pulled her shirt off as he directed.

"God love us," he seemed to pray as her breasts were bared before his eyes. "You make me lose my mind, Carmella."

He pushed his seat farther back, reclining it fully, creating a bed of sorts. Searching the side of her seat for the lever, Carmella did the same.

Ryder raised a narrow padded extension from the floor that fitted between the two wide bucket seats, making a complete bed. Carmella raised her brows in surprise. "Nice," she murmured.

"Effective," he corrected. "Undress."

"Demanding, aren't you?" she suggested, fighting to keep the smile from her voice.

The dominance in his tone did something to her that she knew it shouldn't. It turned her on, made her weak with arousal, with need. She had never known such a level of excitement before Ryder. She feared she never would again with any other man. There was something different about Ryder. Something that reached deeper than the physical, and that terrified her more than the thought of betrayal did.

"I can be more than demanding, Carma." His voice whispered over her senses as he pulled his boots and pants off before coming to his knees.

Carmella had just pulled her own off, and turned back to him, when his hands caught in her hair and he lowered his head to take her lips in a rapacious kiss. She moaned into the blistering, demanding possession. Her mouth opened for his spearing tongue as she met it with her own. They clashed in a duel of lust and need that had her quivering in anticipation.

Ryder didn't ask for anything. He was surging with lust, his body tense with it, hungry for her response. That knowledge had her heart swelling with feelings she didn't want to recognize. And somewhere deeper, she felt a connection, a bond to him that burned hotter than mere emotion.

His kiss was like a flame itself. Hot and moist, his lips and tongue stroking, tasting, drawing her deeper into the inferno *he* was creating, rather than her. Her hands moved to his neck, releasing the small leather thong that held the thick strands back from his face. As it fell forward, she moaned in satisfaction, in pleasure. Until he drew back from her.

She bit at his lips as he pulled away, needing more. His kiss was like an elixir of passion. She was becoming addicted. But what he presented seconds later wasn't bad either.

He rose before her, his knees on the makeshift bed, his head bending low to accommodate the roof of the Hummer as his cock nudged at her lips. His moan was a rough, demanding growl as her lips opened, her mouth covering the bulging head as her tongue stroked the underside hungrily.

"Yes, baby," he whispered roughly, his fingers tunneling into her hair, clenching on the strands to hold her in place. "Your mouth is damned near as hot as your sweet cunt."

She tightened on him, suckling slowly at the turgid flesh, feeling the hard throb of lust that pulsed just under the velvety skin. She stroked the satin expanse of extra-sensitive skin just under the head of his erection, glorying in his strangled moan as she did so.

She wrapped her fingers around the thick shaft, caressing the bold shape of his cock as she sucked as much as possible into her mouth. He tasted of heat and desire, of hard hot male and aching passion and Carmella couldn't get enough of him.

She drew slowly, wickedly, on the throbbing cock, feeling the slick dampness of his pre-cum as he moaned in pleasure above her.

"Yeah," he sighed roughly as she tongued the head. "So good, Carmella. Your mouth is so damned good."

His fingers clenched tighter in her hair, his breath rasping in his throat as she licked and suckled his cock like a favorite treat. And it was. A treat she had never known. Clean, male passion—hot and rich—making her body tighten, making her heart swell with each rough groan from his chest.

He held himself still as her lips moved over him, stroking him. Her tongue whipped across the sensitive underside, probing beneath the flared head before suckling him in hard and deep once again.

"I want to come in your sweet mouth, Carmella," he groaned out explicitly, his cock throbbing in warning of the eminent release. "I want to feel you sucking the life out of me."

Carmella whimpered. She suckled harder, faster, feeling him begin to move, to fuck her mouth with quick, hard thrusts as his body tightened. His hands held her head still, steady. She could feel his gaze on her, the naked lust she knew would fill it urging her on.

Her hands stroked the now damp shaft, her lips tightening as his thrusts became harder, faster. She was starved for him. The taste of him, the heat of his ejaculation.

When it came, she moaned as deeply as he did. Hard, fierce jets of rich semen spurted into her throat as he drove his cock as deep between her lips as he dared. He trembled, biting off a rough curse, holding her head firmly in place as he shot another thick stream of his seed inside her mouth.

His muscles were bunched, his cock twitching and throbbing in her hands as he moaned her name. Carmella cried out, the sound throttled, hoarse with need as she licked the flared head clean of the last trace of his semen.

"God, you're going to kill me." He was still hard, his cock still pulsing with life as he drew back from her. "You make me crazy, Carmella."

Chapter Fifteen

Carmella lay back on the surprisingly comfortable bed the seats had made, staring up at Ryder as he moved between her thighs. Her body was sensitized, primed for his possession. The empty ache in her pussy was mind destroying, desperate. She needed him now. No preliminaries, no hesitations.

Her hips arched for just that, a cry tearing from her throat as she felt the head of his cock at the weeping entrance of her cunt. He pushed into her slowly, stretching the sensitive tissue with exquisite pleasure/pain as he worked his cock into her.

Carmella arched into him, fighting for breath as the erotic intensity rippled through her body. She was on fire for him. Her flesh heated as her need became desperate, so close to orgasm she could feel her womb tightening in preparation for it.

She stared up at Ryder, the brooding sexuality in his features shadowed by the dim lights of the virtual windshield, his blue eyes glittering with passion, his bearded face appearing rough, rakish, as he watched her vagina swallow the thick length of his cock.

It was amazing, shattering, the sensations that rocked over her body as he thrust inside her. The piercing pleasure of the slow thrusts had her panting for more as his erection widened the small entrance. Each inch was an agonizing pleasure as she waited for the moment he would fill her completely.

Her pussy ached, throbbed. The tissue, sensitive to every touch, echoed with the hard pulse of his cock as he filled her, heating her vagina, increasing the sensitivity of the inner channel.

"I could fuck you forever." His voice was a harsh, dark growl. "You're so hot and tight around my cock it's all I can do not to come inside you now."

"Did I ask you to wait?" She could barely speak for the rioting waves of pleasure washing through her body. "Oh God, Ryder, don't wait."

He slid into her to the hilt. She could feel the head of his cock throbbing, flexing in the depths of her pussy, making her insane to feel him moving, thrusting hard and deep inside her.

He bent over, one arm bracing her shoulder, the other wrapping beneath her as he covered her. His weight was a sensually heated blanket of desire. Every touch of his body along hers stroked nerve endings, awakening them to the pleasure of his touch.

Carmella could feel the blood singing through her veins, throbbing in an explicit demand for his driving thrusts. Her hands rose to his shoulders, clenching the hard muscles that tightened beneath her touch. Her head lowered, her lips caressing his chest, her tongue stroking, licking at his skin as he groaned above her.

"Leave me some control." He was panting as his hips flexed, pressing his cock deeper into the sensitive tissue that cupped his flesh.

She bit at his chest. Her teeth nipped, her tongue stroked as he moaned in defeat. He began to move in long, slow thrusts that had her crying out in clawing hunger. She had never known passion so intense, lust so hot and all consuming.

"Do it," she cried out breathlessly, her hips writhing beneath him as he stroked slowly into her body. "Please, Ryder, fuck me."

One broad hand tunneled into her hair, the other gripping her hips tightly to hold her in place as he drove her insane with the deep, slow strokes into her pussy. She could feel her moisture there gathering, frothing, creaming with the blistering carnal hunger flaying her body.

"God, you're so soft and tight," he whispered at her ear, his breathing hard and quick. "I don't want to come, Carmella. I don't want to ever stop fucking you."

She lifted her legs, clamping them around his waist as he rode her with a leisurely pace. It wasn't enough. It was driving her crazy, making her scream, her voice hoarse with the arousal pounding through her veins.

Their flesh was slick with the effects of the lust burning through their systems, the smell of sex, the sound of suckling female tissue and hard driving male filling the interior of the vehicle.

"If you don't move your ass, I'm going to burn blisters on it." She tried to scream her outrage that he was deliberately, cruelly taunting her, but the words only came out as a gasping plea.

She tightened the muscles of her cunt around his invading erection, feeling her flesh ripple around him as he groaned hard and deep in her ear. It was effective. He began to move harder, faster, holding her still beneath him as the pleasure intensified to a level bordering pain.

Carmella gasped for breath, feeling the surging sensations gathering in her womb, tightening it as her pussy clenched around Ryder's thrusting cock. Slowly, every cell in her body became taut, sensitized, hot…

Her eyes flew open as the surging orgasm exploded low in her stomach and began to rush through her body. Her wailing cry was forced from her throat, the hard pulse of her release gushing through her cunt. Ryder moaned thickly, his body stiffening, his own climax tearing through his body.

It felt never-ending. Rippling and surging, a tidal wave of intensity that swept past her control, her shields and her blocks, leaving her open. Aware. Broken.

He had betrayed her. In that one blinding moment when the heart and soul opened, connecting with Ryder's, Carmella knew a sweeping, all consuming rush of fury and pain. The son of a bitch had betrayed her.

The orgasm rushing through her had barely stilled before fire erupted from her hands, sweeping down his back only to be absorbed just as quickly by his body.

Hard hands slammed her wrists to the makeshift bed as she screamed out her fury, twisting beneath him, desperate to be released.

"You bastards!" She cursed him and Torren together. "You son of a bitch bastards, I'll kill you."

Carmella stared up at Ryder's hard, savage features as he held her down easily. His eyes were narrowed, his expression calm, stern. His cock was still lodged inside her, hot and thick, despite his release.

"You have lousy timing," he told her softly as she felt bands of power encircling her body, holding her still, defenseless, as he moved back from her body.

"Fucking PSI agent." She shook her head as bitterness overwhelmed her. "You and Torren both. You betrayed me, Ryder."

She struggled against the bonds, hating herself for trusting him or Torren, but hating them more. She fought her tears. Damn them, she would not cry over either of them.

"Amazing how you can see only those things you want to see," he remarked as he got dressed.

The Hummer moved along the road, growing steadily closer to their destination, to Torren. She knew now why her commander had been so damned hard to find, why he had sent Ryder to her. The elaborate plot made her almost as sick as the truth she had glimpsed in Ryder's soul.

The unique shield that all Fyrebrands possessed had only one key. There was one way to see into her soul, into the part of her that could never lie, even to herself. That key was love. Only a true disarmer would reach the lock and use that emotion to open the doors into her heart. But in doing so, she had glimpsed his as well. What she saw destroyed her.

He hadn't just betrayed her. She ignored the love staring her in the face, the need and the dreams. She had seen the betrayal, the truth of why he had come for her. As judge and jury. As the last step between her and death. She had seen that her secret was no longer safe, even from herself. And she knew, in one blinding second, that none of it mattered without trust. And Ryder didn't trust her.

Chapter Sixteen

"The Tyrea was an elemental. The strongest ever known with the power to pull together all the forces of the elements with just a thought."

Carmella tried to ignore him hours later, but there was no stopping the sound of his voice. "Tyre could control the minds of men, with the secondary elemental powers as well as disarming talents. He was the most powerful man to ever live. So far, of all the little bastards he planted behind the Tyrea's back, only a few have been blessed with both power and honor. We couldn't take the chance that you were one of the few."

As an explanation, it sucked. He had played her. Every moment they had been together he had been lying to her, drawing her in, easing her, reassuring her until the moment her soul accepted what her mind didn't want to see, and opened for him. Love. She had fallen in love with him in one blinding instant, and in the next everything inside her had shattered.

Her insides felt raw, ripped away by the stark, blinding truth of what she had seen in his heart and the pain of knowing it existed. God, had she ever hurt so badly in her life? Had she ever known such desolation within her own soul? Even as the rage had built inside her, the flames erupting from her hands, she had pulled back on the power, trying to control it, to extinguish it. Even though a part of her relished the overriding satisfaction of knowing that at least for an instant, she had caused him pain as well.

"I'm not in the mood for a history lesson, Ryder. This has nothing to do with Tyre and everything to do with you being a jackass. Get over it. I will."

She wouldn't look at him as he drove the vehicle, concentrating instead on the visual display screen as she anticipated facing Torren as well. She had glimpsed his expression earlier. His face was lined, heavy with regret as he watched her. But she knew he didn't regret his actions. It was what she had done that he regretted. What he had seen inside her soul that ate at him. What had he seen that would make him lock her in invisible chains, make him watch her with such anger?

She wouldn't cry, she promised herself as she stared back at him. She would not let him see the tears that were damned near choking her right now. Her stomach was roiling with the pain, her heart ready to explode with it. Son of a bitch, it was just her luck to fall in love with a PSI agent. She thought she was smarter than that; thought her powers would be enough to protect her. She had been wrong.

It was the curse of Fyrebrands. Of the few documented, each had told of the moment their lovers had touched their souls. There were no secrets, no apprehensions between such couples. They were bonded.

It was said it had been the way of Tyre and the Tyrea. That before Tyre convinced himself he was a god, he had first been a man, and his soul had touched the Tyrea's. Carmella's great-grandmother. But even as great as that love had been, it had done nothing to stem the evil inside Tyre.

"I wasn't a jackass, Carmella," he growled. Satisfaction surged through her as she heard the anger growing in his voice. "I let you see the truth. You chose to overlook my feelings for you. All you could see was the deceit."

"Are you fucking crazy?" It was a rhetorical question. Of course he was crazy, he was demonstrating that now. "You think this is about your job with PSI? Do you think I was so stupid that I didn't already suspect, Ryder? Do you think you're the only PSI agent to have ever come after me?"

He lowered his brows into a brooding frown, a question in his eyes that he refused to voice. She smiled slowly, mockingly, as she watched his jaw bunch with fury.

He, of course, wanted to know if she had fucked any of the agents sent out after her. Let him wonder. The mental exercise would do him good.

"You're a descendent of Tyre Leyton and his lover, the Tyrea," he said softly. "You couldn't be trusted without testing, Carmella."

"And did I pass your little test, Ryder?" she asked him softly. "When I let you into my soul did you see the monster you expected to see?"

He didn't show surprise, but he would be too good for that. At least he was now aware that she knew how he saw her. A monster. There, lurking behind his deceit, what he thought was his love for her, had been the twisting, deformed image he thought resided inside her. The image of what he expected to see, even after she had opened herself to him, had nearly destroyed her. He had never believed in her, not completely. He had never thought she was honorable or innocent of Tyre's crimes, and she feared, after seeing the strength of that shadow, that he never would.

"I never thought you were a monster, Carmella." He shook his head, though he avoided her gaze.

She wedged herself uncomfortably into the corner of the seat watching him, her insides burning with pain as she tried to come to grips with everything she had lost in the space of a few, fragile seconds.

"You're such a self-righteous bastard. You and Torren both," she breathed out, resigned. "Have you managed to convince yourself that I deserve to die now? Another monster put away, isn't that how it works, Ryder?"

"Goddammit, Carmella, where do you come up with this crap?" He was fuming, watching her with such brooding anger that it set off a firestorm of fury inside her. He had no right to be furious with her. No right to hold her in chains or in shields. She hadn't lied to him. He had lied to her.

"How did it feel fucking a monster, Ryder?" she snarled, baring her teeth as she fought her pain. "Was the novelty worth it? Do we fuck different than normal women?"

She could feel Torren's presence strengthening around her and fought to keep a shield between her and the man she had once welcomed into her heart and her mind. He had lied to her as well, and she couldn't forget it.

"I won't continue this argument with you." Ryder shook his head, his expression troubled. She liked that. Liked seeing the sudden, internal conflict in his gaze.

"What argument, Ryder? Am I proclaiming my innocence? I want to cut your fucking heart from your chest, I'm not denying it."

"Stop it, Carmella." He breathed in heavily.

"Do you think these chains will stop me, Ryder?" She lifted her hands, the invisible bands of energy cutting a wound in her soul that she feared would never heal. "Do you think you're not the first bastard to try to restrain me?"

"Dammit, Carmella, I just want you to cool off," he snapped. "You're in no frame of mind to follow me and most likely more than capable of attacking. Give yourself time to cool off."

"You son of a bitch, you put me in chains," she screamed, her fury overwhelming her. "You fucking lied to me and on top of it all you didn't even have the decency to try to believe in me. And you expect me not to be angry?"

"You washed my fucking back in flames, Carmella," he yelled back at her. "I'm not in the mood to be roasted tonight, baby."

"You deserved it." She moved forward until they were nearly nose-to-nose. "And don't fool yourself, moron. If I wanted you roasted you would be toast now, not sitting there with the little added power you managed to absorb. You were just waiting on an excuse, just waiting to lock me down and to convince yourself how dangerous I was. The blood of Tyre," she snarled. "A monster, just like he was."

She watched his face closely, his gaze becoming cool, shuttered.

"Get some rest." His voice was perfectly pitched, even and firm. "We have a long ride ahead of us."

Carmella threw herself back in the seat, staring at him with a sneer on her lips. "You won't keep me restrained much longer, Ryder."

"You're disarmed for the moment, Carmella. Try using your powers and you'll only hurt yourself."

She smiled. A tight sarcastic curve of her lips that she noticed had him frowning in suspicion. "I have never depended solely on my powers, Ryder. I will get out of these chains, and when I do, you will never get the chance to get them back on me."

He stared at her for a long, tense moment before he sighed deeply and turned away from her. Carmella drew in a hard breath as she pushed back the pain, the tears. It didn't help to cry. Tears solved nothing. She laid her head against the side of the Hummer and closed her eyes.

Ryder's shield was reinforced with her own. She wasn't powerless, no matter what he thought. He was stronger; she had no doubt. His disarming abilities gave him an edge she couldn't fight with her gifts, but there were times when stealth and cunning far exceeded physical power. Times when a woman just had to show a man how stupid he was, whether she enjoyed the exercise or not. Ryder was about to learn.

* * * * *

Fix it. Or else. Ryder breathed in deeply as Torren's thoughts smacked into his brain with the force of a fist against his head. He nearly swayed with the pain and the shock of having his shield overtaken so easily. He was stronger than Ryder had thought.

Bad move, Torren. Never show your greatest strength. Remember? Torren had pounded it into his brain years before.

Let me past that shield, Ryder. You're killing her. Fury, a friend's pain, it all echoed in the thought.

Ryder glanced back at Carmella again. She looked so small, huddled in the corner of the seat, her eyes closed, her face pale.

I'm not controlling that shield, Torren. He ached with that knowledge. *The only shield I have around her is the one controlling her powers. Carmella is blocking herself.*

Torren's shock, his worry, filled Ryder's brain. Ryder could feel the other man gathering his strength, and sending himself back toward Carmella. Psychic frustration filled the interior of the Hummer.

Goddammit! I warned you. Torren's thought was cold, bitter. *What the hell did you do to her, Ryder? What did she see in your soul?*

Ryder frowned. Love. His deception. What more could she have seen?

There had to be more. Torren's force was nearly demonic in its anger, its fear. *She's known deception before. She would have seen the truth of your heart, whatever it was. What was it?*

You're making excuses for her, Torren. His own thoughts were bleak. *She struck out in anger alone. Because I deceived her. Because you did. She released her power because of that anger, just as Tyre did. The world had yet to heal from that wound.*

There was silence. A complete numbing silence as he felt Torren stepping out of his thoughts slowly, shock resounding around him. What had he said to so surprise the man who had once sworn he could never be surprised?

You're a fool. Torren was in no way pleased. Not that Ryder cared, but still... *Now fix it. Fix it, or you'll deal with me.*

The other man was gone as quickly as he had invaded Ryder's mind. He sighed deeply, tiredly. He'd be damned if he knew what to do now.

Fix it, he grunted silently. Torren was strong...stronger perhaps than Ryder had suspected. But no amount of strength could just fix this.

Chapter Seventeen

They arrived at Torren's location two days later. The beach house was sheltered behind large dunes and swaying palms, its weathered outer planks bleached by salt and wind.

The sturdy, one-story house looked inviting, comfortable, but Carmella was not relaxed. The Hummer came to a stop outside the opened front door as Ryder turned from her, his gaze going to her wrists and ankles. A surge of power enfolded the invisible shackles and within seconds they had fallen to the floor.

Time's almost up, she thought to herself a bit sadly as Ryder exited the vehicle before opening the door for her to step out as well.

"Torren's here?" The shield she had placed around herself kept her from sensing the psychic path she often used with her commander.

"Come in and find out." He gripped her arm as he led her into the beach house.

And there stood Torren. Just inside the large living room, watching their entrance with hooded hazel eyes. His expression was as calm and tranquil as she had ever seen it, but she knew those eyes. He was seething with anger. With her, or with Ryder?

"Try both," he answered her silent thought with a whiplash of harsh fury.

And she didn't really give a damn. He was as handsome as ever. His flowing, dark brown hair rippling to the middle of his shoulders, his hard muscular body standing straight and tall, as perfect and confident as always. Seeing it—seeing him—only made the fury burn hotter inside her.

She stalked across the room, and came face to face with the man who had saved her life and her soul more than once.

She smiled up at him, baring her teeth as he frowned. Before he could flinch she had clenched her fist and drove it with all her remaining strength into the side of his face.

Torren stumbled back, his eyes rounding first in surprise then narrowing furiously as he stared down at her.

"I deserved that," he growled. "But you deserve this."

Before she could evade him, one hand locked in her hair, the other at her hip as he jerked her to him, his lips grinding down on hers. Carmella could only whimper as she struggled against him. His tongue plunged into her mouth, staking his claim on her senses and her mind as he held her tight against his hard body.

The length of his cock seared her through the confining shields of their clothing. His hard hands were a brand at her hip and her head, his passion a blazing conqueror as he tried to possess her soul with the kiss.

Carmella quaked inside. She thought she could resist him. Thought her love for Ryder would make her immune. Unfortunately, in that instant, she realized that Torren, too, had the key to her soul. He always had.

She whimpered in distress. There was no escape. Her hands tightened on his shoulders as she fought the response she was giving him. She was trapped between the two men, heart, body and soul.

"Not trapped, Carmella. Protected. Always protected." Ryder whispered at her back, his hands smoothing along the curves of her rear as his lips stroked over her bare shoulder.

Protected? They had betrayed her. Never trusted her. She moaned into the kiss, fighting them and herself as emotion and sensation overwhelmed her.

She had fought for so long. Fighting was a necessary part of her, but in this instance, her body refused to draw the necessary strength to do anything but revel in each caress it was being given.

Finally, when she thought she would pass out from the fiery heat running rampant between the three of them, Torren lifted his head. He stared down at her, his eyes dark, his expression carnal.

"Now, we can talk. You hit me again, Carmella, and I'll paddle your ass."

Carmella jerked away from the two of them, stalking to the other side of the room before she turned back to face them.

"What is this fascination you two have with spanking me?"

She didn't like the sudden dark intensity that swept over their expressions.

"Oh, you'd like it. Eventually," Ryder promised her, his smile a bit too ruthless to suit her.

She snarled back at him. "Don't bet on getting the chance to try it. I've had my fill of lies from both of you. Now tell me what the hell is going on here or I'm gone."

She watched them, amazed at the differences between the two men, and yet, how much they were alike. Carmella blinked, suddenly realizing how much she cared for each man. How much she loved them, both.

Torren, for obvious reasons. They had been lovers as well as friends. He had covered her back, protected her, helped her survive. Ryder had just taken her over. Her heart had given her no choice when he had shown her both the dominance and the gentleness he held for her. But he didn't trust her. Torren couldn't trust her. Not really. Not if he had set this plan up to begin with.

"Carmella." Torren breathed in deeply. "I know you're angry. Very angry. And I know little of this is making sense to you right now."

"Now there's an understatement," she snapped as she crossed her arms over her breasts.

"Do you trust me, Carmella?" he asked her, his voice soft, reflective.

Did she? She stared back at him, seeing the softness in his hazel eyes, seeing the man she had loved, in so many ways, for so long.

"You know I do, Torren. I wouldn't be here if I didn't." She would have run as hard and as fast as her legs would have carried her the moment she realized Ryder was a PSI agent if she hadn't trusted him.

Ryder crossed his arms over his chest as he watched them, his gaze soft. She didn't want him soft. She wanted him angry. She wanted them all angry so she could rid herself of the fury rushing through her.

"How far do you trust me?" Torren asked her.

Carmella could feel her heart speeding up in her chest at his tone of voice. It was hot, sexual. A tone he had used only rarely with her, even while they had been lovers.

She swallowed tightly, her gaze swinging between the two of them. Torren and Ryder both would be aware of her conflicting emotions right now. Her inability to decide which man held more of her heart. Which she could bear letting go? From the looks of them, neither intended to let her go.

"Right now, only about as far as I can see you," she snorted. "Either of you, if you want the truth."

"You know I've studied the advanced psychic phenomena," Torren told her softly. "The old records, and many of my own suspicions."

She nodded slowly. She was well aware of that.

"Fyrebrands are often unique in many ways." He shrugged. "Their passions are hotter, more tempestuous, requiring a greater amount of control from the person possessing them."

"I'm aware of your theories, Torren." She had never bothered to worry overmuch about them until now.

"The personal control eventually weakens a person without an outlet. It breaks down. It breeds a loss of emotion, a loss of joy." He speared her with a hard, intense look. "I've noticed both in you."

"I'm loyal." She braced herself for whatever came next. "You've never had reason to question that, Torren."

"And I don't question it now." Command, stern and unflinching, filled his voice. "Your soul touched Ryder's, but you held back. Just as you did with me before all this began. You kept your control rather than giving it to him. That was what caused the shadows of distrust that you saw."

She shot Ryder a hateful look. "What have you convinced him of?" she snapped furiously. "You didn't trust me."

"You didn't trust me." He shrugged lazily. "If you had, you would have first, been honest with me. Second, you would not have shadowed that inner part of yourself, Carmella. The part that reveals everything you are."

She was breathing hard and fast now, looking between the two men who each held a part of her soul. Both men too handsome, too damned sexual. Being caught between them, even like this, was too intense for her to handle.

"I'm not one of your experiments." She turned on Torren then, knowledge flooding her mind. They wanted her to feel helpless. Caught between them. Controlled. Bound to them both.

"Unfortunately, you are." Ryder's voice was a rough, sexual caress across her nerve endings. "Your life depends on it, Carmella. I won't let you throw it away because of stubbornness."

She fought to still her breathing, to control the anger beginning to flood her.

"And exactly how does my life depend on whatever the hell you two are hatching up?" She looked from one to the other, seeing more than just concern, more than just desire.

"When you go in with us for testing at PSI headquarters, Carmella, there will be no hiding who and what you are.

Without evidence of control, you'll be signing your own death sentence. You know that."

She fought the tremble that threatened to shake her body. "Then I won't go in. I have no intention of going in." She turned to Torren, trembling now as she saw the truth on his face. "What have you done, Torren?"

"Wrong." Ryder's voice rose at her declaration. "You're mine too, Carmella. Mine and Torren's. You know it, and I know it. I won't let you take the easy way out on this. Goddammit it. PSI headquarters sent me out to look for you. They know you exist."

She could feel the blood draining from her face. They knew who she was. They knew where she was. How? Could they be right about her shields, her controls? Or had Torren betrayed her? She watched him, felt him, but couldn't believe he would do so.

"Ryder can disarm you, as you've seen, and what powers he can't absorb, I can. But if you give up control, together we can amplify those powers as well as still the unprovoked anger that sometimes fills you, Carmella. But we can't do that unless you open to us completely. You have to open to us willingly."

Us? She screamed the thought at Torren. Her gaze swung between the two men, realizing...knowing, that neither man planned to let her go. She wouldn't be a lover to one; she would love two.

Us, Carmella. Ryder's response was a sensual caress through her mind, leaving her trembling in the aftermath.

"How?" She ran her fingers through her hair in desperation. "For God's sake, Torren. He has never trusted me. Ever."

"Because you haven't let him in. You haven't truly let either of us in," Torren snapped. "You are not normal, Carmella, no matter how much you wish you were. Neither are we. The very talents that make you different make your emotional processes more difficult. We will complete you. To do that, we need you just as you need us. Ryder opened himself completely to you, just as I did. It's the reason you can feel my honesty and see his suspicions, otherwise you would have never seen those shadows, which rose when you blocked him."

"No..." It couldn't be that easy.

"I was there!" Torren yelled back at her, furious now. "Do you understand me, Carmella? I was there. Do you think I would have trusted your mind to anyone without observing it? Do you actually believe I wasn't there when you gave him the last part of your heart that I could never seem to hold?"

Her eyes widened, equal parts fury and arousal filling her in one blinding instant. He had been there? Watching? In her mind... She swallowed tightly, her gaze moving slowly to Ryder. She had fought to keep Torren blocked during their trip to his location. Had fought to try to make sense of her needs for both men, when she knew—or thought she knew—she could have only one.

"You're too complacent," Ryder told her softly. "You aren't blocking nearly as well as you should, and you're getting careless. Your frustration level is too high, Carmella. It affects your objectivity and your performance. It's too high, because you refuse to submit to what you know you want."

She laughed. She couldn't help it. In their faces, more amused than really offended, she laughed at both of them. They intended to share her. There had never been a danger of losing either man. The whole elaborate plot was to cement Ryder's hold on her before they slapped her with the truth.

"You're joking? Right? You're turning this into something sexual. Something that you can so obviously help me with," she sneered. "What do you have in mind, Ryder? Double-teaming me? Let's see, I've already fucked Torren." She shot him a distasteful look. "Not that it ever did me much good. And I'm not real pleased with you at the moment, either."

"Didn't do you much good?" Torren kept his voice soft, a warning in and of itself. "Carmella, it's not like you to lie, baby.

You forget; I'm a seer, among other things. I knew what was coming. I knew who was coming. I wasn't about to screw it up by giving you the illusion that you could get anywhere else, what you will only get one way."

Carmella bit her lip. She didn't like the sharp contraction that fisted her womb as he spoke. She sure as hell didn't like the way her juices seemed to flood her pussy.

She turned to Ryder as he moved, walking to her slowly, his expression filled with determination.

"You said you loved me," she whispered. "This isn't love. From either of you."

"Isn't it?" His expression turned immeasurably gentle as he reached her, his hand rising to touch her face. "Does love have a definition, Carmella? Isn't it acceptance, complete acceptance of the one you love? Complete protection and the fulfillment of their needs? No matter those needs? You need what we have to offer. Not just for yourself, but for us as well."

Chapter Eighteen

Carmella fought to breathe just as hard as she fought the heat tingling under her skin. Her muscles tightened as the sensations gathered in the pit of her stomach, working their way over her body.

She looked at Torren, seeing the heat in his gaze, the affection, his concern.

"You don't love me." She shook her head as she turned back to Ryder. "Neither of you can possibly love me. This doesn't make sense."

Confusion didn't sit well with her. The morass of longings, fantasies and desires that had always tormented her had been something she had never thought to actually experience. She could have, at any given time, but her fear of allowing herself that greatest fantasy had always held her back. Now, faced with the only two men she had ever cared for, Carmella was terrified.

"Carmella, I love you beyond life. I did months ago, when I first touched your mind, first entered your fantasies. In all those fantasies, Torren lingered just out of view. You didn't even realize yourself what you were doing. For a while, I didn't realize what you needed."

She shook her head desperately, fighting him, fighting herself. She flinched as Torren came closer. His eyes, usually a cool, tranquil hazel, now glittered with darker highlights as he watched her.

"He holds your woman's soul," he whispered as Ryder's hands moved to the hem of her blouse. "But you and I both know, Carmella, that I too hold a part of your heart."

"No." She wanted to jerk away from them as she felt the heat intensifying under her skin. "You don't understand. It was a just fantasy."

Her nipples were so hard, so filled with longing, she felt as though they would burst as the cloth of her shirt raked over them. Torren gripped her wrists, raising them a second before his mouth covered one swollen peak.

"Oh God." Her knees weakened. Her gaze flew to Ryder. He pulled the shirt up her arms, his hand gripping her wrists as Torren released them. All the while, he watched the other man suckle the smooth, supple flesh.

His eyes darkened in arousal and when he looked at her, they were filled with approval.

"Every Fyrebrand has her weakness," he whispered as he dropped her shirt to the floor. "This is yours, Carmella. And I give it to you, whenever you want it, however you want it."

As he finished speaking, Torren gripped her nipple between his teeth, exerting just enough pressure to leave her gasping on the edge of pain as his tongue flicked over the little tip with sensuous delight. Carmella's eyes widened at the sensations, a breathless scream issuing from her throat as her body jerked, shuddered in the embrace of the two men.

"Easy, Carmella." Ryder's lips brushed hers, the warm rasp of his beard causing her to whimper at the added sensation. "I want you to let go. Just let go. Let me and Torren take care of you, baby. It's okay."

Carmella shook her head, though she couldn't control her gasp as Torren began to suckle greedily at her flesh once more. She had to have control. She couldn't lose it. She couldn't take the chance. To relinquish it to either of them meant the power surging through her body—flames erupting, scorching her—would then be their responsibility to tame. Her control, her need to control, was too much a part of her.

"Please, Ryder." Tears welled in her eyes as she stared back at him. "I can't do this."

"You don't have a choice." For all its gentleness, his voice was firm. "When I return to the agency with you, Carmella, there will be no doubt in anyone's mind that you have bonded with both of us. That your powers are controlled. That I control that part of you. That you are no danger to them or to anyone else. I will not risk your life."

He didn't give her time to answer. He took her lips in a kiss that effectively stilled any other argument. Not that she would have argued further. Torren's hands were pushing the waistband of her pants over her hips, Ryder's tongue was devouring hers, and all Carmella could do was hold on and pray she could at least hold a measure of her restraint close. Dear God, she didn't want to hurt them.

She had already burned Ryder in her fury. What was she capable of with no control whatsoever?

"Shush your fears, baby," Ryder whispered against her lips. "I'll take care of you this time. I promise. Just trust me. Me and Torren. We won't let anything happen."

Cool air chilled her tender nipple as Torren released it, moving back as Ryder picked her up in his arms. Carmella held onto him, caught in the dizzying knowledge of what was to come. Torren knew her powers. He wouldn't falter. Surely he wouldn't. He never had. And Ryder knew the damage she could cause. He could disarm her. He could keep her from hurting any of them. Couldn't he?

She whimpered as they laid her on the bed, quickly removing her boots and her clothing before removing their own. Her head was whirling with the knowledge of what was coming. Fears and desires, fantasies and reality, collided with such chaos that she couldn't seem to find an anchor to hold her tumultuous emotions stable.

She could feel her flesh prickling with power, heating her, intensifying the sensations of Ryder and Torren's hands smoothing over her body. Ryder came up beside her, one arm going under her shoulders as he lifted her into his embrace.

"I'm just going to hold you, baby," he whispered at her ear as he reclined against the headboard, pulling Carmella against his chest as Torren eased her legs apart. "Just hold you, and show you that you have nothing to fear."

Nothing to fear? She could feel the lust scorching her insides, flooding her pussy. It was all she could do to hold back her cries as she watched Torren lower himself between her thighs while he gazed at her cunt in hungry fascination. Torren loved driving her insane with his mouth when they had been lovers. She could have handled it. She had before. But before, she hadn't had Ryder's back bracing hers, his hands cupping her breasts, his fingers tweaking her nipples as he whispered encouragement in her ear.

"Easy, baby," Ryder soothed her as Torren pushed his hands under her rear, lifting her to his mouth. "Slow and easy. You like that, don't you?"

His fingers tightened on the hard points of her breasts as Torren's tongue distended and began a slow, lazy swipe up her soaking slit.

She felt her scalp prickle in warning. The flames were building in her mind, terrifying her.

"No. No, please..." She thrashed her head against Ryder's chest, fighting it, terrified of the consequences.

"Trust me, Carmella," Ryder whispered at her ear. "You have to trust me, baby. Let me have the heat. I can take it. Give it to me, Carma."

Torren's lips covered her clit, his tongue stroking around it, never touching it, causing it to swell further as the pressure echoed through her body. Each caress felt deliberately timed, slow and intense, provoking the ultimate pleasure.

Carmella tightened fighting the sensations, the pleasure. She had never given control of herself or her powers to another living person. To do so now terrified her. They could use her. Could destroy her.

"Carmella." Ryder's voice was stern, the sound of it causing her pussy to clench in need.

Torren moved one hand from beneath her buttocks, sliding slowly along her flesh until it stopped between her thighs. She shuddered.

"Torren... Please..." She was panting now, a fine film of perspiration coating her body as she felt his fingers stop at the entrance to her greedy cunt. "Torren, I can't do this..."

He moaned against her clit. Carmella couldn't stop the strangled scream that escaped her throat as she arched closer to his mouth. Oh God, it was too good. He was destroying her with his touch. She lowered her hands, trying to push him away, only to have Ryder catch her wrists again and stretch them behind her head as he moved her quickly.

Before she could do more than cry out, he had her on her knees as Torren turned on his back, pushing her thighs wide, his tongue spearing hard and fast inside the soaked depths of her cunt. Pleasure spasmed through her womb, raced through her bloodstream.

Torren's body was stretched out before her as Ryder knelt beside her, holding her arms behind her back, staring down at her with an expression of savage sensuality.

She struggled against his grip, then screamed out as Torren's hand landed heavily on her buttock. Her entire body stilled an instant before she felt the flames beginning to rise from her skin.

"God, no!" she screamed out, trying to move away from Ryder, terrified of what would happen now.

Torren wouldn't stop, wouldn't allow her to control her response. He slapped her ass again, then did the unthinkable. His fingers parted the cheeks of her rear, one running down the cleft until it speared the tiny little hole waiting below. His finger slid in deep, hard, pushing through the sensitive tissue, stretching her, opening her.

"Torren." She tried to scream his name, but her wail was one of such pleasure it shocked her own ears.

Torren's tongue was a demon of lust. Spearing into her sensitive cunt, thrusting through the thick juices, lapping at her greedily as he slid his finger easily into her back hole.

"Beautiful, baby." Ryder held her steady as his head lowered to lap at her nipples. His teeth raked them, his lips covered them, suckling deeply as Torren continued to fuck her tormented pussy with his wicked tongue.

She was shaking, sweat dripping from her body, as she held onto her control with the thinnest of threads.

"Let go, Carmella," Ryder whispered from her breast. "Give it to me, baby. Let go."

She shook her head, gasping for breath. A hand landed on her buttock again. She wasn't certain whose. The little sting only deepened the pleasure of Torren's tongue thrusting rapidly into her spasming pussy, and Ryder's little nips at her sensitive nipples.

She couldn't hold on. She knew she couldn't.

When she felt them moving her again, she could only whimper, her body following their commands easily as her mind scrambled for balance. There was none. Before she could do more than scream his name, Ryder had stretched out on the bed as Torren moved up beside her, helping her to straddle the other man's body. Carmella stared into his dark eyes as he held her hips down, encouraging her darkly as Ryder's cock began to sink slowly into the tormented depths of her cunt.

"Torren, please…" Her voice was a ragged plea as her body began to greedily suck Ryder's thick cock into it. "I'm scared."

Her head was resting on Torren's chest as he knelt beside her, his arms supporting her as Ryder began to work his erection inside her. Too much. Too good. She was crying, tears falling slowly down her cheeks as the pleasure became unbearable and the heat inside her began rising once again.

"You're so tight," Torren whispered in her ear. "I remember how tight your sweet pussy is, Carmella. I know how he's stretching it. How good it's making you feel. When he's in—all the way in—your sweet cunt gloving every inch of his cock, I'm going to take your ass. I'm going to take it, Carmella, and you're going to love it."

Torren's hand slid down her back, his finger sliding inside the little hole once again as Ryder groaned out beneath her. She bucked, driving Ryder further inside her as she fought for more of the hot pressure from Torren's finger.

It was too much. She needed it too much. She bent over Ryder's body, going into the arms that opened for her, then enfolded her, screaming out against Ryder's chest as his cock and Torren's finger stole her sanity. She was lost. Adrift. She could do nothing now but trust them to do what was best. To protect her and themselves.

She was only vaguely aware of Torren moving. The feel of cool lubricating gel being worked inside her anus. Long, broad fingers stretching her, preparing her, as Ryder lodged every inch of his cock deep inside her.

Carmella whimpered, awaiting the final invasion. The ecstatic pain she knew would be more than her mind could control. She turned her head on Ryder's shoulder, her tears wetting his flesh.

"Please," she whispered as she felt Torren move behind her, the head of his cock pressing against her rear entrance. "Please, don't let me hurt you."

In that second she lost her breath, and her control. Torren gave little concession to her anal virginity or her fears. With steady, intense pressure he began to ease the thick length of his cock into the ultra tight entrance, his fingers spreading her rear cheeks apart, his groan echoing around her.

It was pleasure and pain. Heated rapturous agony. An inferno.

As Carmella felt Torren's cock slide inside her in a stroke of lightning-hot pleasure, she lost the last remaining shreds of control. She was a vessel now. Pleasure so rich and intense it bordered on pain. Impaled, penetrated, taken. She felt her soul splinter and images she could have never imagined began to ripple through her as Ryder and Torren began to move inside her with deep, powerful strokes. Torren laughing with her as he fucked her during the months they were lovers. She saw his laughter but felt his sadness. She was partly his, partly another's. Without Ryder, without his natural balance, his ability to make her love, none of them had truly been whole.

He completed the circle they were meant to be. Ryder, watching her from afar, impatience and fear driving him as he dreamed of her, searched for her, felt her anger and her grief until the moment he saw her picture in a file. Then he knew her. All of her. Ached for her.

Power swirled around her, through her, inside her, until it erupted, as she had always feared it would. They held her tight, fucking into her, driving her insane with the pleasure until it exploded. She exploded. Heart, body, mind and soul. The orgasm that swept through her entered the soul of each man, just as they, too, reached the fiery peak of their releases.

Hot blasts of semen poured into her body as flames tickled along her flesh, only to be absorbed by the two men. Pleasure speared through her pussy, her womb, stealing her breath, her silent screams a mere breath of sound as she flew from her own body and mingled with the souls of the men who had finally pierced the boundaries of her power. Completed.

Darkness swirled around her then as the violence of her release stole her awareness. She could feel the ripples surging through her body, the power pouring from her mind, only to be absorbed by the men sheltering her. With it the last of the dark restlessness that haunted her evaporated, and she felt the peace that began to take its place.

Carmella came to long seconds later; held between Ryder and Torren as they gasped for breath, sweat dripping from their bodies as Torren finally eased his cock from the tight grip of her anus. Ryder was still buried inside her, though the steel-hard insistence of his erection had eased somewhat. His hand clasped her head to his chest, his lips whispered over her ear, her cheek.

"We love you, Carmella. We both love you," he told her, his voice tender, immeasurably soft. "We're bound now, always."

And they were. He eased her to his side, sighing deeply as drowsiness began to overtake them all. Clasped to Ryder's chest, Torren warming her back, she was protected. Safe. For the first time in all the years she could remember, Carmella slept easily, at peace.

Epilogue

Shannon Reidel stared at the closed file on her desk, smoothing her hand over each one, a sense of accomplishment filling her. Three down. So many more to go. The stamp on the outside of the files proclaimed them completed. Inside, the final tests on the three women were evaluated, notated and determined as a "Safe Risk".

She thought of the three woman and the agents she had sent after them. Testing hadn't been easy on them. It was exhausting, but they had come through it perfectly. And happily.

They were beautiful young women. Each possessing characteristics so reminiscent of their mother that it was heart-breaking. Their reunion had been joyous. They had been filled with laughter, with tears and joy, as they all embraced beneath the protective regard of the men who accompanied them. Men who loved them, completed them, eased them.

The three women, direct descendents of the two most powerful psychics the world had ever known, were safe. But they weren't the last of Tyre's seed. There were others.

She pulled the files across the desk, her hand laying on each, pausing for long seconds as she closed her eyes and breathed in deeply. So many were out there. So many of the children had already perished. Fine, honorable men and women who had been bequeathed the power of Tyre, without the cerebral damage he had incurred during the experiments to advance his powers.

So long ago. So long. She lowered her head, shaking it, her chest aching with her pain.

He had been a good man once. Long, long ago. Before the experiments. Before he had been driven insane by his own power, his own fears. Before he had been taken from her.

She rose to her feet, walking slowly to the small bathroom off her office to the mirror above the sink. She touched her face. It was still unlined. Still as perfect as it had been the day she had walked away from the man who held her soul.

Her eyes were still clear, her body perfectly toned. For nearly a century and a half in age, she looked damned good. She tilted her head, wondering if the scientists who tried to rate her powers, who tried to tamper with them, could have ever envisioned what they created. There wasn't a gray hair on her head. Nothing to indicate she was more than the thirty years of age her file proclaimed.

The Tyrea.

She gripped the sink tightly. Tyre. Dear God, how long and empty the years had been without him. How desolate her life had been, until she had come up with a way to heal in part, the wounds he had created.

Sweet Tyre, she thought, *how I miss you.*

She lowered her head, remembering his kisses, so bold and dominant, his touch firing every cell in her body to life as their souls mingled. The gift and the curse of an elemental whose main power was that of fire. A Fyrebrand.

But it had all been over so quickly. Her fists clenched as she fought back her tears. Tears were for the deepest part of the night. The long black hours when she had nothing else to do but to remember. His touch. The sound of his voice. The curve of his cheek. And she had never forgotten a moment, a touch.

She breathed in hard and deep, staring back into the office, thinking of the lives that had yet to be saved. And those that would be lost. So many innocent lives. So much left to accomplish. And it was her payment. Her atonement. Her curse for ever convincing the man she loved that such power could be controlled. That the experiments could aid the world. Her fault.

On her shoulders lay the near destruction of the world, and now on her shoulders lay the reparation of it. It had begun with these three. But it would be a long time before she would see the end.

About the author:

Lora Leigh is a 36-year-old wife and mother living in Kentucky. She dreams in bright, vivid images of the characters intent on taking over her writing life, and fights a constant battle to put them on the hard drive of her computer before they can disappear as fast as they appeared.

Lora's family, and her writing life co-exist, if not in harmony, in relative peace with each other. An understanding husband is the key to late nights with difficult scenes, and stubborn characters. His insights into human nature, and the workings of the male psyche provide her hours of laughter, and innumerable romantic ideas that she works tirelessly to put into effect.

Lora Leigh welcomes mail from readers. You can write her c/o Ellora's Cave Publishing at P.O. Box 787, Hudson, Ohio 44236-0787.

Also by Lora Leigh:

Bound Hearts 1: Surrender
Bound Hearts 2: Submission
Bound Hearts 3: Seduction
Feline Breeds 1: Tempting The Beast
Law and Disorder 1: Moving Violations
Legacies 1: Shattered Legacy
Legacies 2: Shadowed Legacy
Men of August 1: Marly's Choice
Men of August 2: Sarah's Seduction
Men of August 3: Heather's Gift
Menage a Magick
Wolf Breeds 1: Wolfe's Hope
Wolf Breeds 2: Jacob's Faith
Wolf Breeds 3: Aiden's Charity

Why an electronic book?

We live in the Information Age—an exciting time in the history of human civilization in which technology rules supreme and continues to progress in leaps and bounds every minute of every hour of every day. For a multitude of reasons, more and more avid literary fans are opting to purchase e-books instead of paperbacks. The question to those not yet initiated to the world of electronic reading is simply: *why?*

1. *Price.* An electronic title at Ellora's Cave Publishing runs anywhere from 40-75% less than the cover price of the <u>exact same title</u> in paperback format. Why? Cold mathematics. It is less expensive to publish an e-book than it is to publish a paperback, so the savings are passed along to the consumer.

2. *Space.* Running out of room to house your paperback books? That is one worry you will never have with electronic novels. For a low one-time cost, you can purchase a handheld computer designed specifically for e-reading purposes. Many e-readers are larger than the average handheld, giving you plenty of screen room. Better yet, hundreds of titles can be stored within your new library—a single microchip. (Please note that Ellora's Cave does not endorse any specific brands. You can check our website at www.ellorascave.com for customer recommendations we make available to new consumers.)

3. *Mobility.* Because your new library now consists of only a microchip, your entire cache of books can be taken with you wherever you go.

4. *Personal preferences are accounted for.* Are the words you are currently reading too small? Too large? Too...ANNOYING? Paperback books cannot be modified according to personal preferences, but e-books can.

5. *Innovation.* The way you read a book is not the only advancement the Information Age has gifted the literary community with. There is also the factor of what you can read. Ellora's Cave Publishing will be introducing a new line of interactive titles that are available in e-book format only.

6. *Instant gratification.* Is it the middle of the night and all the bookstores are closed? Are you tired of waiting days—sometimes weeks—for online and offline bookstores to ship the novels you bought? Ellora's Cave Publishing sells instantaneous downloads 24 hours a day, 7 days a week, 365 days a year. Our e-book delivery system is 100% automated, meaning your order is filled as soon as you pay for it.

Those are a few of the top reasons why electronic novels are displacing paperbacks for many an avid reader. As always, Ellora's Cave Publishing welcomes your questions and comments. We invite you to email us at service@ellorascave.com or write to us directly at: 1056 Home Avenue, Akron OH 44310-3502.

THE
ELLORA'S CAVE
LIBRARY

Stay up to date with Ellora's Cave Titles
in Print with our Quarterly Catalog.

TO RECIEVE A CATALOG,
SEND AN EMAIL WITH YOUR NAME
AND MAILING ADDRESS TO:

CATALOG@ELLORASCAVE.COM
OR SEND A LETTER OR POSTCARD
WITH YOUR MAILING ADDRESS TO:
CATALOG REQUEST
C/O ELLORA'S CAVE PUBLISHING, INC.
1337 COMMERCE DRIVE #13
STOW, OH 44224

Discover for yourself why readers can't get enough of the multiple award-winning publisher Ellora's Cave. Whether you prefer e-books or paperbacks, be sure to visit EC on the web at www.ellorascave.com for an erotic reading experience that will leave you breathless.

www.ellorascave.com

Printed in the United States
30777LVS00001B/46-438